Edward Edwards

Lives of the founders of the British Museum

With notices of its chief augmentors and other benefactors, 1570-1870

Edward Edwards

Lives of the founders of the British Museum
With notices of its chief augmentors and other benefactors, 1570-1870

ISBN/EAN: 9783742840790

Manufactured in Europe, USA, Canada, Australia, Japa

Cover: Foto ©Andreas Hilbeck / pixelio.de

Manufactured and distributed by brebook publishing software
(www.brebook.com)

Edward Edwards

Lives of the founders of the British Museum

LIVES OF

THE FOUNDERS

OF THE

BRITISH MUSEUM;

WITH

NOTICES OF ITS CHIEF AUGMENTORS
AND OTHER BENEFACTORS.

1570—1870.

By EDWARD EDWARDS.

———

PART II.

———

LONDON:

TRÜBNER AND CO., 60, PATERNOSTER ROW.

1870.

PRINTED BY J. E. ADLARD, BARTHOLOMEW CLOSE.

CHAPTER III.

A GROUP OF BOOK-LOVERS AND PUBLIC BENEFACTORS.

'If we were to take away from the Museum Collection [of Books] the King's Library, and the collection which George the Third gave before that, and then the magnificent collection of Mr. Cracherode, as well as those of Sir William Musgrave, Sir Joseph Banks, Sir Richard Colt Hoare, and many others,—and also all the books received under the Copyright Act,—if we were to take away all the books so given, I am satisfied not one half of the books [in 1836], nor one third of the *value* of the Library, has been procured with money voted by the Nation. The Nation has done almost nothing for the Library. . . . .

'Considering the British Museum to be a National Library for research, its utility increases in proportion with the very rare and costly books, in preference to modern books. . . . . I think that scholars have a right to look, for these expensive works, to the Government of the Country. . . . .

'I want a poor student to have the same means of indulging his learned curiosity,—of following his rational pursuits,—of consulting the same authorities,—of fathoming the most intricate inquiry,—as the richest man in the kingdom, as far as books go. And I contend that Government is bound to give him the most liberal and unlimited assistance in this respect. I want the Library of the British Museum to have books of both descriptions. . . . .

'When you have given a hundred thousand pounds,—in ten or twelve years,—you will begin to have a library worthy of the British Nation.'—

ANTONIO PANIZZI—*Evidence before Select Committee on British Museum*, 7th June, 1836. (Q. 4785—4795.)

Notices of some early Donors of Books.—The Life and Collections of Clayton Mordaunt CRACHERODE.—*William* PETTY, *first Marquess of Lansdowne, and his Library of Manuscripts.—The Literary Life and Collections of Dr. Charles* BURNEY.—*Francis* HARGRAVE *and his Manuscripts.—The Life and Testamentary Foundations of Francis Henry* EGERTON, *Ninth Earl of Bridgewater.*

THE Reader has now seen that, within some twelve or fifteen years, a Collection of Antiquities, comparatively small and insignificant, was so enriched as to gain the aspect of a National Museum of which all English-speaking men might be proud, and mere fragments of which enlightened Foreign Sovereigns were under sore temptation to covet. He has seen, also, that the praise of so striking a change was due, in the main, to the public spirit and the liberal endeavours of a small group of antiquarians and scholars. They were, most of them, men of high birth, and of generous education. They were, in fact, precisely such men as, in the jargon of our present day, it is too much the mode to speak of as the antitheses of ' the People,' although in earlier days men of that strain were thought to be part of the very core and kernel of a nation.

But if it be undeniably true that the chief and primary merit of so good a piece of public service was due to the HAMILTONS, TOWNELEYS, ELGINS, and KNIGHTS of the last generation, it is also true that the Public, through their representatives, did, at length, join fairly in the work by bearing their part of the cost, though they could share neither the enterprise, the self-denial, nor the wearing toils, which the work had exacted.

Now that the story turns to another department of the National Museum, we find that the same primary and salient characteristic—private liberality of individuals, as distinguished from public support by the Kingdom—still holds good. But we have to wait a very long time indeed, before we perceive public effort at length falling into rank with private, in the shape of parliamentary grants for the purchase of books, calculated even upon a rough approximation towards equality.

As COTTON, SLOANE, HARLEY, and Arthur EDWARDS, were the first founders of the Library, so BIRCH, MUSGRAVE, TYRWHITT, CRACHERODE, BANKS, and HOARE, were its chief augmentors, until almost ninety years had elapsed since the Act of Organization. Of the Collections of those ten benefactors, eight came by absolute gift. For the other two, much less than one half of their value was returned to the representatives of the founders. And that, it has been shown, was provided, not by a parliamentary grant, but out of the profits of a lottery.

The first important addition to the Library, subsequent to those gifts which have been mentioned in a preceding chapter as nearly contemporaneous with the creation of the Museum, was made by the Will of Dr. Thomas Birch, one of the original Trustees. It comprised a valuable series of manuscripts, rich in collections on the history, and especially the biographical history, of the realm, and a considerable number of printed books of a like character.

Dr. Birch was born in 1705, and died on the ninth of January, 1766. He was one of the many friends of Sir Hans Sloane, in the later years of Sir Hans' life. When the Museum was in course of organization, Birch acted not only as a zealous Trustee, but he occasionally supplied the place of Dr. Morton as Secretary. His literary productions have real and enduring value, though their value would probably have been greater had their number been less. His activity is sufficiently evidenced by the works which he printed, but can only be measured when the large manuscript collections which he bequeathed are taken into the account. Very few scholars will now be inclined to echo Horace Walpole's inquiry—made when he saw the Catalogue of the Birch MSS.—'Who cares for the correspondence of Dr. Birch?'

Soon after the receipt of the Birch Collection, a choice assemblage of English plays was bequeathed to the Museum by David Garrick. Its formation had been one of the favourite relaxations of the great actor. And the study of the plays gathered by GARRICK had a large share in mould-ing the tastes and the literary career of Charles LAMB. Thence he drew the materials of the volume of *Specimens* which has made the rich stores of the early drama known to thousands of readers who but for it, and for the Collection which enabled him to compile it, could have formed no fair or adequate idea of an important epoch in our literature.

Sir William MUSGRAVE was another early Trustee whose gifts to the Public illustrated the wisdom of SLOANE's plan for the government of his Museum and of its parliamentary adoption. MUSGRAVE shared the predilection of Dr. BIRCH for the study of British biography and archæology, and he had larger means for amassing its materials. He was descended from a branch of the Musgraves of Edenhall, and was the second son of Sir Richard MUSGRAVE of Hayton Castle, to whom he eventually succeeded. He made large and very curious manuscript collections for the history of portrait-painting in England (now *Additional MSS*. 6391-6393), and also on many points of the administrative and political history of the country. He was a zealous Trustee of the British Museum, and in his lifetime made several additions to its stores. On his death, in 1799, all his manu-scripts were bequeathed to the Museum, together with a Library of printed British Biography—more complete than anything of its kind theretofore collected.

This last-named Collection extended (if we include a partial and previous gift made in 1790) to nearly two thousand volumes, and it probably embraced much more than twice that number of separate works. For it was rich in those biographical ephemera which are so precious to the historical inquirer, and often so difficult of obtain-ment, when needed. Nearly at the same period (1786) a valuable Collection of classical authors, in about nine hundred volumes, was bequeathed by another worthy Trustee, Mr. Thomas TYRWHITT, distinguished both as a scholar and as the Editor of CHAUCER.

But all the early gifts to the Museum, made after its parliamentary organization, were eclipsed, at the close of the century, by the bequest of the Cracherode Collections. That bequest comprised a very choice library of printed books; a cabinet of coins, medals, and gems; and a series of original drawings by the great masters, chosen, like the books and the coins, with exquisite taste, and, as the auctioneers say, quite regardless of expense. It also included a small but precious cabinet of minerals.

The collector of these rarities was wont to speak of them with great modesty. They are, he would say, mere 'specimen collections.' But to amass them had been the chief pursuit of a quiet and blameless life.

Clayton Mordaunt CRACHERODE was born in London about the year 1730. And he was 'a Londoner' in a sense and degree to which, in this railway generation, it would be hard to find a parallel. Among the rich possessions which he inherited from Colonel CRACHERODE, his father—whose fortune had been gathered, or increased, during an active career in remote parts of the world—was an estate in Hertfordshire, on which there grew a certain famous chestnut-tree, the cynosure of all the country-side for its size and antiquity. This tree was never seen by its new owner, save as he saw the poplars of Lombardy, or the cedars of Lebanon—in an etching. In the course of a long life he never reached a greater distance from the metropolis than Oxford. He never mounted a horse. The ordinary extent of his travels, during the prime years of a long life, was from Queen Square, in Westminster, to Clapham. For almost forty years it was his daily practice to walk from his house to the shop of ELMSLY, a bookseller in the Strand, and thence to the still more noted shop of Tom PAYNE, by 'the Mews-Gate.' Once a week, he varied the daily walk by calling on MUDGE, a chronometer-maker, to get his watch regulated. His excursions had, indeed, one other and not infrequent variety—dictated by the calls of Christian benevolence—but of these he took care to have no note taken.

Early in life, and probably to meet his father's wish, he received holy orders, but he never accepted any preferment in the Church. He took the restraints of the clerical profession, without any of its emoluments. His classical attainments were considerable, but the sole publication of a long life of leisure was a university prize poem, printed in the *Carmina Quadragesimalia* of 1748. The only early tribulation of a life of idyllic peacefulness was a dread that he might possibly be called upon, at a coronation, to appear in public as the King's cupbearer—his manor of Great Wymondley being held by a tenure of grand-serjeantry in that onerous employment. Its one later tinge of bitterness lay in the dread of a French invasion. These may seem small sorrows, to men who have had a full share in the stress and anguish of the battle of life. But the weight of a burden is no measure of the pain it may inflict. Mr. CRACHERODE looked to his possible cupbearership, with apprehension just as acute as that with which COWPER contemplated the awful task of reading in public the Journals of the House of Lords. And the sleepless nights which long afterwards were brought to CRACHERODE by the horrors of the French revolutionary war were caused less by personal fears than by the dread of public calamities, more terrible than death. During one year of the devastations on the other side of the Channel, chronicled by our daily papers, Mr. CRACHERODE was thought by his friends to have 'aged' full ten years in his aspect.

BOOK II,
Chap. III.
BOOK-
LOVERS AND
PUBLIC
BENEFAC
TORS.

The one active and incessant pursuit of this noiseless career was the gathering together of the most choice books, the finest coins and gems, the most exquisite drawings and prints, which money could buy, without the toils of travel. Our Collector's liberality of purse enabled him to profit, at his ease, by the truth expressed in one of the wise maxims of John SELDEN :—'The giving a dealer his price hath this advantage;—he that will do so shall have the refusal of whatsoever comes to the dealer's hand, and so by that means get many things which otherwise he never should have seen.' The enjoyment—almost a century ago—of six -hundred pounds a year in land, and of nearly one hundred thousand pounds invested in the 'sweet simplicity' of the three per cents., enabled Mr. CRACHERODE to outbid a good many competitors. His natural wish that what he had so eagerly gathered should not be scattered to the four winds on the instant he was carried to his grave, and also the public spirit which dictated the choice of a national repository as the permanent abode of his Collections, has already made that long course of daily visits to the London dealers in books, coins, and drawings, fruitful of good to hundreds of poorer students and toilers, during more than two generations. From stores such as Mr. CRACHERODE'S— when so preserved—many a useful labourer gets part of his best equipment for the tasks of his life. He, too, would enjoy a visit to the 'PAYNES' and the 'ELMSLYS' of the day as keenly as any book-lover that ever lived, but is too often, perhaps, obliged to content himself with an outside glance at the windows. Public libraries put him practically on a level with the wealthiest connoisseur. When, as in this case—and in a hundred more—such libraries derive much of their best possessions from private liberality, a life like Mordaunt Cracherode's has its ample vindication, and the sting is taken out of all such sarcasms as that which was levelled — in the shape of the query, ' In all that big library is there a single book written by the Collector himself?'—by some snarling epistolary critic, when commenting on a notice that appeared in *The Times* on the occasion of Mr. Cracherode's death.

On another point our Collector was exposed to the shafts of sarcastic comment. He loved a good book to be printed on the very choicest material, and clothed in the richest fashion. The treasure within would not incline him to tolerate blemishes without.—

> ' Nusquam blatta, vel inquinata charta,
> Sed margo calami notæque purus,
> Margo latior, albus integerque,
> Nec non copia larga pergainenæ.—
> Adsint Virgilius, paterque Homerus,
> Mundi pumice, purpuraque culti ;
> Et quicquid magica quasi arte freti
> Faustusque Upilioque præstiterunt.
>
> . . . .
>
> Hic sit qui nitet arte Montacuti,
> Aut Paini, Deromique junioris ;
> Illic cui decus arma sunt Thuani,
> Aut regis breve lilium caduci.'

In Cracherode's eyes, external charms such as these were scarcely less essential than the intrinsic worth of the author. ' Large paper' and broad pure margins are fancies which it needs not much culture or much wit to banter. But now and then, they are ridiculed by those who have just as little capacity to judge the pith and substance of books, as of taste to appreciate beauty in their outward form.*

The solidity of those three per cents., and the plodding perseverance of their owner, were in time rewarded by the collection (1) of a library containing only four thousand five hundred volumes, but of which probably every volume —on an average of the whole—was worth, in mercantile eyes, some three pounds ; (2) of seven portfolios of drawings, still more choice ; (3) of a hundred portfolios of prints, many of which were almost priceless ; and (4) of coins and gems—such as the cameo of a lion on sardonyx, and the intaglio of the *Discobolos*—worthy of an imperial cabinet.

The ruling passion kept its strength to the last. An agent was buying prints, for addition to the store, when the Collector was dying. About four days before his death, Mr. CRACHERODE mustered strength to pay a farewell visit to the old shop at the Mews-Gate. He put a finely printed *Terence* (from the press of FOULIS) into one pocket, and a large paper *Cebes* into another ; and then,—with a longing look at a certain choice *Homer*, in the course of which he mentally, and somewhat doubtingly, balanced its charms with those of its twin brother in Queen Square,—parted finally from the daily haunt of forty peripatetic and studious years.

Clayton Mordaunt CRACHERODE died towards the close of 1799. He bequeathed the whole of his collections to the Nation, with the exception of two volumes of books. A polyglot *Bible* was given to Shute BARRINGTON, Bishop

Book II,
Chap. III.
Book-
Lovers and
Public
Benefac-
tors.

* " Or must I, as a wit, with learned air
    Like Doctor Dibdin, to Tom Payne's repair,
    Meet Cyril Jackson and mild Cracherode there ?
    'Hold !' cries Tom Payne, 'that margin let me measure,
    And rate the separate value of the treasure '
    Eager they gaze. ' Well, Sirs, the feat is done.
    Cracherode's *Poetæ Principes* have won !"
                    Mathias, *Pursuits of Literature.*

of Durham; a princeps *Homer* to Cyril JACKSON, Dean of Christ Church. Those justly venerated men were his two dearest friends.

The next conspicuous donor to the Library of the British Museum was a contemporary of the learned recluse of Queen Square, but one whose life was passed in the thick of that worldly turmoil and conflict of which Mr. CRACHE-RODE had so mortal a dread. To the Collector of the 'Lansdowne Manuscripts,' political excitement was the congenial air in which it was indeed life to live. But he, also, was a man beloved by all who had the privilege of his intimate friendship.

William PETTY FITZMAURICE, third Earl of Shelburne, and first Marquess of Lansdowne, was born in Dublin, in May, 1737. He was the son of John, Earl of Shelburne in the peerage of Ireland, and afterwards Baron Wycombe in the peerage of Great Britain. The Marquess's father united the possessions of the family founded by Sir William PETTY with those which the Irish wars had left to the ancient line of Fitzmaurice.

William, Earl of SHELBURNE, was educated by private tutors, and then sent to Christ Church, Oxford. He left the University early, to take (in or about the year 1756) a commission in the Guards. He was present in the battles of Campen and of Minden. At Minden, in particular, he evinced distinguished bravery. In May, 1760, and again in April, 1761, he was elected by the burgesses of High Wycombe to represent them in the House of Commons. But the death of Earl John, in the middle of 1761, called his son to take his seat in the House of Lords. He soon evinced the possession of powers eminently fitted to shine in Parliament. The impetuosity he had shown on the field of Minden did not desert him in the strife of politics. Those who had listened to the early speeches of PITT might well think that the army had again sent them a 'terrible cornet of horse.' So good a judge of political oratory as was Lord CAMDEN thought SHELBURNE to be second only to CHATHAM himself.

Lord SHELBURNE's first speech in Parliament—the first, at least, that attracted general notice—was made in support of the Court and the Ministry (November 3, 1762). Within less than six months after its delivery he was called to the Privy Council, and placed at the head of the Board of Trade and Plantations. This appointment was made on the 23rd of April, 1763. Just before it he had taken part in that delicate negotiation between Lord BUTE and Henry Fox (afterwards Lord HOLLAND) which has been kept well in memory by a jest of the man who thought himself the loser in it. This early incident is in some sort a key to many later incidents in Lord SHELBURNE's life.

For, in all the acts and offices of a political career, save only one, Lord SHELBURNE was characteristically a lover of soft words. In debate, he could speak scathingly. In conversation, he was always under temptation to flatter his interlocutor. In this conversation of 1763 with Fox, SHELBURNE's innate love of smoothing asperities co-operated with his belief that it was really for the common interest that BUTE and Fox should come to an agreement, to make him put the premier's offer into the most pleasing light. When Fox found he was to get less than he thought to have, he fiercely assailed the negotiator. Lord SHELBURNE's friends dwelt on his love of peace and good-fellowship. At worst, said they, it was but a 'pious fraud.' 'I can see the fraud plainly enough,' rejoined Fox, 'but where is the piety?'

Book II, Chap. III. Book-Lovers and Public Benefactors.

Beginning of Lord Shelburne's Career in Parliament.

Shelburne and Henry Fox.

BOOK II,
Chap. III.
BOOK-
LOVERS AND
PUBLIC
BENEFAC-
TORS.

The office accepted in April was resigned in September, when the coalition with 'the BEDFORD party' was made. Lord SHELBURNE's loss was felt in the House of Lords. But it was in the Commons that the Ministry were now feeblest. 'I don't see how they can meet Parliament,' said CHESTERFIELD. 'In the Commons they have not a man with ability and words enough to call a coach.'

In February, 1765, SHELBURNE married Lady Sophia CARTERET, one of the daughters of the Earl of GRANVILLE. The marriage was a very happy one. Not long after it, he

FORMATION
OF LORD
SHEL-
BURNE'S
LIBRARY.

began to form his library. Political manuscripts, state papers of every kind, and all such documents as tend to throw light on the arcana of history, were, more especially, the objects which he sought. And the quest, as will be seen presently, was very successful. For during his early researches he had but few competitors.

THE SECRE-
TARYSHIP
OF STATE.

1766-1768.

On the organization of the Duke of GRAFTON's Ministry in 1766 (July 30) Lord SHELBURNE was made Secretary of State for the Southern Department, to which at that time the Colonial business was attached. His colleague, in the Northern, was CONWAY, who now led the House of Commons. As Secretary, Lord SHELBURNE's most conspicuous and influential act was his approval of that rejection of certain members of the Council of Massachusetts by Governor BERNARD, which had so important a bearing on colonial events to come.

SHELBURNE, however, was one of a class of statesmen of whom, very happily, this country has had many. He was able to render more efficient service in opposition than in office. Of the Board of Trade he had had the headship but a few months. As Secretary of State, under the GRAFTON Administration, he served little more than two years. His opponents were wont to call him an 'impracticable' man.

But if he shared some of CHATHAM's weaknesses, he also shared much of his greatness.   And on the capital question of the American dispute, they were at one.   They both thought that the Colonies had been atrociously misgoverned. They were willing to make large concessions to regain the loyalty of the Colonists.   They were utterly averse to admit of a severance.

Book II, Chap. III. Book-Lovers and Public Benefactors.

Under circumstances familiar to all readers, and by the personal urgency of the King, Lord SHELBURNE was dismissed from his first Secretaryship in October, 1768.   His dismissal led to CHATHAM's resignation.   SHELBURNE became a prominent and powerful leader of the Opposition, an object of special dislike to a large force of political adversaries, and of warm attachment to a small number of political friends.   His personal friends were, at all times, many.

Lord Shelburne in Opposition.

The nickname under which his opponents were wont to satirize him has been kept in memory by one of the many infelicities of speech which did such cruel injustice to the fine parts and the generous heart of GOLDSMITH.   The story has been many times told, but will bear to be told once again. The author of the *Vicar of Wakefield* was an occasional supporter of the Opposition in the newspapers.   One day, in the autumn of 1773, he wrote an article in praise of Lord SHELBURNE's ardent friend in the City, the Lord Mayor TOWNSHEND.   Sitting, in company with Topham BEAUCLERC, at Drury Lane Theatre, just after the appearance of the article, GOLDSMITH found himself close beside Lord SHELBURNE.   His companion told the statesman that his City friend's eulogy came from GOLDSMITH's pen.   'I hope,' said his Lordship—addressing the poet—'you put nothing in it about Malagrida?'   'Do you know,' rejoined poor GOLDSMITH, 'I could never conceive the reason why they call you "Malagrida,"—*for* Malagrida was a very good

1773. November.

Hardy, *Life of Lord Charlemont,* vol. i, p. 177.

sort of man.' This small misplacement of an emphasis was of course quoted in the clubs against the unlucky speaker. 'Ah!' said Horace WALPOLE, with his wonted charity, 'that's a picture of the man's whole life.'

Lord SHELBURNE's library profited by his long release-ment from the cares of office. He bestowed much of his leisure upon its enrichment, and especially upon the acqui-sition of manuscript political literature. In 1770, he was fortunate enough to obtain a considerable portion of the large and curious Collection of State Papers which Sir Julius CÆSAR had begun to amass almost two centuries before. Two years later, he acquired no inconsiderable portion of that far more important series which had been gathered by BURGHLEY.

Whilst Lord SHELBURNE was serving with the army in Germany, the 'Cæsar Papers' had been dispersed by auction. There were then—1757—a hundred and eighty-seven of them. About sixty volumes were purchased by Philip Cartaret WEBB, a lawyer and juridical writer, as well as antiquary, of some distinction. On Mr. WEBB's death, in 1770, these were purchased by SHELBURNE from his executors. On examining his acquisition, the new possessor found that about twenty volumes related to various matters of British history and antiquities; thirty-one volumes to the business of the British Admiralty and its Courts; ten volumes to that of the Treasury, Star Chamber, and other public departments; two volumes con-tained treaties; and one volume, papers on the affairs of Ireland.

The 'Burghley papers,' acquired in 1772, had passed from Sir Michael HICKES, one of that statesman's secre-taries, to a descendant, Sir William HICKES, by whom they were sold to CHISWELL, a bookseller, and by him to

Book II,
Chap. III.
Book-
Lovers and
Public
Benefac-
tors.

Strype, the historian. These (as has been mentioned in a former chapter) were looked upon with somewhat covetous eyes by Humphrey Wanley, who hoped to have seen them become part of the treasures of the Harleian Library. On Strype's death they passed into the hands of James West, and from his executors into the Library at Shelburne House. They comprised a hundred and twenty-one volumes of the collections and correspondence of Lord Burghley, together with his private note-book and journal.

Another valuable acquisition, made after Lord Shelburne's retirement in 1768 from political office, consisted of the vast historical Collections of Bishop White Kennett, extending to a hundred and seven volumes, of which a large proportion are in the Bishop's own untiring hand. Twenty-two of these volumes contain important materials for English Church History. Eleven volumes contain biographical collections, ranging between the years 1500 and 1717. All that have been enumerated are now national property.

Other choice manuscript collections were added from time to time. Among them may be cited the papers of Sir Paul Rycaut—which include information both on Irish and on Continental affairs towards the close of the seventeenth century; the correspondence of Dr. John Pell, and that of the Jacobite Earl of Melfort.

These varied accessions—with many others of minor importance—raised the Shelburne Library into the first rank among private repositories of historical lore. To amass and to study them was to prove to its owner the solace of deep personal affliction, as well as the relief of public toils. At the close of 1770, he lost a beloved wife, after a union of less than six years. He remained a widower until 1779.

Another source of solace was found in labours that have an inexhaustible charm, for those who are so happy as to have means as well as taste for them. Lord SHELBURNE lived much at Loakes—now called Wycombe Abbey—a delightful seat, just above the little town of High Wycombe. Its striking framework of beech-woods, its fine plane-trees and ash-trees, and its broad piece of water, make up a lovely picture, much of the attraction of which is due to the skill and judgment with which its then owner elicited and heightened the natural beauties of the place.* But those of Bowood exceeded them in Lord SHELBURNE's eyes. There. too, he did very much to enhance what nature had already done, and he had the able assistance of Mr. HAMILTON of Pains-Hill. In consequence of their joint labours, almost every species of oak may be seen at Bowood, with great variety of exotic trees of all sorts. Both wood and water combine to make, from some points of view, a resemblance between Wycombe and Bowood. And both differ from many much bepraised country seats in the wise preference of natural beauty—selected and heightened—to artificial beauty. Lord SHELBURNE himself was wont to say: 'Mere workmanship should never be introduced where the beauty and variety of the scenery are, in themselves, sufficient to excite admiration.'

But, in their true place, few men better loved the productions of artistic genius. He collected pictures and sculpture, as well as trees and books. He was the first of

---

* Loakes had been purchased from the last owner of the Archdall family by Henry, Earl of Shelburne. Earl William (first Marquess of Lansdowne) eventually sold it to the ancestor of the present Lord Carrington.

his name who made Lansdowne House in London, as well as Loakes and Bowood in the country, centres of the best society in the intellectual as well as in the fashionable world.

Book II, Chap. III
Book-Lovers and Public Benefactors.

Years passed on. The course of public events—and especially the death of Lord CHATHAM and the issues of the American war—together with many conspicuous proofs of his powers in debate, tended more and more to bring Lord SHELBURNE to the front. Between him and Lord ROCKINGHAM, as far as regards real personal ability—whether parliamentary or administrative—there could, in truth, be little ground for comparison. But in party connection and following, the claims of the inferior man were incontestible. Lord SHELBURNE, towards the close of 1779, signified his readiness to waive his pretensions to take the lead—in the event of the overthrow of the existing Government—and his willingness to serve under Lord ROCKINGHAM; so little truth was there in the assertion, made by Horace WALPOLE to his correspondent at Florence, that SHELBURNE 'will stick at nothing to gratify his ambition.'

H. Walpole to Mann; 1780. March 21.

But that very charge is, in fact, a tribute. WALPOLE's indignation had been excited just at that moment by the zealous assistance which SHELBURNE had given, in the House of Lords, to the efforts of BURKE in the lower House in favour of economical reforms. He had brought forward a motion on that subject on the same night on which BURKE had given notice for the introduction of his famous Bill (December, 1779). He continued his efforts, and presently had to encounter a more active and pertinacious opponent of retrenchment than Horace WALPOLE.

In the course of a vigorous speech on reform in the

administration of the army, Lord Shelburne had censured a transaction in which Mr. Fullerton, a Member of the House of Commons, was intimately concerned. Fullerton made a violent attack, in his place in the House, upon his censor. But his speech was so disorderly that he was forced to break off. In his anger he sent Lord Shelburne a minute, not only of what he had actually spoken, but of what he had intended to say, in addition, had the rules of Parliament permitted. And he had the effrontery to wind up his obliging communication with these words:—'You correspond, as I have heard abroad, with the enemies of your country.' His letter was presented to Lord Shelburne by a messenger.

The receiver, when he had read it, said to the bearer : 'The best answer I can give Mr. Fullerton is to desire him to meet me in Hyde Park, at five, to-morrow morning.' They fought, and Shelburne was wounded. On being asked how he felt himself, he looked at the wound, and said: 'I do not think that Lady Shelburne will be the worse for this.' But it was severe enough to interrupt, for a while, his political labours.

On the formation in March, 1782, of the Rockingham Administration, he accepted the Secretaryship of State, and took with him four of his adherents into the Cabinet. But the most curious feature in the transaction was that Lord Shelburne carried on, personally, all the intercourse in the royal closet that necessarily preceded the formation of the Ministry, although he was not to be its head. George the Third would not admit Lord Rockingham to an audience until his Cabinet was completely formed. The man whose exclusion from the Grafton Ministry the King had so warmly urged a few years before, was now not less warmly urged by him to throw over his party, and to head a cabinet of his own. He resisted all blandishment, and virtually told the King that the triumph of the Opposition must be its triumph as an unbroken whole ; though he doubtless felt, within himself, that the cohesion was of singularly frail tenacity.

On the 24th of March, SHELBURNE had the satisfaction of conveying to Lord ROCKINGHAM the royal concession of his constitutional demands—obtained after a wearisome negotiation, and only by the piling up of argument on argument in successive conversations at the 'Queen's House,' lasting sometimes for three mortal hours. Three months afterwards, the new Premier was dead. And with him departed the cohesion of the Whigs.

As Secretary of State, Lord SHELBURNE's chief task had been the control of that double and most unwelcome negotiation which was carried on at Paris with France and with America.* For it had fallen to the lot of the utterer of the 'sunset-speech,'†—' if we let America go, the sun of Great Britain is set'—to arrange the terms of American pacification. And the obstructions in that path which were created at home were even more serious stumbling-blocks than were the difficulties abroad. The cardinal points of Lord SHELBURNE's policy, at this time, were to retain, by hook or crook, some amount or other of hold upon America, and at the worst to keep the Court of France from enjoying the prestige, or setting up the pretence, of having dictated the terms of peace.

That the split in the Whig party was really and alto-

Book II,
Chap. III.
Book-
Lovers and
Public
Benefac-
tors.

Death of
Lord Rock-
ingham,
1782, 1 July.

Formation
of Lord
Shel-
burne's
Ministry.

* See, here
after, in life
of T. Gren
ville,
Book III, c. 2.

† This famous speech was delivered on the 5th of March, 1778. ' _Then_,' said Lord Shelburne, after denouncing measures which would sever the Colonies from the Kingdom, ' the sun of Great Britain is set. We shall be no more a powerful or even a respectable people.'—_Parliamentary Debates_, vol. xix, col. 850.

Book II,
Chap. III.
Book.
Lovers and
Public
Benefac-
tors.

Walpole to
Mann (from
an eye wit-
ness), 1782,
July 7.

gether inevitable, now that ROCKINGHAM'S death had placed SHELBURNE above reasonable competition for the premiership, was made known to him when at Court, in the most abrupt manner. On the 7th of July (six days after the death of the Marquess), Fox took him by the sleeve, with the blunt question : ' Are you to be First Lord of the Treasury ?' When SHELBURNE said 'Yes,' the instant rejoinder was, 'Then, my Lord, I shall resign.' Fox had brought the seals in his pocket, and proceeded immediately to return them to the King.

In his first speech as Premier, Lord SHELBURNE spoke thus :—' It has been said that I have changed my opinion about the independence of America. . . . My opinion is still the same. When that independence shall have been established, the sun of England may be said to have set. I have used every effort, public and private—in England, and out of it—to avert so dreadful a disaster. . . . But though

Parliamen-
tary Debates,
vol. xxiii,
col. 194.

this country should have received a fatal blow, there is still a duty incumbent upon its Ministers to use their most vigorous exertions to prevent the Court of France from being in a situation to dictate the terms of Peace. The sun of England may have set. But we will improve the twilight. We will prepare for the rising of that sun again. And I hope England may yet see many, many happy days.'

The best achievements of the brief government of Lord SHELBURNE were (first) the resolute defence, in its diplomacy at Paris and Versailles, of our territories in Canada, and (secondly) its consistent assertion of the principle that underlay a sentence contained in a former speech of the Premier—a sentence which, at one time, was much upon

Merits of
the Shel-
burne
Ministry.

men's lips :—' I will never consent,' he had said, ' that the King of England shall be a King of the Mahrattas.' The merits, I venture to think, of that short Ministry, have had scant acknowledgment in our current histories. And the reason is, perhaps, not far to seek.

The popular history of GEORGE THE THIRD's reign has been, in a large degree, imbued with Whiggism. The historians most in vogue have had a sort of small apostolical succession amongst themselves, which has had the result of giving a strong party tinge to those versions of the course of political events in that reign which have most readily gained the public ear. When the full story shall come to be told, in a later day and from a higher stand-point, Lord SHELBURNE, not improbably, will be one among several statesmen whose reputation with posterity (in common—in some measure—with that of their royal master himself, it may even be) will be found to have been elevated, rather than lowered, by the process.

But, be that as it may, party intrigue, rather than ministerial incapacity, had to do, confessedly, with the rapid overthrow of the Government of July, 1782.

Personally, Lord SHELBURNE was in a position which, in several points of view, bears a resemblance to that in which another able statesman, who had to fight against a powerful coterie, was to find himself forty years later. But in SHELBURNE's case, the struggle of the politician did not, as in CANNING's, break down the bodily vigour of the man. Lord SHELBURNE had twenty-two years of retirement yet before him, when he resigned the premiership in 1783. And they were years of much happiness.

Part of that happiness was the result of the domestic union just adverted to. Another part of it accrued from the rich Library which the research and attention of many years had gradually built up, and from the increased leisure that had now been secured, both for study and for the enjoyment of the choice society which gathered habitually at Lansdowne House and at Bowood.

Lord SHELBURNE's retirement had been followed, in 1784, by his creation as Earl Wycombe and Marquess of Lansdowne. In the following year, he sold the Wycombe mansion and its charming park to Lord CARRINGTON. Thenceforward, Bowood had the benefit, exclusively, of his taste and skill in landscape-gardening. Unfortunately, his next successor, far from continuing his father's work, did much to injure and spoil it. But the third Marquess, in whom so many of his father's best qualities were combined with some that were especially his own, made ample amends.

The exciting debates which grew out of the French Revolution and the ensuing events on the Continent, called Lord LANSDOWNE, now and then, into the old arena. But the domestic employments which have been mentioned, together with that which was entailed by a large and varied correspondence, both at home and abroad, were the things which chiefly filled up his later years. The Marquess died in London on the seventh of May, 1805. He was but sixty-eight years of age, yet he was then the oldest general officer on the army list, having been gazetted as a major-general just forty years before.

In order to acquire for the nation that precious portion of Lord LANSDOWNE's Library which was in manuscript, the national purse-strings were now, for the first time, opened on behalf of the literary stores of the British Museum. Fifty-three years had passed since its complete foundation as a national institution, and exactly twice that number of years since the first public establishment of the Cottonian Library, yet no grant had been hitherto made by Parliament for the improvement of the national collections of books.

Four thousand nine hundred and twenty-five pounds was the sum given to Lord LANSDOWNE's executors for his manuscripts. Besides the successive accumulations of State Papers heretofore mentioned, the LANSDOWNE Collection included other historical documents, extending in date from the reign of HENRY THE SIXTH to that of GEORGE THE THIRD; the varied Collections of William PETYT on parliamentary and juridical lore; those of WARBURTON on the topography and family history of Yorkshire, and of HOLLES, containing matter of a like character for the local concerns of the county of Lincoln; the Heraldic and Genealogical Collections of SEGAR, SAINT GEORGE, DUGDALE, and LE NEVE; and a most curious series of early treatises upon music, which had been collected by John WYLDE, who was for many years precentor of Waltham Abbey, in the time of the second of the Tudor monarchs.

The Lansdowne Collection did not contain very much of a classical character. Its strength, it has been seen already, lay in the sections of Modern History and Politics. The next important addition to the Library of the Museum —that of the manuscripts and printed books of Francis HARGRAVE—was likewise chiefly composed of political and juridical literature. But the third parliamentary acquisition brought to the Museum a store of classical wealth, both in manuscripts and in printed books. HARGRAVE's Legal Library was bought in 1813. Charles BURNEY's Classical Library was bought in 1818. In the biographical point of view neither of these men ran a career which offers much of narrative interest. The one career was that of a busy lawyer; the other, that of a laborious, scholar. But to Burney's life a few sentences may be briefly and fitly given.

The second Charles Burney was a younger son of the well-known historian of Music, who for more than fifty years was a prominent figure in the literary circles—and especially in the Johnsonian circle—of London; and in whose well-filled life a very moderate share of literary ability was made to go a long way, and to elicit a very resonant echo. That 'clever dog Burney,' as he was wont to be called by the autocrat of the dinner-table, had the good fortune to be the father of several children even more clever than himself. Their reputation enhanced his own.

Charles Burney, junior, was born at Lynn, in Norfolk, on the 10th of December, 1757. He was educated at the Charter House in London, at Caius College, Cambridge, and at King's College, Aberdeen. At Aberdeen, Burney formed a friendship with Dr. Dunbar, a Scottish professor of some distinction, and an incident which grew, in after-years, out of that connection, determined the scene and character of the principal employments of Burney's life. He devoted himself to scholastic labours, in both senses of the term; their union proved mutually advantageous, and as tuition gave leisure for literary labour, so the successful issues of that labour spread far and wide his fame as a schoolmaster. He was one of the not very large group of men who in that employment have won wealth as well as honour. It was finely said, many years ago— in one of the State Papers written by Guizot, when he was Minister of Public Instruction in France—' the good schoolmaster must work for man, and be content to await his reward from God.' In Burney's case, the combined assiduity of an energetic man at the author's writing-table, at the master's desk, and also (it must in truthful candour be added) at his flogging block,* brought him a large fortune as well as a wide-spread reputation. This fortune enabled him to collect what, for a schoolmaster, I imagine to have been a Classical Library hardly ever rivalled in beauty and value. It was the gathering of a deeply read critic, as well as of an openhanded purchaser.

The bias of Dr. BURNEY's learning and tastes in literature led him to a preference of the Greek classics far above the Latin. Naturally, his Library bore this character in counterpart. He aimed at collecting Greek authors—and especially the dramatists—in such a way that the collocation of his copies gave a sort of chronological view of the literary history of the books and of their successive recensions.

For the tragedians, more particularly, his researches were brilliantly successful. Of *Æschylus* he had amassed forty-seven editions; of *Sophocles*, one hundred and two; of *Euripides*, one hundred and sixty-six.

His first publication was a sharp criticism (in the *Monthly Review*) on Mr. (afterwards Bishop) HUNTINGFORD's Collection of Greek poems entitled *Monostrophica*. This was followed, in 1789, by the issue of an Appendix to SCAPULA's Lexicon; and in 1807 by a collection of the correspondence of BENTLEY and other scholars. Two years later, he gave to students of Greek his *Tentamen de Metris ab Æschylo in choricis cantibus adhibitis*, and to the youthful theologians his meritorious abridgment of Bishop PEARSON's

---

* More than one of Burney's scholars was accustomed to speak feelingly on the topic of ancient school ' discipline' when any passing incident led the talk in that direction in after life.

Exposition of the Creed. In 1812, he published the Lexicon of PHILEMON.

The only Church preferments enjoyed by Dr. BURNEY were the rectory of St. Paul, Deptford, near London, and that of Cliffe, also in Kent. His only theological publication—other than the abridgment of PEARSON—was a sermon which he had preached in St. Paul's Cathedral in 1812. Late in life he was made a Prebendary of Lincoln.

Like his father, and others of his family, Charles BURNEY was a very sociable man. He lived much with PARR and with PORSON, and, like those eminent scholars, he had the good and catholic taste which embraced in its appreciations, and with like geniality, old wine, as well as old books. He was less wise in nourishing a great dislike to cool breezes. 'Shut the door,' was usually his first greeting to any visitant who had to introduce himself to the Doctor's notice; and it was a joke against him, in his later days, that the same words were his parting salutation to a couple of highwaymen who had taken his purse as he was journeying homewards in his carriage, and who were adding cruelty to robbery by exposing him to the fresh air when they made off.

Some of Dr. BURNEY's choicest books were obtained when the Pinelli Library was brought to England from Italy. The prime ornament of his manuscript Collection, a thirteenth century copy of the *Iliad*, of great beauty and rich in scholia, was bought at the sale of the fine Library of Charles TOWNELEY, Collector of the Marbles.

Although classical literature was the strength of the BURNEY Collection, it was also rich in some other departments. Of English newspapers, for example, he had brought together nearly seven hundred volumes of the seventeenth and eighteenth centuries, reaching from the reign of JAMES THE FIRST to the reign of GEORGE THE THIRD.   No such assemblage had been theretofore formed, I think, by any Collector.   He had also amassed nearly four hundred volumes containing materials for a history of the British Stage, which materials have subsequently been largely used by Mr. GENEST, in his work on that subject. For BURNEY's life-long study of the Greek drama had gradually inspired him with a desire to trace what, in a sense, may be termed its modern revival, in the grand sequel given to it by SHAKESPEARE and his contemporaries.   He had also collected about five thousand engraved theatrical portraits, and two thousand portraits of literary personages.

A large number of his printed books contained marginal manuscript notes by BENTLEY, CASAUBON, BURMANN, and other noted scholars.   And in a series of one hundred and seventy volumes BURNEY had himself collected all the extant remains and fragments of Greek dramatic writers— about three hundred in number.   These remains he had arranged under the collective title of *Fragmenta Scenica Græca.*

A splendid vellum manuscript of the Greek orators, in scription of the fourteenth century, had been obtained from Dr. CLARKE, by whom it had been acquired during Lord ELGIN's Ottoman Embassy, and brought into England. It supplied lacunæ which are found wanting in all other known manuscripts.   It completed an imperfect oration of *Lycurgus*, and another of *Dinarchus.*   Another MS. of the Greek orators, of the fifteenth century, is only next in value to that derived from CLARKE's researches in the East, of 1800.   There is also a very fine manuscript of the Geography of PTOLEMY, with maps compiled in the fifteenth century, and two very choice copies of the Greek *Gospels*, one of which is of the tenth, and the other of the twelfth centuries.

In Latin classics, the BURNEY Manuscripts include a fourteenth century *Plautus*, containing no fewer than twenty plays—whereas a manuscript containing even twelve plays has long been regarded as a rarity. A fifteenth century copy of the mathematical tracts collected by PAPPUS ALEXANDRINUS, a *Callimachus* of the same date, and a curious Manuscript of the *Asinus Aureus* of APULEIUS, are also notable. The whole number of Classical Manuscripts which this Collector had brought together was stated, at the time of his death, to be three hundred and eighty-five.

Dr. BURNEY died on the twenty-eighth of December, 1817, having just entered upon his sixty-first year. He was buried at Deptford, amidst the lamentations of his parishioners at his loss.

For in BURNEY, too, the scholar and the Collector had not been suffered to dwarf or to engross the whole man. His parishioners assembled, soon after his death, to evince publicly their sense of what Death had robbed them of. The testimony then borne to his character was far better, because more pertinent, laudation, than is usually met with in the literature of tombstones. Those who had known the man intimately then said of him : ' His attainments in learning were united with equal generosity and kindness of heart. His impressive discourses from the pulpit became doubly beneficial from the influence of his own example.' The parishioners agreed to erect a monument to his memory, ' as a record of their affection for their revered pastor, monitor, and friend ; of their gratitude for his services, and of their unspeakable regret for his loss.'

Another meeting was called shortly afterwards, with a like object, but of another sort. Despite his reverence for Busbeian traditions, Dr. BURNEY had known how to win the love of his pupils. A large body of them met, under the chairmanship of the excellent John KAYE, then Regius Professor of Divinity at Cambridge, and afterwards Bishop of Lincoln, and they subscribed for the placing of a monument to their old master in Westminster Abbey.

On the twenty-third of February, 1818, the Trustees of the British Museum presented to the House of Commons a petition, praying that Dr. BURNEY's Library should be acquired for the Public. The prayer of the petition was supported by Mr. BANKES and by Mr. VANSITTART, and a Select Committee was appointed to inquire and report upon the application.

In order to an accurate estimate of the value of the Library, a comparison was instituted, in certain particulars, between its contents and those of the Collection already in the national Museum. In comparing the works of a series of twenty-four Greek authors, it was found that of those authors, taken collectively, the Museum possessed only two hundred and thirty-nine several editions, whereas Dr. Charles BURNEY had collected no fewer than seven hundred and twenty-five editions.* His Collection of the Greek dramatists was not only, as I have said, extensive, but it was arrayed after a peculiar and interesting manner. By making a considerable sacrifice of duplicate copies, he had brought his series of editions into an order which exhi-

---

* This small fact in classical bibliography is remarkable enough to call for some particular exemplifications, beyond those given in the text, on a former page. Of the three greatest Greek dramatists, Burney had 315 editions against 75 in the Library of the British Museum. Of Homer he had 87 against 45 ; of Aristophanes, 74 against 23 ; of Demosthenes, 50 against 18 ; and of the *Anthologia*, 30 against 19.

bited, at one view, all the diversities of text, recension, and commentary. His Greek grammarians were arrayed in like manner. And his collection of lexicographers generally, and of philologists, was both large and well selected.

The total number of printed books was nearly thirteen thousand five hundred volumes, that of manuscripts was five hundred and twenty; and the total sum given for the whole was thirteen thousand five hundred pounds.

It was estimated that the Collection had cost Dr. BURNEY a much larger sum, and that, possibly, if sold by public auction, it might have produced to his representatives more than twenty thousand pounds.

In the same year with the acquisition of the Burney Library, the national Collections were augmented by the purchase of the printed books of a distinguished Italian scholar long resident in France, and eminent for his con-

tributions to French literature. Pier Luigi GINGUENÉ— author of the *Histoire Littéraire d'Italie* and a conspicuous contributor to the early volumes of the *Biographie Universelle* —had brought together a good Collection of Italian, French, and Classical literature. It comprised, amongst the rest, the materials which had been gathered for the book by which the Collector is now chiefly remembered, and extended, in the whole, to more than four thousand three hundred separate works, of which number nearly one thousand seven hundred related to Italian literature, or to its history. This valuable Collection was obtained by the Trustees — owing to the then depressed state of the Continental book-market—for one thousand pounds. And, in point of literary value, it may be described as the first— in point of price, as the cheapest—of a series of purchases which now began to be made on the Continent.

A more numerous printed Library had been purchased together with a cabinet of coins and a valuable herbarium, at Munich, three years earlier, at the sale of the Collections of Baron Von Moll. His Library exceeded fourteen thousand volumes, nearly eight thousand of which related to the physical sciences and to cognate subjects. The cost of this purchase, with the attendant expenses, was four thousand seven hundred and seventy pounds. The whole sum was defrayed out of the fund bequeathed by Major Arthur Edwards.[*]

These successive purchases, together with the Hargrave Collection—acquired in 1813—increased the theretofore much neglected Library by an aggregate addition of nearly thirty-five thousand volumes. And for four successive years (1812-15) Parliament made a special annual grant of one thousand pounds[†] for the purchase of printed books relating to British History.

The peculiar importance of the Hargrave Collection consisted in its manuscripts and its annotated printed books. The former were about five hundred in number, and were works of great juridical weight and authority, not merely the curiosities of black-letter law. Their Collector was the most eminent parliamentary lawyer of his day, but his devotion to the science of law had, to some degree, impeded his enjoyment of its sweets. During some of the best years of his life he had been more intent on increasing his legal lore than on swelling his legal

---

[*] It was also from the Edwards fund that the whole costs of the Oriental MSS. of Halhed, and of the Minerals of Hatchett, together with those of several other early and important acquisitions, were defrayed. That fund, in truth, was the mainstay of the Museum during the years of parliamentary parsimony.

[†] Of these four thousand pounds, two thousand three hundred and forty-five pounds seem to have been expended in Printed Books; the remainder, probably, in Manuscripts.

profits. And thus the same legislative act which enriched the Museum Library, in both of its departments, helped to smooth the declining years of a man who had won an uncommon distinction in his special pursuit. Francis HARGRAVE died on the sixteenth of August, 1821, at the age of eighty.

Leaving now this not very long list of acquisitions made by the National Library, in the way of purchase, either at the public cost or from endowments, we have again to turn to a new and conspicuous instance of private liberality. Like CRACHERODE, and like BURNEY, Francis Henry EGERTON belonged to a profession which at nearly all periods of our history—though in a very different degree in different ages—has done eminent honour and rendered large services to the nation, and that in an unusual variety of paths.

Each of these three clergymen is now chiefly remembered as a 'Collector.' Each of them would seem to have been placed quite out of his true element and sphere of labour, when assuming the responsibilities of a priest in the Church of England. CRACHERODE was scarcely more fitted for the work, at all events, of a preacher—save by the tacit lessons of a most meek and charitable life—than he was fitted to head a cavalry charge on the field of battle. BURNEY was manifestly cut out by nature for the work of a schoolmaster; although, as we have seen, he was able— late, comparatively, in life—so to discharge (for a very few years) the duties of a parish priest as to win the love of his flock. EGERTON was unsuited to clerical work of almost any and every kind. Yet he, too, with all his eccentricities and his indefensible absenteeism, became a public benefactor. The last act of his life was to make a provision which has been fruitful in good, having a bearing—very real though indirect—upon the special duties of the priestly function, for which he was himself so little adapted. The bequests of Francis EGERTON had, among their many useful results, the enabling of Thomas CHALMERS to add one more to his fruitful labours for the Christian Church and for the world.

It may not, I trust, be out of place to notice in this connection, and as one among innumerable debts which our country owes specifically to its Church Establishment, the impressive and varied way in which the English Church has, at every period, inculcated the lesson (by no means, now-adays, a favourite lesson of 'the age') that men owe duties to posterity, as well as duties to their contemporaries. The fact bears directly on the subject of this book. Into every path of life many men must needs enter, from time to time, without possessing any peculiar and real fitness for it. In a path which (in the course of successive ages) has been trodden by some millions of men, there must needs have been a crowd of incomers who had been better on the outside. They were like the square men who get to be thrust violently into round holes. But, even of these misplaced men, not a few have learnt, under the teaching of the Church, that if they could not with efficiency do pulpit work or parish work, there was other work which they could do, and do perpetually. Men, for example, who loved literature could, for all time to come, secure for the poorest student ample access to the best books, and to the inexhaustible treasures they contain. CRACHERODE did this. BURNEY helped to do it. EGERTON not only did the like, in his degree, in several parts of England, but he en-abled other and abler men to write new books of a sort which are conspicuously adapted to add to the equipment of divines for their special duty and work in the world.

Neglecting to learn many lessons which the Church teaches, to her clergy as well as to laymen, he had at least learnt one lesson of practical and permanent value.

Hence it is that, in addition to the matchless roll of English worthies which, in her best days, the Church has furnished—in that long line of men, from her ranks, who have done honour to her, and to England, under *every* point of view—she can show a subsidiary list, comprising men whose benefactions are more influential than were, or could have been, the labours of their lives; men of the sort who, being dead, can yet speak, and to much better purpose than ever they could speak when alive. Among such is the Churchman whose testamentary gifts have now very briefly to be mentioned.

Francis Henry EGERTON was a younger son of John EGERTON, Bishop of Durham, by the Lady Anna Sophia GREY, daughter and coheir of Henry GREY, Duke of Kent. He was born on the eleventh of November, 1756. The Bishop of Durham was fifth in descent from the famous Chancellor of England, Thomas EGERTON, Viscount Brachley, to whom, as he lay upon his death-bed, BACON came with the news of King JAMES's promise to make him an Earl. Before the patent could be sealed, the ex-chancellor, it will be remembered, was dead, and JAMES, to show his gratitude to the departed statesman, sold for a large sum the Earldom of Bridgewater to the Chancellor's son. Eventually, of that earldom Francis Henry EGERTON was, in his old age, the eighth and last inheritor.

Mr. EGERTON was educated at Eton and at All Souls. He took his M.A. in 1780, and in the following year was presented, by his relative, Francis, Duke of BRIDGEWATER —the father of inland navigation in Britain—to the Rectory of Middle, in Shropshire, a living which he held for eight and forty years.

He was a toward and good scholar. From his youth he was a great reader and a lover of antiquities, as well as a respectable philologist. His foible was an overweening although a pardonable pride in his ancestry. That ancestry embraced what was noblest in the merely antiquarian point of view, along with the grand historical distinctions of state service rendered to Queen Elizabeth, and of a new element introduced into the mercantile greatness of England under George the Third. A man may be forgiven for being proud of a family which included the servant of Elizabeth and friend of Bacon, as well as the friend of Brindley. But the pride, as years increased, became somewhat wearisome to acquaintances; though it proved to be a source of no small profit to printers and engravers, both at home and abroad. Mr. Egerton's writings in biography and genealogy are very numerous. They date from 1793 to 1826. Some of them are in French. All of them relate, more or less directly, to the family of Egerton.

In the year 1796, he appeared as an author in another department, and with much credit. His edition of the *Hippolytus* of Euripides is also noticeable for its modest and candid acknowledgment of the assistance he had derived from other scholars. He afterwards collected and edited some fragments of the odes of Sappho. The later years of his life were chiefly passed in Paris. His mind had been soured by some unhappy family troubles and discords, and as years increased a lamentable spirit of eccentricity increased with them. It had grown with his growth, but did not weaken with his loss of bodily and mental vigour.

One of the most noted manifestations of this eccentricity was but the distortion of a good quality. He had a fondness for dumb animals. He could not bear to see them suffer by any infliction,—other than that necessitated by a love of field sports, which, to an Englishman, is as natural and as necessary as mother's milk. At length, the Parisians were scandalised by the frequent sight of a carriage, full of dogs, attended with as much state and solemnity as if it contained 'milord' in person. To his servants he was a most liberal master. He provided largely for the parochial service and parochial charities of his two parishes of Middle and Whitchurch (both in Shropshire). He was, occasionally, a liberal benefactor to men of recondite learning, such as meet commonly with small reward in this world.* But much of his life was stamped with the ineffaceable discredit of sacred functions voluntarily assumed, yet habitually discharged by proxy.

On the death, in 1823, of his elder brother—who had become seventh Earl of Bridgewater, under the creation of 1617, on the decease of Francis third Duke and sixth (Egerton) Earl—Francis Henry Egerton became eighth Earl of Bridgewater. But he continued to live chiefly in Paris, where he died, in April, 1829, at the age of seventy-two years. With the peerage he had inherited a

---

* To give but one example: Samuel Burder—the author of the excellent work, so illustrative of Biblical literature, entitled *Oriental Customs* —states, in his MS. correspondence now before me, that the *only* effective reward given to him, in the course of his long labours, was given by Lord Bridgewater. The book above mentioned was 'successful;' 'but,' he says, 'the booksellers, as usual, reaped the harvest,' not the author. It is—shall I say?—an amusing comment on this latter clause, to find that in one of his letters to Lord Bridgewater, Burder states that the person who took the most kindly notice of his literary labours, next after Lord Bridgewater himself, was — the Emperor of Russia (Alexander I).

very large estate, although the vast ducal property in canals had passed, as is well known, in 1803, to the LEVESON-GOWERS.

Part of Lord BRIDGEWATER's leisure at Paris was given to the composition of a largely-planned treatise on Natural Theology. But the task was far above the powers of the undertaker. He had made considerable progress, after his fashion, and part of what he had written was put superbly into type, from the press of DIDOT. Very wisely, he resolved to enable abler men to do the work more efficiently. And this was a main object of his remarkable Will.

That portion of the document which eventually gave to the world the well-known 'Bridgewater Treatises' of CHALMERS, BUCKLAND, WHEWELL, PROUT, ROGET, and their fellows in the task, reads thus :—

'I give and bequeath to the President of the Royal Society the sum of eight thousand pounds, to be applied according to the order and direction of the said President of the Royal Society, in full and without any diminution or abatement whatsoever, in such proportions and at such times, according to his discretion and judgment, and without being subject to any control or responsibility whatsoever, to such person or persons as the said President for the time being of the aforesaid Royal Society shall or may nominate or appoint and employ. And it is my will and particular request that some person or persons be nominated and appointed by him to write, print, publish, and expose to public sale, one thousand copies of a work "*On the Power, Wisdom, and Goodness of God, as manifested in the Creation,*" illustrating such work by all reasonable arguments ; as, for instance, the variety and formation of God's creatures, in the animal, vegetable, and mineral kingdoms ;

the effect of digestion, and thereby of conversion ; the construction of the hand of man, and an infinite variety of
arrangements ; as also by discoveries, ancient and modern,
in arts, sciences, and in the whole extent of literature.   And
I desire that the profits arising from and out of the circulation and sale of the aforesaid work shall be paid by the said
President of the said Royal Society, as of right, as a further
remuneration and reward to such persons as the said President shall or may so nominate, appoint, and employ as
aforesaid.   And I hereby fully authorise and empower the
said President, in his own discretion, to direct and cause to
be paid and advanced to such person or persons during
the printing and preparing of the said work the sum of
three hundred pounds, and also the sum of five hundred
pounds sterling to the same person or persons during the
printing and preparing of the said work for the press, out
of, and in part of, the same eight thousand pounds sterling.
And I will and direct that the remainder of the said sum
of eight thousand pounds sterling, or of the stocks or funds
wherein the same shall have been invested, together with
all interest, dividend, or dividends accrued thereon, be
transferred, assigned, and paid over to such person or persons, their or his executors, administrators, or assigns, as
shall have been so nominated, appointed, and employed by
the said President of the said Royal Society, at the instance
and request of the same President, as and when he shall
deem the object of this bequest to have been fully complied with by such person or persons so nominated,
appointed, and employed by him as aforesaid.'

What was done by the Trustees under this part of Lord
Bridgewater's Will, and with what result, is known to all
readers. That other portion of the Will which relates to
his bequest to the British Museum reads thus :—'I give

and bequeath to the Trustees for the time being of the *British Museum* at Montagu House, in London, to be there deposited . . . for the use of the said Museum, in conformity with the rules, orders, and regulations of the said establishment, absolutely and for ever, all and every my Collection of Manuscripts as hereinafter particularly described. That is to say, the several volumes of Manuscripts, and all papers, parchments (written or printed), and all letters, despatches, registers, rolls, documents, evidences, authorities and signatures, and all impressions of seals and marks, of every description and sort, and of what nature or kind, severally and generally belonging to my Collection of Manuscripts, or in my possession, stamped with my arms or otherwise (except such letters, notes, papers, &c., as are hereinafter directed to be burned and destroyed [' *two words cancelled*, BRIDGEWATER '], in the discretion of my Trustees and Executors hereinafter appointed; and also save and except all such letters, papers, and writings as are attached to and accompanying the printed books specifically bequeathed by me to the Library at *Ashridge,* and which said last-mentioned letters, papers, and writings are also, if I mistake not, stamped with my arms. And I also will and require that all and every the aforesaid manuscripts, papers, parchments (written or printed), letters, despatches, registers, rolls, documents, evidences, authorities, signatures, impressions of seals and marks of every description and sort, and every other Manuscript or Manuscripts appertaining to my said Collection whatsoever and wheresoever, or which shall or may hereafter, during my life, be added thereto (but not private letters, notes, or memorandums of any sort or kind, which I direct to be burned or destroyed), shall, within the space of two years from the day of my decease, be collected and removed to the *British Museum* as aforesaid, under the particular care, superintendence, and direction of Eugene Auguste Barbier, one of my Trustees and Executors hereinafter appointed; for which particular service I give and bequeath to him, the said Eugene Auguste Barbier, the sum of two thousand pounds sterling. I also give, bequeath, and demise unto the said Trustees of the *British Museum* all my estate, lands, parcels of land, ground, hereditaments and appurtenances, situate in the parish of *Whitchurch-cum-Marbury*, or in any other parish or place in the Counties of Salop or Chester, or in either or both of the said Counties, and also all the trees growing thereon, and all seats, sittings, and pews in the Parish Church of Whitchurch-cum-Marbury aforesaid, all or any of which I shall or may have bought or purchased, and which now belong to me by right of purchase, descent, or otherwise, to have and to hold the same estate, lands, parcels of land, ground, hereditaments and appurtenances, to them the said Trustees of the said *British Museum* for the time being for ever, upon the trusts nevertheless, and to and for the ends, intents, and purposes hereinafter particularly mentioned, expressed, and declared; that is to say, that the trees growing on the aforesaid estate, lands, parcels of lands, ground, hereditaments, and appurtenances, shall not be cut or brought down or destroyed, but shall and may be suffered to grow during their natural life, and that the smaller trees only may be thinned here and there, with care and judgment, so as to promote the growth of the larger trees; and that the same estate, lands, parcels of land, ground, hereditaments and appurtenances, seats, sittings or pews, or any part thereof, shall not be susceptible of being let, underlet or rented, by or to any person or persons who shall hold, have, take, or rent any estate, farm, lands, or property of or from the family of Egerton, or of or from any person or persons having that name, or of or from the Rector of *Whitchurch-cum-Marbury* aforesaid for the time being; and upon further trust that they the said Trustees of the British Museum for the time being do and shall lay out and apply the rents, issues, and profits which shall from time to time arise from and out of the said estate, lands, parcels of land, ground, hereditaments and appurtenances, in the purchase of manuscripts for the continual augmentation of the aforesaid Collection of Manuscripts.   I further will and direct that my said Trustees hereinafter appointed, within the space of eighteen calendar months after my decease, do lay out and invest in the Three per cent. Consolidated stocks or funds of England, in the names of the Trustees of the *British Museum* for the time being, or in such names and for such account as the said Trustees shall direct, the sum of seven thousand pounds sterling, the interest and dividends whereof, as the same shall from time to time become due and payable, I desire and direct shall and may be paid over by the said Trustees to such person or persons as shall from time to time be charged with the care and superintendence of the said Collection of Manuscripts.   I also give, grant, bequeath, and devise unto my Trustees hereinafter appointed all and singular my house, land, tenements, hereditaments, and appurtenances at or near *Little Gaddesden*, in the County of Herts, upon trust that they my said Trustees do and shall, during their joint lives and the life of the survivor of them, let and demise the same for such term or time as they shall think fit, for the best rent that can be had and gotten for the same; but the same premises, under no circumstances, to be let, underlet, or rented by or to any person or persons who shall have, hold, take, or rent any estate, farm, or property of or from the family of EGERTON, or any person or persons bearing that name, and do and shall pay over the rents, issues, and profits thereof, as and when received, to the Trustees for the time being of the *British Museum* aforesaid, to be laid out and applied by such last-mentioned Trustees in the service and for the continued augmentation of the said Collection of Manuscripts ; and from and after the decease of the survivor of them my said Trustees hereinafter appointed, I give and devise the said house, land, tenements, hereditaments and appurtenances, unto and for the use of the proprietor or proprietors of the Manor and Estate of *Ashridge*, his heirs and assigns for ever.   And as to all the rest, residue and remainder of my real and personal estate and effects, of every nature and kind soever and wheresoever situate, not hereinbefore disposed of, or availably so, for the purposes intended, I give, devise, and bequeath the same to my said Trustees, upon trust that they my said Trustees do pay over and transfer the same to the said Trustees of the *British Museum*, and do otherwise render the same available for the service of and towards maintaining, preserving, keeping up, improving, augmenting, and extending, as opportunities may offer, my said Collection of Manuscripts so deposited in the *British Museum* as aforesaid, in the most advantageous manner, according to their judgment and discretion.'

'The eccentricity of which I have spoken showed itself in the successive changes of detail and other modifications which these bequests underwent before the testator's death. What with the Will and its many codicils, the documents, collectively, came to be of a kind which might task the acumen of a FEARNE or a St. LEONARDS.   But the drift of the Will was undisturbed.   The restrictions as to the under-letting of the Whitchurch estate, and the like, were now limited by codicils to a prescribed term of years after the testator's death; power was given to the Museum Trustees to sell, also after a certain interval, the landed estate bequeathed for the purchase of manuscripts, should it be deemed conducive to the interest of the Library so to do; and an additional sum of five thousand pounds was given to the Trustees for the further increase of the Collection of Manuscripts, and for the reward of its keeper, in lieu of the residuary interest in the testator's personal estate.

On the 10th of March, 1832, the Trustees resolved that the yearly proceeds of the last-named bequest should be paid to the Librarians in charge of the MSS., but that their ordinary salaries, on the establishment, should be diminished by a like amount.

The Manuscripts bequeathed by Lord BRIDGEWATER comprise a considerable collection of the original letters of the Kings, Queens, Statesmen, Marshals, and Diplomatists, of France; another valuable series of original letters and papers of the authors and scientific men of France and of Italy; many papers of Italian Statesmen; and a portion of the donor's own private correspondence. The latter series of papers includes, amongst others, letters by Andres, D'Ansse de Villoisin, the Prince of Aremberg, Auger, Barbier, the Duke of Blacas, Bodoni, Boissonade, Bonpland, Canova, Cuvier, Ginguené, Humboldt, Valckenaer, and Visconti. Some of these are merely letters of compliment. Others—and, in an especial degree, those of D'Ansse de Villoisin, of Boissonade, of Ginguené, of Humboldt, and of Visconti—contain much interesting matter on questions of archæology, art, and history.

The earliest additions to the Egerton Collection were made by the Trustees in May, 1832. In the selection of MSS. for purchase the Trustees, with great propriety, have given a preference—on the whole; not exclusively—to that class of documents of which the donor's own Collection was mainly composed—the materials, namely, of Continental history.   Amongst the earliest purchases of 1832 was a curious Venetian *Portolano* of the fifteenth century.   In the same year a large series of Irish Manuscripts, collected by the late John HARDIMAN, was acquired.   This extends from the Egerton number '74' to '214'; and from the same Collector was obtained the valuable *Minutes of Debates in the House of Commons*, taken by Colonel CAVENDISH, between the years—so memorable in our history—from 1768 to 1774.*   In the year 1835, a large collection of manuscripts illustrative of Spanish history was purchased from Mr. RICH, a literary agent in London, and another large series of miscellaneous manuscripts—historical, political, and literary—from the late bookseller, Thomas RODD.   From the same source another like collection was obtained in 1840.   An extensive series of French State Papers was acquired (by the agency of Messrs. BARTHES and LOWELL) in 1843; and also, in that year, a collection of Persian MSS.   In the following year a curious series of drawings, illustrating the antiquities, manners, and customs of China, was obtained; and, in 1845, another valuable series of French historical manuscripts.

Meanwhile, the example set by Lord BRIDGEWATER had incited one of those many liberal-minded Trustees of the British Museum who have become its benefactors by aug-mentation, as well as by faithful guardianship, to follow it in exactly the same track.   Charles LONG, Lord Farn-borough, bequeathed (in 1838) the sum of two thousand eight hundred and seventy-two pounds in Three per cent. Consols, specifically as an augmentation of the Bridgewater

---

* These form the Egerton MSS. 215 to 262 inclusive.

fund. Lord FARNBOROUGH's bequest now produces eighty-six pounds a year; Lord BRIDGEWATER's, about four hundred and ninety pounds a year. Together, therefore, they yield five hundred and seventy pounds, annually, for the improvement of the National Collection of Manuscripts.

In 1850 and 1852, an extensive series of German *Albums* —many of them belonging to celebrated scholars—was acquired. These are now 'Egerton MSS. 1179' to '1499,' inclusive, and '1540' to '1607.' A curious collection of papers relating to the Spanish Inquisition was also obtained in 1850. In 1857, the important historical collection, known as 'the Bentinck Papers,' was purchased from Tycho MOMMSEN, of Oldenburgh. In the following year, another series of Spanish State Papers, and also the Irish Manuscripts of HENRY MONCK MASON;—in 1860, a further series of 'Bentinck Papers;'—and in 1861, an extensive collection of the Correspondence of POPE and of Bishop WARBURTON, were successively acquired.

To these large accumulations of the materials of history were added, in the succeeding years, other important collections of English correspondence, and of autograph MSS. of famous authors; and also a choice collection of Spanish and Portuguese Manuscripts brought together by Count DA PONTE, and abounding with historical information. To this an addition was made last year (1869) of other like papers, amongst which are notable some Venetian *Relazioni;* papers of Cardinals Carlo CARAFFA and Flavio ORSINI ; and some letters of Antonio PEREZ. In 1869, there was also obtained, by means of the conjoined Egerton and Farnborough funds, a curious parcel of papers relating to the early affairs of the Corporation and trade of Dover, from the year 1387 to 1678; together with some other papers illustrative of the cradle-years of our Indian empire.

BOOK II,
Chap. III.
BOOK-
LOVERS AND
PUBLIC
BENEFAC-
TORS.

THE 'BYRON
MSS.' IN THE
EGERTON
COLLECTION
(1867).

Amongst the latest accessions obtained from the Bridge-water fund are some MSS. from the hand of a famous English poet of the last generation. These have now an additional, and special, interest in English eyes, from a recent lamentable occurrence. The pen of a slanderer has aimed at gaining a sort of celebrity, more enduring than anything of its own proper production could hope to secure, by attempting to affix on BYRON and on Augusta LEIGH—after both the great poet and the affectionate sister have lain many years in their several graves, and can no longer rebut the slander—the stain of an enormous guilt. Some, however, are yet alive, by whom the calumny *can*, and will, be conclusively exposed. Meanwhile, the slanderer's poor aim will, probably, have been reached—but in an unexpected and unenviable way.

> 'The link
> *Thou* formest in his fortunes, bids us think
> Of thy poor malice, naming thee with scorn.'

Very happily, the calumniating pen was not held in any English hand.

Much more might, and not unfitly, be said in illustration of the historical and literary value of those manuscript accessions to the National Library which, in these later years, have accrued out of the proceeds of Lord BRIDGEWATER's gift. Enough, however, has been stated, to serve by way of sample.

OTHER BENE-
FACTIONS OF
LORD
BRIDGE-
WATER.

Nor were these the only literary bequests and foundations of the last Earl of BRIDGEWATER. He bequeathed, as heir-looms, two considerable Libraries, rich both in theology and in history—to the respective rectors, for ever, of the parishes of Middle and of Whitchurch. These, I learn—from MS. correspondence now before me—are of great value, and are gladly made available, by their owners for the time being, to the use of persons able and willing to profit by them.   He also founded a Library, likewise by way of heirloom, at Ashridge. Book II, Chap. III. Book-Lovers and Public Benefactors.

Whilst the National Library was thus being gradually improved, both by increased liberality on the part of Parliament and, far more largely, by the munificent gifts of individuals, other departments of the Museum had not been neglected.

Charles Greville, the nephew of Sir William Hamilton, had collected, in his residence at Paddington Green, a noble cabinet of minerals.   It was the finest assemblage of its kind which had yet been seen in England.   For the purchase of this Collection Parliament made a grant, in the year 1810, of thirteen thousand seven hundred and twenty-seven pounds. The acquisition of the Greville Minerals ;

In 1816, a valuable accession came to the zoological department, by the purchase, for the sum of eleven hundred pounds, of a Collection of British Zoology, which had been formed at Knowle, in Devonshire, by Colonel George Montagu.   The Montagu Collection was especially rich in birds. of the Montagu Museum ; [See, hereafter, Book III, c. I.]

Nine years later, the Library was further benefited, in the way of gift, by a choice Italian Collection, gathered and given by Sir Richard Colt Hoare, of Stourhead ; and, in the way of Parliamentary grant, by the acquisition of the collection of manuscripts, coins, and other antiquities, which had been made in the East, during his years of Consulship at Baghdad, by Claudius James Rich. and of the Collections of Sir R. C. Hoare

Sir Richard Hoare was not less distinguished for the taste and judgment with which he had collected the historical literature of Italy, than for the zeal and ability with which he cultivated, both as author and as patron, the—in Britain—too much neglected department of provincial topography.   He had spent nearly five years in Italy—partly during the reign of NAPOLEON—and amassed a very fine collection of books illustrative of all departments of Italian history.   In 1825, Sir Richard presented this Collection to the Trustees of the British Museum in these words:—'Anxious to follow the liberal example of our gracious monarch GEORGE THE FOURTH, of Sir George BEAUMONT, and of Richard Payne KNIGHT (though in a very humble degree), I do give unto the British Museum my Collection of Topography, made during a residence of five years abroad; and hoping that the more modern publications may be added to it hereafter.'   The Library so given included about seventeen hundred and thirty separate works.   Sir Richard did something, himself, to secure the fulfilment of the annexed wish, by adding to his first gift, made in 1825, in subsequent years.

The researches of Claudius RICH merit some special notice.   He may be regarded as the first explorer of Assyria.   Had it not been for his early death, it is very probable that he might have anticipated some of the brilliant discoveries of Mr. LAYARD.   But his quickly intercepted researches will be best described, in connection with the later explorations in the same field.   Here it may suffice to say that from Mr. RICH's representatives a Collection of Manuscripts, extending to eight hundred and two volumes—Syriac, Arabic, Persian, and Turkish—was obtained, by purchase, in 1825, together with a small Collection of Coins and miscellaneous antiquities.

To the Oriental Manuscripts of RICH, an important addition was made in the course of the same year by the bequest of Mr. John Fowler HULL—another distinguished

Orientalist who passed from amongst us at an early age—
who also bequeathed a Collection of Oriental and Chinese
printed books. Mr. HULL's legacy was the small beginning of that Chinese Library which has now become so
large.

It was also in the year 1825 that Sir Gore OUSELEY
presented a Collection of Marbles obtained from Persepolis.
These will be mentioned hereafter in connection with the
antiquarian explorations of Claudius RICH and his suc-
cessors. The donor of the Persepolitan Marbles died on
the eighteenth of November, 1844.

In addition to these many liberal benefactions made
during the earlier years of the present century, a smaller
gift (virtually a gift, though in name a ' deposit') of the
same period claims brief notice, on account both of its
artistic value and of its curious history. I refer to that
exquisite monument of ancient art known, for many years,
as the ' Barberini Vase,' but now more commonly as the
' Portland Vase,' from the name of its last individual
possessor.

This vase is one of the innumerable acquisitions which
the country owes to the intelligent research and cultivated
taste of Sir William HAMILTON. It had been found more
than a century before his time (probably in the year 1640),
beneath the Monte del Grano, about three miles from
Rome, on the road to Tusculum. The place of the discovery was a sepulchral chamber, within which was found a
sarcophagus containing the vase, and bearing an inscription
to the memory of the Emperor ALEXANDER SEVERUS (*A.D.*
222-235) and to his mother. About this sarcophagus and
its inscription there have been dissertations and rejoinders,
essays and commentaries, illustrative and obscurative, in

Book II,
Chap. III.
Book-
Lovers and
Public
Benefac-
tors.

sufficient number to immortalise half a dozen Jonathan Oldbucks and 'Antigonus' Mac-Cribbs. And the controversy is still undetermined.

After having been long a conspicuous ornament of the Barberini Palace, the 'Barberini Vase' was bought by Hamilton. When, in December, 1784, he paid one of his visits to England, the vase came with him. Its fame had previously excited the desires of many virtuosi. By the Duchess of Portland it was so strongly coveted, that she employed a niece of Sir William to conduct a negotiation with much more solemnity and mystery than the ambassador would have thought needful in conducting a critical Treaty

Correspond-
ence of Mrs.
Delany, vol.
ii (in many
places).

of Peace. The Duchess's precautions foiled the curiosity of not a few of her fellow-collectors in virtû. 'I have heard,' wrote Horace Walpole, 'that Sir W. Hamilton's renowned vase, which had disappeared with so much mystery, is again recovered; not in the tomb, but the treasury, of the Duchess of Portland, in which, I fancy, it had made ample room for itself. Sir William told me it would never go out of England. I do not see how he could warrant *that*. The Duchess and Lord Edward have both shown how little stability there is in the riches of that family.' As yet,

II. Walpole to
Lady Upper-
Ossory, 10
August, 1785.
(Cunn. Edit.,
vol. ix, p. 3.)

the reader will remember, that 'Portland Estate,' which was so profitably to turn farms into streets, was but in expectancy.

And then Walpole adds: '*My* family has felt how insecure is the permanency of heir-looms,'—the thought of that grand 'Houghton Gallery,' and its transportation to Russia, coming across his memory, whilst telling Lady Upper-Ossory the story of the coveted vase, just imported from the Barberini Palace at Rome.

The Duchess of Portland enjoyed the sight of her beautiful purchase only during a few weeks. It was bought

in by the family (at the nominal price of £1029*) at the
sale of her famous museum of curiosities—a sale extending
to more than four thousand lots—and twenty-four years
afterwards, it was lent, for exhibition (1810), by the third
Duke of PORTLAND, to the Trustees of the British Museum,
where it has since remained.

When WEDGWOOD set about imitating the Portland
Vase in his manufactory at Etruria—for which purpose the
then Duke liberally lent it to him—he discovered that the
vase had been broken and skilfully put together again.
After it had been publicly exhibited during almost thirty-
five years in London, the frenzy of a maniac led—as it
seemed at the moment—to its utter destruction.   But,
mainly by the singular skill and patience of the late John
DOUBLEDAY (a craftsman attached to the Department of
Antiquities for many years), it was soon restored to its pris-
tine beauty.   That one act of violence in 1845 is the only
instance of very serious injury arising from open exhibition
to all comers which the annals of the Museum record.

* Horace Walpole, at this sale, purchased the fine MS., with drawings
by Julio Clovio, which was long an ornament of the villa at Strawberry
Hill, and also a choice cameo of Jupiter Serapis, for which he gave a
hundred and seventy-three pounds. He preferred, he said, either of
them to the vase.   So, at least, he fancied when he found it unattainable.
‘I am glad,’ he wrote to Conway (18 June, 1786), ‘ that Sir Joshua saw
no more excellence in the *Jupiter* than in the Clovio, or the Duke, I
suppose, would have purchased it as he did the Vase—for £1000.   I told
Sir William and the late Duchess—when I never thought that it would
be mine—that I would rather have the head than the vase.’

CHAPTER IV.

THE KING'S OR 'GEORGIAN' LIBRARY;— ITS COLLECTOR, AND ITS DONOR.

'A crown,
Golden in show, is but a wreath of thorns;
Brings dangers, troubles, cares, and sleepless nights,
To him who wears the regal diadem.'

———

'O polish'd perturbation! golden care !
That keep'st the ports of slumber open wide
To many a watchful night ! '—
Henry IV, Part 2, iv, 4.

Notices of the Literary Tastes and Acquirements of King GEORGE THE THIRD.—*His Conversations with Men of Letters.*—*History of his Library and of its Transfer to the British Nation by* GEORGE THE FOURTH.

BOOK II, Chap. IV. THE KING'S OR 'GEORGIAN' LIBRARY.

THE CONTRASTS BETWEEN GEORGE III AND GEORGE IV.

THE strong antagonisms in mind, in disposition, and in tastes, which existed between GEORGE THE THIRD and GEORGE THE FOURTH, may be seen in the small and incidental acts of their respective lives, almost as distinctly, and as sharply defined, as they are seen in their private lives, or in their characteristic modes of transacting the public business. GEORGE THE THIRD regretted the giving away of the old 'Royal Library' of the Kings his ancestors, not because he grudged a liberal use of royal books by private scholars, but because he thought a fine Library was the necessary appendage of a palace. He occasionally stinted himself of some of his personal enjoyments in life, in order to have the more means to amass books. He formed, during his own lifetime, a Library which is probably both larger and finer than any like Collection ever made by any one man, even under the advantageous conditions of royalty. When he had collected his books, he made them liberally accessible. To himself, as we all know, Nature had not given any very conspicuous faculty for turning either books or men to good account; nor had education done much to improve the parts he possessed.

GEORGE THE FOURTH, as it seems, regretted the formation of the new Royal Library by the King his father, because, when he inherited it, he found that its decent maintenance and upkeeping would demand every year a sum of money which he could spend in ways far more to his taste. He had been far better educated than his father had been. And to him Nature had given good abilities; but study was about the last and least likely use to which, at any time, he was inclined to apply them. If he saw any good at all in having, on his accession, the ownership of a large Library, it lay, not in the power it afforded him of benefiting literature, and the labourers in literature, but in the possibility he saw that so fine a collection of books might be made to produce a round sum of money. One of his first thoughts about the matter was, that it would be a good thing to offer his father's beloved Library for sale— to the Emperor of Russia. By what influences that shrewd scheme of turning a penny was diverted will be seen in the sequel.

If GEORGE THE THIRD was, in respect to his parts, only slenderly endowed, he had in another respect large gifts. Both his industry and his power of sustained application were uncommon. And his conscientious sense of responsibility for the use of such abilities as he had was no less remarkable. Whatever may have been his mistakes in government, no man ever sat on the British throne who was more thoroughly honest in his intentions, or more deeply anxious to show, in the discharge of his duties, his consciousness of being

'Ever in his great taskmaster's eye.'

That his public acts did not more adequately correspond with his good desires was due, in large measure, to an infelicitous parentage and a narrow education.

As the father of lies sometimes speaks truth, so a mere party manifesto may sometimes give sound advice, though clothed in a discreditable garb. When public attention came first to be attracted to the character of the peculiar influences which began to mould the training of the young Prince of WALES soon after his father's death, a Court Chamberlain received, one morning, by the post, an unsigned document, which he thought it his duty to place in the hands of the Prime Minister, and he, when he had read it, thought the paper important enough to be laid before the King. This anonymous memorial denounced, as early as in the winter of 1752 (when the Prince was but fourteen years old), the sort of education which GEORGE THE THIRD was receiving as being likely to initiate an unfortunate reign.

The paper (which I have now before me) is headed: '*A Memorial of several Noblemen and Gentlemen of the first rank*,' and in the course of it there is an assertion—as being already matter of public notoriety—' that books inculcating the worst maxims of government, and defending the most avowed tyrannies, have been put into the hands of the Prince of Wales,' and such a fact, it is said, ' cannot but affect the memorialists with the most melancholy apprehensions when

they find that the men who had the honesty and resolution
to complain of such astonishing methods of instruction are
driven away from Court, and the men who have dared to
teach such doctrines are continued in trust and favour.'*

Making all allowance for partisan feeling and for that
tinge of Whig oligarchism which peeps out, as well in the
very title, as in the contents of this 'Memorial,' there was
obvious truth in the denunciation, and a modicum of true
prophecy in the inference.   But such a remonstrance had
just as little effect, in the way of checking undue influences,
as it had of wisdom in the form given to it, or in the mode
of its presentation at Court.

The Prince's education was not merely imbued with
ideas and maxims little likely to conduce towards a prosperous reign. It was intellectually narrow and mean. He
grew up, for example, in utter ignorance of many of the
great lights of English literature.   In respect to all books,
save one (that, happily, the greatest of all), he became one
of those who, through life, draw from the small cisterns,

Book II,
Chap. IV.
The
King's or
'Georgian'
Library.

A *Memorial,*
&c.; MS.
Addit. 6271,
fol. 3.

Narrow
range of
George the
Third's
tastes for
books.

---

* Lord Harcourt resigned his office of Governor to the Prince at the
beginning of December, 1752.   Scott, then the Prince's tutor, was
recommended to his office by Bolingbroke.   The Bishop of Peterborough's appointment as Preceptor was made in January, 1753.
Among the books complained of, the *Histoire de la Grande Bretagne*
of Father Orléans, and the *Introduction à la vie du Roi Henri IV* of
another Jesuit, Father Péréfixe, are said to have been included. Another
and more famous book, which was much in Prince George's hands in his
early years, was also obnoxious to the Whigs—Bolingbroke's *Idea of a
Patriot King*.   But it would scarcely have been prudent in the malcontents to have put a work which (whatever its faults) ranks, to some extent,
among our English classics, in the same expurgatory, or prohibitory,
index with the books of Orléans and of Péréfixe.   If George the Third
got some harm out of Lord Bolingbroke's book, he probably obtained
also some good.   Pure Whiggism—pure but not simple—has never been
noted for any discriminating tolerance of spirit.   And, in 1752, it was
furious at the prospect that the continuance of its long domination was
imperilled.

instead of going to the deep wells. He seems to have been trained to think that the literary glories of his country began with the age of Queen ANNE.

In after years, GEORGE THE THIRD attained to some dim consciousness of his own narrowness of culture. The ply, however, had been too early taken to be got rid of. No training, probably, could have made him a scholar. But his powers of application under wise direction would have opened to him stores of knowledge, from which unwise influences shut him out for life. His faculty of perseverance in study, it must be remembered, was backed by thorough honesty of nature, and by an ability to withstand temptations. When he was entering his nineteenth year, a sub-preceptor, who had watched him sedulously, said of him : ' He is a lad of good principle. He has no heroic strain, and no turn for extravagance. He loves peace, and, as yet, has shown very virtuous principles. He has the greatest temptation to gallant with ladies, who lay themselves out in the most shameless manner to draw him on, but to no purpose.' Certainly this last characteristic was neither an inherited virtue nor an ancestral tradition. And it stands in curious contrast with the tendencies of all his brothers and of almost all his sons.

From youth upwards the Prince read much, though he did not read wisely. No sooner was he King than he began to set about the collection of his noble Library. In the choice of a librarian he was not infelicitous, though the selection was in part dictated by a feeling of brotherly kindness. For he chose a very near relative—Mr. afterwards Sir Frederick Augusta BARNARD. Mr. BARNARD had many qualities which fitted him for his task.

The foundation of the Library was laid by a very fortunate purchase on the Continent. Its increase was largely promoted by a political revolution which ensued shortly afterwards ; and, in order to turn his large opportunities to most account, the King's Librarian modestly sought and instantly obtained the best advice which that generation could afford him—the advice of Samuel JOHNSON.

In 1762, the fine Library of Joseph SMITH, who had been British Consul at Venice during many years, was bought for the King.   It cost about ten thousand pounds. SMITH had ransacked Italy for choice books, much as his contemporary, Sir William HAMILTON, had ransacked that country for choice vases.   And he had been not less successful in his quest.   In amassing early and choice editions of the classics, and also the curiosities and rarities of fifteenth-century printing, he had been especially lucky. From the same source, but at a later date, GEORGE THE THIRD also obtained a fine gallery of pictures and a collection of coins and gems.   For these he gave twenty thousand pounds.   For seven or eight years the shops and warehouses of English booksellers were also sedulously examined, and large purchases were made from them.   In this labour JOHNSON often assisted, actively, as well as by advice.

When the suppression of the Jesuits in many parts of Europe made the literary treasures which that busy Society had collected—often upon a princely scale and with admirable taste, so far as their limitations permitted—both the King and his librarian were struck with the idea that another fine opportunity opened itself for book-buying on the Continent.   It was resolved that Mr. BARNARD should travel for the purpose of profiting by it.   Before he set out on his journey, he betook himself to JOHNSON for counsel as to the best way of setting about the task.

JOHNSON's counsel may be thus abridged : The litera-

Book II, Chap. IV. THE KING'S OR 'GEORGIAN' LIBRARY.

Dactyliotheca Smithiana ; 1707; Lady M. W. Montagu, Letters, vol. iii, p. 89.

ture of every country may be best gathered on its native soil. And the studies of the learned are everywhere influenced by peculiarities of government and of religion. In Italy you may, therefore, expect to meet with abundance of the works of the Canonists and the Schoolmen; in Germany with store of writers on the Feudal Laws; in Holland you will find the booksellers' shops swarming with the works of the Civilians. Of Canonists a few of the most eminent will suffice. Of the Schoolmen a liberal supply will be a valuable addition to the King's Library. The departments of Feudal and Civil Law you can hardly render too complete. In the Feudal Constitutions we see the origin of our property laws. Of the Civil Law it is not too much to say that it is a regal study.

In respect to standard books generally, continued JOHNSON, a Royal Library ought to have the earliest or most curious edition, the most sumptuous edition, and also the most useful one, which will commonly be one of the latest impressions of the book. As to the purchase of entire libraries in bulk, the Doctor inclined to think—even a century ago—that the inconvenience would commonly almost overbalance the advantage, on the score of the excessive accumulation of duplicate copies.

And then he added a remark which (long years afterwards) Sir Richard Colt HOARE profited by, and made a source of profit to our National Museum. 'I am told,' said JOHNSON, 'that scarcely a village of Italy wants its historian. And it will be of great use to collect, in every place, maps of the adjacent country, and plans of towns, buildings, and gardens. By this care you will form a more valuable body of geography than could otherwise be had.'

On that point—as, indeed, on all the points about which

he gave advice—JOHNSON's counsel bore excellent fruit. The 'body of geography' contained in the Georgian Library has never, I think, been surpassed in any one Collection (made by a single Collector) in the world. It laid, substantially, the foundation of the noble assemblage of charts and maps which now forms a separate Department of the Museum, under the able superintendence of Mr. Richard Henry MAJOR, who has done much for the advancement of geographical knowledge in many paths, but in none more efficiently than in his Museum labours.

BOOK II, Chap. IV. THE KING'S OR 'GEORGIAN' LIBRARY.

Like good counsel was given to BARNARD by the great lexicographer, in relation to the gathering of illustrated books. He told the King's Librarian that he ought to seek diligently for old books adorned with woodcuts, because the designs were often those of great masters.

When to this remark the Doctor added the words: 'Those old prints are such as cannot be made by any artist now living,' he asserted what was undoubtedly true, if he limited that high praise to the best class of the works of which he was speaking. But his words carry in them also an indirect testimony of honour to GEORGE THE THIRD. If, in the century which has passed since Samuel JOHNSON discussed with Frederick BARNARD the wisest means of forming a Royal Library, a great stride has been made by the arts of design in Britain, a share of the merit belongs to the patriotic old King. He was amongst the earliest in his dominions to encourage British art with an open hand. He was not only the founder of the Royal Academy, but a most liberal patron to artists ; and he did not limit his patronage to those men alone who belonged to his own Academy. If for a series of years the Royal Academy did less for Art, and did its work in a more narrow spirit of coterie than it ought to have done, the fault was not in the

JOHNSON'S REMARK ON MODERN ILLUSTRATED BOOKS.

founder. And, of late years, the Academy itself has, in many ways, nobly vindicated its foundation and the aid it has received from the Public. Towards the foundation of the Academy, GEORGE THE THIRD gave, from his privy purse, more than five thousand pounds. To many of its members he was a genial friend, as well as a liberal patron.

Many other institutions of public education shared his liberality. Some generous benefactions which he gave to the British Museum itself, in the earlier years of his reign, have been mentioned already. But there were a crowd of other gifts, both in the earlier and in the later years, of which the limits of this volume at present forbid me to make detailed mention.

The Continental tour of Mr. BARNARD was very successful as to its main object. He obtained such rich accessions for the Library as raised it—especially in the various departments of Continental history and literature — much above all other Libraries in Britain.

Within a few years of his return to England the very choice Collection which had been formed by Dr. Anthony ASKEW came into the market. For this Library, in bulk, the King offered ASKEW's representatives five thousand pounds. They thought they could make more of the Collection by an auction, but, in the event, obtained less than four thousand pounds. The Askew Library extended only to three thousand five hundred and seventy separate printed works, but it contained a large proportion of rare and choice books. The chief buyers at the sale were the Duke of LA VALLIÈRE and (through the agency of DE BURE) LEWIS THE SIXTEENTH. The King of England bought comparatively little, although on this occasion Mr. BARNARD could scarcely have withholden his hand on the score of the special injunctions which the King had formerly laid down for his guidance in such public competitions.

For it deserves to be remembered that GEORGE THE THIRD's conscientious thoughtfulness for other people led him, early in his career as a Collector, to give to his librarian a general instruction such as the servants of wealthy Collectors rarely receive. 'I do not wish you,' he said, ' to bid either against a literary man who wants books for study, or against a known Collector of small means.' He was very free to bid, on the other hand, against a Duke of ROXBURGHE or an Earl SPENCER.

The King's kindness of nature was also shown in the free access which he at all times afforded to scholars and students in his own Library. To this circumstance we owe some of the most interesting notices we have of his opinions of authors and of books.

In the earliest years of the Royal Collectorship part of the Library was kept in the old palace at Kew, which has long since disappeared, the site of it being now a gorgeous flower-bed.   Afterwards, and on the acquisition for the Queen, of Buckingham House,* the chief part of the Collection was removed to Pimlico, and arranged in the handsome rooms of which a view appears, by way of vignette, on the title-pages of the sumptuously printed catalogue prepared by BARNARD.   It was at Buckingham House that JOHNSON's well-known conversation with the King took place, in February, 1767.

When JOHNSON first began to use the Royal Collection it

Book II,
Chap. IV.
THE
KING'S OR
'GEORGIAN'
LIBRARY.

THE OLD
LOCALITIES
OF THE
GEORGIAN
LIBRARY.

* The mansion for which the Trustees of the British Museum had been asked to give £30,000 was sold, five years afterwards, to the King for £20,000.   It was purchased for the Queen as a jointure-house in lieu of her proper mansion, Somerset House, then devoted to public purposes. All the royal princes and princesses were born in Buckingham House, except George IV, and one, perhaps, of the younger children.

Book II,
Chap. IV.
The
King's or
'Georgian'
Library.

was still in its infancy. He was surprised both at its extent and at the number of rare and choice books which it already included. He had seen Barnard's assiduity, and had helped him occasionally in his book-researches, long prior to the tour of 1768. But it astonished him to see that the King, within six or seven years, had gathered so fine a Library as that which he saw in 1767. He became a frequent visitor. The King, hearing of the circumstance, desired his librarian to let him know when the literary autocrat came again.

The inter-
view at
Bucking-
ham House
between
George III
and Dr.
Johnson.

1767, Febru-
ary.

The King's first questions were about the doings at Oxford, whence, he had been told, Johnson had recently returned. The Doctor expressed his inability to bestow much commendation on the diligence then exhibited by the resident scholars of the University in the way of any conspicuous additions to literature. Presently, the King put to him the question, 'And what are you about yourself?' 'I think,' was the answer—given in a tone more modest than the strict sense of the words may import—'that I have already done my part as a writer.' To which the King rejoined, 'I should think so too, had you not written so well.' After this happy retort, the King turned the conversation on some recent theological controversies. About that between Warburton and Lowth he made another neat though obvious remark—'When it comes to calling names, argument, truly, is pretty well at an end.' They then passed in review many of the periodical publications of the day, in the course of which His Majesty displayed considerable knowledge of the chief books of that class, both English and French. He showed his characteristic and kingly attention to minutiæ by an observation which

Croker's
Boswell, pp.
181-186.

he made when Johnson had praised an improved arrangement of the contents of the *Philosophical Transactions*—

oblivious, at the moment, that he had himself suggested the change. 'They have to thank Dr. Johnson for that,' said the King.

Book II, Chap. IV. The King's or 'Georgian' Library.

Another remark made by George the Third during this conversation deserves to be remembered. 'I wish,' said he, 'that we could have a really well-executed body of British Biography.' This was a desideratum in the seventh year of the old King, and it is a desideratum still in the thirty-fourth year of his granddaughter. The reign of Queen Victoria was comparatively young when the late Mr. Murray first announced, not without some flourish of trumpets, a forthcoming attempt at such a labour, but the little that was said as to the precise plan and scope of the work then contemplated, gave small promise of an adequate performance; and hitherto there has been no performance at all.

Six years after the interview with Johnson, another literary conversation, of which we have a record, was held in the Royal Library. But on this occasion the scene was Kew. Dr. Beattie's fame is now a thing of the past. There is still, however, some living interest in the account of the talk between the author of *The Minstrel* and his sovereign, held in 1773, about liturgies, about prayers occasional and prayers *ex tempore*, and about the methods of education adopted in the Scottish universities.

The King's conversation with Dr. Beattie; 1773. August. Forbes, *Life of Beattie*, vol. i, pp. 347-354.

The King's least favourable—but not least characteristic —appearance, as a talker on literary subjects, is made in that conversation with Miss Burney, in which he uttered his often-quoted remark on Shakespeare :—' Was there ever such stuff as great part of *Shakespeare*—only one must not say so?' The sense of the humorous seems in George III to have been wholly lacking. And some part of the sadness of his life has probably a vital connexion with that deficiency.

And with Miss Burney. 1785. December.

*Book II,
Chap. IV.
The
King's or
'Georgian'
Library.*

*D'Arblay,
Diary, vol. ii,
pp. 395–398.*

In the last-mentioned conversation, the King evinced considerable acquaintance with French literature. He shared, to some extent, the then very general admiration for Rousseau, on whom he had bestowed more than one act of kindness during the brief English exile of the author of *Emile*. He shared, also, the common impression as to the absence of gratitude in the brilliant Frenchman's character. When Miss Burney told him that his own portrait had been seen to occupy the most conspicuous place in Rousseau's living-room after his return to France, the King was both surprised and touched.

Next after the large and choice acquisitions made for the King's Library on the Continent, some of its most conspicuous and valuable literary treasures were acquired at the several sales, in London, of the Libraries of James West (1773), of John Ratcliffe (1776), and of Richard Farmer (1798). It was at the first of these sales that George the Third laid the foundation of his unequalled series of the productions of the father of English printing.

George the Third's series of books from Caxton's Press.

The *Caxtons* bought for the King at West's sale included the dearly prized *Recuyell of the Histories of Troye* (1472-1474?), the *Booke of the Chesse* (1476?), the *Canterbury Tales* of Chaucer (1478?), the *Dictes and Sayinges of the Philosophers* (1480), the *Mirrour of the World* (1481), the *Godfrey of Boloyne* (1482), the *Confessio Amantis* (1483), the *Paris and Vienne* (1485), and the *Royal Booke* (1487?). Of these, the lowest in price was the *Confessio* of 1483, which the King acquired for nine guineas, and the highest in price was the *Chaucer* of 1478, which cost him forty-seven pounds fifteen shillings.

At the same sale, he also acquired another Caxton, which has a peculiar interest. The King's copy of the *Troylus and Creside* (probably printed in the year 1484) formerly belonged

> 'To Her, most gentle, most unfortunate,
> Crowned but to die—who in her chamber sate
> Musing with Plato, though the horn was blown,
> And every ear and every heart was won,
> And all, in green array, were chasing down the sun ;'

and it bears her autograph.

Three years after the dispersion of WEST's Library came that of the extraordinary Collection which had been made by a Bermondsey ship-chandler, John RATCLIFFE by name. This worthy and fortunate Collector has been said, commonly, to have amassed his black-letter curiosities by buying them, at so much a pound, over his counter. *   But of such windfalls no man has ever been so lucky as to have more than a few.   John RATCLIFFE was, like his King, a large buyer at WEST's sale, and at many other sales, upon the ordinary terms.

By pains and perseverance he had collected of books printed by CAXTON the extraordinary number of forty-eight.   No Collector ever surpassed, or even reached, that number, except Robert HARLEY, in whose days books that are now worth three hundred pounds could, not infrequently, be bought for much less than the half of three hundred pence.

RATCLIFFE's forty-eight *Caxtons* produced at his sale two hundred and thirty-six pounds.   The King bought twenty of them at an aggregate cost of about eighty-five pounds.   Amongst them were the *Boethius*, of 1478 ; the *Reynarde the Foxe*, of 1481 ; the *Golden Legende*, and the

---

* The story, I observe, has been endorsed in Mr. Blades' excellent *Life of Caxton* (see part 2, p. 268), but it is undoubtedly a distortion or exaggeration of some chance occurrence.   No such series could have been formed otherwise than, in the main, by systematic research.

BOOK II,
Chap. IV.
THE
KING'S OR
'GEORGIAN'
LIBRARY.

Curial, both of 1484; and the *Speculum Vitæ Christi*, probably printed in 1488. The *Boethius* is a fine copy, and was obtained for four pounds six shillings. A few years ago an imperfect copy of the same book brought more than sixteen times that sum.

GIFTS TO
THE KING'S
LIBRARY.

Two others of the King's *Caxtons* were the gift of Jacob BRYANT. One of these is Ralph LEFEVRE's *Recueil des histoires de Troye*, printed, probably, in 1476. The other is the *Doctrinal of Sapience*, printed in 1489. This last-named volume is on vellum, and is the only copy so printed which is known to exist. A third Caxton volume was bequeathed to GEORGE THE THIRD by Mr. HEWETT, of Ipswich. This is the *Æsop* of 1484, and is the only extant copy. It was delivered to the King by Sir John HEWETT

GEORGE III
AND THE
BIBLIO-
MANIA.

and Mr. Philip BROKE, the legator's executors. GEORGE THE THIRD was very sensitive to the special triumphs of collectorship, and would be sure to prize the *Æsop* all the more for its attribute of uniqueness.

A story in illustration of this specific tinge of the biblio-mania in our royal Collector was wont to be told by Sir Walter SCOTT, and is mentioned in his interesting obituary notice of the King, printed in the *Edinburgh Weekly Journal* * immediately after the King's death. According to SCOTT, GEORGE THE THIRD was fond of crowing a little over his brother-collector, the Duke of ROXBURGHE, on the score that the royal copy of the famous *Recuyell of the Histories of Troye* had a pre-eminence over the Roxburghe copy. The pre-eminence was of a sort, indeed, to which no one but a thorough-paced Collector would be sensible. For it consisted in the 'locking,' or wrong imposing, of certain pages, afterwards corrected at press. The fault, therefore,

---

* *Edinburgh Weekly Journal*, Feb. 1820. The article is reprinted in *Miscellaneous Prose Works*, Edition of 1841, vol. ii, p. 184.

indicated priority of working off. But I do not find in the King's *Recuyell*—which now lies before me—the peculiarity spoken of in the poet's story. Such a fault does exist in the Roxburghe copy, which now belongs to the Duke of DEVONSHIRE. Other and authenticated anecdotes, however, are abundant, which suffice to show the close knowledge of, and the keen interest in, his books, by which GEORGE THE THIRD was characterised. It was a still better trait in him that he found real pleasure in knowing that the treasures and rarities of his Library subserved the inquiries and studies of scholars. Nor did he make narrow limitations. Men like JOHNSON and Bishop HORSLEY profited by the Collection. So, too, did men like GIBBON and PRIESTLEY.

The total number of Caxton prints amassed by GEORGE III was thirty-nine. Of these three are in the Royal Library at Windsor—namely, the *Recueil* (1476?), the *Æsop* (1484), and the *Doctrinal* (1489).

To a keen enjoyment of the pleasures of collectorship, the King added, in 1787, a passing taste of those of authorship. As a Collector, the bibliomania did not engross him. He had a delight in amassing fine plants as well as fine books. The *Hortus Kewensis* (in both applications of the term) was largely indebted to his liberality of expenditure and to his far-spread research. He sent botanic missionaries to the remotest parts of Asia, as well as to Africa. He took the most cordial interest in those varied voyages of discovery which—as I have observed in a former chapter—cast so distinctive a lustre on his reign, and in consequence of which such large additions were made to our natural history collections, public and private. And he did much to promote scientific agriculture, both by precept and by example.   It was as a practical agriculturist that the King (under a slight veil of pseudonymity *) made his bow to the reading public by the publication of seven articles in Arthur YOUNG's useful and then well-known periodical, the *Annals of Agriculture*.

Those articles have a threefold aim.   They inculcate the wisdom, for certain soils, of an intermediate system of treatment and of cropping, midway between the old routine and the drill-husbandry, then of recent introduction; they describe several new implements, introduced by DUCKET of Esher and of Petersham; and they advocate an almost entire rejection of fallows.   They further describe a method, also introduced by Farmer DUCKET, and then peculiar, of destroying that farmer's pest, couch-grass (*triticum repens*), by trench-ploughing it deep into the ground, and contain many other practical suggestions, some of which seem to have been empirical, and others so good that they have become trite.

But the best service rendered by GEORGE THE THIRD to the agricultural pursuits, of which he was so fond, was his introduction of the Merino flocks, which became conspicuous ornaments to the great and little parks at Windsor.   Part of the success which, for a time, attended the importation of those choice Merino breeds was due to the zealous co-operation of Lord SOMERVILLE and of Sir Joseph BANKS [see the next chapter], but the King himself took a real initiative in the matter; acquired real knowledge about it; and deserved, by his personal efforts, the cognomen given him (by some of those worthy farmers who used to attend the annual sales at Windsor) of 'the Royal Shepherd.'

---

* 'Ralph Robinson' is the name signed to the communications to the *Annals of Agriculture*, but they are dated from Windsor. (See *Annals*, vol. vii, 1787.)

The recreative pursuits, alike of the book-collector and of the agriculturist, as well as the labours of the conscientious monarch, were at length to be arrested by that great calamity which, after clouding over some months of the years of vigour, was destined to veil in thick gloom all the years of decline—the years when great public triumphs and crushing family afflictions passed equally unnoted by the recluse of Windsor.

> ' Thy lov'd ones fell around thee.
> . . . . . . Thou, meanwhile,
> Didst walk unconscious through thy royal towers,
> The one that wept *not*, in the tearful isle!
>
> . . . .
> But who can tell what visions might be thine?
> The stream of thought, though broken, still was pure.
> Still on that wave the stars of Heaven might shine
> Where earthly image would no more endure.
> Nor might the phantoms to thy spirit known,
> Be dark or wild,—creations of Remorse,—
> Unstain'd by thee, the blameless Past had thrown
> No fearful shadows o'er the Future's course.'

When GEORGE THE THIRD died at Windsor Castle, on the 29th of January, 1820, the public mourning was sincere.   During its ten years of rule, the Regency had done very much to heighten and intensify regret for the calamity of 1810.   The errors of the old monarch came, naturally, to be dwarfed to the view, when his private virtues acquired all the sharp saliency of contrast.

Since his death, political writers have usually been somewhat harsh to his memory.   But the verdict of history has not yet been given in.   When the time for its delivery shall at length come, there will be a long roll of good deeds to set off against many mistakes in policy.   Nor will the genuine piety, and the earnest conscientiousness of the individual man—up to the measure of the light vouchsafed to him—be forgotten in the preliminary summing up. What George the Third did for Britain simply in conferring upon it the social blessings of a pure Court, and of a bright personal example, is best to be estimated by contemplating what, in that respect, existed before it, and also what came immediately after it. Comparisons of such a sort will serve, eventually, to better purpose than that of feathering the witty shafts of reckless satirists, whether in prose or in verse. Meanwhile, it is enough to say that no honester, no more God-fearing man, than was George the Third, ever sat upon the throne of England.

During all the time of his long illness, the King's Library had continued, more or less, to grow. When he died, it contained sixty-five thousand two hundred and fifty volumes, besides more than nineteen thousand unbound tracts. These have since been bound severally. The total number of volumes, therefore, which the Collection comprised was about eighty-four thousand. At the time of the King's decease, the annual cost of books in progress, and of periodical works, somewhat exceeded one thousand pounds. The annual salaries of the staff—four officers and two servants—amounted to eleven hundred and seventy-one pounds. The Library occupied a fine and extensive suite of rooms in Buckingham Palace. One of them was large enough to make a noble billiard-room.

The Royal Library, therefore, embarrassed King George the Fourth in two ways. It cost two thousand two hundred pounds a year, even without making any new additions to its contents. It occupied much space in the royal residence which could be devoted to more agreeable purposes. Then came the welcome thought that, instead of being a charge, it might be made a source of income. The

Emperor of Russia was known to covet, as a truly imperial luxury, what to the new King of Great Britain was but a costly burden.   He broached the idea—but met, instead of encouragement, with strong remonstrance.

The news of the royal suggestion soon spread abroad. Amongst those who heard of it with disgust were Lord FARNBOROUGH (who is said to have learnt the design in talking, one day, with Princess LIEVEN) and Richard HEBER.   Both men bestirred themselves to prevent the King from publicly disgracing the country in that way. Lord FARNBOROUGH betook himself to a conference with the Premier, Lord LIVERPOOL.   Mr. HEBER discussed the matter with Lord SIDMOUTH.   By the ministers, public opinion upon the suggested sale was pretty strongly and emphatically conveyed to His Majesty, whatever may have been the courtliness of tone employed about it.

GEORGE THE FOURTH, however, was not less strongly impressed by the charms of the prospective rubles from Russia.   He felt that he could find pleasant uses for a windfall of a hundred and eighty thousand pounds, or so. And he fought hard to secure his expected prize—or some indubitably solid equivalent.   'If I can't have the rubles,' said the King, 'you must find me their value in pounds sterling.'   The Ministers were much in earnest to save the Library, and, in the emergency, laid their hands upon a certain surplus which had accrued from a fund furnished some years before by France, to meet British claims for losses sustained at the date of the first French Revolution. But the expedient became the subject of an unpleasant hint in the House of Commons.   And the Government, it is said, then resorted to that useful fund, the 'Droits of Admiralty.'   By hook or crook, GEORGE THE FOURTH received his 'equivalent.'   He then sat down to his writing-table (at Brighton), to assure Lord LIVERPOOL—in his official capacity—of the satisfaction he felt in having 'this means of advancing the Literature of my Country.' Then he proceeded to add :—' I also feel that I am paying a just tribute to the memory of a Parent, whose life was adorned with every public and private virtue.'

The Executors or Trustees of King GEORGE THE THIRD knew well what the monarch's feelings about his Library would, in all reasonable probability, have been, had he possessed mental vigour when preparing for his last change. They exacted from the Trustees of the Museum a pledge that the Royal Library should be preserved apart, and entire.

Parliament, on its side, made a liberal provision for the erection of a building worthy to receive the Georgian Library. The fine edifice raised in pursuance of a parliamentary vote cost a hundred and forty thousand pounds. It provided one of the handsomest rooms in Europe for the main purpose, and it also made much-needed arrangements for the reception and exhibition of natural-history Collections, above the books.

The removal of the Royal Library from Buckingham House was not completed until August, 1828. All who saw the Collection whilst the building was in its first purity of colour—and who were old enough to form an opinion on such a point—pronounced the receptacle to be eminently worthy of its rich contents. The floor-cases and the heavy tables—very needful, no doubt—have since detracted not a little from the architectural effect and elegance of the room itself.

Along with the printed books, and the extensive geographical Collections, came a number of manuscripts—on historical, literary, and geographical subjects.* By some transient forgetfulness of the pledge given to Lord Farnborough, the manuscripts, or part of them, were, in March, 1841, sent to the 'Manuscript Department' of the Museum. But Mr. Panizzi, then the Keeper of the Printed Books, successfully reclaimed them for their due place of deposit, according to the arrangement of 1823. Nor was such a claim a mere official punctilio.

In every point of view, close regard to the wishes of donors, or of those who virtually represent them, is not more a matter of simple justice than it is a matter of wise and foreseeing policy in the Trustees of Public Museums. The integrity of their Collections is often, and naturally, an anxious desire of those who have formed them. In a subsequent chapter (C. ii of Book III) it will be seen that the wish expressed by the representatives of King George the Third was also the wish of a munificent contemporary and old minister of his, who, many years afterwards, gave to the Nation a Library only second in splendour to that which had been gathered by George the Third.

Not the least curious little fact connected with the Georgian Library and its gift to the Public, is that the gift was *predicted* thirty-one years before George the Fourth wrote his letter addressed to Lord Liverpool from the Pavilion at Brighton, and twenty-eight years before the death of George the Third.

In 1791, Frederick Wendeborn wrote thus:—'The King's private Library . . . can boast very valuable and magnificent books, which, as it is said, will be one time or another

Book II,
Chap. IV.
The
King's or
'Georgian'
Library.

*Minutes of
Evidence*
(1850), as
above.

---

* Curiously enough, three volumes of the Georgian MSS. had belonged to Sir Hans Sloane, and had, in some unexplained way, come to be separated from the bulk of his Collection. They now rejoined their old companions in Great Russell Street.

joined to those of the British Museum.' WENDEBORN[*] was a German preacher, resident in London for many years. He was known to Queen CHARLOTTE, and had occasional intercourse with the Court. May it not be inferred that on some occasion or other the King had intimated, if not an intention, at least a thought on the matter, which some courtier or other had repeated in the hearing of Dr. WENDEBORN?

[*] See, before, p. 339.

CHAPTER V.

THE FOUNDER OF THE BANKSIAN MUSEUM AND LIBRARY.

> 'It may be averred for truth that they be not the highest instances that give the best and surest information. . . . . It often comes to pass [in the study of Nature] that small and mean things conduce more to the discovery of great matters, than great things to the discovery of small matters.'—BACON.
>
> 'Not every man is fit to travel. Travel makes a wise man better, but a fool worse.'—OWEN FELLTHAM.

The Life, Travels, and Social Influence, of Sir Joseph BANKS.—*The Royal Society under his Presidency.— His Collections and their acquisition by the Trustees of the British Museum.—Notices of some other contemporaneous accessions.*

WE have now to glance at the career—personal and scientific—of an estimable public benefactor, with whom King GEORGE THE THIRD had much pleasant intercourse, both of a public and a private kind. Sir Joseph BANKS was almost five years younger than his royal friend and correspondent, but he survived the King by little more than three months, so that the Georgian and the Banksian Libraries were very nearly contemporaneous accessions. The former, as we have seen, was given in 1823, and fully received in 1828; the latter was bequeathed (conditionally) in 1820, and received in 1827. These two accessions, taken conjointly, raised the Museum collection of books (for the first time in its history) to a respectable rank amongst the National Libraries of the day. The Banksian bequest made also an important addition to the natural-history collections, especially to the herbaria. It is as a cultivator and promoter of the natural sciences, and pre-eminently of botany, that Sir Joseph won for himself endur-ing fame. But he was also conspicuous for those personal and social qualities which are not less necessary to the man, than are learning and liberality to the philosopher. For the lack of such personal qualities some undoubted public benefactors have been, nevertheless, bad citizens. In this public benefactor both sets of faculties were harmoniously combined. They shone in his form and countenance. They yet dwell in the memory of a survivor or two, here and there, who were the contemporaries of his closing years.

Joseph BANKS was born at Reresby Abbey, in Lincoln-shire, on the thirteenth of December, 1743. He was the only son of William BANKS-HODGKENSON, of Reresby Abbey, by his wife Sophia BATE.

Mr. BANKS-HODGKENSON was the descendant of a York-shire family, which was wont, of old, to write itself 'Banke,' and was long settled at Banke-Newton, in the wapentake of Staincliffe. The second son of a certain Henry BANKE, of Banke-Newton, acquired, by marriage, Beck Hall, in Giggleswick ; and by his great grandson, the first Joseph BANKES, Reresby Abbey was purchased towards the close of the seventeenth century. His son (also Joseph) sat in Parliament for Peterborough, and served as Sheriff of Lincolnshire in 1736. The second (and eldest surviving) son of the Member for Peterborough took the name of HODGKENSON, as heir to his mother's ancestral estate of Overton, in Derbyshire, but on the death of his elder brother (and his consequent heirship) resumed the paternal name, and resigned the Overton estate to his next brother, who became Robert HODGKENSON, of Overton. Mr. BANKS-HODGKENSON died in 1761, leaving to his son, afterwards Sir Joseph BANKS, a plentiful estate.

The youngster was then little more than beginning his career at Oxford, whither he had recently come from Eton, though his schooling had been begun at Harrow. He was 'lord of himself,' and of a fine fortune, at the critical age of eighteen. To many, such an inheritance, under like circumstances, has brought misery. To Joseph BANKS, it brought noble means for the prosecution of a noble aim. It was the ambition of this young Etonian—not to eclipse jockies, or to dazzle the eyes of fools, but—to tread in the footsteps of LINNÆUS. Rich, hardy, and handsome in person, sanguine in temperament, and full of talent, he resolved that, for some years to come, after leaving the University, the life that might so easily be brimmed with enjoyments should incur many privations and face many hardships, in order to win both knowledge and the power of benefiting the Public by its communication. That object of early ambition, it will be seen, was abundantly realised in the after-years.

There is no reason to think that a resolution, not often formed at such an age as eighteen, was come to in the absence of temptation to a different course. BANKS was no ascetic. Nor was it his fortune, at any time, to live much with ascetics. One of his earliest friends was that Lord SANDWICH* whose memory now chiefly connects itself with the unsavoury traditions of Medmenham Abbey, and with the peculiar pursuits in literature of John WILKES. With SANDWICH he spent many of the bright days of

* John Montagu, fourth Earl of Sandwich (1729-1792).

youth in fishing on Whittlesea Mere. BANKS had the good fortune—and the skill—to make his early acquaintanceship with the future First Lord of the Admiralty conducive to the interests of science. The connexion with the Navy of another friend of his youth, Henry PHIPPS, afterwards Earl of MULGRAVE, was also turned, eventually, to good account in the same way.

Part of young BANKS' vacations were passed at Reresby and in frequent companionship with Lord SANDWICH; part at his mother's jointure-house at Chelsea, very near to the fine botanic garden which, a few years before, had been so much enriched by the liberality of Sir Hans SLOANE. In that Chelsea garden, and in other gardens at Hammersmith, BANKS studied botany with youthful ardour. And he made frequent botanic excursions in the then secluded neighbourhood. In the course of one of these rambles he fell under suspicion of felony.

He was botanizing in a ditch, and his person happened to be partially concealed by a thick growth of briars and nettles, at a moment when two or three constables, who were in chase of a burglar, chanced to approach the spot. The botanist's clothes were in a miry condition, and his suspicious posture excited in the minds of the local Dogberries the idea that here they had their man. They were deaf to all expostulations. The future President of the Royal Society was dragged, by ignominious hands, before the nearest justice. The magistrate agreed with the constables that the case looked black, but, before committing either the prisoner or himself, he directed that the culprit's pockets should be searched. They contained little money, and no watches; but an extraordinary abundance of plants and wild flowers. The explanations which before had been refused were now accepted, and very courteous apologies were tendered to the victim of an excess of official zeal. But the awkwardness of the adventure failed to deter the sufferer from his eager pursuit, in season and out of it, of his darling science. A botanist he was to be.

He left Oxford in 1763, and almost instantly set out on a scientific voyage to Newfoundland and Labrador. Here he laid the first substantial groundwork of his future collections in natural history. He sailed with PHIPPS, who was already a captain in the Navy, and had been charged with the duty of protecting the Newfoundland fisheries. The voyage proved to be one of some hardship, but its privations rather sharpened than dulled the youthful naturalist's appetite for scientific explorations. He had learned thus early to endure hardness, for a worthy object.

His second voyage was to the South Seas, and it was made in company with the most famous of the large band of eighteenth-century maritime discoverers—James Cook, and also with a favourite pupil of LINNÆUS (the idol of BANKS' youthful fancy), Daniel Charles SOLANDER, who, though he was little above thirty years of age, had already won some distinction in England, and had been made an Assistant-Librarian in the British Museum.*

To make the voyage of *The Endeavour* as largely conducive as was possible to the interests of the natural sciences, Mr. BANKS incurred considerable personal expense, and he induced the Admiralty to make large efforts, on its

* Solander, who was afterwards to be so intimately connected with the Banksian Collections, had been for some years in this country when he was selected by Banks to be one of his companions in the voyage of *The Endeavour*. He was born in Sweden, in the year 1736. He came to England in July, 1760. He succeeded Dr. Maty, as Under-Librarian of the British Museum, in 1773, when Maty was made Principal Librarian. At that date he had already served the Trustees for many years as one of their Assistant-Librarians.

part, to promote and secure the various objects of the new expedition. One of those objects was the observation at Otaheite of a coming transit of Venus over the Sun; another was the further progress of geographical discovery in a quarter of the world to which public interest was at that time specially and strongly turned. Banks, individually, was also bent on collecting specimens in all departments of natural history, and on promoting geographical knowledge by the completest possible collection of drawings, maps, and charts of all that was met with. He engaged Dr. Solander as his companion, and gave him a salary of four hundred pounds a year. With them sailed two draughtsmen and a secretary, besides four servants.

The Endeavour set sail from Plymouth on the twenty-sixth of August, 1768, and from Rio-de-Janeiro on the eighth of December. On the fourteenth of January, 1769, the naturalists landed at Terra-del-Fuego, and they gathered more than a hundred plants theretofore unknown to European botanists. Proud of their success, they resolved that, after a brief rest, they would explore the higher regions, in hope to reap a rich harvest of Alpine plants. Solander, as a Swede and as a traveller in Norway, knew something of the dangers they would have to face. Banks himself was not without experience. But both were enterprising and resolute men. They set out on their long march in the night of the fifteenth of January, in order to gain as much of daylight as possible for the work of botanizing. They hoped to return to the ship within ten hours. As they ascended, Solander warned his companions against the temptation that he knew awaited them of giving way to sleep when overcome by the toil of walking. 'Whoever sits down,' said he, 'will be sure to sleep, and whoever sleeps will wake no more.' But the fatigue proved to be excessive. The foreseeing adviser was borne down by it, and was the first to throw himself upon the snow. BANKS was the younger man by six or seven years, and had a strong constitution. He fought resolutely against temptation, and, with the help of the draughtsmen, exerted himself with all his might to keep SOLANDER awake. They succeeded in getting him to walk on for a few miles more. Then he lay down again, with the words, ' Sleep I must, for a few minutes.' In those few minutes the fierce cold almost paralysed his limbs. Two servants (a seaman and a negro) imitated the Swede's example, and were really paralysed. With much grief, it was found that the servants must, inevitably, be left to their fate. The party had wandered so far that when they set about to return they were—if the return should be by the way they had come—a long day's journey from the ship. And their route had lain through pathless woods. Their only food was a vulture. A third man seemed in peril—momentarily—of death by exhaustion. Happily, a shorter cut was found. Their journey had not been quite fruitless. But they all felt that they had bought their botanical specimens at too dear a rate. Two men were already dead. One of the draughtsmen seems to have suffered so severely that he never recovered from the effects of the journey. Mr. BUCHAN died, three months afterwards, in Otaheite, just four days after they had landed in the celebrated island, to visit which was among the especial objects of their mission.

The transit of Venus over the Sun's disc was satisfactorily observed on the third of June, but the observation had been nearly foiled by the roguery of a native, who had carried off the quadrant. The thief was found amongst several hundred of his fellows, and, but for a characteristic combination in BANKS of frank good humour and of firm hardi-

BOOK II,
Chap. V.
THE FOUNDER OF THE BANKSIAN MUSEUM AND LIBRARY.

THE STAY IN OTAHEITE.
1769.

hood, the spoil would not have been recovered. On this, as upon many other occasions, both his fine personal qualities and his genial manners marked him as a natural leader of men. On occasions, however, of a more delicate kind they brought him into a peculiar peril. Queen Oberea fell in love with him. She was not herself without attractions. And they were clad in all the graces of un-adorned simplicity. The poetical satirists of his day used Sir Joseph—after his return—with cruel injustice if he was really quite so successful, in resisting feminine charms in Otaheite, as he had formerly been at home.

But however that may have been, his researches, as a naturalist, at Otaheite were abundantly successful. And to the island, in return, he was a friend and benefactor. After a stay of three months the explorers left Otaheite for New Holland on the 15th of August, 1769. In Australia their collections were again very numerous and valuable. But their long stay in explorations exposed them to two great dangers, each of which was very nearly fatal to Mr. Banks and to most of his companions. They struck upon a rock, while coasting New South Wales. Their escape was wonderful. The accident entailed an amount of injury to the ship which brought them presently within a peril more imminent still. Whilst making repairs in the noxious climate of Batavia, a pestilence seized upon nearly all the Europeans. Seven, including the ship's surgeon, died in Batavia. Twenty-three, including the second draughts-man, Mr. Parkinson, died on shipboard afterwards. Banks and Solander were so near death that their recovery seemed, to their companions, almost miraculous.

After leaving New South Wales and Batavia they had a prosperous passage to the Cape—prosperous, save for the loss of those whom the pestilence had previously stricken—

and made some additions to their scientific stores. *The Endeavour* anchored in the Downs on the 12th of June, 1771, after an absence of nearly three years. Beyond the immediate and obvious scientific results of the voyage, it was the means, eventually, of conferring an eminent benefaction on our West Indian Colonies. It gave them the Bread-Fruit tree (*Artocarpus incisa*). The transplantation of God's bounties from clime to clime was a favourite pursuit—and a life-long one—with Sir Joseph Banks, and its agencies cost him much time and thought, as well as no small expenditure of fortune.

The hardships and sufferings of Terra-del-Fuego and of Batavia had not yet taken off the edge of his appetite for remote voyages. He expended some thousands of pounds in buying instruments and making preparations for a new expedition with Cook, but the foolish and obstructive conduct of our Navy Board inspired him with a temporary disgust. He then turned his attention to Northern Europe. He resolved that after visiting the western isles of Scotland he would explore Iceland. Solander was again his companion, together with two other northern naturalists, Drs. Lind and Von Troil. Banks chartered a vessel at his own cost (amounting, for the ship alone, to about six hundred pounds).

Before starting for the cold north, they refreshed their eyes with the soft beauties of the Isle of Wight. There, said one of the delighted party, 'Nature has spared none of her favours;' and a good many of us have unconsciously repeated his remark, long afterwards. They reached the Western Isles of Scotland before the end of July, and, after a long visit, explored Staffa, the wonders of which were then almost unknown. Scientific attention, indeed,

Book II,
Chap. V.
The Foun-
der of the
Banksian
Museum
and
Library.

The Visit to
Staffa.

1772.
August 12.

was first called to them by Banks, when he communicated to Thomas Pennant, of Downing, his minute survey, and his drawings of the basaltic columns.

He thought that the mind can scarcely conceive of anything more splendid, in its kind, than the now famous cave. When he asked the local name of it, his guide gave him an answer which, to Mr. Banks, seemed to need explanation, though the name has nowadays become but too familiar to our ears. 'The Cave of Fiuhn,' said the islander. 'Who or what is " Fiuhn" ?' rejoined Banks. The stone, he says, of which the pillars are formed, is a coarse kind of basalt, much resembling the 'Giants' Causeway' in Ireland, 'though

Banks to
Pennant;
Aug., 1772.

none of them so neat as the specimens of the latter which I have seen at the British Museum. . . . Here, it is dirty brown; in the Irish, a fine black.' But he carried away with him the fullest impression of the amazing grandeur of the whole scene.

The Tour in
Iceland.

The tourists reached Iceland on the twenty-eighth of August. They explored the country, and saw everything notable which it contained. On the twenty-first of September they visited the most conspicuous of the *geysers*, or hot-springs, and spent thirteen hours in examining them. On the twenty-fourth, they explored Mount Hecla.

The most famous geyser described by Von Troil (who acted usually as penman for the party) was situate near a farm called Harkaudal, about two days' journey from Hecla. You see, he tells us, a large expanse of fields shut in, upon one side, by lofty snow-covered mountains, far away, with their heads commonly shrouded in clouds, that occasionally sink (under the force of a prevalent wind) so as to conceal the slopes, while displaying the peaks. The peaks, at such moments, seem to spring out of the clouds themselves. On another hand, Hecla is seen, with its three ice-capped summits, and its volcanic vapours; and then, again, a ridge of stupendous rocks, at the foot of which the boiling springs gush forth, with deafening roar, and are backed by a broad marsh containing forty or fifty other springs, or 'geysers,' from which arise immense columns of vapour, subject of course to all the influences and lightings-up of wind and sky. Our tourists carefully watched the 'spoutings' of the springs—which are always fitful—and, according to their joint observations, some of these rose to the height of sixty feet. Occasionally—it has since been observed by later explorers—they reach to an elevation of more than three times that number of feet.

Nor did Mr. Banks neglect the literature of Iceland, which abounds with interest. He bought the Library of Halfdan Einarsson, the literary historian of Iceland, and made other large and choice collections. And he presented the whole to the British Museum—after bestowing, I believe, some personal study on their contents—upon his return to England at the close of the year.

For many generations, it has been very conducive to the possession of social prestige in this country that a man should have acquired the reputation of an adventurous traveller. Even if the traveller shall have seen no anthropophagi, no men 'whose heads do grow beneath their shoulders,' he is likely to attain to some degree of social eminence, merely as one who has explored those

' Antres vast and desarts idle,'

of which home-keeping people have no knowledge, save from the tales of voyagers. To prestige of this kind, Mr. Banks added respectable scientific attainments, a large fortune, and a liberal mind. He was also the favoured

32

Book II, Chap. V.
THE FOUN-
DER OF THE
BANKSIAN
MUSEUM
AND
LIBRARY.

Von Troil to
Bergmann;
7 Sept., 1773.
(Abridged.)

SOCIAL
POSITION
AND INFLU-
ENCE OF SIR
JOSEPH
BANKS.

possessor of graceful manners and of no mean powers of conversation. It was, therefore, quite in the ordinary course of things that his house in London should become one of the social centres of the metropolis. It became much more than that. From the days of his youth Banks had seen much of foreigners; he had mixed with men of European distinction. An extensive correspondence with the Continent became to him both a pursuit and an enjoyment, and one of its results, in course of time, was that at his house in Soho Square every eminent foreigner who came to England was sure to be seen. To another class of persons that house became scarcely less distinguished as the abode, not only of the rich Collections in natural history which their owner had gone so far to seek, and had gathered with so much toil and hardship, but of a noble Library, for the increase of which the book-shops of every great town in Europe had been explored.

The possessor of such manifold distinctions and of such habits of mind seemed, to most men, marked out as the natural head of a great scientific institution. Such a man would be sure to reflect honour on the Society, as well as to derive honour from his headship. But at this particular epoch the Royal Society (then the one conspicuous scientific association in the kingdom) was much embroiled. Mr. Banks was, in many respects, just the man to assuage dissensions. But these particular dissensions were of a kind which his special devotion to natural history tended rather to aggravate than to soften.

Mathematicians, as all men know, have been illustrious benefactors to the world, but—be the cause what it may— they have never been famous for a large-minded estimate of the pursuits and hobbies of other men, whom Nature had not made mathematical. At the time when Joseph

BANKS leaped—as one may say—into eminence, both scientific and social, in London, Sir John PRINGLE was President of the Royal Society, and his position there somewhat resembled the position in which we have seen Sir Hans SLOANE to have been placed. Like Sir Hans, PRINGLE was an eminent physician, and a keen student of physics. He did not give umbrage to his scientific team, exactly in the way in which SLOANE had given it—by an overweening love of reading long medical papers. But natural, not mathematical, philosophy, was his forte; and the mathematicians were somewhat uneasy in the traces whilst Sir John held the reins. If PRINGLE should be succeeded by BANKS, there would be a change indeed on the box, but the style of coachmanship was likely to be little altered. It is not surprising that there should have been a good deal of jibbing, just as the change was at hand, and also for some time after it had been made.

Mr. BANKS was elected to the chair of the Royal Society on the 30th of November, 1777. He found it to be a very difficult post. But, in the end, the true geniality of the man, the integrity of his nature, and the suavity of his manners, won over most, if not quite all, of his opponents. The least that can be said of his rule in that chair is that he made the Royal Society more famous throughout Europe, than it had ever been since the day when it was presided over by NEWTON.

For it was not the least eminent quality of BANKS' character that, to him, a touch of *science* 'made the whole world kin.' He was a good subject, as well as a good man. He knew the blessings of an aristocratic and time-honoured monarchy. He had that true insight which enables a man to discriminate sharply between the populace and the People.

Book II,
Chap. V.
THE FOUNDER OF THE BANKSIAN MUSEUM AND LIBRARY.

See before,
Book I,
c. 6.

THE ELECTION TO THE PRESIDENCY.

1777.
30 Nov.

But, when the interests of science came into play, he could say—with literal and exactest truth,—

' Tros Tyriusve mihi nullo discrimine agetur.'

He took a keen and genial delight both in watching and in promoting the progress of science on the other side of the Channel, whether France itself lay under the loose rule of the republican and dissolute Directory, or under the curbing hand of the First Consul, who was already rapidly aspiring towards empire.

On ten several occasions, Banks was the means of inducing our Government to restore scientific collections, which had been captured by British cruisers, to that magnificent Botanic Garden (the *Jardin des Plantes*, at Paris) for which they had been originally destined.   Such conduct could not but win for him the affectionate reverence of Frenchmen.   On one eminent occasion his good services went much further.

Men yet remember the European interest excited by the adventurous expedition and the sad fate of the gallant seaman, John Francis De La Pérouse.   When the long search for La Pérouse, which had been headed by the French Admiral Bruni d'Eutrecasteaux, came by discords to an untimely end, the collection of specimens of natural history which had been made, in the course of it, by De La Billardière, was brought into an English port. The commander, it seems, felt much as Sloane's captain * had felt at the time of our own Revolution of 1688.   From Lewis the Sixteenth he had received his commission. He was unprepared to yield an account of its performance to anybody else.   He brought his cargo to England, and

* See Book I, c. 6.

placed it at the absolute disposal of the French emigrant Princes.

By the eldest Prince, afterwards LEWIS THE EIGHTEENTH, directions were given that an offer should be made to Queen CHARLOTTE to place at Her Majesty's disposal whatever she might be pleased to select from the Collections of LA BILLARDIÈRE, and that all the remainder of them should be given to the British Museum.

To the interests of that Museum no man of sense will think that Sir Joseph BANKS was, at any time, indifferent. At this particular time, he had been, repeatedly, an eminent benefactor to it. By the French Prince the Collections were put at his orders for the advantage of the Museum, of which he was now a Trustee, as well as a benefactor. But his first thought was for the national honour of Britain, not for the mere aggrandizement of its Museum. 'I have never heard,' said BANKS, 'of any declaration of war between the philosophers of England and the philosophers of France. These French Collections must go to the French Museum, not to the British.' And to France he sent them, without a moment's hesitation. Such an act, I take it, is worthy of the name of 'cosmopolitanism.' The bastard imitation, sometimes current under that much abused term—that which knows of no love of country, except upon a clear balance of mercantile profit—might be more fitly called by a plainer word.

Nor were Frenchmen the only persons to benefit by the largeness of view which belonged to the new President of the Royal Society. At a later period, he heard that Collections which had been made by William VON HUMBOLDT, and subsequently seized by pirates, had been carried to the Cape, and there detained. BANKS sent to the Cape a commission for their release, and restoration to the Collector.

He defrayed the expenses, and refused to accept of any reimbursement. Such actions might well reflect honour on the Royal Society, as well as on the man whom the wisest among its fellows had placed at their head.

The Royal Society had but a share of its President's attention, though the share was naturally a Benjamin's portion. He worked assiduously on the Board of Agriculture. He helped to found the Horticultural Society and the Royal Institution of London. He became, also, in 1788, a co-founder of that 'African Institution' which contributed so largely, in the earlier years of this century, to promote geographical discovery in Africa, and to spread —of dire necessity, at but a snail's pace—some of the blessings of Christian civilization to those dark places of the earth which are full of cruelty.

BANKS' close intercourse with the Continent enabled him to do yeoman's service to the African Institution. Many ardent and aspiring young men in all parts of Europe were fired, from time to time, with an ambition to do some stroke or other of good work in an enterprise which was, at once, scientific and, in its ultimate issues, evangelical. Some of the aspirants were, of course, but very partially fitted or equipped for such labours. But among those who entered on it with fairest promise the protégés of BANKS were conspicuous. Some brief notice of the services he was enabled to render in this direction belongs, however, more fitly, to a somewhat later date than that at which we have, as yet, arrived.

Among the Fellows of the Royal Society there had been much division of opinion as to the eligibility of Joseph BANKS for their Presidency. At Court, there was none. GEORGE THE THIRD, with all his genuine good nature, had been unable to restrain a lurking dislike of Sir John PRINGLE's friendly intercourse with Benjamin FRANKLIN. He was pleased to see PRINGLE retire to his native Scotland, and to receive BANKS at Court, in Sir John's place. He did not then anticipate that the new President would, one day, offend (for a moment) his irrepressible prejudices in a somewhat like manner.

Sometimes, Sir Joseph's attendance at Court brought him into company which had become to him, in some degree, unwonted. We have seen him making a very favourable impression in the feminine circles at Otaheite. But the ladies in attendance on Queen CHARLOTTE were less charmed with him. In March, 1788, I find Fanny BURNEY diarizing (at Windsor Castle) thus :—' Sir Joseph BANKS was so exceedingly shy that we made no acquaintance at all. If, instead of going round the world, he had only fallen from the moon, he could not appear less versed in the usual modes of a tea-drinking party. But what, you will say, has a tea-party to do with a botanist, a man of science, and a President of the Royal Society ?'

In March, 1779, Mr. BANKS made a happy marriage with Dorothea HUGESSEN, daughter and coheir of William Weston HUGESSEN, of Provender, in Kent. Two years afterwards, the King made him a Knight Grand Cross of the Order of the Bath, and cultivated his familiar and frequent acquaintance both in town and at Windsor. Ere long, he was still further honoured with the rank of a Privy Councillor. Both men were deeply interested in agriculture and in the improvement of stock. Sir Joseph shared his sovereign's liking for the Merino breeds ; took an active part in managing those in Windsor Park, and for many years presided, very successfully, over the annual sales. The King had been willing to give away his surplus stock, for the mere sake of promoting improvement, but he was made to see that more good was likely to accrue from sales than from gifts. When in Lincolnshire Sir Joseph Banks laboured hard for the more complete drainage of the fens, and in many ways furthered the introduction of sound agricultural methods. He was a good neighbour; though not a very keen sportsman. And most of his time was now necessarily passed either in London or in its neighbourhood. But, among other acts of good fellowship, he rarely visited Reresby Abbey without patronising a picnic ball at Horncastle, for the benefit of the public dispensary of that town. And it was noted by Lincolnshire people that when, in the after-years, Sir Joseph's severe sufferings from gout kept him much away from Reresby, the dispensary suffered also—from depletion—until Mr. Dymoke, of Scrivelsby, had revived, after Banks' example, the good old annual custom of the town.

It was in the year 1797, and again in 1806, that Sir Joseph was enabled to render special service to that African enterprise which lay near his heart, by enlisting in its toils a zealous German and a not less zealous Swiss—Frederick Hornemann and John Lewis Burckhardt. It was the fate of both of those enterprising men to pay the usual penalty of African exploration. Hornemann succumbed, after six years' service. Burckhardt was spared to work for ten years. Some among the minor scientific results of his well-known travels are preserved in the Public Library at Cambridge (to which he bequeathed his manuscripts). Others of them are in the British Museum. The latter would deserve record in these pages, were it now practicable. Burckhardt died at Cairo on the seventeenth of

October, 1817, just eleven years after his arrival in London, from Göttingen, with that letter to Sir Joseph BANKS in his pocket which, under Divine Providence, determined his work in life. Another great public service of a like kind, rendered by Sir Joseph BANKS to his country and to mankind, was his zealous encouragement of explorations in Australia.

Meanwhile, a new outburst of discord in the Royal Society arose out of a well-merited honour conferred on its President by the Institute of France, in 1802. It was inevitable that a body so eminent and illustrious as the French Institute should not only feel gratitude to Sir Joseph BANKS for that liberality of spirit which had dictated, in the midst of war, his many gracious and generous acts of service to Frenchmen, but should long since have reached the conviction that they would be honouring themselves, not less than honouring him, by his reception in their midst. During the momentary lull afforded by the Peace of Amiens—when the Institute was reorganized by the hand of the great man who was proud of its badge of fellowship, even when clad in the dalmatica—they placed BANKS at the head of their eight Foreign Members. BANKS' estimate of the honour of membership was much like NAPOLEON's. 'I consider this mark of your esteem,' said BANKS, in his reply, 'the highest and most enviable literary distinction which I could possibly attain. To be the first elected as an Associate of the first Literary Society in the world surpasses my most ambitious hopes.'

Several Fellows of the Royal Society resented these warm acknowledgments. They thought them both unpatriotic, and uncomplimentary to themselves. The mathematical malcontents, with Bishop HORSLEY at their head, eagerly profited by so favourable an opportunity of renewing the expression of their old and still lurking dissatisfaction with the choice of their President. HORSLEY addressed to Sir Joseph a letter of indignant and angry remonstrance. Somewhat discreditably, the Bishop chose a pseudonymous signature instead of manfully affixing his own. '*Misogallus*'* was the mask under which he made an appeal to those anti-Gallican prejudices which so many of us imbibe almost with our mother's milk, and have in after-years to get rid of. He aimed a poisoned dart at his old antagonist, when pointing one of his many passionate sentences in a way which he knew would arrest the special attention of the King. The shaft hit the mark. But the King was presently appeased. He knew BANKS, and he knew the Bishop of St. Asaph.

From time to time Sir Joseph BANKS contributed many interesting articles to the *Philosophical Transactions*, and to the *Annals of Agriculture*. His able paper on the Blight in Wheat did service in its day, and was separately published. But it is not as an author that this illustrious man will be remembered. He knew how to fructify the thoughts and to disseminate the wisdom of minds more largely gifted than his own. Necessarily, space and prominence in the public eye is—more especially after a man's death— a good deal determined by authorship. Hence, in our *Biographical Dictionaries*, a crowd of small writers occupy a disproportionate place, and some true and illustrious public benefactors remain almost unnoticed. Undeniably,

* Bishop Horsley certainly forgot the ever-memorable words which he had so often read—Matt. v, 44—when he, a prelate, signed himself ' Misogallus.'

the fame of one such benefactor as a Joseph BANKS ought to outweigh, and must, intrinsically, outweigh, that of many scores of minor penmen. His benefactions were world-wide. And by them he, being dead, yet speaks, and will long continue to speak, to very good and lofty purpose. He died in London on the ninth of May, 1820, at the venerable age of eighty-one years completed.

He died without issue, and was succeeded in his chief Lincolnshire estates by the Honourable James Hamilton STANHOPE (afterwards Mr. STANHOPE BANKS), and by Sir Henry HAWLEY. His Kentish estates were bequeathed to Sir Edward KNATCHBULL.

His Library, Herbarium, Manuscripts, Drawings, Engravings, and all his other subsisting Collections, he bequeathed to the Trustees of the British Museum, for public use for ever, subject to a life-use and a life-interest in them which, together with an annuity, he specifically bequeathed to the eminent botanist, Robert BROWN, who was, for many years, both his friend and his librarian. He also gave an annuity of three hundred pounds a year to Mr. BAUER, an eminent botanical draughtsman; and he added, largely, to the innumerable benefactions he had made in his lifetime to the Botanical Gardens at Kew. To Mr. BROWN he also left the use, for life, of his town house in Soho Square, subject to the life-interest, or the voluntary concession, of the testator's widow.

In his first Codicil, Sir Joseph BANKS made a proviso that, if it should be the desire of the Trustees of the British Museum—and if that desire should also receive the approval of Mr. BROWN—the life-possessor should be at full liberty to cause the Collections to be transferred to the Museum during his lifetime. That, in fact, was the course which, by mutual consent, was eventually taken, to the manifest advantage of the British Public and the promotion of Science.

Part of Sir Joseph's personal Manuscripts were bequeathed to the Royal Society; another portion to the British Museum; and a third portion (connected with the Coinage of the Realm) to the Royal Mint. A minor part of his Collections in Natural History had been given to the British Museum in his own lifetime, and he had personally superintended their selection and arrangement. He had also been a bene-factor to the Hunterian Museum at Glasgow, to the Museum of the London College of Surgeons, and to that, also in London, formerly known as ' Bullock's Museum.' He was, throughout life, as eager to give, as he was diligent to get.

 About the year 1825, negotiations were opened by the Trustees of the British Museum with Mr. Robert Brown, with the view of obtaining for the Public the immediate use of the Banksian Library and the other Collections, and, along with them, the public services of the eminent botanist under whose charge they then were. The then President of the Royal Society, Sir Humphrey Davy, acted for the Public in that negotiation; but some delays intervened, so that it was not brought to a close until nearly the end of the year 1827.

At that date, the transfer was effected. Mr. Brown became the head of the Botanical Department of the Museum, and his accession to the Staff added honour to the institution—in the eyes of all scientific Europe—as well as eminent advantage to the public service. Mr. Brown acted as Keeper until nearly the time of his decease. He died in the year 1858, full of years and of botanical fame.

The Library of Sir Joseph BANKS comprised the finest collection of books on natural history which had ever been gathered into one whole in England. It was also pre-eminently rich in the transactions, generally, of learned societies in all parts of the world; and there is a masterly Catalogue of the Collection, by Jonas DRYANDER, which was printed, at Sir Joseph's cost, in the years 1798-1800. That Catalogue, I venture to hope, will, some day, become—with due modification—the precedent for a printed Catalogue of the whole Museum Library—vast as it already is, and vaster as it must needs become before that day shall have arrived.

The Banksian Herbaria comprise BANKS' own botanical collections in his travels, and those of CLIFFORT, HERMANN, CLAYTON, AUBLET, MILLER, JACQUIER, and LOUREIRO, together with part of those made by TOURNEFORT, the friend and fellow-botanizer of SLOANE, and the author of the *Corollarium*. They also include many valuable plants gathered during those many English Voyages of Discovery which, from time to time, BANKS' example and his liberal encouragement so largely fostered. From the Collections now seen in the Botanical Room of the British Museum not a few of the great works of LINNÆUS, GRONOVIUS, and other famous botanists, derived some of their best materials. These Collections are at present under the zealous and faithful care of Mr. John Joseph BENNETT, long the assistant and the friend of BROWN.

Among nearly contemporaneous accessions which would well merit some detailed notice, were the space for it available, are a valuable assemblage of Marbles from Persepolis, which had been collected by Sir Gore OUSELEY, and were given to the Museum by the Collector, and a small but

BOOK II, Chap. V. THE FOUNDER OF THE BANKSIAN MUSEUM AND LIBRARY.

THE BANKSIAN LIBRARY.

THE BANKSIAN HERBARIA.

BRIEF NOTICE OF SOME OTHER NEARLY CONTEMPORANEOUS ACCESSIONS.

choice Collection of Minerals from the Hartz Mountains, given to the Public by King GEORGE THE FOURTH. The Persepolitan sculptures were received in the year 1825; the Minerals from the Hartzgebirge, in the year 1829.

BOOK THE THIRD.

LATER AUGMENTORS AND BENEFACTORS.

1829—1870.

CONTENTS OF BOOK III:—

'THE comprehensive character of the British Museum—
the origin of which may be traced to the heterogeneous
nature of Sir Hans SLOANE's bequest—doubtless makes it
difficult to provide for the expansion of its various branches,
according to their relative demands upon the space and
light which can be applied to their accommodation. Any
attempt, however, now to diminish that difficulty by segre-
gating any portion, or by scattering in various localities the
components of the vast aggregate, would involve a sacrifice
of great scientific advantages which are not the less inhe-
rent in their union because that union was, in its origin,
fortuitous. . . . .

'Some passages of our evidence . . . illustrate the difficulty
of drawing a line of separation, for purposes of management
and superintendence, between certain Collections. . . . .
Its occurrence [*i. e.* the occurrence of such a difficulty]
indicates strongly the value to Science, of the accidents
which have placed in near juxtaposition the Collections of
mineralogy [and] of forms of existing and extinct animal
and vegetable life. The immediate connexion of all alike
with the Library of the Museum is too important to allow
us to contemplate its dissolution.'—*Report of the Commissioners appointed to inquire into the Constitution and Management of the British Museum* (1850), p. 36.

CHAPTER I.

GENERAL VIEW OF THE HISTORY OF THE BRITISH MUSEUM, UNDER THE ADMINISTRATION, AS PRINCIPAL-LIBRARIAN, OF JOSEPH PLANTA.

> . . . Perséverance keeps honour bright.
> To have done, is to hang
> Quite out of fashion, like a rusty mail
> In monumental mockery.
>
> *Troilus and Cressida.*

> ' Signor, mirate, come 'l tempo vola,
> E siccome la vita
> Fugge, e la Morte nè sovra le spalle,
> Voi siete or qui : pensate alla partita
> Che l' alma ignuda e sola
> Conven ch' arrive a quel dubbioso calle.' . . . .
>
> PETRARCH (*Italia mia*, &c.).

Notices of the Life of Joseph PLANTA, *third Principal-Librarian.—Improvements in the Internal Economy of the Museum introduced or recommended by Mr.* PLANTA.—*His labours for the enlargement of the Collections — and on the Museum Publications and Catalogues.—The Museum Gardens and the Duke of* BEDFORD.

HITHERTO these pages have chiefly had to do with the history of the integral parts of the British Museum, and with that of the men by whom these integral parts, taken severally, were first founded or first gathered. We have now to glance at the organic history of the whole, after the primary Collections and the early additions to them came, by aggregation, to be combined into the existing national establishment. It may, at best, be only by glances that so wide a subject can (within the limits of this one volume) be looked over, in retrospect. That necessity of being brief suggests a connection of the successive epochs in the story of the Museum, for seventy years, with the lives of the three eminent men who have successively presided over the institution since the beginning of the present century. Those three official lives, I think, will be found to afford succinct divisions or breakings of the subject, as well as to possess a distinctive personal interest of their own. Our introductory chapters will therefore—in relation to the chapters which follow them—be, in part, retrospective, and, in part, prospective.

When Dr. Charles Morton died (10 February, 1799), Joseph Planta was, by the three principal Trustees, appointed to be his successor. The choice soon commended itself to the Public by the introduction of some important improvements into the internal economy of the institution. It is the first librarianship which is distinctively marked as a reforming one. In more than one of his personal qualities Mr. Planta was well fitted for such a post as that of Principal Officer of the British Museum. He had been for many years in the service of the Trustees. He had won the respect of Englishmen by his literary attainments. He was qualified, both by his knowledge of foreign languages and by his eminent courtesy of manners, for that salient part of the duties of librarianship which consists in the adequate reception and the genial treatment of strangers.

Joseph Planta was of Swiss parentage. He was of a

race and family which had given to Switzerland several worthies who have left a mark in its national history. He was born, on the twenty-first of February, 1744, at Castasegna, where his father was the pastor of a reformed church. The boy left Switzerland before he had completed the second year of his age. He began his education at Utrecht, and continued it, first at the University of Göttingen, and afterwards by foreign travel—whilst yet open to the formative influences of youthful experience upon character—both in France and in Italy. It was thus his fortune to combine what there is of good in the characteristics of the cosmopolite with what is better in those of a patriotic son of the soil. It was Joseph PLANTA's fortune never to live in Switzerland, as a resident, after the days of early infancy, but, for all that, he remained a true Swiss. And one of the acts of his closing years in England was to make a most creditable contribution to Helvetic history.

Andrew PLANTA, father of Joseph, came to London in 1752. He was a man of good parts and of pleasing address. He established himself as pastor of a German congregation, and was also made an Assistant-Librarian in the British Museum. Afterwards, he was chosen to be a Fellow of the Royal Society and a ' reader ' to Queen CHARLOTTE. That appointment brought with it, in course of time, a measure of Court influence by which young PLANTA profited. His youthful ' *Wanderjahre* ' had inspired the growing man with a keen desire to see more of foreign countries. When the father's favour at Court put him in a position to represent at head-quarters the youth's fancy to see life abroad, and to state (as he truthfully could) that neither talent nor industry were lacking in his character, the statement obtained for Joseph PLANTA the secretaryship of legation at Brussels. There, he felt himself

Book III,
Chap. I.
History
of the
Museum
under
Mr. Planta.

to be in an element which suited him; but his filial affection brought him back to England in 1773, in order that he might solace the last days, on earth, of his father. In that year the elder PLANTA died.

It was also in 1773 that Joseph PLANTA became an Assistant-Librarian. In the next year he was appointed to succeed Dr. MATY in both of his then offices. At the Royal Society he succeeded him as Secretary; at the Museum, he succeeded him as an Under-Librarian—when the Doctor was made head of the establishment. His new post at the Museum brought to PLANTA the special charge of the Department of MSS.

Joseph PLANTA had already made—immediately after his first appointment as Assistant-Librarian—his outset in authorship by the publication of his *Account of the Romansch Language.* It is a scholarly production, though (it need hardly be said) not what would be expected, on such a subject, after the immense stride made in linguistical studies during the ninety-five years which have elapsed since it was given to literature, in pages in which nowadays such a treatise would hardly be looked for. Its first appearance was in the *Philosophical Transactions.* In 1776 it was translated into German and printed at Chamouni.

Phil. Trans.,
vol. lxvi, pp.
129-160.

The subsequent years were devoted, almost exclusively, to the proper duties of his Museum office—on the days of service—and to those of the Paymastership of Exchequer Bills, a function to which Mr. PLANTA was appointed in 1788, and the duties of which he discharged, with efficiency and honour, for twenty-three years. Authorship had but little of his time until a much later period of life.

A little before his appointment in the administrative service of the country, PLANTA had married Miss Elizabeth ATWOOD. For him, marriage did just the opposite of what it has, now and then, been said to do for some other men. It took off the edge of his liking for foreign travel. For it gave him a very happy home. Their union endured for twenty-four years. PLANTA was not a man of the gushing sort. But, to intimates, he would say—in the lonely years; there were to be but few of them—'She was an angel in spirit and in heart.' Mrs. PLANTA died in 1821.

On the death of Charles MORTON, Mr. PLANTA, as we have seen already, was made Principal Librarian. He found the Museum still in its infancy, although no less than forty-six years had passed since the bequest of Sir Hans SLOANE was made to the British Public, and more than forty years since that Public had entered upon its inheritance. The collections had kept pace with the growth of science only in one or two departments. In others the arrear was enormous. The accessibility was hampered with restrictions. The building was in pressing need of enlargement, gradual as had been the growth of some sections, and glaring as was the deficiency of other sections.

PLANTA put his shoulders to the wheel, and met with support and encouragement from several of the Trustees. But the feeling still ran strongly against any approach to indiscriminate publicity in any department of the Museum. Men did not carry that restrictive view quite so far in 1800, as it had been expressed by Dr. John WARD —an able and good man—in 1760, and earlier; but they still looked with apprehension upon the combined ideas of a crowd of visitors, and irreplaceable treasures of learning and of art. A good many of the men of 1800 possessed, it must in candour be remembered, living recollections of the sights and the deeds of 1780. Residents in Bloomsbury were likely, on that score, to have particularly good memories. They had seen with their eyes precious manuscripts, which treasured up the lifelong lore of a MANSFIELD, given by the populace to the flames.

Under the influence of such memories as these, Mr. PLANTA had to propose abolition of restrictions, with a gentle and very gradual hand. He began by improving the practice, without at first greatly altering the rules. By and by he brought, from time to time, before the Trust, suggestions for relaxations in the rules themselves.

From the outset he administered the Reading Room itself with much liberality. When he became Principal Librarian the yearly admissions were much under two hundred. In 1816, they had increased to two hundred and ninety-two. In 1820, to five hundred and fifteen. As respects the Department of Antiquities, the students admitted to draw were in 1809 less than twenty; in 1818 two hundred and twenty-three were admitted. In 1814 he recommended the Trustees to make provision for the exhibition every Thursday, 'to persons applying to see them,' the Engravings and Prints;—the persons admitted not exceeding six at any one time, and others being admitted in due succession. He also recommended a somewhat similar system of exhibition for adoption in the Department of Coins and Medals. And the Trustees gave effect to both recommendations. Eventually Mr. PLANTA proposed, for the *general* show Collections of the Museum, a system of entirely free admission at the instant of application, abolishing all the hamper of preliminary forms.

It was also, I believe, at Mr. PLANTA's instance, or partly so, that the Trustees applied to Parliament, in 1812, for special grants to enable them to improve the Collection of Printed Books, with reference more particularly to the endeavour to perfect the National Library in the National

History—to that very limited extent to which the monu- ments and memorials of our history are to be found in print. Virtually, the grants on behalf of the Manuscript Department, not those on behalf of the Printed Book Department, were, in 1812, as they still are in 1870, the grants which mainly tend to make the British Museum what, most obviously, it ought to become, the main store-house of British History and Archæology, both in literature and in art.

The magnificent additions made by private donors to every section of the British Museum during the administration of PLANTA, have been sufficiently passed under review in the closing chapters of Book II. Several of them, it has been seen, were the fruits of the public spirit of individual Trustees. Such gifts amply vindicated the wisdom both of Sir Hans SLOANE and of Parliament, when both Founder and Legislature gave to men of exalted position a preference as peculiarly fit, in the judgment of each, for the general guardianship of the Museum.

But private gifts—munificent as they were—left large gaps in the National Collections. It is one of Mr. PLANTA's distinctive merits that his tastes and sympathies embraced the Natural History Department, as well as those literary departments with which, as a man of letters, he had a more direct personal connection. He supported, with his influence, the wise recommendation to Parliament—made in 1810—for the purchase of the GREVILLE Collection of Minerals. He recommended, in 1822, the purchase, from the representatives of the naturalist MONTICELLI, of a like, though minor Collection, which had been formed at Naples. The Cavaliero MONTICELLI's Collection was, in the main, one that had been undertaken in imitation of an earlier assemblage of volcanic products which had been also gathered at

Naples by Sir William HAMILTON, and by the Collector given (as I have already recorded) to the Trustees. In a similar spirit he promoted the acquisitions which were made from time to time, by the instrumentality of Claudius RICH, of Henry SALT, and of several other workers in the fruitful field of Classical, Assyrian, and Egyptian archæological exploration. Both in the literary and scientific departments of the Museum he also gave some special attention to the due continuance and completion of the various collections bestowed on the Public by the munificence of Sir Joseph BANKS.

Another conspicuous merit belongs to Joseph PLANTA. He supported the Trustees in that wise and large-minded policy which induced them to regard *publication*, as well as accumulation, to be one of the chief duties of their Trust for the Nation. He thought it not enough, for example, to show to groups of Londoners, from time to time, and to occasional foreign visitants, in almost solitary state, the wealth of Nature and of Art in the Museum Collections. He saw it to be no less the duty of the faithful trustees of such treasures to show them to the world at large by the combined labours of the painter, the draughtsman, the engraver, and the printer. It will ever be an honourable distinction—in the

briefest record of his Museum labours—that he promoted the publication of the beautiful volumes entitled *Description of the Ancient Marbles in the British Museum;* of the *Catalogue of the Anglo-Gallic Coins;* of the *Mausoleum and Cinerary Urns;* of the *Description of Terra Cottas;* and other like works. The first-named work in particular is an especial honour to the Trustees of the Museum, and to all who were concerned in its production. Beautifully engraved, and ably edited, it made the archæological treasures of the Nation widely known even to such foreigners,

interested in the study of antiquity, as circumstances pre-
cluded from ever seeing the marbles themselves. When
watching—in the bygone years—the late Henry CORBOULD
busy at the work into which he threw so much of his love,
as well as of his skill in drawing, I have been tempted, now
and then, to envy the craft which, in its results, made our
national possessions familiarly known, in the far parts of
the world, to students who could never hope to see the
wonderful handicraft of the old Greek sculptors, otherwise
than as it is reflected and transmitted by the handicraft of
the skilled modern draughtsman. CORBOULD had the eye
to see artistic beauty and the soul to enjoy it. He was
not one of the artists who are artisans, in everything but
the name. In the '*Ancient Marbles in the British Museum,*'
published under the active encouragement of the Trustees
and of their Principal Librarians, during a long series of
years, CORBOULD, as draughtsman, had just the work for
which Nature had pre-eminently fitted him.

Joseph PLANTA also took his share in the compilation of
the Catalogues both of Printed Books and of Manuscripts.
In this department, as in the archæological one, he extended
the benefits of his zealous labour to the scholar abroad as
well as to the scholar at home. What was carefully prepared was liberally *printed* and liberally circulated. PLANTA
wrote with his own hand part of the published *Catalogue
of the Printed Books,* and much of the *Catalogue of the
Cottonian Manuscripts.* To the latter he prefixed a brief
life of the Founder, by which I have gladly and thankfully
profited in my own more extended labour at the beginning
of this volume.

One incidental employment which Mr. PLANTA's office
entailed upon him—as Principal Librarian—was of a less
grateful kind. It merits notice on more than one account,

very trivial as is the incident of Museum history that occasioned it, when looked at intrinsically.

In 1821, the then Duke of Bedford (John, ninth Duke) filed in Chancery an injunction against the Trustees to restrain them from building on the garden-ground of the Museum. To build was—at that time—an undoubted injury to the Bloomsburians, and, consequently, a not less undoubted depreciation of the Duke's estate. It is hard, nowadays, to realise to one's fancy what the former Museum gardens were in the olden time. They not only adorned every house that looked over them, but were—in practice, and by the indulgence of the Trustees and officers—a sort of small public park for the refreshment of the vicinity at large. Their neighbourhood made houses more valuable in the market.

Almost seventy years before the filing of the Chancery injunctions of 1820-21, a predecessor of the Duke (John, seventh Duke) had compelled Parliament—and with great reason—to enact that the 'New Road' should be made a broad road ; not a narrow lane. He had carried a proviso for the construction of gardens in front of all the houses along the road. Were public property, and public enjoyments, protected by English law with one tenth part of the efficiency with which private property and private enjoyments are protected, that clause in the 'New Road Act' of 1750 would have proved, in our own present day, a measure advantageous to public health. But public easements are unknown, or nearly unknown, to English law. And the Duke's clause has come, in course of time, to teem with public nuisance, instead of public benefit. Englishmen build at the national cost magnificent cathedrals, and then permit railway-jobbers to defile them, at pleasure, with railway 'architecture.' They construct, by dint of large taxation, magnificent river-embankments, and permit every sort of smoke-belching chimney and eye-killing corrugated-iron-monstrosity to spoil the view. What the old Duke of BEDFORD intended to make a metropolitan improvement, as well as a defence to his own property, has come to be a cause of public detriment,—simply because our legislation, in the year of Grace 1870, affords protection to no kind of public property that is insusceptible, by its nature, of direct valuation in pounds and pence.

The action of the ninth Duke of BEDFORD was in contrast with that of his predecessor. It was not altogether selfish, since there was an actual abatement of public enjoyment in that step which he was opposing. The Trustees of the British Museum were really compelled to take something from the Public with one hand;—but, with the other, they gave a tenfold equivalent. Their contention, of course, prevailed against the Duke's opposition.

It may not be intrusive here to mention that it is known that by the present Duke of BEDFORD very generous and liberal furtherance would be given to new schemes of extension for the Museum, were Parliament, on full consideration, to think enlargement at Bloomsbury the right course to be taken in pending matters. But this subject will demand a few words hereafter.

PLANTA's energies seem for several years to have been given, almost exclusively, to his Museum duties, in combination (as was perfectly practicable and befitting, under the then circumstances) with his Exchequer Paymastership. But in the closing years of his Under-Librarianship many months were (not less fitly) given to a worthy literary undertaking. He wrote his *History of the Helvetic Confederacy* towards the end of the last century, and published it soon after his appointment to the Principal-Librarianship. In the next year he published a supplement to it, under the title of *A View of the Restoration of the Helvetic Confederacy*. The *History* reached its second edition in 1807.

Based primarily on the great work of Johannes Von Müller, Planta's *History of the Helvetic Confederacy* is both a very able production and one that is animated by a spirit of patriotism which is wise as well as strong. It was an enduring contribution to the literature of the author's fatherland. After its appearance, his official duties mainly engrossed his attention. He died, full of years and honours, in the year 1827, leaving a son, who, like his father and his grandfather, distinguished himself in the civil service of their adopted country.

Joseph Planta, in his fifty-three years of service, had seen the British Museum pass from its infancy into the early stages of its maturity. But it still, at the time of his death, was too much regarded, both by the general Public and by Parliament, as, in the main, a place of popular amusement. His next successor saw the beginning of further improvements, such as lifted the Museum upon a level with the best of its fellow-institutions in all Europe. His second successor saw it lifted far above them, in several points of view. And what he witnessed of augmented improvement—when leaving office three or four years ago —was, in a very large measure, the result of his own zealous labours and of his eminent ability.

CHAPTER II.

INTRODUCTION TO BOOK III *(Continued)*:—GROWTH, PROGRESS, AND INTERNAL ECONOMY, OF THE BRITISH MUSEUM, DURING THE PRINCIPAL-LIBRARIANSHIP OF SIR HENRY ELLIS.

> 'It is expedient that the Trustees should revise the salaries of the Establishment, with the view of ascertaining what increase may be required for the purpose of . . . . obtaining the whole time and services of the ablest men, independently of any remuneration from other sources; and that, when such scale of salary shall have been fixed, it shall not be competent to any Officer of the Museum, paid thereunder, to hold any other situation conferring emolument or entailing duties.'
>
> REPORT FROM SELECT COMMITTEE ON BRITISH MUSEUM, 14 July, 1836.

Internal Economy of the Museum at the time of the death of Joseph PLANTA.—*The Literary Life and Public Services of Sir Henry* ELLIS.—*The Candidature of Henry* FYNES CLINTON.—*Progress of Improvement in certain Departments.—Introduction of Sir Antonio* PANIZZI *into the Service of the Trustees.—The House of Commons' Committee of* 1835-36.—PANIZZI *and Henry Francis* CARY.—*Memoir of* CARY.—PANIZZI'S *Report on the proper Character of a National Library for Britain, made in October,* 1837.—*His successful labours for Internal Reform.—And his Helpers in the work.—The Literary Life and Public Services of Thomas* WATTS.—*Sir A.* PANIZZI'S *Special Report to the Trustees of* 1845, *and what grew thereout.—Progress, during Sir H.* ELLIS'S *term of office, of the several Departments of Natural History and of Antiquities.*

WHEN Sir Henry ELLIS was appointed to be the successor of Mr. PLANTA (20th December, 1827), the British Museum was still composed of but four departments, in conformity with the organization of 1809. It was publicly open on three days in each week, but only during forty weeks of every year. This was a great improvement of the previous arrangements, as we have seen, under MATY and MORTON. But Mr. PLANTA's most conspicuous improvements lay in the (admittedly more important) direction of access to the Medal, Print, and Reading Rooms. To his administration, students in all these departments were much indebted. Sir Henry ELLIS was to witness and to carry out, very efficiently as Principal Librarian, some more extensive modifications of the old system of things; but he, in his turn, was to be quite eclipsed (so to speak) in the character of Museum improver, by his successor in office. And it was, in fact, to the latter that such among the conspicuous improvements of the last twenty years of Sir Henry's official administration as related to the Department of Printed Books—and in no department were the improvements more striking—were pre-eminently due.

Sir Henry ELLIS (who has but so recently departed from amongst us) entered the service of the Trustees, as a temporary assistant in the Library, in the year 1806, having had already three years' experience in Bodley's Library at Oxford. When coming occasionally to London during his employment at Oxford he would see Dr. Charles MORTON, who had helped to organize the Museum almost fifty years before. The *public* life of those two acquaintances spread, conjointly, over a period of a hundred and twenty years.*

* Morton died at eighty-three; Planta, at eighty-four; Ellis, at ninety-two. Morton, as we have seen, was known to Sir Hans Sloane. Sloane was already a noted man in the days of Charles the Second; and he also lived to be ninety-two. The joint lives of Sloane, Morton, and Ellis extended over nearly two hundred and ten years.

Had it never fallen to the lot of Henry ELLIS to render to the Public any service at all, in the way of administering and improving the National Museum, he would still have earned an honourable niche in our literary history. His contributions to literature are, indeed, very unequal in their character. Some of them are fragmentary; some might be thought trivial. But very many of them have sterling value. And his archæological labours, in particular, were zealous and unremitting. He began them in 1798. He had not entirely ceased to add to them in 1868. In the closing year of the eighteenth century he was giving further-ance to the labours on British history of Richard GOUGH. In the sixty-eighth year of the nineteenth century he was still taking an intelligent and critical interest in the large undertakings of Lord ROMILLY and of Mr. DUFFUS HARDY, for affording to future historians the means of basing the reconstruction of our national history upon the one firm foundation of an exhaustive search of our national records.

The fourth Principal Librarian of the British Museum was born at Shoreditch, in London, on the 29th of November, 1777. He was of a Yorkshire family long settled (and still flourishing) at Dewsbury. Henry ELLIS was educated at Merchant Taylors' School, and at St. John's College, Oxford, where he graduated B.C.L. in 1802. His first book (but not, perhaps, his first publica-tion) was the *History of the Parish of St. Leonard, Shore-ditch*, printed in 1798. He became F.S.A. in 1800; one of its Secretaries in 1813; and its Director in 1854. To the *Archæologia* he was a contributor for more than fifty years. In 1800, he sent to the first Record Commission a Report on the Historical Manuscripts at St. John's. For the same Commission he wrote, in the year 1813, and the three following years, an *Introduction to Domesday Book.*

Of this he would speak very modestly in after-days, saying: 'I have worked on *Domesday* for years; but only in making an opening into the mine. Other men will have yet to bring out the metal.' For the second Record Commission he re-edited his *Introduction* and considerably improved it. This was done in 1832; and, to say the least, it brought some very good ore to the surface. When both these Commissions had given way to the better organization recently framed by Lord ROMILLY, he edited, for the series of *Chronicles and Memorials of Great Britain*, the Latin Chronicle of John of Oxenedes, from a MS. belonging to Sir Robert COTTON's Library. When *Oxenedes* was published, just sixty years had passed from the publication of Sir Henry's first Record labour, undertaken at the instance of Lord COLCHESTER.

In the interval, he had had a great opportunity, the first glimpse of which needs must have dilated the heart of so genuine a lover of antiquity. The publication of an improved edition of the *Monasticon Anglicanum* of DODSWORTH and DUGDALE ought to have made a new epoch in British archæology. But the opportunity was lost. In those days, there was no encouragement for such labours at the Treasury; no enlightened promoter of them at the Rolls House. The control of the new *Monasticon* passed into the hands of mere tradesmen. Neither of Mr. ELLIS's co-editors ever buckled to the work. ELLIS himself became simply the servant of the associated publishers, who had no aim whatever beyond turning a golden penny out of the traditional prestige of Sir William DUGDALE's name, and out of the standing advertisement that the *Monasticon* was indubitably one of those books 'which no gentleman's library ought to be without.' Heaps of crude, untranslated, and unelucidated information were thrust into the book, against the editor's own clear conviction of his duty, and in spite of his remonstrance. 'We must retrench,' was the one answer to all editorial recommendations of real improvement. And meanwhile the publishers were actually netting fair profits from a long list of confiding subscribers. What might well have been a 'broadstone of honour' to English literature became its glaring disgrace.* No one would more gladly have striven for a better result—had the power lain with him—than would Sir Henry ELLIS. As to his nominal co-editors, they did almost nothing, from first to last.

To far better result did ELLIS labour upon his successive editions of *Hall, Hardyng, Fabyan,* and *Polydore Vergil,* among our chroniclers, and of BRAND's *Observations on Popular Antiquities,* of DUGDALE's *History of Saint Paul's Cathedral,* and of NORDEN's *Essex,* among the standard illustrations of our archæology and topography. But his most enduring contribution to historical literature is, beyond doubt, his *Original Letters, illustrative of English History,* the publication of which began in 1824, and was completed in 1846. That work alone would suffice to keep his name in honourable memory for a long time to come.

* I do not make this statement without ample warrant. When preparing, under Lord Romilly's direction, my humble contribution of the lost *Liber de Hyda* to the series of *Chronicles and Memorials,* I had competent occasion to test the *Monasticon* of 1813-1824, and found it to teem with errors and oversights in that part of it which I had then to do with. I had had other occasions to study it somewhat closely twenty years before, and with like result. At the interval of twenty years, one could hardly stumble twice upon exceptionally ill-edited portions of such a book. For the new 'Dugdale,' thus truthfully characterised, subscribers paid a hundred and thirty pounds for small paper, two hundred and sixty pounds for large paper, copies ; and the number of subscribers was considerable. So much for the 'We must retrench' of the publishers.

At the British Museum he had a considerable advantage over his predecessor in the Principal Librarianship. He enjoyed the assistance, almost from the first, of an abler staff, in more than one of the departments, than Mr. Planta had commanded during the earlier years of his administration. And an improved order of service had been established before Mr. Ellis's rule began. In this way appliances lay already under his hand which facilitated the work of progress, when—more especially—a strong demand for improvement came from without, as well as from the action of the Trustees themselves within.

At that date the Department of Printed Books was under the charge of the Rev. Henry Hervey Baber (the eminent editor of the 'Alexandrian MS.' of the Septuagint). He was assisted by Mr. Henry Francis Cary, the translator of Dante, and also by Mr. Walter, who had been one of the Librarians of King George the Third, and who, in 1831, was succeeded by Mr. Antonio Panizzi. In the Department of MSS. Mr. Ellis's Assistant-Keeper, the Rev. Josiah Forshall, had succeeded to the charge, and the new Keeper had the able assistance of Sir Frederick Madden, whose labours for the improvement of his department are well known to scholars. The Antiquities were confided to Mr. Edward Hawkins; the various Natural History Collections to Messrs. König and Children. The Botanical Department was, as I have shown at the close of the preceding Book, just about to be re-organized (almost to be created) by the transfer of the Collections of Sir Joseph Banks, and with them of the services of their distinguished Keeper. Taken altogether, such a staff as this was of threefold efficiency to that with which Mr. Planta had started at the beginning of the century.

Mr. Ellis enjoyed an additional advantage from the

great familiarity with the whole service of the Museum which he had acquired during his labours as Secretary from the year 1814. The secretarial duty had been combined with the functions of keepership during thirteen years. Great punctuality, a conspicuous faculty for method and memory, and very courteous manners, were qualifications which are not always, or necessarily, found in union with conspicuous industry. In him they were combined. Nevertheless, he narrowly escaped losing the merited reward of long and assiduous labours. For he had a formidable competitor.

At this time, a most accomplished scholar, who deservedly possessed large influence, both social and political, had obtained the virtual promise of almost the highest personage in the realm that whenever Mr. PLANTA died he should receive the offer of successorship. Mr. Henry FYNES CLINTON, in those quiet ante-reform days, had been able, for twenty years, to unite the functions of a Member of Parliament with the assiduous pursuits of scholarship in one of its highest forms. Learning had higher charms for him than Politics, and he had no turn for debate, but he had steadily attended the House of Commons while giving to the world his *Fasti Hellenici* and *Fasti Romani*. Six months before Mr. PLANTA's decease, the Archbishop of CANTERBURY had, in effect, promised Mr. FYNES CLINTON that he would nominate him to be Principal Librarian, and the Archbishop well knew that, as far as learning went, such an appointment would be applauded throughout Europe. The Archbishop (Dr. Charles MANNERS SUTTON), did not forget his promise, and his vote carried that of the then Speaker of the House of Commons, who was the Archbishop's son. Their joint communication with the Lord Chancellor procured his assent also. ' We have made,'

Book III,
Chap. II.
HISTORY
OF THE
MUSEUM
UNDER SIR
H. ELLIS.

THE CANDIDATURE OF
MR. H.
FYNES
CLINTON.

the Archbishop told Mr. Fynes Clinton, 'your recommendation to the King as strong as possible.' The practice,
as the reader will perhaps remember, was that the then
Principal Trustees should in all such cases recommend to
the Sovereign *two* names, with such observations upon them
as to those Trustees might seem appropriate.

As Mr. Ellis was now the senior officer; had had the
care successively of two several departments (MSS. and
Printed Books); had also served as Secretary, and, in all
these employments, had acquitted himself with diligence
and credit, there could, of course, be no difficulty as to the
name which should be submitted to George the Fourth
in company with that of Mr. Fynes Clinton. Other
Trustees interested themselves in supporting, indirectly but
efficiently, the claims of one who had served the Board so
long. And the King was pleased to prefer the second
name which had been placed before him by the Principal
Trustees rather than the first. Lord Lansdowne received
His Majesty's commands to signify to the Archbishop that
it was upon the ground of 'long service in the Museum'
that the King had made his choice.

Those who had (like the writer) opportunity to watch,
during most of the succeeding thirty years, the continuance
of that service, know that the King's selection was justified.
Sir Henry Ellis was not gifted with any of those salient
abilities which dazzle the eyes of men; but he had great
power of labour, the strictest integrity of purpose, and a
very kind heart. He was ever, to the Trustees, a faithful
servant, up to the full measure of his ability. To those
who worked under him he was always courteous, conside-
rate, and very often he was generous. He would sometimes expose himself to misconstruction, in order to appease
discords. He would at times rather seem wanting in

firmness of will than, by pressing his authority, wound the feelings of well-intentioned but irritable subordinates. No one could receive from him a merited reproof—I speak from personal experience—without perceiving that the duty of giving it was felt to be a painful duty. The Commissioners of 1850 had ample warrant for hinting, in their Report to the Crown—when alluding to certain internal disputes—that the qualities least abounding in Sir Henry Ellis's composition were those which equip a man 'for such harsher duties of his office, as cannot be accomplished by the aid of conciliatory manners, the index of a benevolent disposition.'

A man of that temper will now and then, in his own despite, get forced into a somewhat bitter controversy. One sharp attack on Sir Henry's administration of his Principal-Librarianship had a close connection with discords of an anterior date which had broken out in the Society of Antiquaries. The late Sir Harris Nicolas would scarcely have criticised, with so much vehemence, what he thought to have been a careless indifference on Ellis's part to the acquisition for the British Museum of an important body of historical manuscripts, preserved in a chateau in a distant corner of France (and offered to the Trustees in 1829), but for the circumstance that Sir Henry's kindly unwillingness, evinced a little while before, to desert a very weak colleague at Somerset-House had stood in the way of some much-needed reforms in that quarter. Without in the least intending beforehand to represent things unfairly, Sir H. Nicolas acted under the influence of an unconscious bias or pre-judgment. The Joursanvault story is still worth telling, although it has now become an old story, and one portion of the historical treasures it relates to are now past wishing for, as an English possession.

Book III, Chap. II. History of the Museum under Sir H. Ellis.

Report (1850) p. 32.

The story of the MSS. at Pomard.

In the course of the revolutionary convulsions in France, a great body of historical documents had been abstracted from the famous old Castle of Blois. Eventually, as years passed on, they found their way into the country-seat, at Pomard, of the Baron de JOURSANVAULT, and with them were amalgamated an extensive collection of old family papers, many books on genealogy, and some choice illuminated missals.

An English gentleman long resident in France had formed the acquaintance of the Baron de JOURSANVAULT, and in the course of conversation came to hear of the existence of these historical treasures. He also perceived that their owner had little taste for them, or ability to profit by their contents. Sir Thomas Elmsley CROFT probed his French friend on the subject of parting with them. The Baron lent a willing ear, and, to whet his interlocutor's appetite, told him that a great many of the manuscripts related to the history of the English rule in France. Sir Thomas then apprised an English friend, famous for his love of old MSS., of the existence of the hoards, and of the certainty that the Baron who owned them would greatly prefer a few rouleaux of English gold to a whole castle-full of the most precious parchments that ever charmed the longing eyes of a Jonathan OLDBUCK—or a Harris NICOLAS.

Sir Harris, directly he received this piece of news from Paris, passed it on to his friend the late Lord CANTERBURY, then Speaker, who, in turn, communicated the information to Sir H. ELLIS, for the use of the Trustees. ELLIS was sent to France—whither indeed he had, just at that moment, arranged to go, in order to spend part of his holidays in Paris, according to his frequent custom.

He reached Pomard (two hundred and fifty miles from

Paris) in September, 1829, and found a vast body of charters which had formed the archives of the mediæval Earls of Blois, together with many heraldic and genealogical manuscripts chiefly relating to French families. But he found hardly any manuscripts which bore, directly, upon English history or affairs—the immediate object, it must be remembered, of the mission given him by the Trustees.

Immediately on his return to Paris, Sir Henry wrote thus to the Archbishop of CANTERBURY:—'The Collection is indeed a most extraordinary one of its kind, and would be a treasure in the stores of the British Museum, or of any other public Collection, though, perhaps, for a reason which will presently appear, some of the Trustees may think a public library of France would be its most appropriate repository. It is placed in two attics of the Chateau, of considerable area—and I should say sixteen feet in height—in cartons (or paste-board boxes), each two feet in length by one in depth and width. Each carton contains some hundreds of charters, at least whenever I examined them, and I made here and there my comparison with the catalogue of from twenty to thirty cartons, all answering to the catalogue and to the successive dates upon the outside of the boxes. . . . . . In one room there were above a hundred boxes piled up to the ceiling, the lower ones of which, where I could get at them, were full of instruments arranged as I have described. I counted also, in the same room, near a hundred and fifty bundles, all of single articles, partly piled up for want of room, and placed upon the floors. In the second room I counted a hundred and forty-nine cartons piled up like the former, and no ladder in the house to get at them. I did what I could upon a pair of steps made of two thin boards fastened to two other upright boards, but I had not even a safe pair of steps. Many of the cartons in the second room contained collections of a comparatively recent date, apparently the manuscripts of the Baron's father. Some of these were terriers of lands, others were marked " *Pays Étrangers*," " *Monumens Généalogiques ;*" " *Pièces Historiques ;*" " *Parlement ;*" " *Histoire de l'Église.*"

'Of the great collection of charters (and it appeared to me to be larger than all the collection of charters at present in the British Museum put together), I am bound to say that I believe them to have formed almost the entire muniments of the Earls of BLOIS, containing whatever related to their concern in the wars of Europe in the middle ages, to their prædial possessions, their granting out of property and privileges, sales, feudal or public acts, quittances of money for military services, letters patents, expenses of household, and every act, material or immaterial, likely to be found in the archives of one of the greatest houses of England.

'I looked in vain, however, for anything illustrative of English history, except in a single bundle, tied in paper, which seemed unconnected with the cartons, and was not, as far as I could find, in any of the MS. catalogues. This bundle was entitled, in a modern hand, " Documens relatifs à l'occupation de la France par les Anglais, 1400." It consists of about one hundred vellum instruments, one or two, or perhaps more, so far in the form of letters that they were official announcements; such as the Duke of ORLEANS in England in 1437, that he had obtained safe conducts for his Chancellor and Premier Écuyer d'écurie. Amongst these are various orders of payment and acquittances for money, and several relate to Charles, Duke of ORLEANS, whilst prisoner in England after the fight of Agincourt. There is a payment to the Earl of SUFFOLK; another to

persons fighting against the English; a payment for the
deliverance of the Duc d'ANGOULEME whilst a prisoner in
England in 1412; various orders of John, Duke of BED-
FORD, the Bastard of Salisbury, the Duke of EXETER, &c.,
to persons in the care of military posts under them; the
Duke of BEDFORD concerning musters; HENRY THE
FIFTH's acquittance to the parishioners of certain villages
for payments on account of the war; various grants of
the same King for services in the wars; a grant to Sir
William BOURCHIER of the estates of the Earl of Eu, dated
at Mantes in his seventh year; and an order for a confirma-
tion to be made out of the different grants of the Kings
of England and Dukes of Normandy to the House of
Lepers at Dieppe.'

When Sir Henry ELLIS had completed at Pomard that
rough examination of the Collection which he thus described on his return to Paris, his first inquiry of the
owner was, of course, about price. M. de JOURSANVAULT
was embarrassed. To Sir Thomas CROFT he had already
said that he hoped to get sixty thousand francs. ELLIS
had noticed, as the Baron drove him from Beaune into the
court-yard of the old chateau, that its appearance denoted
wealth in past rather than in present days, but he could
hardly have been prepared for the effect of altered circumstances in turning a gentleman into a chapman. In the
evening the anticipated sixty thousand francs had grown
into a hundred and ten thousand. Nor was this the only
demand. The Duke of WELLINGTON must use his credit
at Paris to transform the Baron into a Count (without any
stipulation for an entailed estate by way of 'majorat'); and
if the task should be beyond the powers even of the conqueror of NAPOLEON, then M. de JOURSANVAULT was to
receive, from the English Government, authority to import

into England five hundred pipes of Beaune wine, grown upon his own estate, free of all customs duties, and for his own profit.

Sir Henry (who with great good sense had already taken precaution that his position at the British Museum should not be known to his host at Pomard, in the hope of precluding any exaggeration of terms) remonstrated against the burden of such a demand, but all entreaty was vain. The Baron was bent on having—in addition to his £4400—either a step in nobility, or, at the least, a handsome remission of customs duty. The Trustees, in the end, declined to treat.

When it came to Sir Harris NICOLAS's knowledge that ELLIS's journey to Pomard was apparently to have no result in the way of bringing historical manuscripts into England, he felt angry as well as disappointed. It was his earnest belief—whether right or wrong—that a valuable occasion had been somewhat trifled with. He told the story,* and

* After stating that Mr. Ellis had made needless proclamation at Paris of the object of his journey, Sir Harris Nicolas proceeds thus :—
' Not contented with this injudicious and useless development of the objects in view, the learned gentleman himself pompously announced wherever he went that he was the " Chief Librarian of the British Museum," sent specially to treat for these manuscripts, thus making a public affair of what should have been kept private. The effect of this folly may easily be imagined. Long before the " Chief Librarian " reached Pomard, the French newspapers expressed their indignation that historical muniments should be sold to the British Government, inferring that England must be anxious to possess the records in question, when the purchase of them was made an official business.

' The effect of all this parade upon the owner of the manuscripts was a natural one; he fancied he had erred in his estimate of their value, and that, as they seemed to be objects of national importance to another Government, he resolved to make that Government pay at a much higher rate, for what they manifested such extraordinary anxiety to obtain, than a private individual. On the " Chief Librarian's " arrival at Pomard, he discovered that the Baron could speak little English; and treasured up the memory, and both the story and the narrator's personal reminiscences of the transaction had their share in bringing about the parliamentary enquiry into the affairs of the British Museum.

Originally, and immediately, that inquiry was proposed to the House of Commons by Mr. Benjamin HAWES, then M.P. for Lambeth, at the instance of a Mr. John MILLARD, who had been employed, for some years, on an Index of MSS., and whose employment (upon very good grounds) had been discontinued. Sir Harris NICOLAS also brought his influence to bear. Mr. HAWES, personally, had a very earnest intention to benefit the Public by the inquiry. But his own pursuits in life were not such as to have given him the literary qualifications necessary for conducting it. With not less wisdom than modesty, when he had carried his motion for a Select Committee, he waived his claim to its chairmanship. The Committee chose for that office Mr. SOTHERON ESTCOURT. The burden of examination, on

the Baron, as he has since asserted, discovered that the " Chief Librarian " could speak less French; hence it was with great difficulty that the latter could understand that the Baron had become so enlightened about his treasures as to expect, not merely double the price he originally asked for them, but as our Government had interfered on the subject, he wished it to advance one step further, by inducing his Most Christian Majesty to raise his Barony into a Comté. Such terms were out of the question ; and after spending two or three hours only in examining the Collection, but which required at least as many weeks, the " Chief Librarian " returned to England *re infecta*, and made his report to the Trustees, who refused to purchase the Collection, but offered to buy a few documents, which the owner, of course, declined. Thus, highly valuable documents are lost to the Museum and to the country, in consequence, solely and entirely, of the absurd measures adopted for their acquisition.'—NICOLAS, *Observations on the State of Historical Literature in England*, pp. 78-80. My long and observant acquaintance with Sir H. Nicolas justifies me in adding to this extract—in which there are such obvious exaggerations of statement—that I am convinced he was writing from insufficient and inaccurate information. He was incapable of wilful misstatement.

behalf of the Trustees, was borne—it need not be said how ably—by men of no less mark than Sir Robert Harry Inglis and the late Earl of Derby, then Lord Stanley.

One of the best results of the appointment of that Committee of 1835-36 was the opportunity it gave to Mr. Baber and to Mr. Panizzi of advocating the claims of the National Library to largely increased liberality on the part of Parliament. The latter, in particular, did it with an earnestness, and with a vivacity and felicity of argument and of illustration, which I believe won for him the respect of every person who enjoyed (as I did) the pleasure of listening to his examination. I do not think that anybody in that Committee Room of 1836 thought his arguments a whit the weaker for being expressed by 'a foreigner.' But it chances to be within my knowledge that pressure was put upon Mr. Hawes, as a conspicuous member of the Committee, to induce him to put questions to a certain witness with the view of enabling that witness to attack the Trustees for appointing a foreigner to an important office in the Museum. The ludicrous absurdity of an objection on that score—in relation to a great establishment of Literature and Science—was not, it seems, felt in those days as it would assuredly be felt in the present day. The absurdity did not strike the mind of Mr. Hawes, but, to his great credit, he steadfastly refused to admit of any impeachment in the Committee of a choice which he believed had been most fitly made in all other respects.*

---

* I was myself present at an interview (in Lambeth), when the most urgent influence was used with Mr. Hawes to induce him to attack Mr. Panizzi's original appointment as an 'Assistant-Librarian'; and I heard him express a strong approval of it, on the ground of the obvious qualifications and abilities of the individual officer—though himself sharing the opinion that in such appointments Englishmen should have the preference.

It is more than probable that the ability which Mr. Panizzi had displayed in the Committee Room of the House of Commons, as well as the zeal for our national honour which he had shown himself to possess, had something to do in preparing the way for the promotion which awaited him within a few months after Mr. Hawes' Committee made its final report to the House. But his labours in the Museum itself had certainly given substantial and ample warrant for that promotion—under all the circumstances of the case—as will be seen presently.

Amongst the duties entrusted to Mr. Panizzi after his entrance (in 1831) into the service of the Trustees as an extra Assistant-Librarian, was the cataloguing of an extra-ordinary Collection of Tracts illustrative of the History of the French Revolution. He had laboured on a difficult task with great diligence and with uncommon ability. In 1835, a Committee of Trustees reported, in the highest terms, on the performance of his duties, and concluded their report with a recommendation which, although the general body of Trustees did not act upon it, became the occasion of a very eulogistic minute. Two years afterwards, the office of Keeper of Printed Books became vacant by the resignation of the Reverend Henry Hervey Baber, who had filled it, with great credit, from the year 1802.

The office of Senior Assistant-Librarian in that Department was then filled by another man of eminent literary distinction, the Reverend Henry Francis Cary, who, as one of the best among the many English translators of Dante, is not likely to be soon forgotten amongst us. Not a few Englishmen of the generation that is now passing away learnt in his version to love Dante, before they were able to read him in his proper garb, and learnt too to love Italy, as Cary loved it, for Dante's sake.

Mr. Cary was the grandson of Mordecai Cary, Bishop of Killaloe, and the son of a Captain in the British Army, who at the time of Henry Cary's birth was quartered at Gibraltar, where the boy was born on the sixth of December, 1772. He was educated at Birmingham and at Christ Church, Oxford. It was in his undergraduate days at Christ Church that he began to translate the *Inferno*, although he did not publish his first volume until he had entered his thirty-third year, and had established himself in 'the great wen' as Reader at Berkeley Chapel (1805). Cary's '*Dante*' soon won its way to fame. Among other blessings it brought about his life-long friendship with Coleridge and with the Coleridgian circle. He now became an extensive contributor to the literary periodicals. In 1816, he was made Preacher at the Savoy. In 1825, he offered himself to the Trustees of the British Museum as a candidate for the Keepership of the Department of Antiquities in succession to Taylor Combe. That office was given, with great propriety, to Mr. Edward Hawkins, who had assisted Mr. Combe, and had, in fact, replaced him during his illness. But Mr. Cary had met with encouragement—especially from the Archbishop of Canterbury—and kept a bright look-out for new vacancies. In May or June, 1826, he wrote to his father that he had learnt that the office of Assistant-Librarian in the Department of Printed Books was vacant. It had been, he added, held by a most respectable old clergyman of the name of Bean, and Mr. Bean was just dead. Within a week or two, Mr. Cary was appointed to be his successor. By a large circle of friends the appointment was hailed as a fitting tribute to a most deserving man of letters.

The homely rooms in the Court-yard of the Museum allotted to the Assistant-Keeper of the Printed Book Department were soon the habitual resort of a cluster of poets. The faces of COLERIDGE, ROGERS, Charles LAMB,* and (during their occasional visits to London) those of SOUTHEY and of WORDSWORTH, became, in those days, very familiar at the gate of old Montagu House. COLERIDGE had always loved CARY, and when the charms of long monologues, delivered at the Grove to devout listeners, withheld him from visits, the correspondence between Highgate and Bloomsbury became so frequent and so voluminous, that he is said to have endeavoured to persuade Sir Francis FREELING that all correspondence to or from the British Museum ought to be officially regarded as ' On His Majesty's Service,' and to be franked, to any weight, accordingly. But those love-enlivened rooms were, in a very few years, to be darkly clouded. CARY lost his wife on the twenty-second of November, 1832, and almost immediately afterwards—so dreadful was the blow to him—' a look of mere childishness, approaching to a suspension of vitality, marked the countenance which had but now beamed with intellect.' Such are the words of his fellow-mourner.

Part of Mr. CARY's duties at the Museum now necessarily fell, for a few months, to be discharged by Mr.

Book III, Chap. II. HISTORY OF THE MUSEUM UNDER SIR H. ELLIS.

Life of H. F. Cary, by his Son, vol. ii, p. 198.

---

* It was in the old rooms in the Court-yard of Montagu House that Charles Lamb enjoyed the last, I think, of his ' dinings-out.' A few days after his final visit (November, 1834) the hand of Death was already upon him. Cary, before writing the well-known epitaph, wrote some other graceful and touching lines on his old friend. They were occasioned by finding, in a volume lent to Lamb by Cary, Lamb's bookmark, against a page which told of the death of Sydney. They begin thus :—

> ' So should it be, my gentle friend,
> Thy leaf last closed at Sydney's end ;
> Thou too, like Sydney, wouldst have given
> The water, thirsting, and near Heaven.'

Panizzi, who, in the preceding year, had been appointed next in office to Cary. The circumstances of that appointment have been thus stated by the eminent Prelate who made it :—

'Mr. Panizzi was entirely unknown to me, except by reputation. I understood that he was a civilian who had come from Italy, and that he was a man of great acquirements and talents, peculiarly well suited for the British Museum. That was represented to me by several persons who were not connected with the Museum, and it was strongly pressed by several of the Trustees, who were of opinion that Mr. Panizzi's appointment would be very advantageous for the institution. Considering the qualifications of that gentleman, his knowledge of foreign languages, his eminent ability and extensive attainments, I could not doubt the propriety of acceding to their wishes.'

When that appointment was made, Mr. Panizzi had already passed almost ten years in England. The greater part of them had been spent at Liverpool, as a tutor in the language and literature of Italy. Born at Brescello, in the Duchy of Modena, Mr. Panizzi had been educated at Reggio and at Parma; in the last-named University he had graduated as LL.D. in 1818; and he had practised with distinction as an advocate. Part of his leisure hours had been given to the study of bibliography, and to the acquisition of a library. But he was an ardent aspirant for the liberty of Italy, and, in 1820, narrowly escaped becoming one of its many martyrs. After the unsuccessful rising of that year in Piedmont, he was arrested at Cremona, but escaped from his prison. After his escape he was sentenced to death. He sought a refuge first at Lugano, and afterwards at Geneva. But his ability had made him a marked man. Austrian spies dogged his steps, and appealed, by turns, to the suspicions and to the fears of the local authorities. Presently it seemed clear that England, alone, would afford, to the dreaded 'conspirator' for Italy, a secure abode. At Liverpool he acquired the friendship successively of Ugo Foscolo, of Roscoe, and of Brougham. In 1828, he received and accepted the offer of the Professorship of Italian Literature in the then London University, now 'University College.' In 1830, he began the publication of his admirable edition of the poems of Bojardo and Ariosto, which was completed in 1834.

When Mr. Baber announced, in March, 1837, his intention to resign his Keepership, Mr. Panizzi made no application for the office, but he wrote to the Principal Trustees an expression of his hope that if, in the event, 'any appointment was to take place on account of Mr. Baber's resignation,' his services would be borne in mind.

One of Mr. Cary's earliest steps in the matter was to apply to his friend and fellow-poet, Mr. Samuel Rogers. Rogers—to use his own words—was one who had known Cary 'in all weathers.' His earnest friendship induced him to write a letter of recommendation to the three Principal Trustees. After he had sent in his recommendation, a genuine conscientiousness—not the less truly characteristic of the man for all that outward semblance of cynicism which frequently veiled it—prompted him to think the matter over again. It occurred to him to doubt whether he was really serving his old friend Cary by helping to put him in a post for which failing vigour was but too obviously, though gradually, unfitting him. His misgiving increased the more he turned the affair over in his mind. He then wrote three letters (to the Archbishop, Chancellor, and Speaker), recalling his recommendation, and stating his reason. With the Speaker, Rogers also conversed on the subject. Mr. Abercromby asked the poet : 'What do you know about a Mr. Panizzi, who stands next to Cary?' 'Panizzi,' said Rogers, 'would serve you very well.' 'To tell you the truth,' rejoined the Speaker, 'we think that, if Mr. Cary is not appointed, Panizzi will be the right man.' At that time, Mr. Panizzi was not personally known either to the Speaker or to the Chancellor.

I give these details, first, because they became, in after-days, a very vital and influential part of the History of the British Museum. No appointment was ever made during the whole of the hundred and fifteen years which have elapsed betwixt the first organization of the establishment in 1755 and the year in which I write (1870) that has had such large influence upon its growth and its improvement ; and, secondly, because in a published life of the excellent man whose temporary disappointment led to a great public benefit a passage appears which (doubtless very unintentionally, but not the less seriously) misrepresents the matter, and hints, mysteriously, at underhanded influence, as though something had been done in the way of treachery to Cary. 'The Lord Chancellor and the Speaker,' writes Cary's biographer, ' acting under information, *the source of which was probably known only to them and their informant*, resolved on passing him over, and appointing his subordinate, Mr. Panizzi, to the vacant place.'

These letters and conversations passed in the interval between the announcement that there would be a vacancy in the Museum staff and its actual occurrence. The Keepership became vacant on the twenty-fourth of June. On that day Mr. Cary made his personal application to the Archbishop. The Archbishop told him that objections were made to his appointment. CARY, immediately after his return, told his brother-officers BABER and PANIZZI what the Archbishop had communicated to him. 'Then,' said Mr. PANIZZI, 'the thing concerns me.' 'Yes,' rejoined CARY, 'certainly it does.' They all knew that applications for the vacant office from outsiders were talked of. Among these were the late Reverend Ernest HAWKINS and the late Reverend Richard GARNETT (who afterwards succeeded to the Assistant-Librarianship). And Mr. PANIZZI then proceeded to say to Mr. CARY: 'You will not, now, object to my asking for the place myself, as there are these objections to you.' CARY replied, 'Not at all.' Instantly, and in CARY's presence, Mr. PANIZZI wrote thus to the Archbishop :—'I hope your Grace will not deem it presumptuous in me to beg respectfully of your Grace and the other Principal Trustees to take my case into consideration, should they think it necessary to depart from the usual system of regular promotion, on appointing Mr. BABER's successor. I venture to say thus much, having been informed by Mr. CARY of the conversation he has had the honour to have with your Grace.' The writer gave his letter into Mr. CARY's hand, received his brother-officer's immediate approval, and had that approval, at a later hour of the day and after a re-perusal of the letter, confirmed.

Within the walls of the Museum, the general feeling was so strongly in favour of Mr. CARY's appointment, despite all objection (and nothing can be more natural than that it should be so—'A fellow-feeling makes us wondrous kind'), that the *public* interest, in having an officer who would use the appointment rather as a working-tool than as a reclining staff, was, for the moment, lost sight of. Sir Henry ELLIS himself, when asked to give a formal testimonial of Mr. PANIZZI's qualifications to be head of the

Printed Book Department, answered: 'If you told me that the Bodleian Librarianship was vacant—or any other outside Librarianship worth your having—you should have my heartiest recommendation. At present, you must excuse me;' or in words to that effect. Edward HAWKINS, then Keeper of the Department of Antiquities, expressed himself (in the hearing of the present writer) to like purpose, when asked what his opinion was on a point which, at the moment, attracted not a little attention in literary circles.*

CARY afterwards—and when it was too late to recall it —regretted his assent to Mr. PANIZZI's application. He applied again to the Archbishop, and obtained something like a promise of support. He wrote several letters to the Lord Chancellor. In one of these he (unconsciously, as it seems) adduced a conclusive argument against his own appointment to the office he sought. He wrote that, as he was informed, the objections of his Lordship and of the Speaker were twofold: the one resting on his age, and the other on the state of his health. He answered the objections in these words:—'My age, it is plain, might rather ask for me that *alleviation of labour* which, *in this as in other public offices, is gained by promotion* to a superior place, than call for a continuance of the same laborious employment.' What must have been a Lord Chancellor's ruminations upon the 'alleviation of labour' which 'a

* It is necessary that I should state, with precision, the sources of the information conveyed in the text. I rely, chiefly, on three several sources, one of which is publicly accessible. My main knowledge of the matter rests (first) upon the *Minutes of Evidence* taken by Lord Ellesmere's Commission of 1848-1850; (secondly) upon conversations with the late Mr. Edward Hawkins, held in July and August, 1837, not long after the appearance of Mr. Cary's letter in *The Times*; (thirdly) upon a conversation, on the same subject, with which I was honoured by Sir Henry Ellis in 1839.

superior place' brings to a public servant, is a somewhat amusing subject of conjecture.

It was with perfect honesty and integrity of purpose that Mr. CARY adduced medical testimony of his fitness for continued but diminished labours. He would have exerted himself to the best of his ability. But it was a blemish in an excellent man that (under momentary irritation) he twice permitted himself to reproach his competitor and colleague with being 'a foreigner.'

One would fain have hoped that our famous countryman Daniel DEFOE had, a hundred years before, put all reproach and contumely on the score of a man's *not* being a 'true-born Englishman' quite out of Court, in all contentions concerning capabilities of public service. But, of all places in the world, a MUSEUM is the queerest place in which to raise petty questions of nationality. If it be at all worthy of its name, its contents must have come from the four quarters of the globe. Men of every race under Heaven must have worked hard to furnish it. It brings together the plants of Australia; the minerals of Peru; the shells of the far Pacific; the manuscripts which had been painfully compiled or transcribed by twenty generations of labourers in every corner of Europe, as well as in the monasteries of Africa and of the Eastern Desert; and the sculptures and the printed books of every civilised country in the world. And then it is proposed—when arrangements are to be made for turning dead collections into living fountains of knowledge —that the question asked shall be: *not* 'What is your capacity to administer?' but 'Where were you born?' I hope, and I believe, that in later years Mr. CARY regretted that he had permitted a name so deservedly honoured to endorse so poor a sophism.

Mr. Antonio Panizzi received his appointment on the fifteenth of July, 1837. If he had worked hard to gain promotion, he worked double tides to vindicate it. In the following month, Mr. Cary resigned his Assistant-Librarianship. He left the Museum with the hearty respect and with the brotherly regrets of all his colleagues, without any exception. Of him, it may very truly be said, he was a man much beloved.

Nor was it otherwise with Mr. Baber. His public services began in old Bodley towards the end of the year 1796, and they were so efficient as to open to him, at the beginning of the present century, a subordinate post in the British Museum, his claims to which he waived the instant that he knew they would stand in the way of Ellis, his early friend of undergraduate days. He became Assistant-Librarian in 1807 ; Keeper of Printed Books in 1812. He, too, was a man with no enemies. In literature he won (before he was fifty) an enduring place by his edition of the *Vetus Testamentum Græcum e Codice MS. Alexandrino . . . . descriptum.*

Of the amiability of character which distinguished Mr. Baber, not less than did his scholarship, the present writer had more than common experience. It was my fortune to make my first intimate acquaintance (1835) with the affairs of the British Museum in the capacity of a critic on that part of Mr Baber's discharge of his manifold functions as Keeper which related to the increase of the Library, both by purchase and by the operation of the Copyright Act. I criticised some of his doings, and some of his omissions to do, with youthful presumption, and with that self-confident half-knowledge which often leads a man more astray, practically, than does sheer ignorance. So far from resenting strictures, a few of which may have had some small validity and value, while a good many were certainly plausible but shallow, he turned the former to profit, and, so far from resenting the latter, repeatedly evinced towards their author acts of courtesy and kindness. It was in his company that I first explored—as we strode from beam to beam of the unfinished flooring—the new Library rooms in which, long afterwards, I was to perform my humble spell of work on the *Catalogue of the Printed Books;* as he had performed his hard-by almost thirty years earlier.

Mr. BABER survived his retirement from his Keepership (in 1837) no less than thirty-two years. He died, on the twenty-eighth of March, 1869, at his rectory-house at Stretham, in the Isle of Ely, and in his 94th year. He had then been F.R.S. for fifty-three years, and had survived his old friend Sir Henry ELLIS by a few weeks. He served his parishioners in Cambridgeshire, as he had served his country in London, with unremitting zeal and punctual assiduity.

One of Mr. PANIZZI's earliest employments in his new office of 1837 was to make arrangements for the formidable task of transferring the whole mass of the old Library from Montagu House to the new Building, but he also did something immediately towards preparing the way for that systematic enlargement of the Collection of Printed Books which he had formerly and so earnestly pressed on the attention, not merely of the Select Committee of the House of Commons in 1835-36, but of every Statesman and Parliament-man whose ear he could gain, whether (in his interlocutor's opinion) in season or out of season. To use the expression of the man who, at a later date, mainly helped him in that task, Mr. PANIZZI's leading thought, in regard to Public Libraries, was that Paris must be surpassed. In common with others of us who, like himself, had been examined before Mr. HAWES' Committee on that subject, he had brought into salient relief some points of superiority which foreign countries possessed over Britain, but the ruling motive of the unsavoury comparison was British improvement, not, most assuredly, British discredit.

In the formidable business of the transfer of the bulk of the National Library, Mr. PANIZZI received his best help from a man now just lost to us, but whose memory will surely survive. Exactly six months after his own appointment to the headship of his Department, he introduced into the permanent service of the Trustees Mr. Thomas WATTS. The readers of such a volume as this will not, I imagine, think it to be a digression if I here make some humble attempt to record what was achieved by my old acquaintance—an acquaintance of almost one and thirty years' standing—both in his varied literary labours and in his long and fruitful service at the Museum.

Thomas WATTS was born in London in the year 1811. He was educated at a private school in London, where he was very early noted for the possession of three several qualities, one or other of which is found, in a marked degree, in thousands of men and in tens of thousands of precocious boys, but the union of all of which, whether in child or in man, is rare indeed. Young WATTS evinced both an astonishing capacity for acquiring languages—the most far remote from his native speech—and an unusual readiness at English composition. He had also a knack for turning off very neat little speeches and recitations. Before he was fifteen, he could give good entertainment at a breaking-up or a 'speech-day.' Before he was twenty, he had gained his footing as a contributor to periodical literature.*

---

* I believe that his earliest contribution consisted of some articles entitled 'Notes of a Reader,' published in 1830, in a periodical (long since defunct) called *The Spirit of Literature*. These were written and

In the autumn of the year 1835, Mr. WATTS' attention was attracted to the publication of the *Minutes of Evidence taken before the Select Committee on the British Museum,* the first portion of which had been ordered to be printed, by the House of Commons, in the preceding August. He read the evidence with great interest, and ere long he wrote (in 1836 and 1837) some valuable comments upon it, which embodied several suggestions for the improvement of the Museum service, and for making it increasedly accessible to the Public. More than two or three of the suggestions so offered, he lived to carry out—long afterwards, by his own exertions, and with the cordial approval of his superior officer, Mr. PANIZZI—into practice, after he had himself entered into the service of the Trustees as an Assistant in the Printed Book Department.

But he chose a very unfortunate medium for his useful communications of 1836 and 1837. He printed them in the columns of the ' *Mechanics' Magazine,*' where, for practical purposes, they were almost buried. Of this fact I am able to give a small illustrative and personal instance. Possibly, it may be thought to have some little biographical value, as a trait of his character.

In both of the years above named Mr. WATTS did the present writer the honour to make some remarks on his humble labours for the improvement of the Museum in 1835 and 1836. Mr. WATTS' remarks were very complimentary and kind in their expression. But I never saw or heard of them, until this year, 1870, after their writer had passed from the knowledge of the many acquaintances and friends who, in common with myself, much esteemed him, and who will ever honour his memory.

printed long before Mr. Watts became a correspondent of the *Mechanics' Magazine,* as mentioned in the text.

One of the communications which my late friend published in that '*Mechanics' Magazine*' contained two suggestions—made contingently, and by way of alternative plans —for the enlargement of the Museum buildings. Nearly eleven years afterwards (August, 1847), I unconsciously repeated those very suggestions, amongst many others, in a pamphlet, entitled *Public Libraries in London and Paris*. I was in complete ignorance that my suggestions of 1847 were otherwise than entirely original. I thought them wholly my own. Of the print which accompanied my pamphlet I give the reader an exact fac-simile, errors included, on the opposite plate. The print embodied very nearly the same thoughts, on the enlargement of the library, which had been expressed, so long before, in the pages of the '*Mechanics' Magazine*.' The first presented copy of that pamphlet and print was given to my friend WATTS. I was then absent, far from London, and I had presently the pleasure of receiving from him a long letter, containing some criticisms and remarks on my publication. But such was his modest reticence about his own prior performance, that the letter contained no word or hint concerning the anticipation of my alternative suggestions for the enlargement of the Library in his prior publication. And, in the long interval between 1837 and 1847, I suppose we had conversed about the improvement of the Museum, and about its buildings, actual and prospective, some thirty or forty times, but (as I have said) those valuable and thoughtful articles of his, printed in 1836-7—and making complimentary mention of my own labours, and of my evidence given before Mr. HAWES' Committee—never came within my knowledge. No part of their contents was even mentioned to me. I saw them, for the first time, in January, 1870. Very few men—within my range of acquaintance

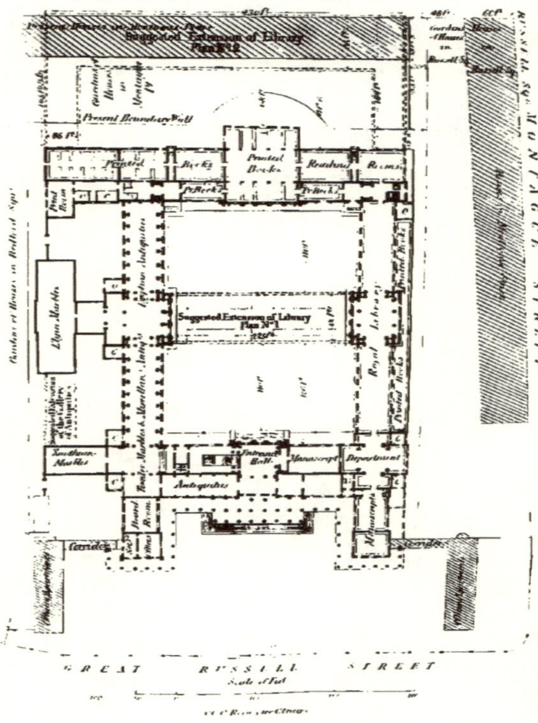

SUGGESTIONS MADE IN 1847
FOR THE ENLARGEMENT OF THE LIBRARY OF THE
— BRITISH MUSEUM —
BEING THE FAC-SIMILE OF A PLAN INSERTED IN A PAMPHLET (WRITTEN IN 1846)
— ENTITLED —
PUBLIC LIBRARIES IN LONDON AND PARIS

—had so much dislike to talk of their performances, as was manifested by Thomas WATTS. To this day, very much of what he did for the Public is scarcely known even by those who (at one time or other) enjoyed the pleasure, and the honour, of his friendship. He was one of the men who 'did good by stealth,' and would have almost blushed to find it fame.

When Thomas WATTS entered the Museum, the immediate task entrusted to him, onerous as it was, did not (for any long time) engross his attention. In common with Mr. PANIZZI, his desire to increase the Library, and to make London surpass Paris—'*Paris must be surpassed*,' are the words which close the best of those articles, printed in 1837, to which I have just now referred—amounted to a positive passion. He did not talk very much about it ; but I fancy it occupied, not only his waking thoughts, but his very dreams.

Mr. PANIZZI had not been at the head of his Department many weeks before he began a Special Report to the Trustees, recommending a systematic increase of the Collection of Printed Books.

In the autumn of 1837 he could hardly foresee that one of the attacks to be made, in the after-years, upon those who had appointed him, or who had promoted his appointment, for the crime of preferring ' a foreigner' to a high post in our National Museum, would be based upon the foreigner's neglect of English Literature. ' An Italian Librarian,' said those profound logicians, ' must, naturally and necessarily, swamp the Library with Italian books. He can't help doing it.' But, strange as it may have seemed to objectors of that calibre, this particular Italian happened to be, not only a scholar—a ripe and good one—

but a man of wide sympathies, and of catholic tastes in literature. He was able himself to enjoy SHAKESPEARE, not less thoroughly than he was able, by his critical acumen, to increase other men's enjoyment of ARIOSTO and of DANTE.

In October, 1837, he wrote thus :—' With respect to the purchase of books, Mr. PANIZZI begs to lay before the Trustees the general principles by which he will be guided, if not otherwise directed, in endeavouring to answer the expectations and wishes of the Trustees and of the Public in this respect. First, the attention of the Keeper of this emphatically British Library ought to be directed, most particularly, to British works, and to works relating to the British Empire ; its religious, political, and literary, as well as scientific history ; its laws, institutions, description, com- merce, arts, &c. The rarer and more expensive a work of this description is, the more indefatigable* efforts ought to be made to secure it for the Library. Secondly, the old and rare, as well as the critical, editions of ancient Classics, ought never to be sought for in vain in this Collection. Nor ought good comments, as also the best translations into modern languages, to be wanting. Thirdly, with respect to foreign literature, arts, and sciences, the Library ought to possess the best editions of standard works for critical purposes or for use. The Public have, moreover, a right to find, in their National Library, heavy as well as expen- sive foreign works, such as *Literary Journals ; Transactions of Societies* ; large Collections, historical or otherwise ; com- plete series of Newspapers ; Collections of Laws, and their best interpreters.' We have, in this brief passage, the germ

---

* In *Minutes of Evidence* (page 596) printed erroneously ' *reasonable.*' To the brief extract, for which alone I can here afford space, were appended, in the original Report, many pertinent amplifications and illustrations. Some of these are given in the *Minutes of Evidence* above referred to.

of the admirable Report on the National Library, written on a far more extended scale, which was afterwards laid before the Government, and, ultimately, before Parliament.

If this Report failed to lead, immediately (or, indeed, for a long time to come), to the increased means of acquisition on which its writer's mind was so much bent, the fault did not lie in the Trustees. It lay with the House of Commons, and with the Chancellor of the Exchequer.

It is hard to realise, in 1870, how entirely the effort for an adequate improvement of the British Museum was an uphill task. Trustees like the late Lord DERBY and the late Sir R. H. INGLIS were earnestly desirous to carry out such recommendations as those of Mr. PANIZZI, but the employment of urging them on the Ministry was an ungrateful one. In those days of reforming-activity, although, in 1837, the average radicals in 'the House' were not quite such devout believers in the faith that a general overturn was the only road to a general millenium as they had been in 1832, they were willing enough to listen to attacks upon the managers of any public institution (no matter how crude were the views of the assailants, or how lopsided their information), but they were not half so ready to open the public purse-strings in order to enable impugned managers or trustees to improve the institution entrusted to them upon a worthy scale.

Three months after writing his Report of 1837, Mr. PANIZZI was enabled to procure the official assistance of Mr. WATTS. The appointment strengthened his hands, by giving to a man of extraordinary powers for organization and government, the services of a man not less extraordinary for his powers of accumulating and assimilating detail. What each man characteristically possessed, was just the right supplement to the special

Book III,
Chap. II.
History
of the
Museum
under Sir
H. Ellis.

faculties of the other. But even such a happy union of personal qualities would have failed to carry into effect the large aspirations for the improvement of the Museum which both men, severally and independently, had cherished (during many years), but for one other circumstance. This was a merely incidental—one might say a fortuitous—circumstance; but it proved very influential upon the fortunes of the British Museum in the course of the years to come. When Mr. PANIZZI began to be known in London society—at first, very much by the instrumentality of the late Mr. Thomas GRENVILLE, who, at an early period, had become warmly attached to him—his acquaintance was eagerly cultivated. In this way he obtained opportunities to preach his doctrine of increased public support for our great national and educational institutions (his advocacy was not limited within the four walls of the Museum) in the ears of very valuable and powerful listeners. It was thought, now and then, that he preached on that topic out of season as well as in season. But the issue amply vindicated the zeal which prompted him to make the pleasures of social intercourse subserve the performance of a public trust. Few men, I imagine—holding the unostentatious post of a librarianship—ever possessed so many social opportunities of the kind here referred to, as were possessed by Mr. PANIZZI. And even those listeners who may have thought him over-pertinacious, sometimes, in pressing his convictions, must needs have carried away with them the assurance that one public servant, at all events, did not regard his duties as 'irksome.' They must have seen that this man's heart was in his official work.

See hereafter,
Chap. V.

So was it also in the instance of Mr. PANIZZI's right-hand man within the Museum itself. Thomas WATTS was not gifted with powers of persuasive argument. His address and manners did no sort of justice to the intrinsic qualities, or to the true heart, of the man himself. To strangers, they often gave a most inaccurate idea of his faculties and character. Under the outward guise of a blunt-spoken farmer, there dwelt, not only high scholarship, but a lofty sense—it would not be too strong to say a passionate sense—of public duty. He had none of the persuasive gifts of vivid talk. But he could preach forcibly, by example. When he had made some way with the first task which was assigned him, that of superintending the removal of the Library, and its due ordering—in some of the details of which he was ably assisted, almost from the outset, by Mr. George BULLEN (who, in January, 1838, was first specially employed to retranscribe the press-marks or symbols of the books, as they stood in old Montagu House, into the new equivalents necessitated by their altered position in the new Library, in which labour he was, in the April following, assisted by Mr. N. W. SIMONS)—and had solved, by assiduous effort and self-denying labour, some of the many difficulties which stood in the way of effecting that removal without impeding, to any serious degree, the service of the Public Reading Room, he turned his attention, at Mr. PANIZZI's instance, to the—to him—far more grateful task of preparing lists of foreign books for addition to the Library. For this task he evinced special qualities and attainments which, I believe, were never surpassed, by any librarian in the world; not even by an AUDIFFREDI, a VAN-PRAET, or a MAGLIABECHI.

Mr. WATTS' earliest schoolfellows had marvelled at his faculty for acquiring with great rapidity such a degree of familiarity with foreign tongues, as gave him an amply sufficient master-key to their several literatures. When yet very young, he showed a scholarly appreciation of the right methods of setting to work. He studied languages in groups—giving his whole mind to one group at a time, and then passing to another. At an age when many men (far from being blockheads) are painfully striving after a literary command of their mother-tongue, young WATTS had showed himself to be master of two several clusters of the great Indo-European family, and to have a very respectable acquaintance with a third. When, as a youthful volunteer at the Museum, he was fulfilling a request made to him by Mr. BABER, that he would catalogue the Collection of Icelandic books given to the Public, half a century before, by Sir Joseph BANKS, and also another parcel of Russian books, which had been bought at his own recommendation, the reading of Chinese literature was the labour of his hours of private study, and the reading of Polish literature was the recreation of his hours of leisure.

What the feelings of an ambitious student of that strain would be when officially instructed by his superior to take under his sole (or almost sole) charge the duty of examining the Museum Catalogues, and of obtaining from all parts of Europe and Asia, and from many parts of America, other catalogues of every kind, in order to ascertain the deficiencies of the Library, and to supply them, the reader can fancy. The new assistant luxuriated in his office. Many of his suggestions were periodically and earnestly supported with the Trustees by Mr. PANIZZI. His labours were appreciated and often (to my personal knowledge) warmly applauded by his superior officer.

He began with making lists of Russian books that were *desiderata* in the Museum Library; then of Hungarian; then of Dutch; then of French, Italian, Spanish, and Portuguese; then of Chinese; then of Welsh; then of the rapidly growing, but theretofore (at the Museum) much neglected, literature of the Americas and the Indies.

I used, now and then, to watch him at his work, and to think that no man could possibly be employed more entirely to his liking. Long after I ceased to enjoy any opportunity of talking with him about his employment, I used occasionally to hear that similar tasks occupied, not infrequently, the hours of evening leisure as well as the hours of official duty. Some who knew him more intimately than—of late years—it was my privilege to know him, believe that his early death was in part (humanly speaking) due to his passion for poring over catalogues and other records of far-off literatures when worn-out nature needed to be refreshed, and to be recreatively interested in quite other occupations.

During the last twenty years alone (1850-1869 inclusive) he cannot have marked and recommended for purchase less than a hundred and fifty thousand foreign works, and in order to their selection he must needs have examined almost a million of book-titles, in at least eighteen different languages.

When little more than half that last-named term of years had expired he was able to write—in a Report which he addressed to Mr. PANIZZI in February, 1861—that the common object of Keeper and Assistant-Keeper had been, during almost a quarter of a century, to 'bring together from all quarters the useful, the elegant, and the curious literature of every language; to unite with the best English Library in England, or the world, the best Russian Library out of Russia, the best German out of Germany, the best Spanish out of Spain, and so with every language from Italian to Icelandic, from Polish to Portuguese. In five of the languages in which it now claims this species of supremacy, in Russian, Polish, Hungarian, Danish, and Swedish, I believe I may say that, with the exception of perhaps fifty volumes, every book that has been purchased by the Museum within the last three and twenty years has been purchased at my suggestion. I have the pleasure of reflecting that every future student of the less-known literatures of Europe will find riches where I found poverty; though, of course, the collections in all these languages together form but a small proportion of the vast accumulations that have been added to the Library during your administration and that of your successor.'*

When the reader comes to add to his estimate of the amount of mental labour thus briefly and modestly indicated by the man who performed it, a thought of the further toil involved in the re-arrangement and careful *classification* of more than four hundred thousand volumes of books, in all the literary languages of the world (without any exception), he will have attained some rough idea of the public service which was crowded into one man's life; and that, as we all have now to regret, not a protracted life. He will have, too, some degree of conception of the amount of acquired knowledge which was taken from us when Thomas WATTS was taken.

To his works of industry and of learning, the man we have lost added the still better works of a kindly, benevolent heart. Many a struggling student received at his hands both wise and loving counsel, and active help. And his good deeds were not advertised. They would not now have been spoken of, but for his loss—in the very thick of his labours for the Public.

In a precious volume, which was first added to the manuscript stores of the British Museum a little before

* The 'successor' referred to is Mr. Winter Jones, then Keeper of Printed Books, now Principal-Librarian of the British Museum.

Mr. Watts' death, there occurs the rough jotting of a thought which is very apposite to our human and natural reflections upon such an early removal from the scene of labour as that just referred to. When somebody spoke to Bacon of the death, in the midst of duty and of mental vigour, of some good worker or other in the vineyard of this world, almost three centuries ago, he made the following entry in his private note-book :—'Princes, when in jousts, triumphs, or games of victory, men deserve crowns for their performance, do not crown them below, where the deeds are performed, but call them up. So doth God by death.'

But these several branches of public duty, onerous as they were, were far from exhausting Mr. Watts' mental activity, either within the Museum walls or outside of them. He was a frequent contributor to periodical literature. To his pen the *Quarterly Review* was indebted for an excellent article on the *History of Cyclopædias;* the *Athenæum*, for a long series of papers on various topics of literary history and of current literature, extending over many years; the various Cyclopædias and Biographical Dictionaries successively edited by Mr. Charles Knight, for a long series of valuable notices, embracing the Language and Literature of Hungary; those of Wales; and more than a hundred and thirty brief biographical memoirs, distinguished alike for careful research and for clear and vigorous expression. These biographies relate, for the most part, to foreign men of letters. To the pages of the *Transactions of the Philological Society* he was a frequent contributor. His Memoir on Hungarian Literature, first read to that Society, procured him the distinction of a corresponding-membership of the Hungarian Academy, and the distinction was enhanced by his being elected on the same day with Lord Macaulay.

Within the Museum itself two distinct and important departments of official labour, both of which he filled with intelligence and zeal, have yet to be indicated. In 1839, he took part—with others—in framing an extensive code of 'rules' for the re-compilation of the entire body of the Catalogues of Printed Books. In May, 1857, he took charge of the Public Reading-Room, as Chief Superintendent of the daily service.

It need hardly be said that the first-named task—that on the Catalogues—was a labour of planning and shaping, not one of actual execution. It was very important, however, in its effects on the public economy of the Library, and it was the one only labour, as I believe, performed by Mr. Watts, whether severally or in conjunction with others, which failed to give unmixed satisfaction to the general body of readers. The *Minutes of Evidence*, taken by the Commissioners of 1848-1850, whilst they abound in expressions of public gratitude both to Mr. Panizzi and, next after him, to Mr. Watts, contain a not less remarkable abundance of criticisms, and of complaints, upon the plan (not the execution) of the *Catalogue of Printed Books* begun in 1839. The subject is a dry one, but will repay some brief attention on the reader's part.

When Mr. Panizzi became Keeper, he had (it will have been seen) to face almost instantly, and abreast, three several tasks, each of which entailed much labour upon himself, personally, as well as upon his assistants. The third of them—this business of the Catalogue—proved to be not the least onerous, and it was, assuredly, not the best rewarded in the shape of its ultimate reception by those concerned more immediately in its performance. I can speak with some sympathy on this point, since it was as a temporary assistant in the preparation of this formidable and keenly-criticised Catalogue, that the present writer entered the service of the Trustees, in February, 1839.

That some objections to the plan adopted in 1839 are well-grounded I entirely believe. But the important point in this matter, for our present purpose, is, not that the plan preferred was unobjectionable, but that the utmost effort was used, at the time and under the circumstances of the time, to prepare such a Catalogue as should meet the fair requirements both of the Trustees and of the Readers. It is within my recollection that, to effect this, Mr. PANIZZI laboured, personally as well as in the way of super-intendance and direction, as it has not often happened to me, in my time, to see men labour for the Public. Assuredly to him promotion brought no lessening of toil in any form.

In shaping the plan of the General Catalogue of 1839-1870 (for it is, at this moment of writing, still in active progress), the course taken was this :—A sort of committee of five persons was formed, each of whom severally was to prepare, in rough draft, rules for the compilation of the projected work, illustrated by copious examples. It was to be entirely new, and to embrace every book contained in the Library up to the close of the year 1838. The draft rules were then freely discussed in joint committee, and wherever differences of opinion failed to be reconciled upon conference, the majority of votes determined the question. Such was Mr. PANIZZI's anxiety to prepare the best Catalogue for the Readers that was practicable, that he never insisted, authoritatively, on his own view of any point whatever, which might be in contention amongst us, when he stood in a minority. On all such points, he voted upon an exact equality with his assistants. The rules that were most called into question (before the Commissioners of 1848-1850) had been severally discussed and determined in this fair and simple way. Beyond all doubt, some of the rules might now be largely amended in the light of subsequent experience. But, when adopted, they seemed to *all* of us the best that were practicable under all the then circumstances.

The committee thus formed consisted of Mr. PANIZZI himself, of Mr. Thomas WATTS, of Mr. John Winter JONES (now Principal-Librarian), of Mr. John Humffreys PARRY (now Mr. Serjeant PARRY), and of the writer of this volume. The labour was much more arduous than the average run of readers in a Public Library have any adequate conception of. It occupied several months. It was pushed with such energy and industry, that many a time, after we had all five worked together, till the light of the spring days of 1839 failed us, we adjourned to work on— with the help of a sandwich and a glass of Burgundy—in Mr. PANIZZI's private apartment above the old gate in the Court-yard. If the result of our joint labours had been printed in the ordinary form of books, it would have made a substantial octavo volume. The code has, no doubt, many faults and oversights, but, be they what they may, it was a vast improvement upon former doings in that direc-

tion ; and not a little of it has been turned to account, of late years, in the Public Libraries of France, of Germany, and of America.

In the labours of this little house-committee my late friend took a very large share. To Mr. PANIZZI, and to him, all their colleagues in the task of 1839 will readily admit that the chief merit of what is good, and the smallest part of the demerit of what may have been injudicious, in the *Rules for the Compilation of the Catalogue of Printed*

Books (now before me) is incontestably due. My own experience in such matters, in the spring of 1839, was small indeed. That of my friend PARRY was even less. Mr. Winter JONES possessed, already, the advantage of a thorough familiarity with the Library about to be catalogued, and also an extensive and thorough general knowledge of books. Of Mr. PANIZZI's qualifications and attainments, for such a labour, it would be supererogatory and idle to say a word more, except that he had already—and single-handed—made so good a Catalogue of the fine Library of the Royal Society that the meddling of half-a-dozen 'revisers' failed to spoil it. But there is no impropriety in saying of Mr. WATTS, that he so delighted in the labour in hand as to make it seem, to those who worked with him, that he looked upon it in the light of a pleasant recreation rather than in the light of a dry task.

But whatever the ultimate differences of opinion, amongst those concerned in such a matter, about the merits of the Museum Catalogue, begun in 1839, there was no difference at all, either in the House or out of it, as to the conspicuous merits of his performance of every subsequent duty. His stores of knowledge were put, with the utmost readiness, at the service of all sorts of readers; and he was not less admirable in the discharge of his office of Superintendent of the Reading Room than afterwards in the more prominent office of Keeper of Printed Books—which he held little more than three years.

When Sir Henry ELLIS retired, in 1856, from the office of Principal-Librarian, the Collection of Printed Books—which he had found, on his accession to that office, extending to less than one hundred and fifty thousand volumes—exceeded five hundred and twenty thousand volumes.

The annual number of Readers admitted had increased from about seven hundred and fifty to nearly four thousand.

The one step which did more than aught else to promote this improvement was the systematic survey of the then existing condition of the Printed Library, in all the great departments of knowledge, which Mr. Panizzi set on foot in 1843, and embodied in a Memoir addressed to the Trustees, on the first of January, 1845.

The principle on which this Memoir was compiled lay in the careful comparison of the Museum Catalogues with the best special bibliographies, and with the Catalogues of other Libraries. In Jurisprudence, for example, the national collection was tested by the *Bibliotheca Juridica* of Lipenius, Senckenberg, and Madahn ; by the list of law-books inserted in Dupin's edition of Camus' *Lettres sur la profession d'Avocat*, and by the *Bibliothèque diplomatique choisie* of Martens. In Political Economy, by Blanqui's list given in the *Histoire de l'Economie politique en Europe*. The Mathematical section of the Library was compared with Rogg's *Handbuch der mathematischen Literatur*. In British History, the *Bibliotheca Grenvilliana*, and the *Catalogue of the Library of the Writers to the Signet*, were examined, for those sections of the subject to which they were more particularly applicable, and so on in the other departments. The facts thus elicited were striking. It was shown that much had been done since 1836 to augment almost every section of the Library ; but that the deficiencies were still of the most conspicuous sort. In a word, the statement abundantly established the truth of the proposition that 'the Collection of Printed Books in the British Museum is not nearly so complete and perfect as the National Library of Great Britain ought to be. . . . .'

and it then proceeded to discuss the further question : ' By what means can the collection be brought with all proper despatch to a state of as much completeness and perfection as is attainable in such matters, and as the public service may require ?'

It was shown that no reliance could be placed upon donations, for the filling up those gaps in the Library which were the special subject of the Memoir. Rare and precious books might thus come, but not the widely miscellaneous assemblage still needed. As to special grants for the acquisition of entire collections, not one of ten such collections, it was thought, would, under existing circumstances, be suitable for the Museum. The Copyright-tax has no bearing, however rigidly enforced, save on current British Literature. There remained, therefore, but one adequate resource, that of annual Parliamentary grants, unfettered by restrictions as to their application, and capable of being depended upon for a considerable number of years to come. Purchases might thus be organized in all parts of the world with foresight, system, and continuity. In the letter addressed by the Trustees to the Treasury, it was stated that, ' for filling up the chasms which are so much to be regretted, and some of which are distinctly set forth in the annexed document, the Trustees think that a sum of not less than ten thousand a year will be required for the next ten years,' in addition to the usual five thousand a year for the ordinary acquisitions of the Library.

The Lords of the Treasury were not willing to recommend to Parliament a larger annual grant than ten thousand pounds, ' for the purchase of books of all descriptions,' but so far they were disposed to proceed, ' for some years to come;' and they strongly inculcated upon the Trustees ' the necessity, during the continuance of such grants, of postponing additions to the other collections under their charge, which, however desirable in themselves, are of subordinate importance to that of completing the Library.'

In 1843, an important series of modern Historical MSS., relating more especially to the South of Europe, was purchased from the RANUZZI family of Bologna. The papers of the Brothers Laurence HYDE, Earl of Rochester, and Henry HYDE, Earl of Clarendon, were also secured. Additions, too, of considerable interest, were made to the theological and classical sections of the MS. Department, by the purchase of many vellum MSS., ranging from the eleventh to the fifteenth centuries. In 1849, the most important acquisitions related to our British History. About three hundred documents illustrative of the English Wars in France (1418 to 1450), nearly a hundred autograph letters of WILLIAM III, and an extensive series of transcripts from the archives at the Hague, were thus gathered for the future historian. In 1850, a curious series of Stammbücker, three hundred and twenty in number, and in date extending from 1554 to 1785, was obtained by purchase. These Albums, collectively, contained more than twenty-seven thousand autographs of persons more or less eminent in the various departments of human activity. Amongst them is the signature of MILTON. The acquisitions of 1851 included some Biblical MSS. of great curiosity ; an extensive series of autograph letters (chiefly from the Donnadieu Collection), and a large number of papers relating to the affairs of the English Mint.

In the year last named Sir Frederick MADDEN thus summed up the accessions to his Department since the year 1836 :

Volumes of Manuscripts	9051
Rolls of Maps, Pedigrees, &c.	668
Manuscripts on Reed, Bark, or other material .	136
Charters and Rolls	6750
Papyri	42
Seals	442

Book III,
Chap. II.
History
of the
Museum
under Sir
H. Ellis.
Tabular
view of the
accessions
to the MSS.
Depart-
ment from
1836-1851.

And he adds :—'If money had been forthcoming, the number of manuscripts acquired during the last fifteen years might have been more than doubled. The collections that have passed into other hands, namely, Sir Robert Chambers' Sanscrit MSS.; Sir William Ouseley's Persian; Bruce's Ethiopic and Arabic; Michael's Hebrew; Libri's Italian, French, Latin, and Miscellaneous; Barrois' French and Latin; as well as the Stowe Collection of Anglo-Saxon, Irish, and English manuscripts, might all have been so united. The liberality of the Treasury becomes very small when compared with the expenditure of individuals. Lord Ashburnham, during the last ten years, has paid nearly as large a sum for MSS. as has been expended on the National Collection since the Museum was first founded.'

Growth of
the Printed
Depart-
ment up to
1851.

The causes which at this period again tended somewhat to slacken the growth of the Printed Collection have been glanced at already. But during the fifteen years from 1836 to 1851, it had increased at the rate of sixteen thousand volumes a year, on the average. When the estimates of 1852 were under discussion, Mr. Panizzi stated, 'that till room is provided, the deficiency must in a great measure continue, and new [foreign] books only to a limited extent be purchased.' The grant for such purchases was therefore, in that year, limited to four thousand pounds. In a subsequent report, Mr. Panizzi added, 'that he could not but deeply regret the ill-consequences which must accrue by allowing old deficiencies to continue, and new ones to accumulate.' From the same report may be gathered a precise view of the actual additions, from all sources, during the quinquennium of 1846-1850. The increase in the printed books, therefore, although it had not quite kept pace with Mr. PANIZZI's hopeful anticipations in 1852, had actually reached a larger yearly average, during that last quinquennium, than was attained in the like period from 1846 to 1850.

The report from which these figures are taken was made in furtherance of the good and fruitful suggestion that a great Reading Room should be built within the inner quadrangle. Judging from the past, argued Mr. PANIZZI, in June, 1852, 'and supposing that for the next ten years from seven thousand to seven thousand five hundred pounds will be spent in the purchase of printed books, the increase .... would be at the average of about twenty-seven thousand volumes a year, without taking into consideration the chance of an extraordinary increase, owing to the purchase or donation of any large collection. It was owing

to the splendid bequest of Mr. GRENVILLE that the additions to the Collection in 1847 reached the enormous amount of more than fifty-five thousand volumes. After the steady and regular addition of about twenty-seven thousand volumes for ten years together, here reckoned upon, the Collection of Printed Books in the British Museum might defy comparison, and would approach, as near as seems practicable in such matters, to a state of completeness. The increase for the ten years next following might be fairly reduced to two thirds of the above sum. At this rate, the collection of books, which has been more than

doubled during the last fifteen years, would be double of what it now is in twenty years from the present time [1852].' At the date of this report the number of volumes was already upwards of four hundred and seventy thousand. At the date at which I now write (January, 1870), the number of volumes, as nearly as it can be calculated, has become one million and six thousand. On the average, therefore, of the whole period, the increase has been not less than thirty-one thousand five hundred volumes in every year. The Collection was somewhat more than doubled during the first fifteen years of Mr. PANIZZI's Keepership. During the next like term of years, when the department was partly under the administration of Mr. PANIZZI, and partly under that of Mr. WINTER JONES, it was nearly doubled again. It follows that the anticipation expressed in the *Report* of 1852 has been much more than fulfilled. Less than seventeen years of labour have achieved what was then expected to be the work of twenty years.

If the other departments of the British Museum cannot show an equal ratio of growth during the term now under review, it has not been from lack of zeal, either in their heads or in the Trustees. Their progress, too, was very great, although it is not capable of being so strikingly and compendiously illustrated. It has also to be borne in mind that the arrears, so to speak, of the Library, were relatively greater than those of some other divisions of the Museum.

At the commencement of Sir Henry ELLIS's term of Principal-Librarianship, the Natural-History Collections were partly under the charge of Dr. LEACH, partly under that of Mr. Charles KÖNIG. Both were officers of considerable scientific attainments. In the instance of Dr. LEACH, certain peculiar eccentricities and crotchets were mixed up in close union with undoubted learning and skill. In not a few eminent naturalists a tendency to undervalue the achievements of past days, and to exaggerate those of the day that is passing, has often been noted. LEACH evinced this tendency in more ways than one. But a favourite way of manifesting it led him many times into difficulties with his neighbours. He despised the taxidermy of Sir Hans SLOANE's age, and made periodical bonfires of Sloanian specimens. These he was wont to call his 'cremations.' In his time, the Gardens of the Museum were still a favourite resort of the Bloomsburians, but the attraction of the terraces and the fragrance of the shrubberies were sadly lessened when a pungent odour of burning snakes was their accompaniment. The stronger the complaints, however, the more apparent became Dr. LEACH's attachment to his favourite cremations.

LEACH was the friend and correspondent of that eminent cultivator of the classificatory sciences, Colonel George MONTAGU, of Lackham. Both of them rank among the early members of the Linnæan Society, and it was under LEACH's editorship that MONTAGU's latest contributions to the Society's *Transactions* were published. MONTAGU's *Synopsis of British Birds* marks an epoch in the annals of our local ornithology, as does his treatise entitled *Testacea Britannica* in those of conchology. His contributions to the National Collections were very liberal. But he did not care much for any books save those that treated of natural history. In addition to a good estate and a fine mansion, he had inherited from his brother a choice old Library at Lackham, and a large cabinet of coins. These, I believe, he turned to account as means of barter for books and specimens in his favourite department of study. His love of the beauties of nature led him to prefer an unpretending abode in Devon to his fine Wiltshire house, and it was at Knowle that he died in August, 1815. His Collections in Zoology were purchased by the Trustees, and were removed from Knowle soon after his death. Scarcely any other purchase of like value in the Natural-History Department was made for more than twenty years afterwards. After the purchase of the Montagu Collection, the growth of that department depended, as it had mainly depended before it, on the acquisitions made for the Public by the several naturalists who took part in the Voyages of Discovery or whose chance collections, made in the course of ordinary duty, came to be at the disposal of the British Admiralty.

Book III, Chap. II. History of the Museum under Sir H. Ellis.

Many of those naturalists were men of marked ability. Of necessity, their explorations were attended with much curious adventure. To detail their researches and vicissitudes would form—without much credit to the writer—an interesting chapter, the materials of which are superabundant. But, at present, it must needs be matter of hope, not of performance.

The distinctive progress of the Natural-History Collections, from comparative and relative poverty, to a creditable place amongst rival collections, connects itself preeminently with the labours of Dr. John Edward GRAY, who will hereafter be remembered as the ablest keeper and organizer those collections have hitherto had. Dr. GRAY is now (1870) in the forty-sixth year of his public service at the British Museum, which he entered as an Assistant, in 1824. He is widely known by his able edition of GRIFFITHS' *Animal Kingdom*, by his *Illustrations of Indian Zoology*, by his account of the famous Derby Menagerie at Knowsley, and by his *Manual of British Shells;* but his least ostensible publications rank among the most conclusive proofs both of his ability and of his zeal for the public service. Dr. GRAY has always advocated the publication—to use Mr. CARLYLE's words when under interrogatory by the Museum

Commissioners of 1848—of 'all sorts of Catalogues.' It is to him that the Public owe the admirable helps to the study of natural history which have been afforded by the long series of inventories, guides, and nomenclators, the publication of which began, at his instance, in the year 1844, and has been unceasingly pursued. A mere list of the various printed synopses which have grown out of Dr. GRAY's suggestion of 1844 would fill many such pages as that which the reader has now before him. The consequence is, that in no department of the Museum can the student, as yet, economise his time as he can economise it in the Natural-History Department. *Printed*, not Manuscript, Catalogues mean time saved; disappointment avoided; study fructified. No literary labour brings so little of credit as does the work of the Catalogue-maker. None better deserves the gratitude of scholars, as well as of the general mass of visitors.

Dr. GRAY became Keeper of Zoology in 1840. Four years earlier, he had given to Sir Benjamin HAWES' Committee a striking account of the condition of that department, illustrating it by comparisons with the corresponding Collections in Paris, which may thus (not without unavoidable injustice) be abridged :—The species of mammalia then in the Museum were four hundred and five; the species of birds were two thousand four hundred, illustrated by four thousand six hundred and fifty-nine individual specimens. At that date, the latest accessible data assigned to the Paris Collection about five hundred species of mammals, and about two thousand three hundred species of birds, illustrated by nearly six thousand specimens. The Museum series of birds was almost equally rich in the orders, taken generally; but in gallinaceous birds it was more than proportionately rich, a large number of splendid examples having been received from India. In the birds of Africa, of Brazil, and of Northern Europe, also, the Museum was already exceptionally well-stored.

Book III, Chap. II. History of the Museum under Sir H. Ellis.

The special value of the Ornithological Collection undoubtedly showed that it had been more elaborately cared for than had been some other parts of natural history. But the extent and richness of the bird gallery, even at this period, is not to be ascribed merely to a desire to delight the eyes of a crowd of visitors. For scientific purposes, a collection of birds must be more largely-planned and better filled than a collection of mammals, or one of fish. In birds, the essential characters of a considerable group of individual specimens may be identical and their colours entirely different. Besides the numerous diversities attendant upon age and sex, the very date at which a bird is killed may produce variations which have their interest for the scientific student.

See *Minutes of Evidence* 1836, p. 238.

The number of species of reptiles was in 1836 about six hundred, illustrated by about one thousand three hundred specimens. This number was much inferior to that of the Museum at Paris, but it exceeded by one third the number of species in the Vienna Museum, and almost by one half the then number at Berlin.

Ibid., p. 242 (Q. 2996-9).

The species of fish amounted to nearly a thousand, but this was hardly the fourth of the great collection at Paris, although it probably exceeded every other, or almost every other, Continental collection of the same date. Of shells, the Museum number of species was four thousand and twenty-five (exclusive of fossils), illustrated by about fifteen thousand individuals. This number of species was at par with that of Paris; much superior both to Berlin and to Leyden; but it was far from representing positive—as distinguished from comparative—wealth. There were already, in 1836, more than nine thousand known species of shells.

It was further shown in the evidence that, even under the arrangements of 1836, the facilities of public access equalled those given at the most liberal of the Continental Museums, and considerably exceeded those which obtained at fully four-fifths of their number.

Among the many services rendered to the Museum by Dr. GRAY, one is of too important a character to be passed over, even in a notice so brief as this must needs be. The large bequest in Zoology of Major-General HARDWICKE grew out of a stipulation made by Dr. GRAY, when he undertook, at General HARDWICKE's request, the editorship of the *Illustrations of Indian Zoology.* A long labour brought to the editor no pecuniary return, but it brought an important collection to the British Public in the first instance, and eventually a large augmentation of what had been originally given.

In March, 1849, the course of inquiries pursued by Lord ELLESMERE's Commission led to a new review of the growth of the Natural-History Collections, and more especially of the Zoology. It applied in particular to the twelve or thirteen years which had then elapsed since the prior inquiries of 1835-1836. The statement possesses much interest, but it is occasionally deficient in that systematic and necessary distinction between species and specimens which characterised the evidence of 1836. In brief, however, it may be said, that in the eight years extending between June, 1840, and June, 1848, twenty-nine thousand five hundred and ninety-five *specimens* of vertebrated animals were added to the Museum galleries and storehouses. Of these, five thousand seven hundred and ninety-seven were mammals; thirteen thousand four hundred and fourteen were birds; four thousand one hundred and twelve reptiles; and six thousand two hundred and seventy-two were fish. The number of specimens of annulose animals added during the same period was seventy-three thousand five hundred and sixty-three: and that of mollusca and radiata, fifty-seven thousand six hundred and ten.

These large additions comprised extensive gatherings made by Dyson in Venezuela, and in various parts of North America; by Gardiner and Clausen in Brazil; by Gosse in Jamaica; by Gould, Gilbert, and Stephenson, in Australia and in New Zealand; by Hartweg in Mexico; by Goudot in Columbia; by Verreaux and Smith in South Africa; by Frazer in Tunis; and by Bridges in Chili and in some other parts of South America.

Of the splendid collections made by Mr. Hodgson in India, some more detailed mention must be made hereafter.

Meanwhile, on the Continent of Europe, political commotion had seriously checked the due progress of scientific collections. Britain had been making unwonted strides in the improvement of its Museum, at the very time when most of the Continental States had allowed their fine Museums to remain almost stationary. In mammals, birds, and shells, the British Museum had placed itself in the first rank. Only in reptiles, fish, and crustacea, could even Paris now claim superiority. Those classes had there engaged for a long series of years the unremitting research and labour of such naturalists as Cuvier, Dumeril, Valenciennes, and Milne-Edwards; and their relative wealth of specimens it will be hard to overtake. In insects, the Museum Collection vies with that of Paris in point of extent, and excels it in point of arrangement.

Not less conspicuous had been the growth of the several Departments of Antiquities. And this part of the story of the Museum teems with varied interest. Within a period of less than thirty years, vast and widely-distant cities, rich in works of art, have been literally disinterred. In succession to the superb marbles of Athens, of Phigaleia, and of Rome, some of the choicest sculptures and most curious minor antiquities of Nineveh, of Calah, of Erech, of Ur-of-the-Chaldees, of Babylon, of Xanthus, of Halicarnassus, of Cnidus, and of Carthage, have come to London.

The growth of the subordinate Collections of Archæology has been scarcely less remarkable. The series of ancient vases—to take but one example—of which the research and liberality of Sir William HAMILTON laid a good foundation almost a century ago, has come at length to surpass its wealthiest compeers. Only a few years earlier, it ranked as but the third, perhaps as but the fourth, among the great vase-collections of Europe. London, in that point of view, was below both Naples and Paris, if not also below Munich. It now ranks above them all; possessing two thousand six hundred vases, as against two thousand at Paris, and two thousand one hundred at Naples.*

Another department, lying in part nearer home—that of British, Mediæval, and Ethnological Antiquities—has been almost created by the labours of the last twenty years. The 'British' Museum can no longer be said to be a misnomer, as designating an establishment in which British Archæology met with no elucidation.

* Birch, *Ancient Pottery*, vol. i, pp. 209, 210.

CHAPTER III.

INTRODUCTION TO BOOK III *(Continued)*:—GROWTH, PROGRESS, AND INTERNAL ECONOMY, OF THE BRITISH MUSEUM DURING THE PRINCIPAL-LIBRARIANSHIP OF SIR ANTONIO PANIZZI.

> 'Whatever be the judgment formed on [certain contested] points at issue, the Minutes of Evidence must be admitted to contain pregnant proofs of the acquirements and abilities, the manifestation of which in subordinate office led to Mr. Panizzi's promotion to that which he now holds under circumstances which, in our opinion—formed on documentary evidence—did credit to the Principal Trustees of the day.'—REPORT OF THE COMMISSIONERS APPOINTED TO INQUIRE INTO THE MANAGEMENT OF THE BRITISH MUSEUM (1850).
>
> 'In consideration of the long and very valuable services of Mr. Panizzi, including not only his indefatigable labours as Principal-Librarian, but also the service which he rendered as architect of the new Reading-Room, the Trustees recommended that he should be allowed to retire on full salary after a discharge of his duties for thirty-four years.'
> HANSARD'S *Parliamentary Debates* (27 July, 1866).

The Museum Buildings.—The New Reading-Room and its History.—The House of Commons' Committee of 1860:—Further Reorganization of the Departments—Summary of the Growth of the Collections in the years 1856-1866, and of their increased Use and Enjoyment by the Public.

NO QUESTION connected with the improvement of the British Museum has, from time to time, more largely engrossed the attention, either of Parliament or of the Public at large, than has the question of the Buildings. On none have the divergences of opinion been greater, or the expressions of dissatisfaction with the plans—or with the want of plan—louder or more general.

Yet there is no doubt (amongst those, at least, who have had occasion to examine the subject closely) that the architects of the new British Museum—first Sir Robert SMIRKE, and then Mr. Sydney SMIRKE—have been conspicuous for professional ability. Nor is there any doubt, anywhere, that the Trustees of the Museum have bestowed diligent attention on the plans submitted to them. They have been most anxious to discharge that part of their duty to the Public with the same faithfulness which, on the whole, has characterised their general fulfilment of the trust committed to them. Why, it is natural to ask, has their success been so unequal?

Without presuming upon the possession of competence to answer the question with fulness, there is no undue confidence in offering a partial reply. Part of their failure to satisfy the public expectations has arisen from a laches in Parliament itself. At the critical time when the character of the new buildings had practically to be decided, parsimoniousness led, not only to construction piecemeal, but to the piecemeal preparation of the designs themselves. Temporary makeshifts took the place of foreseeing plans. And what may have sounded like economy in 1830 has, in its necessary results, proved to be very much like waste, long before 1870.

Had a comprehensive scheme of reconstruction been looked fully in the face when, forty years ago, the new buildings began to be erected, three fourths at most of the money which has been actually expended would have sufficed for the erection of a Museum, far more satisfactory in its architectural character, and affording at least one fourth more of accommodation for the National Collections. The British Museum buildings have afforded a salient instance of the truth of BURKE's words : ' Great expense may be an essential part in true economy. Mere parsimony is *not* economy.' But, in this instance, the fault is plainly in Parliament, not in the Trustees of the establishment which has suffered.

The one happy exception to the general unsatisfactoriness of the new buildings—as regards, not merely architectural beauty, but fitness of plan, sufficiency of light, and adaptedness to purpose—is seen in the new Reading-Room. And the new Reading-Room is, virtually, the production of an amateur architect. The chief merits of its design belong, indubitably, to Sir Antonio PANIZZI. The story of that part of the new building is worth the telling.

That some good result should be eventually derived from the large space of ground within the inner quadrangle had been many times suggested. The suggestion offered, in 1837, by Mr. Thomas WATTS was thus expressed in his letter to the Editor of the *Mechanics' Magazine :*—

Mr. WATTS began by criticising, somewhat incisively, the architectural skill which had constructed a vast quadrangle without providing it even with the means of a free circulation of air. He pinned Sir Robert SMIRKE on the horns of a dilemma. If, he argued, the architect looked to a sanitary result, he had, in fact, provided a well of malaria. If he contemplated a display of art, he had, by consenting to the abolition of his northern portico, spoiled and destroyed all architectural effect. ' The space,' he proceeded to say, which has thus been wasted, ' would have afforded accommodation *for the whole Library,* much superior to what is now proposed to afford it. A Reading-Room of ample dimensions might have stood in the centre, and

Book III,
Chap. III.
History
of the
Museum
under Sir
A. Panizzi.

*Mechanics'
Magazine*
(1837); vol.
xxvi, pp. 295,
seqq.

been surrounded, on all four sides, with galleries for the books.' Afterwards, when adverting to the great expense which had been incurred upon the façades of the quadrangle, he went on to say : ' It might now seem barbarous to propose the filling up of the square—as ought originally to have been done. Perhaps the best plan would be to design another range of building entirely [new ?], enclosing the present building on the eastern and northern sides as the Elgin and other galleries do on the western. To do this, it would be necessary to purchase and pull down one side of two streets,—Montagu Street and Montagu Place.'

Ibid.

See Chap. ii
of Book III,
p. 566, and
the accompanying
fac-simile.

As I have intimated already, this alternative project was unconsciously reproduced, by the present writer, ten years later, without any idea that it had been anticipated. But neither to the mind of the writer of 1837, nor to that of the writer of 1847, did the grand feature of construction which, within another decade, has given to London a splendid building as well as a most admirable Reading-Room, present itself. The substantial merit, both of originally suggesting, and of (in the main) eventually realising the actual building of 1857, belongs to Antonio PANIZZI.

As to the claims on that score advanced by Mr. HOSKING, formerly Professor of Architecture at King's College, they apply to a plan wholly different from the plan which was carried into execution.

Mr. HOSKING's scheme was drawn up, for private circulation, in February, 1848 (thirteen months after the writing of my own pamphlet entitled *Public Libraries in London and in Paris*, and more than six months after its circulation in print), when it was first submitted to Lord ELLESMERE's Commission of Inquiry. It was first published (in *The Builder*) in June, 1850. His object was to provide a grand central hall for the Department of Antiquities.

When Mr. HOSKING called public attention to his design of 1848—in a pamphlet entitled *Some Remarks upon the recent Addition of a Reading-Room to the British Museum* —Mr. Sydney SMIRKE wrote to him thus:—'I recollect seeing your plans at a meeting of the Trustees, . . . shortly after you sent them [to Lord ELLESMERE]. When, long subsequently, Mr. PANIZZI showed me his sketch for a plan of a new Reading-Room, I confess it did not remind me of yours, the purposes of the two plans and the treatment and construction were so different.'* Whilst to Mr. SMIRKE himself belongs the merit of practical execution, that of design belongs no less unquestionably to PANIZZI.

* If the question of mere hints and analogies in construction were to be followed out to its issues, the result, I feel assured, would in no degree tend to strengthen the contention of Mr. Hosking's pamphlet. Something like a first germ of the mere ground-plan of the new Reading-Room may, perhaps, be found in M. Benjamin Delessert's *Projet d'une Bibliothèque circulaire*, printed, at Paris, as far back as the year 1835, when the question of reconstructing the then 'Royal,' now 'Imperial Library,' was under discussion in the French Chambers. 'I propose,' says Delessert, 'to place the officers and the readers in the centre of a vast rotunda, whence branch off eight principal galleries, the walls of which form diverging radii . . . and *have book-cases on both sides*,' &c. His plan may be thus shown, in small. The differences, it

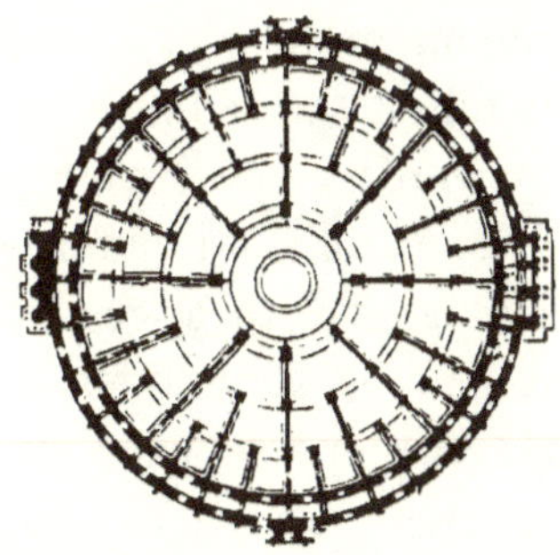

will be seen, between this sketch and Mr. Panizzi's sketch of 1854, are greater than are the resemblances.

Mr. Panizzi himself preferred, at first, the plan of extending the building on the eastern and northern sides. His suggestions had the approval of the Commissioners of 1850. But the Government was slow to give power to the Trustees to carry out the plan of their officer and the recommendation of the Commissioners of Inquiry, by proposing the needful vote in a Committee of Supply. Plan and Report alike lay dormant from the year 1850 to 1854. It was then that, as a last resort, and as a measure of economy, by avoiding all present necessity to buy more ground of the Duke of Bedford, Mr. Panizzi recommended the Trustees to build within the quadrangle, and drew a sketch-plan, on which their architect reported favourably. Sixty-one thousand pounds, by way of a first instalment, was voted on the third of July, 1854. The present noble structure was completed within three years from that day, and its total cost—including the extensive series of book-galleries and rooms of various kinds, subserving almost innumerable purposes—amounted in round numbers to a hundred and fifty thousand pounds. It was thus only a little more than the cost of the King's Library, which accommodates eighty thousand volumes of books and a Collection of Birds. The new Reading-Room and its appendages can be made to accommodate, in addition to its three hundred and more of readers, some million, or near it, of volumes, without impediment to their fullest accessibility.

To describe by words a room which, in 1870, has become more or less familiar, I suppose, to hundreds of thousands of Britons, and to a good many thousands of foreigners, would now be superfluous. But it will not be without advantage, perhaps, to show its character and appearance with the simple brevity of woodcuts.

The following illustrative block-plan shows the general

arrangement of the Museum building at large, at the date of the erection of the new Reading-Room.

Book III,
Chap. III.
History
of the
Museum
under Sir
A. Panizzi.

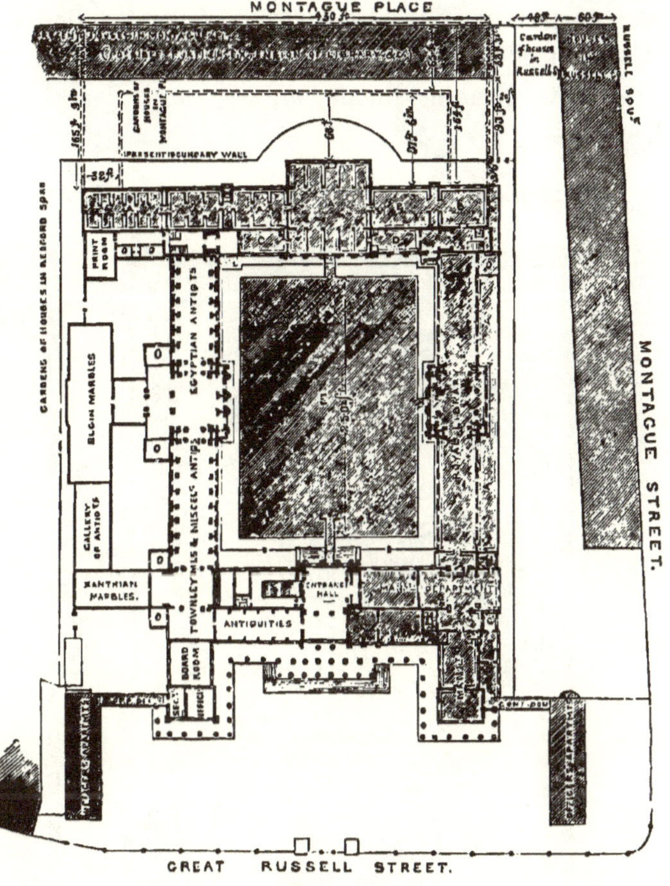

I. General Block-Plan of the British Museum,
as it was in 1857.

Block-plan
of Museum
(1857), dis-
tinguish-
ing the
Libraries
from the
Galleries
of Anti-
quities, &c.

The shaded part of the building itself shows the portions allotted to the *Library*. The unshaded part is assigned, on the ground floor, to the Department of *Antiquities*, and (speaking generally) on the floor above—in common with the upper floors of the Library part—to the Departments of *Natural History*. The '*Print Room*' is shown on the ground-plan between the Elgin Gallery and the north-western extremity of the Department of Printed Books.

The next illustration shows, in detail, the ground-plan of the new Reading-Room and of the adjacent book-galleries :—

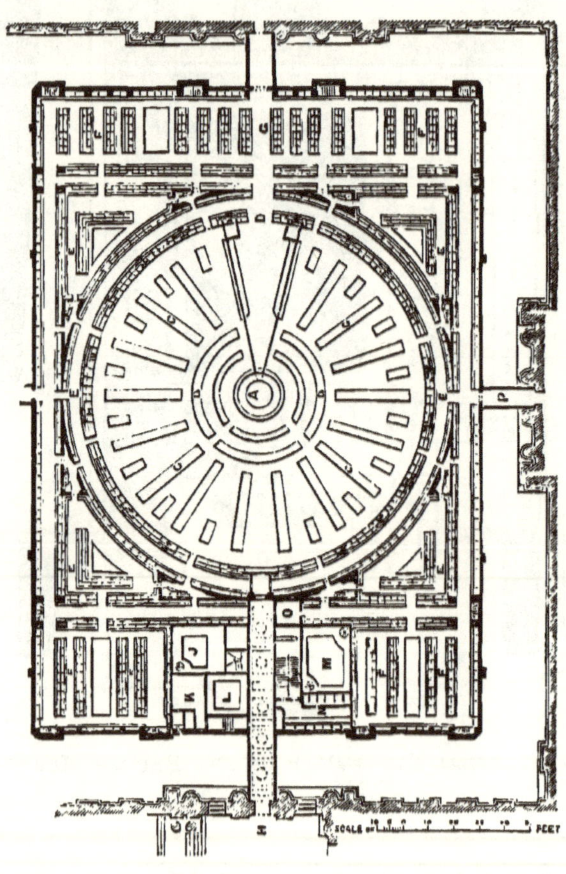

II. Ground-Plan of the new or 'Panizzi' Reading-Room,
and of the adjacent Galleries, 1857.

The general appearance of the interior of the Reading-Room may be shown thus:—

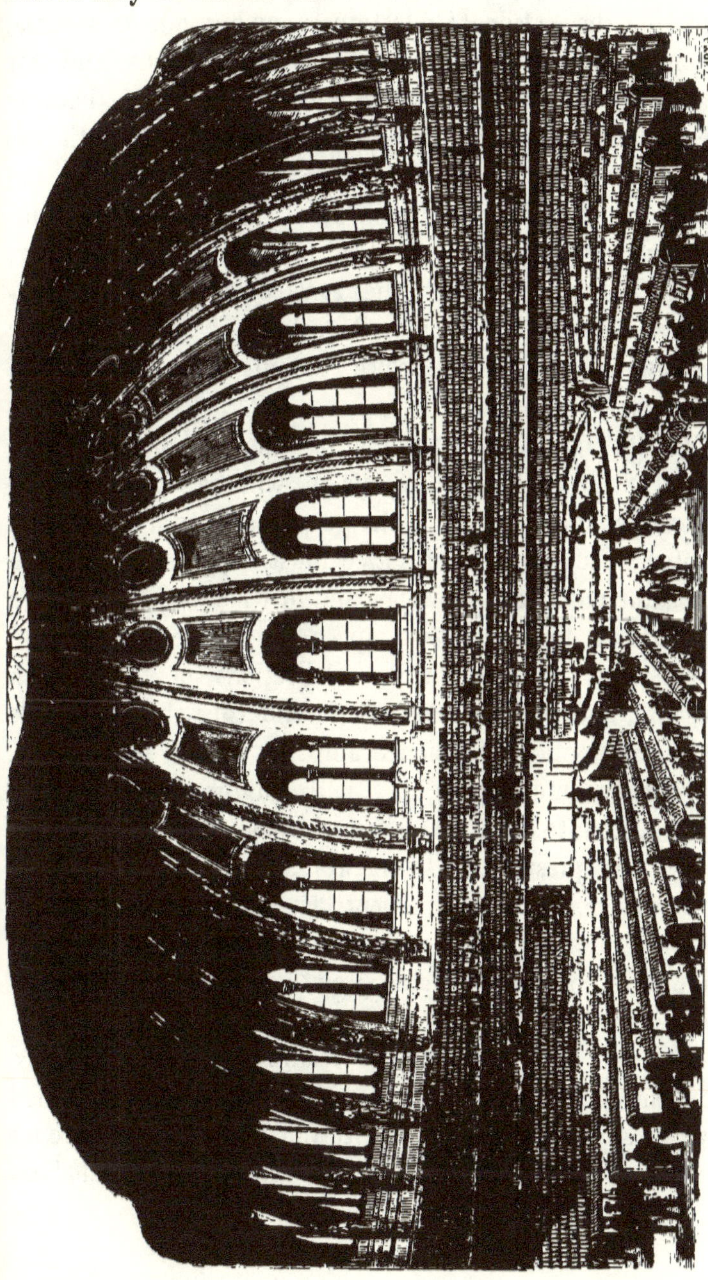

III. INTERIOR VIEW OF THE NEW READING-ROOM, 1857.

Of course, the improvements thus effected did but solve a portion of the difficulty felt, long before 1857, in accommodating the National Collections upon any adequate scale, which should provide alike for present claims and for future extension. This more effectual provision became one of the most pressing questions with which both the Trustees and their officers had now to deal. During the whole term of Sir A. Panizzi's Principal-Librarianship this building question increased in gravity and urgency, from year to year. Both the Trustees and the Principal-Librarian were intent upon its solution. But the latter was enforced, by failing health, to quit office, leaving the matter still unsolved.

Most of the little information on this part of the subject which, within my present limits, it will be practicable for me to offer to the reader, belongs, properly, to a subsequent chapter. But some brief notice must be given here of the important inquiries, 'how far, and in what way, it may be desirable to find increased space for the extension and arrangement of the various Collections of the British Museum, and the best means of rendering them available for the promotion of Science and Art,' which were made, between the months of May and August of 1860, by a Select Committee of the House of Commons.

The first question to be answered by the Committee of 1860 was this: Is it expedient, or not, that the *Natural-History* Collections should be removed from Bloomsbury, to make room for the inevitable growth of the Collections of *Antiquities?*

After an elaborate inquiry, spreading over three months, the Committee reported thus:—'The witnesses examined have, almost unanimously, testified to the preference over the other Collections, with which the Natural-History Collections are viewed by the ordinary and most numerous frequenters of the Museum. This preference is easily accounted for; the objects exhibited, especially the birds, from the beauty of their plumage, are calculated to attract and amuse the spectators. The eye has been accustomed in many instances to the living specimens in the Zoological Gardens, and cheap publications and prints have rendered their forms more or less familiar. It is, indeed, easily intelligible that, while for the full appreciation of works of archæological interest and artistic excellence a special education must be necessary, the works of Nature may be studied with interest and instruction by all persons of ordinary intelligence. It appears, from evidence, that many of the middle classes are in the habit of forming collections in various branches of Natural History, and that many, even the working classes, employ their holidays in the study of botany or geology, or in the collection of insects obtained in the neighbourhood of London; that they refer to the British Museum, in order to ascertain the proper classification of the specimens thus obtained, and that want of leisure alone restrains the further increase of this class of visitors. Your Committee, in order to confirm their view of the peculiar popularity of the Natural-History Collections, beg to refer to a return from the Principal-Librarian, which shows the number of visitors in the several public portions of the Museum, at the same hour of the day, during fifteen open days, from the fifteenth of June to the eleventh of July, 1860. From this it appears that two thousand five hundred and fifty-seven persons were in the Galleries of Antiquities at the given hour, and one thousand and fifty-six in the King's Library and MSS. Rooms, while three thousand three hundred and seventy-eight were in the Natural-History Galleries; showing an excess of two

Book III,
Chap. III.
History
of the
Museum
under Sir
A. Panizzi.

The
Select
Committee
of the
House of
Commons,
1860.

hundred and twenty per cent. in the Natural-History Department over the King's Library and MSS. Rooms, and of thirty-three per cent. over the Galleries of Antiquities, notwithstanding that the latter are of considerably greater extent than the Galleries of Natural History. The evidence received by your Committee induces the belief that the removal of these most popular collections from their present central position to one less generally accessible would excite much dissatisfaction, not merely among a large portion of the inhabitants of the metropolis, but among the numerous inhabitants of the country, who from time to time visit London by railway, and to whom the proximity of the British Museum to most of the railway termini, as compared with the distance of the localities to which it has been proposed to transport such collections, is of great practical importance. Similar evidence shows that the proposed removal of those collections from the British Museum has excited grave and general disapprobation in the scientific world. Your Committee cannot here employ more forcible language than that made use of in a memorial signed by one hundred and fourteen persons, including many eminent promoters and cultivators of science in England, and presented to the Chancellor of the Exchequer in 1848. The following are their words:—" We beg to add the expression of our opinion that the removal of the Natural-History Collections from the site where they have been established for upwards of a century, in the centre of London, particularly if to any situation distant from that centre, would be viewed by the mass of the inhabitants with extreme disfavour, it being a well-known fact that by far the greater number of visitors to the Museum consists of those who frequent the halls containing the Natural-History Collections, while it is obvious that many of

those persons who come from the densely peopled districts of the eastern, northern, and southern parts of London, would feel it very inconvenient to resort to any distant locality." '

After an elaborate examination into the nature and extent of those enlargements which the present growth and probable increase of the several Collections of Antiquities and of Natural History render necessary, the Committee proceed thus :—

The ground immediately surrounding the Museum, says the reporter, speaking of the adjacent streets to the east, west, and north, 'comprises altogether about five and a half acres, valued by Mr. SMIRKE at about two hundred and forty thousand pounds. As the proprietary interest in all this ground belongs to a single owner, your Committee are of opinion that it would be convenient, and possibly even a profitable arrangement, for the State at once to purchase that interest, and to receive the rents of the lessees in return for the capital invested. The State would then have the power, whenever any further extension of the Museum became necessary, to obtain possession of such houses as might best suit the purpose in view.

'Independently, however, of this larger suggestion, your Committee are fully convinced, both from the uniform purport of the papers printed at different times by the House of Commons, and from the statements of the various witnesses whom they have now examined, that it is indispensable, not merely to the appropriate exhibition of our unequalled National Collections, but even to the avoidance of greater ultimate expense, through alterations and re-arrangements, that sufficient space should be immediately acquired in connexion with the British Museum, to meet the requirements of the several departments which have been enumerated under the last head, and that such space

Book III, Chap. III. History of the Museum under Sir A. Panizzi.

Recommendations of the Commons' Committee of 1860.

BOOK III,
Chap. III.
HISTORY
OF THE
MUSEUM
UNDER SIR
A. PANIZZI.

should throughout be adapted, by its position, extent, and facilities of application, to the arrangement of the collections on a comprehensive, and, therefore, probably permanent system. They will now proceed to point out several sites, either on or adjoining the present ground of the Museum, which seem to them to present the greatest advantages for the accommodation of the respective departments.'

NATURAL
HISTORY
COLLEC-
TIONS.

Although, the Committee proceed to say, the amount of space which, on the foregoing estimate, would be requisite for the Natural-History Collections is not so great as to involve the necessity of their removal from the British Museum on that ground alone, your Committee, nevertheless, attach so much weight to the arguments in favour of preserving the various departments of the Museum from the risk of collision with each other, that, should it be determined to provide new space for Natural History in connexion with the Museum, they would make it a primary object to isolate its collections, as far as possible, from all others in the same locality. The chief part of the Natural-History Collections is now on the upper floor, where they occupy, according to the return of Mr. SMIRKE, in November, 1857, forty-eight thousand four hundred and forty-two superficial feet. The remainder of that floor, containing, exclusively of a small space not reckoned by Mr. SMIRKE, twenty-one thousand five hundred and thirty-two feet, is occupied by Antiquities. It appears to your Committee that if, by any adaptation of ground to be acquired adjoining the Museum, adequate space should be provided elsewhere for the Antiquities now on the upper floor, the most expedient arrangement would be to appropriate the whole of that floor to the Natural-History Collections. If this space proved insufficient for all such collections, your Committee would then recommend that the newly acquired portion should be applied exclusively to the Department of Zoology ; and that a sufficient portion of ground should be purchased on the north side of the Museum as a site for galleries to provide for Mineralogy, and thus also indirectly for Geology.

A convenient site for this department would, in the opinion of the Committee, be provided by the suggested acquisition of additional ground on the north side. A building might there be erected in continuation of the present east wing of the Museum, to contain, on its upper floor, the Mineralogical Collections, and on the lower the Prints and Drawings, with adequate space both for their preservation and exhibition.

In determining the site most suitable for the large additional accommodation required for this department, the Committee thought it most prudent that the Trustees of the Museum should be guided, partly by the greater or less cost of purchasing the requisite amount of ground in different directions, but chiefly by the greater or less fitness of the different portions of ground for the best system of arrangement.

In the same year in which Mr. PANIZZI became Principal-Librarian (1856), one of the recommendations of Lord ELLESMERE's Commission-Report of 1850 was carried into effect by the creation of the new office of 'Superintendent of the Natural-History Departments.' And the former partial subdivision and reorganization of those departments was, in the following year, carried further by the formation of a separate Department of Mineralogy. In subsequent years, the old Department of Antiquities was, like the Natural History, divided into four departments, namely, (1) Greek and Roman Antiquities ; (2) Oriental Antiquities ; (3) British and Mediæval Antiquities and Ethnography ; (4) Coins and Medals.

At present (1870), it may here be added, the entire Museum is divided into twelve departments, comprising three several groups of four sections to each. The Natural-History group being comprised of (1) Zoology; (2) Palæontology; (3) Botany; (4) Mineralogy. The Literary group comprising (1) Printed Books; (2) Manuscripts; (3) Prints and Drawings; (4) Maps, Charts, Plans, and Topographical Drawings. Experience has amply vindicated the wisdom of the principle of subdivision. But it is probable that the principle has now been carried as far as it can usefully work in practice.

Increased efficiency and rapidly growing collections brought with them enlarged grants from Parliament. In the first year of Sir A. Panizzi's Principal-Librarianship, the estimate put before the House of Commons for the service of the year 1856-7 was sixty thousand pounds, as compared with a grant for the service of the year immediately preceding of fifty-six thousand one hundred and eighty pounds. In his last year of office, the estimate for the service of the year 1866-67 amounted to one hundred and two thousand seven hundred and forty-four pounds, against a grant in the year preceding of ninety-eight thousand one hundred and sixty-four pounds.

There had also been, in that decade, a marked degree of increase—though one of much fluctuation—in the number of visits, both to the General Collections and, much more notably, to the Reading-Rooms and the Galleries for Study. In 1856, the number of general visitors was three hundred and sixty-one thousand seven hundred and fourteen; in 1866, it was four hundred and eight thousand two hundred and seventy-nine. But in the 'Exhibition Year' (1862), it had reached eight hundred and ninety-five thousand and seventy-seven, which was itself little more than one-third of the exceptionally enormous number of visitors recorded* in the year of the first of the great Industrial Exhibitions (1851).

BOOK III,
Chap. III.
HISTORY
OF THE
MUSEUM
UNDER SIR
A. PANIZZI.

It was during Sir A. PANIZZI's decade that the largest number of visitors ever recorded to have entered the Museum within one day was registered. This exceptional number occurred on the 'Boxing Day' of the Londoners, 26th December, 1858, when more than forty-two thousand visitors were admitted. Under the old system there had been a dread of holiday crowds, and the largest number ever admitted on any one day, prior to 1837, was between five thousand eight hundred and five thousand nine hundred. That number had been looked upon as a marvel. On the Easter Monday of 1837, twenty-three thousand nine hundred and eighty-five were admitted. Neither then nor on the 1858 'Boxing Day' was any injury or disorderly conduct complained of.

The highest number of visits for study made to the Reading-Room, prior to 1857, occurred in 1850, when the number was seventy-eight thousand five hundred and thirty-three. The number in the year 1865 was one hundred thousand two hundred and seventy-one, but in the interval it had risen (1861) to one hundred and thirty thousand four hundred and ten. For several years, between 1856 and 1866, the average number of visits for study to the Galleries of Antiquities averaged about one thousand nine hundred annually; those to the Print Room, about two thousand eight hundred; those to the Coin and Medal Room, about one thousand nine hundred.

---

* Namely, two millions five hundred and twenty-seven thousand two hundred and sixteen visits, which *included* seventy-eight thousand two hundred and eleven visits to the Reading-Room for study.

The rapid growth of the Collection of Printed Books, more especially between the years 1845-1865, which had, as we have seen, resulted from the unremitting labours of Mr. Panizzi, was well kept up, both under his immediate successor, Mr. John Winter Jones, and (after Mr. Jones' promotion to the Principal-Librarianship, towards the close of 1866) by the next Keeper, Mr. Watts. As is well known, the increase of the Library is still more remarkable for the character of the additions purchased than for their mere number. But recent years have afforded no such instance of individual munificence in this department of the Museum as that which will presently call for detailed notice when we record the acquisition (in 1846) of the Grenville Library, nor could any such instance, indeed, be reasonably looked for.

Sir Frederick Madden's energetic researches and labours for the improvement of the Collection of MSS. would well merit a fuller account than it is here practicable to give of them. They have been perseveringly and worthily continued by his successor, Mr. Edward Augustus Bond, to whom students also owe the great and distinctive debt of the commencement of an admirable " Index of Matters " to the Collection generally. No greater boon, in the way of Catalogues, was ever given within the walls of the Museum, though, as yet, it is necessarily a beginning only. The special labours of Dr. Gray in that sphere, for the Natural-History Collections, comprised the extended advantage of printing and sale. Not less, I hope, will eventually be done for the service of manuscript students. There is the desire to do it, and the means must, sooner or later, follow.

The wonderful growth and development of the Collections of Antiquities in recent years is the special subject of the next chapter. That growth derives no small part of its permanent scientific interest and value from the impressive way in which it illustrates the teachings of Holy Scripture. *Some* of the collections amassed in the British Museum have, more than once, by dint of human vanity, been made to subserve a laudation of the wonderful achievements of Man, rather than of the power, wisdom, and goodness of God; but for the ebullitions of human vanity there is extremely little room when a visitor stands beside the sculptured memorials of that vast empire which 'the cedars in the garden of GOD could not hide,' which was 'lifted up in the pride of its height,' only to become a marvel for desolation, so that upon its ruin 'the fowls of the heaven remain.' When before our own eyes and ears the very stones cry out in the wall, and the beams out of the timber answer them, the man vainest of his science or of his philosophy must needs be led to ask himself: 'What hath GOD wrought?'

Some very advanced men of science have become, of late, fond of 'Sunday-evening Lectures' *for the instruction of the working classes.* That would be a tolerably impressive Sunday-evening Lecture which a competent scholar could give in the Assyrian Gallery of the British Museum.

Here, and now, the recent increase of the Department of Antiquities may be wholly passed over. But to that part of the history of accessions which bears upon the Natural-History Galleries some attention must needs be given, by way of continuing our former brief epitome of the improvements made between the years 1836 and 1850.

Of the state of the Department of Zoology, during the earlier part of the decade now more immediately under review, a good and instructive account was given in Pro-

Book III, Chap. III. History of the Museum under Sir A. Panizzi.

Ezek. xxxi, 8 to 13. Comp. Habak. ii, 14.

fessor Owen's Annual Report of 1861.   Its most material portions run thus :—

'The proportion of the stuffed specimens of the class Mammalia, exhibited in the glazed cases of the Southern Zoological Gallery and Mammalian Saloon, is in good condition.   The stuffed specimens, which, from their bulk, or from want of space in the cases, stand on the floor, have suffered in a certain degree from exposure to the corrosive smoke-dust of the metropolis, the effects of which cannot be wholly prevented.'

The proportion, continues Mr. Owen, of the Collection of Mammalia consisting of skins preserved in boxes, the Osteological specimens, including the horns and antlers, and the specimens kept in spirit, are all in a good state of preservation.   The unstuffed, Osteological and bottled specimens are unexhibited and restricted in use, as at present located, to scientific investigation and comparison ; but it is with difficulty that the special visitor for such purposes can now avail himself of these materials, owing to their crowded accumulation in the Basement Rooms in which they are stored.

'The exhibited Collection of Birds is in a good state of preservation, is conveniently arranged for public inspection, and is usefully and instructively named and labelled.   The interest manifested by visitors, and the satisfaction generally expressed in regard to this gallery, indicate the amount of public instruction and gratification which would result from a corresponding serial arrangement and exposition of the other classes of the animal kingdom.

'The stuffed and exhibited selections from the classes of Reptilia and Fishes, are in a very good state of preservation ; they suffer less from the requisite processes of cleaning than the classes covered by hair, fur, or feathers.

'Of these cold-blooded Vertebrates the proportion preserved in spirits is much greater than in Mammals and Birds, and, consequently, through the present allotment of space, the majority of the singular specific forms of Reptiles and Fishes are excluded from public view. Upwards of two thousand specimens in spirits of these classes have been added in the past year to the previously crowded shelves of the basement store-rooms, where access to any individual specimen is a matter of some difficulty, if not hazard. Of the above additions, fourteen hundred and fifty-six have accrued from the donation of the Secretary of State for India in Council. The interest and novelty of the specimens have constrained their acceptance, and the same reason has led to the acquisition of many additions from other sources.

'Amongst them deserve to be specified two specimens of that singular snake, the *Herpeton tentaculatum*, known for a century past only by a single discoloured example in the Paris Museum; those now in the stores of the British Museum were acquired from Siam, and have served to enrich Zoology with a complete knowledge of the species, through the descriptions and figures by Dr. GÜNTHER.

'The following may be also specified, namely, the burrowing Snake from South Africa, *Uriechis microlepidotus*; a new genus of tree-snake, *Herpetoreas*; a new genus, *Barycephalus*, of Saurian, from an altitude in the Himalayas of fifteen thousand feet above the level of the sea; also two new species of freshwater Tortoise, the *Emys Livingstonii*, dedicated to its discoverer in Africa, and the *Emys Siamensis*. Among the additions to the class of Fishes has been acquired a new genus, *Hypsiptera*, of the Scomberoid family; with several new species, including one, *Centrolophus Britannicus*, belonging to this country.

'The specimens of the Molluscous classes showing the entire animal, preserved in spirits, and stored in the basement room, are in good condition. The entire class of *Tunicata* is so preserved; also the families or genera devoid of, or with rudimental, shells, in the other Molluscous classes. A small proportion of such "naked" Mollusca, and the soft parts of a few of the testaceous kinds, are represented by coloured wax models in the exhibited series of shells arranged in the Bird Gallery.

'The whole of the exhibited collection is in an excellent state of preservation. The system or scale on which the genera, species, and local varieties of shells are exhibited, with their names and localities, gives to the ordinary visitor a power of comparing his own specimens, and, in most instances, of determining them, without the necessity of special application to the keeper or assistant in the department. The extent to which students and others avail themselves of this facility of comparison, and the value attached to it, show that the above principle and scale of exhibition of specimens are proper to be adopted in a National Museum for public use.'

In the year following the presentation of this Report, Professor OWEN made a more elaborate review, both of the condition and of the needs of the Zoological Department, from which I gather broadly, and by abridgement, the following striking results :—

The number of *species* of Mammals possessed by the British Museum was a little over two thousand, exemplified by about three thousand individual specimens. In the year 1830, the number of *specimens* had been about one thousand three hundred and fifty; in 1850, it had risen to nearly two thousand. It follows that, within thirty-two years, the number of specimens in the Museum Collection had been somewhat more than doubled. But still the number of *species* adequately illustrated was only about two thousand against three thousand five hundred species of Mammals which are known, named, and have been more or less adequately described, by zoologists.

Of Birds, about two thousand five hundred species were, in 1862, exhibited in the galleries of the British Museum, and in its store-rooms there were the skins of about four thousand two hundred species. The number of species already known and described, in 1862, was not less than eight thousand three hundred. And, it is hardly necessary to add, vast explorations have since been undertaken, in the years which have elapsed, or are now about to be undertaken, in Africa, in Madagascar, in Borneo, in New Guinea, and in many parts of Australia.

Of Fishes, the Museum contained, in 1862, about four thousand species. These were then represented, by way of public exhibition, irrespectively of the unexhibited stores, by about one thousand five hundred stuffed specimens, illustrating about one thousand species. The total number of recorded species, already at that date, amounted to more than eight thousand.

Of Reptiles, little more than two hundred and fifty species were publicly shown in the Museum Galleries, but its collections, unexhibited for want of space, were already much larger. The number of known species of *Reptilia*, in 1862, exceeded two thousand.

Coming to the Invertebrata, it appears that, in 1862, about ten thousand species of molluscs, illustrated by about one hundred thousand specimen shells, were publicly exhibited. This, it will be remembered, was anterior to the great accession of the CUMING Collection, which already, in 1862, contained more than sixteen thousand *species*— and is the finest and most complete series ever brought together.

Book III, Chap. III. History of the Museum under Sir A. Panizzi.

See, hereinafter, Chap. VI.

Book III,
Chap. III.
History
of the
Museum
under Sir
A. Panizzi.

About forty-five thousand specimens of molluscs were, in 1862, stored in the drawers of the galleries and other rooms, or in the vaults beneath. These, on a rough computation, may have illustrated about four thousand five hundred species.

Within the *two years only*, 1860-1862, the registered number of specimens of Fossils was increased from one hundred and twenty thousand to one hundred and fifty-three thousand, but of these it was found possible to exhibit to the Public little more than fifty thousand specimens.

Growth
of the
Mineralo-
gical Col-
lections.
1858-1862.

Coming to the Department of Mineralogy, we find that the registered specimens had increased, within about four years, from fifteen thousand to twenty-five thousand. This increase was mainly due to the acquisition of the noble ALLAN-GREG Cabinet formed at Manchester. But large as this increase is, the national importance of the Mineralogical Collections is very far from being adequately represented by the existing state of the Museum series, even after all the subsequent additions made between the years 1862-1870. A Museum of Mineralogy worthy of England must eventu-
Owen,
Report, as
above (1862).
ally include five several and independent collections. There must be (1) a Classificatory Collection, for general purposes ; (2) a Geometrical Collection, to show the crystalline forms ; (3) an Elementary Collection, to show the degrees of lustre and the varieties of cleavage and of colour ; (4) a Technological Collection, to show the economic application of minerals—the importance of which, to a commercial, manufacturing, and artistic country, can hardly be exaggerated. Last of all, there is needed a special collection of an ancillary kind; that, I mean, which has been
Ibid.)
called sometimes a 'teratological' collection, sometimes a 'pseudomorphic' collection. Call it as you will, its object

is important.   Such a series serves to show both the defective and the excessive forms of minerals, and their transitional capacities.   These five several collections are, it will be seen, over and above that other special Collection of Sky-stones or 'Meteorites,' which is already very nobly represented in our National Museum.

CHAPTER IV.

ANOTHER GROUP OF ARCHÆOLOGISTS AND EXPLORERS.—THE SPOILS OF XANTHUS, OF BABYLON, OF NINEVEH, OF HALICARNASSUS, AND OF CARTHAGE.

> 'She doted upon the Assyrians her neighbours, ...
> when she saw men pourtrayed upon the wall,—the images
> of the Chaldeans pourtrayed with vermilion, girded with
> girdles upon their loins, exceeding in dyed attire upon
> their heads; all of them princes to look to, after the
> manner of the Babylonians of Chaldea.'
>
> EZEKIEL xxiii, 12-15.

> 'I do love these ancient ruins;
> We cannot tread upon them, but we set
> Our foot upon some reverend history.
>
> . . . .
>   But all things have their end,
> Castles and cities (which have diseases like to men)
> Must have like death which we have.'
>
> WEBSTER, *The Duchess of Malfi.*

The Libraries of the East.—The Monasteries of the Nitrian Desert, and their Explorers.—William CURETON *and his Labours on the MSS. of Nitria, and in other Departments of Oriental Literature.—The Researches in the Levant of Sir Charles* FELLOWS, *of Mr.* LAYARD, *and of Mr. Charles* NEWTON.—*Other conspicuous Augmentors of the Collection of Antiquities.*

WE have now to turn to that vast field of research and exploration, from which the national Museum of Antiquities has derived an augmentation that has sufficed to double, within twenty-five years, its previous scientific and literary value to the Public. In this chapter we have to tell of not a little romantic adventure; of remote and perilous explorations and excavations; sometimes, of sharp conflicts between English pertinacity and Oriental cunning; often, of great endurance of hardship and privation in the endeavour at once to promote learning—the world over—and to add some new and not unworthy entries on the long roll of British achievement.

Two distinct groups of explorers have now to be recorded. The labours of both groups carry us to the Levant. What has been done of late years by the searchers after manuscripts, in their effort to recover some of the lost treasures of the old Libraries of the East, will be most fairly appreciated by the reader, if, before telling of the researches and the studies of CURZON, TATTAM, CURETON, and their fellow-workers in Eastern manuscript archæology, some brief prefatory notice be given of the earlier labours, in the same field, of HUNTINGTON, BROWNE, and other travellers in the seventeenth and eighteenth centuries. Mention must also be made of the explorations of SONNINI and of ANDRÉOSSI.

About the year 1680, Robert HUNTINGTON, afterwards Bishop of Raphoe, visited the Monasteries of the Nitrian Desert, and made special and eager research for the Syriac version of the *Epistles of St. Ignatius*, of the existence of which there had been wide-spread belief amongst the learned, since the time of Archbishop USSHER. But his quest was fruitless, although, as it is now well known, a Syriac version of some of those epistles did really exist in one of the monasteries which HUNTINGTON visited. The monks, then as afterwards, were chary of showing their MSS., very small as was the care they took of them. The

39

only manuscripts mentioned by Huntington, in recording his visits to three of the principal communities—St. Mary Deipara, St. Macarius, and El Baramous—are an *Old Testament* in the Estrangelo character; two volumes of Chrysostom in Coptic and Arabic; a Coptic Lectionary in four volumes; and a *New Testament* in Coptic and Arabic.

Towards the close of the following century, these monasteries received the successive visits of Sonnini, of William George Browne, and of General Count Andréossi. Sonnini says nothing of books. Browne saw but few—among them an Arabo-Coptic *Lexicon*, the works of St. Gregory, and the *Old* and *New Testaments* in Arabic—although he was told by the superior that they had nearly eight hundred volumes, with none of which they would part. General Andréossi, on the other hand, speaks slightingly of the books as merely 'ascetic works, ... some in Arabic, and some in Coptic, with an Arabic translation in the margin;' but adds, 'We brought away some of the latter class, which appear to have a date of six centuries.' This was in 1799. Browne died in 1814; Sonnini de Manoncourt, in 1812; Count Andréossi survived until 1828.

In the year 1827, the late Duke of Northumberland (then Lord Prudhoe) made more elaborate researches. His immediate object was a philological one, his Lordship desiring to further Mr. Tattam's labours on a Coptic and Arabic Dictionary. Hearing that 'Libraries were said to be preserved, both at the Baramous and Syrian convents,' he proceeded to El Baramous, accompanied by Mr. Linart, and encamped outside the walls. "The monks in this convent,' says the Duke, 'about twelve in number, appeared poor and ignorant. They looked on us with great jealousy, and denied having any books, except those in the church, which they showed us.'   But having been judiciously mollified by some little seductive present, on the next day, 'in a moment of good humour, they agreed to show us their Library.   From it I selected a certain number of Manuscripts, which, with the *Lexicon (Selim)* already mentioned, were carried into the monk's room. A long deliberation ensued, ... as to my offer to purchase them.'   Only one could write, and at last it it was agreed that he should copy the *Selim*, which copy and the MSS. I had collected were to be mine, in exchange for a fixed sum of dollars, to which I added a present of rice, coffee, tobacco, and such other articles as I had to offer.'   After narrating the acquisition of a few other MSS. at the Syrian convent, or Convent of St. Mary Deipara, his Lordship proceeds :—' These manuscripts I presented to Mr. TATTAM, and gave him some account of the small room with its trap-door, through which I descended, candle in hand, to examine the manuscripts, where books, and parts of books, and scattered leaves, in Coptic, Ethiopic, Syriac, and Arabic, were lying in a mass, on which I stood. . . . In appearance, it seemed as if, on some sudden emergency, the whole Library had been thrown down this trap-door, and they had remained undisturbed, in their dust and neglect, for some centuries.'

Ten years later, Mr. TATTAM himself continued these researches.   But in the interval they had been taken up by the energetic and accomplished traveller Mr. Robert CURZON, to whose charming *Visits to the Monasteries of the Levant* it is mainly owing that a curious aspect of monastic life, which theretofore had only interested a few scholars, has become familiar to thousands of readers of all classes.

Mr. CURZON'S researches were much more thorough

than those of any of his predecessors. He was felicitous in his endeavours to win the good graces of the monks, and seems often to have made his visits as pleasant to his hosts as afterwards to his readers. But, how attractive soever, only one of them has to be noticed in connexion with our present topic—that, namely, to the Convent of the Syrians mentioned already. 'I found,' says Mr. CURZON, 'several Coptic MSS. lying on the floor, but some were placed in niches in the stone wall. They were all on paper, except three or four; one of them was a superb MS. of the Gospels, with a commentary by one of the early fathers. Two others were doing duty as coverings to large open pots or jars, which had contained preserves, long since evaporated. On the floor I found a fine Coptic and Arabic Dictionary, with which they refused to part.' After a most graphic account of a conversation with the Father Abbot— the talk being enlivened with many cups of rosoglio—he proceeds to recount his visit to a 'small closet, vaulted with stone, which was filled to the depth of two feet or more with loose leaves of Syriac MSS., which now form one of the chief treasures of the British Museum.' The collection thus 'preserved' was that of the Coptic monks; the same monastery contained another which was that of the Abyssinian monks. 'The disposition of the manuscripts in the Library,' continues Mr. CURZON, 'was very original. . . . The room was about twenty-six feet long, twenty feet wide, and twelve feet high; the roof was formed of the trunks of palm-trees. A wooden shelf was carried, in the Egyptian style, around the walls, at the height of the top of the door, ... underneath the shelf various long wooden pegs projected from the wall, ... on which hung the Abyssinian MSS., of which this curious Library was entirely composed. The books of Abyssinia are bound in the usual way—sometimes in red leather, and sometimes in wooden boards, . . . they are then enclosed in a case, . . . to which is attached a strap, . . . and by these straps the books are hung on the wooden pegs, three or four on a peg, or more, if the books were small ; their usual size was that of a small, very thick quarto. . . . Almost all Abyssinian books are written upon skins. . . . They have no cursive writing ; each letter is therefore painted, as it were, with the reed-pen. . . . Some manuscripts are adorned with the quaintest and grimmest illustrations conceivable, ... and some are worthy of being compared with the best specimens of caligraphy in any language.' Then follows an amusing account of the 'higgling of the monks,' after a truly Abyssinian fashion, ending in the acquisition of books, of the whole of which the travellers could not, by any packing or stuffing, make their bags containable. 'In this dreadful dilemma, . . . seeing that the quarto was the most imperfect, I abandoned it ; and I have now reason to believe, on seeing the manuscripts of the British Museum, that this was the famous book, with the date of *A.D.* 411, the most precious acquisition to any Library that has been made in modern times, with the exception, as I conceive, of some in my own Collection. . . . This book, which contains some lost works of Eusebius, has . . . fallen into better hands than mine.'

In the following year (1838), the Rev. Henry TATTAM (afterwards Archdeacon of Bedford), in furtherance of the purpose which had previously enlisted Lord PRUDHOE's co-operation, set out upon his expedition into Egypt. He arrived at Cairo in October, and in November proceeded up the Nile as far as Esneh, visiting many monasteries, and inspecting their Libraries, in most of which he only met with liturgies and service-books. Sanobon was an ex-

BOOK III,
Chap. IV.
ANOTHER
GROUP OF
ARCHÆOLO-
GISTS AND
EXPLORERS.

Curzon,
Visits, &c.,
as above.

ception, for there he found eighty-two Coptic MSS., some of them very fine.

Continuing the narrative, we find that on the 12th of January they started across the desert for the valley of the Natron Lakes, and pitched their tent at a short distance from the Monastery of Macarius. The monks told them that of these convents there had once been, on the mountain and in the valley of Nitria, no less than three hundred and sixty. Of fifty or thereabouts the ruins, it is said, may still be seen. At the Convent of the Syrians, the Archdeacon was received with much civility, not, however, unaccompanied by a sort of cautious circumspection. After a look at the church, followed by the indispensable pipes and coffee, the monks asked the cause to which they were indebted for the honour of his visit. He told them discreetly that it was his wish to see their books. 'They replied that they had no more than what he had seen in the church; upon which he told them plainly that he knew they had.' A conference ensued, and, on the next day, they 'conducted him to the tower, and then into a dark vault, where he found a great quantity of very old and valuable Syriac MSS. He selected six quarto volumes, and took them to the superior's room. He was next shown a room in the tower, where he found a number of Coptic and Arabic MSS., principally liturgies, with a beautiful copy of the *Gospels*. He then asked to see the rest. The monks looked surprised to find he knew of others, and seemed at first disposed to deny that they had any more, but at length produced the key of the apartment where the other books were kept, and admitted him. After looking them over, he went to the superior's room, where all the priests were assembled, fifteen or sixteen in number; one of them brought a Coptic and Arabic *Selim*, or *Lexicon*, which Mr.

TATTAM wished to purchase ; they informed him they could not part with it, ... but consented to make him a copy. He paid for two of the Syriac MSS. he had placed in the superior's room, for the priests could not be persuaded to part with more. . . . . The superior would have sold the Dictionary, but was afraid, because the Patriarch had written in it a curse upon any one who should take it away.' [It was the same volume which had been vainly coveted by Mr. CURZON, as well as by several preceding travellers, and of which he tells us he ' put it in one of the niches of the wall, where it remained about two years, when it was purchased and brought away for me by a gentleman at Cairo.'] ' In the Convent of El Baramous,' continues Miss PLATT, ' Mr. TATTAM found about one hundred and fifty Coptic and Arabic liturgies, and a very large Dictionary in both languages.   In the tower is an apartment, with a trap-door in the floor, opening into a dark hole, full of loose leaves of Arabic and Coptic manuscripts.'   At the Monastery of Amba-Bichoi, Mr. TATTAM saw a lofty vaulted room, so strewn with loose manuscripts as scarcely to afford a glimpse of the floor on which they lay, ' in some places a quarter of a yard deep.'   At Macarius Convent a similar sight presented itself, but of these Mr. TATTAM was permitted to carry off about a hundred.

As the reader may well imagine, the charms of the Syriac MSS. had made too deep an impression on Mr. TATTAM's heart to admit of an easy parting.   Many were the longing, lingering looks, mentally directed towards them.   Almost at the moment of setting out on his return to Cairo, he added four choice books to his previous spoils. In February, he resolved to revisit the convents, and once more to ply his most persuasive arguments.   He was manfully seconded by his Egyptian servant, MAHOMMED, whose favourite methods of negotiation much resembled those of Mr. Curzon. 'The Archdeacon soon returned,' says Miss Platt, 'followed by Mahommed and one of the Bedouins, bearing a large sack full of splendid Syriac MSS. on vellum. They were safely deposited in the tent.' At Amba-Bischoi a successful bargain was struck for an old *Pentateuch* in Coptic and Arabic, and a beautiful Coptic *Evangeliary*. On the next day, 'Mahommed brought from the priests a Soriana, a stupendous volume, beautifully written in the Syriac characters, with a very old worm-eaten copy of the *Pentateuch* from Amba-Bischoi, exceedingly valuable, but not quite perfect.' The remainder of the story, or rather the greater part of what remains, must here be more concisely told than in the words of the reviewer.

The manuscripts which Mr. Tattam has thus obtained, in due time arrived in England. Such of them as were in the Syriac language were disposed of to the Trustees of the British Museum. . . Forty-nine manuscripts of extreme antiquity, containing some valuable works long since supposed to have perished, and versions of others written several centuries earlier than any copies of the original texts now known to exist, constituted such an addition as has been rarely, if ever, made at one time to any Library. The collection of Syriac MSS. procured by Mr. Rich had already made the Library of the British Museum conspicuous for this class of literature; but the treasure of manuscripts from Egypt rendered it superior to any in Europe.

From the accounts which Lord Prudhoe, Mr. Curzon, and Mr. Tattam had given of their visits to the Monastery of the Syrians, it was evident that but few of the manuscripts belonging to it had been removed since the time of Assemani; and probable that no less a number than nearly two hundred volumes must be still remaining in the hands of the monks.   Moreover, from several notes in the manuscripts . . already brought to England, it was certain that most of them must be of very considerable antiquity . . . In several of these notices, Moses of Tecrit states that, in the year 932, he brought into the convent from Mesopotamia about two hundred and fifty volumes.   As there was no evidence whatever to show that even so many as one hundred of these MSS. had ever been taken away (for those which were procured for the Papal Library by the two Assemani, added to those which Mr. Curzon and Mr. Tattam had brought to England, do not amount to that number), there was sufficient ground for supposing that the Convent of the Syrians still possessed not fewer than about one hundred and fifty volumes, which, at the latest, must have been written before the tenth century. Application, accordingly, was made by the Trustees to the Treasury ; a sum was granted to enable them to send again into Egypt, and Mr. Tattam readily undertook the commission. The time was most opportune.   Had much more delay been interposed, these manuscripts, which, perhaps, constitute the greatest accession of valuable literature which has been brought from the East into Europe since the taking of Constantinople, would, in all probability, have been now the pride of the Imperial Library at Paris.

Mr. Tattam thought he could work most effectively through the influence of a neighbouring Sheikh with the superior of the convent.   By which means he obtained, after some delays, a promise that all the Syriac MSS. should be taken to the Sheikh's house, and there bargained for.   'My servant,' he says, 'had taken ten men and eight donkeys from the village ; had conveyed them, and already bargained for them, which bargain I confirmed.   That night

Book III,
Chap. IV.
Another
Group of
Archæolo-
gists and
Explorers.

Treasury
grant, in
1841, for
further re-
searches.

Quart.
Review,
as before.

Mr.
Tattam's
expedition
to Nitria
in 1842.

Book III,
Chap. IV.
Another
Group of
Archæolo-
gists and
Explorers.

we carried our boxes, paper, and string, and packed them all. .... Before ten in the morning they were on their way to Alexandria.' But, as will be seen in the sequel, the monks were too crafty for Mr. Tattam to cope with.

Tischen-
dorf's visit
in 1844.

In 1844, Tischendorf visited the monasteries already explored by Curzon and Tattam. His account reproduces the old characteristics :—'Manuscripts heaped indiscriminately together, lying on the ground, or thrown into large baskets, beneath masses of dust. . . . . The excessive suspicion of these monks renders it extremely difficult to induce them to produce their MSS., in spite of the extreme penury which surrounds them. . . . . But much might yet be found to reward the labour of the searcher.'

In truth, the monks, poor and simple as they sometimes seemed to be, had taken very sufficient care to keep enough of literary treasures in their hands to reward 'further researches.' Nearly half of their collection seems to have been withheld.

Pacho's
negotia-
tion for
the reco-
very of the
MSS. with-
held by the
monks of
St. Mary
Deipara.

A certain clever Mr. Pacho now entered on the scene as a negotiator for the obtainment or recovery of the missing 'treasures of the tombs.' They had been virtually purchased before, but the Lords of the Treasury very wisely re-opened the public purse, and at length secured for the Nation an inestimable possession. The new accession completed, or went far towards completing, many MSS. which before See page 622, in this Chapter. were tantalizingly imperfect. It supplied a second ancient copy of the famous Ignatian *Epistles* (*to St. Polycarp, to the Ephesians*, and *to the Romans*); many fragments of palimpsest manuscripts of great antiquity, and among them the greater part of St. Luke's *Gospel* in Greek; and about four thousand lines of the *Iliad*, written in a fine square uncial letter, apparently not later than the sixth century. The total number of volumes thus added to the previous Nitrian Collections were calculated, roundly, to be from a hundred and forty to a hundred and fifty.

That the rich accession to our sacred literature, thus made amidst many obstacles, should be turned speedily to public advantage, two conditions had to be fulfilled. Skilful labour had first to be employed in the arrangement of a mass of fragments. Scholars competently prepared, by previous studies in Oriental literature and more especially in Syriac, must then get to work on their transcription, their gloss, and their publication. It could scarcely have been expected, beforehand, that any one man would be able to undertake both tasks, and to keep them, for some years to come, well abreast. The fact, however, proved to be so. The right man was already in the right place for the work that was to be done.

The late William CURETON had entered the service of the Trustees of the British Museum in 1837, at the age of twenty-nine, when he had been already for about eight years in holy orders. He was a native of Westbury, in Shropshire. His education, begun at Newport School, had been matured at Christ-Church, Oxford. He had been just about to enter himself at Christ-Church in the ordinary way, when his father died, suddenly, leaving the family fortunes under considerable embarrassment. CURETON, and a brother of his, showed the metal they were both made of, by instantly changing their youthful plans. That the whole of the diminished patrimony might be at their mother's sole disposal, William CURETON went to Oxford as a servitor. His brother, instead of waiting for his expected commission in the Army, enlisted as a private dragoon. And certainly, in the issue, neither of these young men lost any ‘dignity’—in any sense of that word—

on account of the step so unselfishly taken at their start in life.

William CURETON began his literary labours as a Coadjutor-Under-Librarian in old Bodley. Dr. GAISFORD introduced him to Dr. BANDINEL, in 1834, with the words:—'I bring you a good son. He will make a good librarian.' It was at Oxford that he laid the substantial foundation of his Oriental studies. After three years, he followed the fashion already set him by some of the best and ablest officers the Bodleian has ever had—ELLIS, BABER, and H. O. COXE, for example—by transferring, for a time, his services from the great Library of Oxford to that of London. His first (or nearly his first) Museum task was to set to work on the cataloguing of the Arabic and Persian MSS. In 1842, he began his earliest Oriental publication (undertaken for the 'Oriental Text Society,' to be mentioned presently), namely, AL SHARASTANI's *Book of Religious and of Philosophical Sects.*

At the British Museum, he became quite as notable for the amiability of his character, and the genial frankness of his manners, as for his scholarly attainments and his power of authorship. I have a vivid recollection of my own introduction to him, in the February of 1839, and of the impression made on me by his kindly and cordial greeting. When I noted that pleasant face, which beamed with good nature as well as with intellect, I instantly appreciated the force of the words used by my introducer: 'Let me make you known,' said he, 'to my father-confessor.' I thought the choice to be obviously a felicitous one. Not less vivid is my memory of the delight Mr. CURETON manifested on receiving, within the Museum *vaults*, the first importation from the Nitrian Desert. The sight of such a mass of torn, disorderly, and dirty fragments, would have appalled many men not commonly afraid of labour, but to William Cureton the scholarly ardour of discovery made the task, from the first, a pleasure. When successive fresh arrivals gave new hope that many gaps in the manuscripts of earliest importation would, in course of time, be filled up, the laborious pleasure ripened into joy.

The collection, obtained by the long succession of labours already narrated, reached the British Museum on the first of May, 1843. When the cases were opened, very few indeed of the MSS. were perfect. Nearly two hundred volumes had been torn into separate leaves, and then mixed up together, by blind chance and human stupidity. It was a perplexing sight. But the eyes that looked on it belonged to a seeing head. Even into a little chaos like this, almost hopeless as at the first glance it seemed, the learning, assiduity, and patience of Mr. Churton gradually brought order. Of necessity, the task took a long time. First came the separation of the fragments of different works, and then the arrangement of the leaves into volumes, with no aid to pagination or catchwords. With translations of extant Greek works, the collection of their originals gave, of course, great help. But in a multitude of cases every leaf had to be read and closely studied.

Within about eighteen months of the reception of the MSS., Mr. Cureton had ascertained the number of volumes —reckoning books made up of fragments, as well as complete works—to amount to three hundred and seventeen, of which two hundred and forty-six were on vellum, and seventy on paper; all in Syriac or Aramaic, except one volume of Coptic fragments. With the forty-nine volumes previously acquired, an addition was thus made to the MS. Department of the National Library of three hundred and sixty-six volumes. Many of these volumes contain two, three, or four distinct works, of different dates, bound together, so that probably, in the whole, there were of manuscripts and parts of manuscripts, upwards of one thousand, written in all parts of Mesopotamia, Syria, and Egypt, and at periods which range from the year 411 to the year 1292. Of the specific character and contents of some of the choicest of these MSS., mention will be made hereafter.

For several years, the labour on the Syriac fragments did but alternate with that on the larger body of the Arabic MSS., a classed catalogue of which Mr. CURETON published in 1846,—only a month or two after he had contributed to the *Quarterly Review* a deeply interesting and masterly article on the Syriac discoveries. This paper was quickly followed by his first edition of the *Three Epistles of St. Ignatius* (I, to Polycarp; II, to the Ephesians; III, to the Romans). In an able preface, he contended that, of these genuine *Epistles*, all previous recensions were, to a considerable extent, interpolated, garbled, and spurious; and also that the other Ignatian *Epistles*, so-called, are entirely supposititious. In the year 1870 it need hardly be said either that this publication excited much controversy, or that competent opinion is still divided on some parts of the subject. But on two points there has never been any controversy whatever:—As an editor, William CURETON displayed brilliant ability; as a student of theology, he was no less distinguished by a single-minded search after truth. He was never one of those noisy controversialists of whom Walter LANDOR once said, so incisively,* that they were less angry with their opponents for withstanding the truth, than for doubting their own claims to be the channels and the

* In—unless a memory more than thirty years old deceive me—that noble masterpiece of English prose, the ' *Citation of Shakespeare for Deer-stealing*' (1835).

champions of Truth. To his dying day, CURETON owned himself to be a learner—even in Syriac.

Within three years of the publication of his *Ignatius*, CURETON gave to the world his precious edition of the fragmentary *Festal Letters* of ATHANASIUS, which Richard BURGESS soon translated into English, and LASSOW into German. The Syriac version was one of its editor's earliest discoveries amongst the spoils of the Nitrian monasteries, and it was published at the cost of a new society, of which CURETON himself was the main founder. For the old Oriental publication society * limited itself, as its name imports, to the publication of translations. The new one —the claims of which to liberal support CURETON was never weary of vindicating—was expressly founded to print Oriental texts. This new body had his strongest sympathies, but he co-operated zealously with the 'Translation Fund' as well as with the 'Text Society.'

Among his other and early labours, was the publication of a Rabbinical Comment on the *Book of Lamentations*, and of the Arabic text of EN NASAFI'S *Pillar of the Creed of the Sunnites* ('Umdat Akidat ahl al Sunnat wa al Tamaat'), both of which books were printed in 1843. After 1845, CURETON's literary labours were almost exclusively devoted to that Syriac field in which he was to be so large and so original a discoverer. The first distinctively public recognition of his services was his appointment as a Chaplain to the Queen, in 1847. Two years afterwards, he was made a Canon of Westminster and Rector of St. Margaret's. Thenceforward, his energies were divided. The charms of Syriac discovery were not permitted to obstruct the due performance of the appropriate work of a parish-priest; though it is much to be feared that they

* The Oriental Translation Fund.

were but too often permitted to interfere, more than a little, with needful recreation and rest.

Among those of his parochial labours which demanded not a small amount of self-sacrifice were the rebuilding and the improved organization of the schools; the building of a district church—St. Andrew's—in Ashley Place; and the establishment of Working-Class Lectures, upon a wise and far-seeing plan.

In 1851, he gave to scholars the curious palimpsest fragments of HOMER from a Nitrian manuscript (now ADDIT. MS., 17,210), and, two years afterwards, the *Ecclesiastical History* of JOHN, Bishop of Ephesus. This was quickly translated into German by SCHÖNFEHLER, and into English by Dr. R. Payne SMITH. Then came the *Spicilegium Syriacum*, containing fragments of BARDESANES, of MELITO of Sardes, and the inexpressibly precious fragments of an ancient recension of the Syriac *Gospels*, believed by CURETON to be of the fifth century, and offering considerable and most interesting divergences from the Peshito version.

In a preface to these evangelical fragments of the fifth century, their editor contends that they constitute a far more faithful representation of the true Hebrew text than does the Peshito recension, and that the remark holds good, in a more especial degree, of the *Gospel of St. Matthew*. This publication appeared in 1858.

Enough has been said of these untiring labours to make it quite intelligible, even to readers the most unfamiliar with Oriental studies, that their author had become already a celebrity throughout learned Europe. As early as in 1855, the Institute of France welcomed Dr. CURETON, as one of their corresponding members, in succession to his old master, GAISFORD, of Christ-Church. In 1859, the Queen conferred on him a distinction, which was especially appropriate and dear to his feelings. He became 'Royal Trustee' of that Museum which he had so zealously served as an Assistant-Keeper of the MSS., up to the date of his appointment to his Westminster parish and canonry. No fitter nomination was ever made. Unhappily, he was not to be spared very long to fill a function so congenial.

Yet one other distinction, and also one other and most honourable labour, were to be his, before another illustrious victim was to be added to the long list of public losses inflicted on the country at large by the gross mismanagement, and more particularly by what is called—sardonically, I suppose—the 'economy' of our British railways. CURETON's life too, like some score of other lives dear to literature or to science, was to be sacrificed under the car of our railway Juggernaut.

In 1861, he published, from another Nitrian manuscript, EUSEBIUS' *History of the Martyrs in Palestine*. Early in 1863, he succeeded the late Beriah BOTFIELD in the Chair of the Oriental Translation Fund. On the twenty-ninth of May, of the same year, a railway 'accident' inflicted upon him such cruel injuries as entailed a protracted and painful illness of twelve months, and ended—to our loss, but to his great gain—in his lamented death, on the seventeenth of June, 1864.

He died where he was born, and was buried with his fathers. The writer of these poor memorial lines upon an admirable man well remembers the delight he used to express (thirty years ago) whenever it was in his power to revisit his birthplace, and knows that the delight was shared with the humblest of its inhabitants. Dr. CURETON was one of those genuine men who (in the true and best sense of the words) are not respecters of persons. He had a frank, not a condescending, salutation for the lowliest ac-

BOOK III,
Chap. IV.
ANOTHER
GROUP OF
ARCHÆOLO-
GISTS AND
EXPLORERS.

THE
REMOVAL,
AND ITS
CIRCUM-
STANCES.

quaintances of youthful days.   And those lowliest were not among the least glad to see his face again at his holiday-visits ; nor were they among the least sorrowful to see it, when it bore the fatal, but now to most of us quite familiar, traces of victimism to the mammon-cult of our railway directors.

Just as we have to go very far back indeed in the history of the Manuscript Department of the British Museum, in order to find an accession quite as notable as are—taking them as a whole—the manuscripts of the Nitrian monasteries, so have we also to do in the history of the several Departments of Antiquities, in order to find any parallel to the acquisitions of monuments of art and archæology made during the thirty years between 1840 and 1870.   In point of *variety* of interest, in truth, there is no parallel at all to be found.

In archæology, however—as in scientific discovery, or in mechanical invention—every great burst of new light will be seen, if we look closely enough, to have had its remote precursive gleams, howsoever faint or howsoever little noticed they may have been.

Austen Henry Layard, for example, is a most veritable 'discoverer.'   Nevertheless, the researches of Layard link themselves with those of Claudius Rich, and with the still earlier glimpses, and the mere note-book jottings, of Carsten Niebuhr, as well as with the explorations of Layard's contemporary and most able French fellow-investigator, Monsieur Botta.   In like manner, Nathan Davis is the undoubted disinterrer of old Carthage, but the previous labours of the Italian canon and archæologist Spano, of Cagliari, and those of the French geographers De Dreux and Dureau de La Malle, imperfect as they all were, helped to put him upon the quest which was destined to receive so rich a reward.

It is obvious, therefore, that a tolerably satisfactory account of the researches of the renowned archæologists mentioned at the head of this chapter must be prefaced with some notices of much earlier and much less successful labours than theirs; and a thorough account would need greatly more than that. But, at present, I cannot hope to give either the one or the other. Rapid glances at the recent investigations are all that, for the moment, are permitted me, and for the perfunctory manner of these 1 shall have to make not a little demand on the reader's indulgence. The subject-matter is rich enough to claim a volume to itself; nor would the story be found to lack well-sustained and varied interest, even if retold at large.

The first inquiries and explorations in *Lycia* of Sir Charles FELLOWS began several years earlier than those in *Assyria* of Mr. Austen LAYARD, but an intelligible narrative of what LAYARD did, in 1845, must needs start with a notice, be it ever so brief, of what BOTTA had been doing in 1842. The Lycian excavations were also effectively begun in 1842. They were, in fact, contemporaneous with the first excavations at Nineveh. I begin, therefore, with the closely-linked labours of BOTTA and of LAYARD, prefacing them with a glance at the previous pursuits and aims in life of our distinguished fellow-countryman.

Austen Henry LAYARD is an Englishman, notwithstanding his birth in Paris (5th of March, 1817), and his descent from one of the many Huguenot families who (in one sense) do honour to France for their sufferings for conscience sake, and who (in many more senses than one) do honour to England by the way in which zealous and persevering exertions in the service of their adopted country have

BOOK III, Chap. IV. ANOTHER GROUP OF ARCHÆOLOGISTS AND EXPLORERS.

AUSTEN HENRY LAYARD AND HIS EARLY CAREER.

BOOK III,
Chap. IV.
ANOTHER
GROUP OF
ARCHÆOLO-
GISTS AND
EXPLORERS.
enabled them to pluck the flowers of fame, or of distinction, from amidst the sharp thorns of adversity. Austen LAYARD is the grandson of the honoured Dr. LAYARD, Dean of Bristol, and he began active life, whilst yet very young, in a solicitor's office in the City of London. But he had scarcely reached twenty-two years of age before family circumstances enabled him to gratify a strong passion for Eastern travel. Archæology had no share, at first, in the attractions which the Levant presented to his youthful enterprise. But a fervid nature, a good education, and a wonderful power of self-adaptation to new social circumstances, made the mind of the young traveller a fitting seedplot for antiquarian knowledge, whenever the opportunity of acquiring it should come.

THE
JOURNEY
THROUGH
ASIA MINOR
AND SYRIA
IN 1839-1840.
To a man of that stamp it would be impossible that he should tread near those ancient ruins, every stone of which must needs connect itself with some 'reverend history' or other—when the discerning eye should at length pore upon it and ponder it—without the ambition stirring within him to make at least an earnest attempt to explore and to decipher. To this particular man and his companion in travel, Fortune was propitious, by dint of her very parsimony. As he says himself: 'No experienced dragoman measured our distances or appointed our stations. We were honoured with no conversations by pashas, nor did we seek any civilities from governors. We neither drew tears nor curses from the villagers by seizing their horses, Nineveh and
its Remains
(1849), vol. i,
p. 2. or searching their houses for provisions; their welcome was sincere; their scanty fare was placed before us; we ate, and came, and went in peace.'

It was almost thirty years ago—about the middle of April, 1840—that Mr. LAYARD looked upon those vast ruins on the east bank of the Tigris, opposite Mósul, which include the now famous mounds of Konyunjik and of Nebbi Yunus. Having gazed on them with an incipient longing—even then—to explore them thoroughly, he and his companion rode into the desert, and looked with new wonder at the great mound of Kàlàh Sherghat, the site of which is by some geographers identified with the Assur of the book Genesis.* After that hasty and tantalising visit, in the spring of 1840, LAYARD did not again see Mósul until the summer of 1842, when he was again travelling Tatar, and hurrying to Constantinople. In the interval, he had often thought of his early purpose, and had talked of it to many travellers. Now, in 1842, he heard that what he had hitherto been able only to contemplate, as the wished-for task of the future, Monsieur BOTTA, the new French Consul at Mósul, had, for some months, been actually working upon; although, as yet, with very small success. Our countryman encouraged the French Consul in his undertaking, and presently learned that by him the first real monument of old Assyria had been uncovered. This primary discovery was not made at Kouyunjik, but at Khorsabad, near the river Khauser, many miles away from the place at which the first French excavations had been made, early in 1842.

The delighted emotions of Monsieur BOTTA, when he found himself, very suddenly, standing in a chamber in which—to all probability—no man had stood since the Fall of Nineveh, and saw that the chamber was lined with sculptured slabs of 'gypsum-marble' or alabaster, full of historic scenes from the wars and triumphs of Assyria, a

---

* Comp. 'Asshur builded Nineveh, and the city Rehoboth, and *Calah*.' —*Gen.* x, 11. Mr. Layard quotes this passage, in *Nineveh and its Remains* (vol. i, p. 4, edit. 1849), and seems to identify 'Kalah Sherghat' as retaining its ancient name.

reader can better imagine than a writer can describe. BOTTA himself rather indicates than depicts them, in the deeply interesting letters which he speedily addressed to his friend MOHL at Paris (and which by MOHL were not less promptly published in the *Journal Asiatique,* to be within a month or two pondered and wondered over by almost every archæologist in Europe). The delight, and also the surprise, were enhanced when the discoverer saw that almost every slab had a line of wedge-shaped characters carved above it, giving hope of history in legible inscriptions, as well as history in ruins. For, unhappily, nearly all the sculptures *first* discovered at Khorsabad were fractured. The durability of the Assyrian style of building had brought about the defacement of the sculptured records. The walls were formed of blocks of gypsum, backed and lined, so to speak, with enormous masses of clay. When the weight of such large earth-banks pressed down upon the sculptured slabs, these were thrust from their place. Many that were still in position, when first seen, fell, or crumbled, as the explorer was looking at them. He had to shore-up and underpin, as he went on; and to do this by unpractised hands. Else, the more diligent his excavations, the more destructive they would have been of the very end he had in view.

LAYARD was at Constantinople when the news came of M. BOTTA's increasing successes. His detention there had been unexpected, as well as unavoidable. But he wrote to England without delay. He had a foresight that BOTTA would not lack encouragement in France. He felt no unworthy jealousy on account of the fact that it was a Frenchman who was now disinterring historic treasures of a hitherto unexampled kind, and who was rapidly securing historic fame for himself.* Mr. LAYARD knew— few men just then knew more fully—that in all matters of learning and of discovery the gains of France are the gains of the world. For the staunchest of John Bulls amongst us must acknowledge that in the arts of scientific dissemination and exposition a Frenchman (other things being equal) has usually twice the expertness of an Eng- lishman. But he was naturally desirous that France should not have *all* the glory of Assyrian discovery. What, then, was the reception with which his first overtures were met? 'With a single exception,' in the person of his London correspondent, 'no one,' he tells us, 'in England' .... 'seemed inclined to assist or take any interest in such an undertaking.'

What, on the other hand, were the encouragements given to the French explorer by the Government and the Nation of France? They were large; they were ungrudgingly given; and they were instantaneously sent. In Mr. LAYARD's words: 'The recommendation was attended to with that readiness and munificence which [has] almost invariably distinguished the French Government in under- takings of this nature. Ample funds to meet the cost of extensive excavations were at once assigned to M. BOTTA, and an artist of acknowledged skill was placed under his orders, to draw such parts of the monuments discovered as could not be preserved or removed.' Who will wonder

BOOK III, Chap. IV.
ANOTHER GROUP OF ARCHÆOLO- GISTS AND EXPLORERS.

LAYARD'S OVERTURES TO THE BRITISH GOVERN- MENT.

Nineveh and its Remains, vol. i, p 10.

LIBERAL AID EXTENDED TO M. BOTTA BY THE FRENCH GOVERN- MENT.

---

* Nor was there any petty or unworthy jealousy in the distinguished French explorer. 'During the entire period of his excavations,' writes Mr. Layard, 'M. Botta regularly sent me, not only his [own] descriptions, but copies of the inscriptions, without exacting any promise as to the use I might make of them. That there are few who would have acted thus liberally, those who have been engaged in a search after Antiquities in the East will not be inclined to deny.'— *Nineveh and its Remains,* vol. i, p. 14.

that at first it seemed as though France would carry off all the stakes, and England have no place at all in the archæological race ?

Mr. LAYARD, however, was otherwise minded. And he found, presently, a powerful helper in the person of the British Ambassador at Constantinople, Sir Stratford CANNING (now Lord Stratford de Redcliffe). Had it not been for the union, in that ambassador, of a large intellect, a liberal mind, and a strong will, and also for the *absence*, in him, of that shrinking from extra-official responsibilities which in so many able men has often emasculated their ability, Mr. LAYARD's efforts, earnest and unremitting as they were, would assuredly have been foiled.

The reader will perceive that for what was achieved, in 1845 and in the subsequent years, on the banks of the Tigris, the British public owe a debt of gratitude to Lord STRATFORD DE REDCLIFFE, the encourager of the enterprise, as well as to Mr. LAYARD, its originator.

But neither does this fact, nor does the like of it, five years earlier, in the help given by Lord PONSONBY to the Lycian researches of Sir Charles FELLOWS, invalidate or weaken the remark I have ventured to make (on pages 348 ; 381, of the present volume, and elsewhere) about the discreditable and long-continued apathy of our Foreign Office in matters of art and literature ; especially if we compare on that head British practice with French practice. Perhaps, at first blush, it might be thought somewhat presumptuous, in a private person, to remark so freely on what seem to him the shortcomings of statesmen. But it has to be borne in mind that, in such cases as this, outspoken criticism is rather the expression of known public opinion, than of mere individual judgment. The one writer, how humble soever, is very often the mouthpiece of the thoughts of many minds. Nor is other warrant for such criticism lacking.

Three years after beginning his excavations at Nimroud, Mr. LAYARD himself wrote thus (from Cheltenham) :—' It is to be regretted that proper steps have not been taken for the transport to England of the sculptures discovered at Nineveh. Those which have already reached this country, and (it is to be feared) those which are now on their way, have consequently suffered *unnecessary* injury ; . . . . . yet, . . . they are almost the only remains of a great city and of a great nation.'

Part of the injury now observable in the Assyrian sculptures of the British Museum was, of course, inseparable from circumstances attending the discovery. Besides the injury already spoken of—from the pressure of the earth-banks—all the low-reliefs of one great palace had suffered from intense heat. From this cause, Mr. LAYARD's experiences recall, in one particular, the impressive accounts we have all read of the opening of ancient tombs in Egypt and in Italy. The fortunate excavator suddenly beheld a kingly personage, in fashion as he lived. The royal forehead was still encircled by a regal crown. The fingers were decked with rings ; the hand, mayhap, grasped a sceptre. But whilst the discoverer was still gazing in the first flush of admiration, the countenance changed ; the ornaments crumbled ; the sceptre and the hand that held it alike became dust. So it was, at times, at Nimroud. Some of the calcined slabs presented, for a moment, their story in its integrity. Presently, they fell into fragments.

None the less, when the reader goes into the Kouyunjik Gallery ; looks at the sculptures from SENNACHERIB's palace ; observes the innumerable 'joinings,' and then glances at his official ' *Guide*' (which tells him, at page 85,

Book III, Chap. IV. ANOTHER GROUP OF ARCHÆOLOGISTS AND EXPLORERS.

Nineveh and its Remains, vol. i, p. xiii.

MIXED NATURE OF THE CAUSES OF THE MUTILATIONS OU-

Book III,
Chap. IV.
Another
Group of
Achæolo-
gists and
Explorers.

Servable
in the
Museum
Sculptures
from
Assyria.

'many single slabs reached this country in three hundred or four hundred pieces'), he is bound for truth's sake to remember that, whilst some of the breakage is ascribable to the action of fire at the time of the Fall of Nineveh, another portion of it is ascribable to the want or absence of action, on the part of some worthy officials in the public service of Britain, just twenty-five centuries afterwards.

With Sir Stratford Canning's help, and with the still better help of his own courage and readiness of resource, Mr. Layard surmounted most of the obstacles which lay in his path. There was a rich variety of them. To quote but a tithe of his encounters with Candian pashas, Turcoman navvies, Abou-Salman visitors, and Mósul cadis and muftis, would ensure the reader's amusement beyond all doubt; but the temptation must be overcome. Happily, the original books are well known, though the anecdotes are more than racy enough to bear quotation and requotation.

Layard's
first dis-
covery,
28th Nov.,
1845.

Two incidents of the first explorations (1845-46) must needs be told. The earliest discovery was made on the twenty-eighth of November. The indications of having approached, at length, a chamber lined with sculpture, rejoiced the Arab labourers not less than it rejoiced their employer. They kept on digging long after the hour at which they were accustomed to strike work. The slab first uncovered was a battle scene. War chariots drawn by splendidly equipped horses contained three warriors apiece, in full career. The chief of them (beardless) was clothed in complete mail, 'and wore a pointed helmet on his head, from the sides of which fell lappets covering the ears, the lower part of the face, and the neck. The left hand (the arm being extended) grasped a bow at full stretch; whilst the right, drawing the string to the car, held an arrow ready to be discharged.   A second warrior urged, with reins and whip, three horses to the utmost of their speed. . . . A third, without helmet and with flowing hair and beard, held a shield for the defence of the principal figure.   Under the horses' feet, and scattered about, were the conquered, wounded by the arrows of the conquerors.   I observed with surprise the elegance and richness of the ornaments, the faithful and delicate delineation of the limbs and muscles, both in the men and horses, and the knowledge of art displayed in the grouping of the figures and the general composition.   In all these respects, as well as in costume, this sculpture appeared to me, not only to differ from, but to surpass, the bas-reliefs of Khorsabad.'

Thus cheered, the work of digging went on with fresh vigour, and in new directions.   Parts of a building which had suffered from decay, not from fire, were at length uncovered.   Slabs of still greater beauty were disclosed.   'I now thought,' says the explorer, 'I had discovered the earliest palace of Nimroud.'

On the morning after the discovery of these new and more choice sculptures—middle of February, 1846—Mr. LAYARD rode away from the mound to a distant Arab encampment—wisely cultivating, as was his manner, a good understanding with a ticklish sort of neighbours.   Two early Arabs, from this camp, had already paid a morning visit to the mound.   They hastened back at a racing pace.   Before they could well pull up their horses, or regain their own Oriental composure, the riders shouted at sight of Layard : 'Hasten, O Bey, to the diggers.   They have found great NIMROD himself.   Wallah ! it is wonderful, but it is true ! We have seen him with our eyes.'

The 'Bey' did not wait for lucid explanations ; but

Book III,
Chap. IV.
Another
Group of
Archæolo-
gists and
Explorers.

Nineveh and
its Remains
(1849), vol. i,
p. 41.

Book III,
Chap. IV.
Another
Group of
Archæolo-
gists and
Explorers.

Ibid., p. 65.

1846,
February.

urged his horse to emulate the speed with which the grateful, though mysterious, tidings had been brought to him. No sooner had he entered the new trench at the mound, than he saw a splendidly sculptured head, the form of which assured him at a glance that it must belong to a winged bull or lion like to those of Persepolis and of Khorsabad. Its preservation was perfect, its features sharply cut. The Arab workmen stood looking at it with intent and fear-expressing eyes—but with open palms. The first word that came from their lips begged a ' back-sheesh,' in honour of the auspicious occasion. The terror of one of them, only, had led him to scamper at full speed to his tent, that he might hide himself from the frightful monster whose aspect seemed to threaten vengeance on those rash men who had dared to disturb his long repose, in the bowels of the earth.

Scarcely had Mr. Layard glanced at ' Nimrod ' before he found that more than half the tribe whose encampment he had just left had followed hard at his heels. They were headed by their Sheikh. It would be difficult to depict, in few words, the conflict of their feelings. Admiration, terror, anger, had each a part in the emotion which was evinced, no less in their gestures than in their words. ' There is no God but God, and Mahomed is his prophet! This is not the work of men's hands, but of those infidel giants whom the Prophet—peace be with him!—has said, that " they were higher than the tallest date-tree." This is one of the idols which Noah—peace be with him!—cursed before the Flood.' Such were the words of Sheikh Abd-ur-rahman himself. He showed great reluctance, at first, to enter the trench. But when once in, he examined the image with great and continued earnestness. All his followers echoed his verdict.

Ibid., p. 66.

But the townspeople of Mósul were more difficult to deal with. The Cadi called a meeting of the Mufti and the Ulema, to discuss the most effectual protest against such an atrocious violation of the Koran as that committed by the unbelieving explorer and his mercenary labourers. Their notions about NIMROD were very vague. Some thought him to have been an ancient true-believer; others had a strong misgiving that he, like his unearther, was but an infidel. They were all clear that the digging must be stopped. It tasked all Mr. LAYARD's skill, experience, and force of character, to surmount these new difficulties. When they had been at length overcome—with the brilliant results known now to most Englishmen—he had to face the enormous difficulties of transport. The great human-headed lions he was obliged to leave in their original position. A multitude of smaller sculptures (many of them reduced in bulk by sawing) were safely brought to England. The first arrivals came in 1847.* In 1849 and in 1850, the excavations in the mounds first opened were vigorously resumed, and new researches were made in several directions. Early in 1850, the explorers buckled to the task of removing the lions. That chapter in Mr. LAYARD's familiar narrative is not the least interesting one.

* It is a slight blemish in Mr. Layard's otherwise admirable books that they are loose in the handling of dates. It is sometimes necessary to turn over hundreds of pages in order to be sure of the year in which a particular excavation was made, or in which an interesting incident occurred. Sometimes, again, there is an actual conflict of dates, e. g. *Discoveries in the Ruins*, &c. (1853), p. 3, 'After my departure from Mósul in 1847,' and again, p. 66, 'On my return to Europe in 1847;' but at p. 162, we read : 'Having been carefully covered up with earth, previous to my departure in 1848, they [the lions] had been preserved,' &c. I mention this simply because it is possible that error may thus, once or twice, have crept into the marginal dates given above, though pains has been taken about these.

Book III,
Chap. IV.
Another
Group of
Archæolo-
gists and
Explorers.

*Discoveries in
the Ruins of
Nineveh and
Babylon*
(1853),
pp. 162, 163;
201-209; scqq.
Dec., 1849.

The explorations partially interrupted in 1847 were resumed in 1849. From the October of that year until April, 1851, they were carried on with even more than the old energy, for the means and appliances were more ample, and the encouragements drawn from success followed each other in far quicker succession.

The suspension had been but partial, for Mr. Hormuzd Rassam, then British Vice-Consul at Mósul, had been empowered to keep a few men still digging at Kouyunjik. He had there unearthed several new sculpture-lined chambers of no small interest. But at Nimroud nothing worthy of mention had been done during Layard's absence. That was now his first object. Kouyunjik, however, for a long time gave the best yield.

1849,
Oct. and Nov.

In December the south-east façade of the Kouyunjik Palace was uncovered. It was found to be a hundred and eighty feet in length, and contained, among other sculptures, ten colossal bulls and six human figures. The accompanying inscriptions contained the early annals of Sennacherib, and of his wars with Merodach Baladan.*

Presently, the labours on the north-west palace at Nimroud were also richly rewarded. The somewhat higher antiquity of that building, as compared with the homogeneous structures of Kouyunjik and Khorsabad, had already impressed itself with the force of conviction on Mr. Layard's individual mind. The fact now became manifest to all eyes that had the capacity to see.

These Nimroud monuments belong,—according to the opinion of the best archæologists,—most of them, to the

* The Berodach-Baladan of 2 Kings, xx, 12, who 'sent letters and a present unto Hezekiah, when he had heard that Hezekiah had been sick.'

eighth, some of them, however, to the earlier part of the seventh centuries *B.C.* They now occupy the most central of the Assyrian Galleries in the British Museum. The monuments of Kouyunjik and of Khorsabad are probably but little anterior to the supposed date (625 *B.C.*) of the destruction of Nineveh. These are exhibited in galleries adjacent to the 'Nimroud Central Saloon.' To describe only a few of them in connection with the interesting circumstances of their respective disclosures would demand another chapter. A word or two, however, must be given to one among the earlier discoveries (October, 1846), and to one among the latest of those made (in the spring of 1851), whilst Mr. LAYARD himself remained in the neighbourhood of Mósul.

At Nimroud many trenches had, in those early days, been opened unprofitably. Mr. LAYARD doubted whether he ought to carry them further. Half inclined to cease, in this direction, he resolved, finally, that he would not abandon a cutting on which so much money and toil had been spent, until the result of yet another day's work was shown. 'I mounted my horse,' he says—to ride into Mósul—'but had scarcely left the mound when a corner of black marble was uncovered, lying on the very edge of the trench.' It was part of an obelisk seven feet high, lying about ten feet below the surface. Its top was cut into three gradines, covered with wedge-shaped inscriptions. Beneath the gradines were five tiers of sculpture in low-relief, continued on all sides. Between every two tiers of sculpture ran a line of inscription. Beneath the five tiers, the unsculptured surface was covered with inscriptions. These, as subsequent researches have shown, contain the Annals of SHALMANESER, King of Assyria, during thirty-one years towards the close of the ninth century before our Lord. The tribu-

Book III,
Chap. IV.
ANOTHER
GROUP OF
ARCHÆOLO-
GISTS AND
EXPLORERS.

DISCOVERY
OF THE
BLACK-
MARBLE
OBELISK,
1846,
October
(found in
centre of
the great
mound).

*Nineveh and
its Remains,*
vol. i, p. 345.
(1849 edit.)

Book III,
Chap. IV.
Another
Group of
Archæolo-
gists and
Explorers.

Ibid., 346.

taries of the great monarch are seen in long procession, bearing their offerings. In the appended cuneiform record of these tributaries are mentioned Jehu, ' of the House of Omri,' and his contemporary Hazael, King of Syria. Well may the proud discoverer call his trophy a ' precious relic.'

We now leap over more than four eventful years. Mr. Layard is about to exchange the often anxious but always glorious toils of the successful archæologist, for the not less anxious and very often exceedingly inglorious toils of the politician. He will also henceforth have to exchange many a pleasant morning ride and many a peaceful evening 'tobacco-parliament' with Arabs of the Desert, for turbulent discussions with metropolitan electors, and humble obeisances in order to win their sweet voices. Just before he leaves Mósul come some new unearthings of Assyrian sculpture, to add to the welcome tidings he will carry into England.

The dis-
coveries at
Kouyunjik
of the
spring of
1851.

He found, he tells us—in one of the closing chapters of his latest book—that to the north of the great centre-hall four new chambers, full of sculpture, had been discovered. On the walls of a grand gallery, ninety-six feet by twenty-three, was represented the return of an Assyrian army from a campaign in which they had won loads of spoil and a long array of prisoners. The captured fighting men wore a sort of Phrygian bonnet reversed, short tunics, and broad belts. The women had long tresses and fringed robes. Sometimes they rode on mules or were drawn—

*Discoveries
at Nineveh
and Babylon*
(edit. 1853),
pp. 582-584.

by men as well as by mules—in chariots. The captives were the men and women of Susiana. The victor was Sennacherib.

In several subsequent years—1853, 1854, 1855, when most Englishmen were intently acting, or beholding with suspended breath, the great drama in the Crimea—a famous compatriot was continuing the task so nobly initiated by Austen LAYARD. Sir Henry RAWLINSON (made by this time Consul-General at Baghdad) carried on new excavations, both at Nimroud and at Kouyunjik. In these he was ably assisted by Mr. W. K. LOFTUS, as well as by Mr. Hormuzd RASSAM, the helper and early friend of LAYARD, and (in the later stages) by Mr. TAYLOR. Another obelisk, with portions of a third and fourth; thirty-four slabs sculptured in low-relief; one statue in the round; and a multitude of smaller objects, illustrating with wonderful diversity and minuteness the manners and customs, the modes of life and of thought, as well as the wars and conquests, the luxury and the cruelty, of the old Assyrians, were among the treasures which, by the collective labour of these distinguished explorers, were sent into Britain. Another 'recension,' so to speak, of the early Annals of SENNACHERIB, King of Assyria, inscribed upon a cylinder, was not the least interesting of the monuments found under the direction of Sir Henry RAWLINSON, whose name had already won its station—many years before his consulship at Baghdad—beside those of GROTEFEND, of BURNOUF and of LASSEN, in the roll of those scientific investigators by whose closet labours the researches and long gropings of the RICHES, the BOTTAS, and the LAYARDS, were destined to be interpreted, illustrated, and fructified for the world of readers at large.

For it is not the least interesting fact in this particular and most richly-yielding field of Assyrian archæology—that several men in Germany;—more than one man in France;—and one man, at least, in Persia, had been working simultaneously, but entirely without concert, at those hard and, for a time, almost barren studies which were eventually to supply a master-key to vast libraries of inscriptions brought to light after an entombment of twenty-five hundred years.

Scarcely smaller than the debt of gratitude which Britain owes to Mr. LAYARD and to Lord STRATFORD DE REDCLIFFE, for the Marbles and other antiquities of Assyria, is the debt which she owes to the late Sir Charles FELLOWS for those of Lycia. Nor ought it to be passed over without remark that the admirably productive mission to the Levant of Mr. Charles NEWTON seems to have grown, in germ, out of the applications made at Constantinople on behalf of Sir Charles FELLOWS. In that merit he has but a very small share. The merit of the Lycian discoveries is all his own. He has now gone from amongst us,—like most of the benefactors whose public services have been recorded in this volume. How inadequate the record; how insufficient for the task the chronicler; no one will be so painfully conscious, as is the man whose hand—in the absence of a better hand—has here attempted the narrative. The Museum story has been long. What remains to be said must needs be put more briefly. But because Sir Charles FELLOWS has been so lately removed from the land he served with so much zeal and ability, I shall still venture to claim the indulgence of my readers for a somewhat detailed account of the work done in Lycia, and of the man who did it.

In one respect, it was with Charles FELLOWS as with Austen LAYARD. A youthful passion for foreign travel, and what grew out of that, lifted each of them from obscurity into prominence. But LAYARD achieved fame at a much earlier age than did Sir Charles FELLOWS. Sir Charles was almost forty before his name came at all before the Public. LAYARD was already a personage at eight and twenty. This small circumstantial difference between the fortune of two men whose pursuits in life were, for a time, so much alike, deserves to be kept in mind, on this account : Sir Charles lived scarcely long enough to see any fair appreciation of what he had accomplished. Even those whose political sympathies incline them to a belief that Mr. LAYARD's *official* services will never suffice to console Englishmen for the interruption of his archæological services, hope that he may live long enough to enjoy a rich reward for the latter in their yearly-increasing estimation by his countrymen at large. They will delight to see the fervid member for Southwark utterly eclipsed in the fame of the great discoverer of long-entombed Assyria.

BOOK III,
CHAP. IV.
ANOTHER
GROUP OF
ARCHÆOLO-
GISTS AND
EXPLORERS.

Sir Charles FELLOWS was the son of Mr. John FELLOWS, of Nottingham. He was born in 1799. In the year 1837, he set out upon a long tour in Asia Minor. Archæological discovery no more formed any part of a preconcerted plan in Mr. FELLOWS' case than it did, two or three years afterwards, in Mr. LAYARD's. Both were led to undertake their respective explorations in a way that (for want of a more appropriate word) we are all accustomed to call ' accidental.'

THE
TRAVELS IN
ASIA MINOR,
AND WHAT
GREW
THEREOUT.

In February, 1838, he found himself at Smyrna. After a good deal of observation of men and manners, he betook himself to an inspection of the buildings. He soon found that not a little of the modern Smyrna was built out of the ruins of the Smyrna of the old world. Busts, columns, entablatures, of white marble and of ancient workmanship, were everywhere visible, in close admixture with the recently-quarried building-stone of the country and the period. But not only had the old marbles been built into the new edifices ; they had been turned into tombstones.

*Journal
written
during an
Excursion in
Asia Minor,*
pp. 8, seqq.
(edit. 1852).

Book III,
Chap. IV.
Another
Group of
Archæolo-
gists and
Explorers.

Ibid., p. 9.

Certain Jews, of an enterprising and practical turn of mind, had bought, in block, a whole hill-full of venerable marbles, in order to have an inexhaustible supply of new tombstones close at hand.   In another part of the suburbs of the town, the walls of a large corn-field turned out, on close examination, to·be built of thin and flat stones, of which the inner surface was formed of richly-patterned mosaic, black, white, and red.   From that day, the traveller, wheresoever he journied, was a scrutinising archæologist.   And the traveller, thus equipped for his work, was busied, two months afterwards, in exploring that most interesting part of Asia Minor (a part now called 'Anadhouly'), which includes Lydia, Mysia, Bithynia, Phrygia, Pisidia, Lycia, Pamphylia, and Caria; and much of which was never before trodden— so far as is known, and the knowledge referred to is that of the best geographers in England, discussing this matter expressly, at a meeting of the Geographical Society—by the feet of any European.*

The ex-
plorations
in Anti-
phellus
and its
vicinity.
1838, April.

On the eighteenth of April, Mr. Fellows found himself in the romantically beautiful, but rugged and barren, neighbourhood of Antiphellus.   The ancient town of that name possessed a theatre, and a multitude of temples, grandly placed on a far-outjutting promontory.   For miles around, the rocks and the ravines were strewn with marble fragments.   The face of the cliff, which, on one side, overhangs the town, was seen to be deeply indented with rock-tombs, richly adorned.   They contained sarcophagi of a special

---

* And in which not a few readers will be sure to feel all the more interest, because of its sacred associations, when they call to mind those first-century travels of certain famous travellers who, 'after they had passed throughout Pisidia, came to Pamphylia, and . . . . . . when they had gone through Phrygia, . . . and were come to Mysia, assayed to go into Bythinia, but the Spirit suffered them not ;'—having work for them to do in another quarter.

form. The lid of each of them bore a rude resemblance to a pointed arch. It sounds at first almost grotesquely, in the ear of a reader of Mr. FELLOWS' *Journal* of 1839, to hear him speak of Lycian tombs as 'Elizabethan' in their architecture. But, in the sense intended, the term is strictly apposite. If the reader will but glance at one of Mr. FELLOWS' many beautiful plates of those rock-tombs, he will see at once that they look not unlike the stone-mullioned windows of our own Tudor age.

But the discovery which eclipsed all Mr. FELLOWS' previous researches was that of the ancient capital of Lycia —Xanthus. Next in importance to that was his disinterment of Tlos. He saw the ruins of other and, in their day, famous towns. It was plain that he had now before him a fine opening to add to the stores of human knowledge in some of its grandest departments—artistic, historical, biblical. But, in 1838, he had not the most ordinary appliances of minute research. He went back to England ; found (as LAYARD was also destined to find, very shortly afterwards) only a very little encouragement, at official hands ; much more than a little, however, in his own reflections and foresight. In 1839, he went back to Lycia, taking with him George SCHARF, then carefully described as 'a young English artist,' now widely known as an eminent archæologist. FELLOWS explored. SCHARF drew. Early in 1840, ten Lycian cities were added to the previous discoveries. Each of them contained many precious works of ancient art.

In order to effectual excavation, and in order also to the safety of what was found from destruction by Turkish barbarities, the Sultan's firman was essential. The difficulties were much like those which, as I have had occasion to show

Book III, Chap. VI. ANOTHER GROUP OF ARCHÆOLOGISTS AND EXPLORERS.

Journal of an Excursion, &c., as above, p. 164.

FURTHER DISCOVERIES IN THE VALLEY OF THE XANTHUS, AND IN OTHER PARTS OF LYCIA ; 1840-42.

in 'Book Second,' lay in the path of Lord Elgin, under similar circumstances, more than forty years earlier. By Lord Ponsonby's zealous efforts, they were at length sur-mounted. At the earnest instance of the Museum Trustees, the Government at home seconded the exertions of their ambassador at Constantinople; and this combination of endeavour made that feasible which the best energies of Sir Charles Fellows, single handed, must have utterly failed to secure.

The reader will not, I incline to think, regard as an instance of overmuch detail, if I here add—for instructive comparison with the terms of the official letter procured by Lord Elgin—the words in which Rifaat Pasha, in June, 1841, describes the antiquities, the removal whereof was to be graciously permitted. In 1800, Lord Elgin (after enormous labour) was empowered to 'take away any pieces of stone, from the Temples of the Idols, with old inscriptions or figures thereon.' Now—in 1841—the 'pieces of stone' are described as 'antique remains and rare objects.' The schoolmaster, it will be seen, had been at work at Constantinople.

The explorations at Cadyanda, at Pinara, and at Sidyma, richly merit the reader's attention, as an essential part of our present subject. But happily Sir Charles Fellows' books are both accessible and popular. Here we must hasten on to Xanthus, and Sir Charles' story must now be told in his own expressive and graphic words :

'Xanthus certainly possesses some of the earliest Archaic sculpture in Asia Minor, and this connected with the most beautiful of its monuments, and illustrated by the language of Lycia. These sculptures to which I refer must be the work of the sixth or seventh centuries before the Christian era, but I have not seen an instance of these remains having been despoiled for the rebuilding of walls ; and yet the decidedly more modern works of a later people are used as materials in repairing the walls around the back of the city and upon the Acropolis ; many of these have Greek inscriptions, with names common among the Romans. The whole of the sculpture is Greek, fine, bold, and simple, bespeaking an early age of that people.   No sign whatever is seen of the works of the Byzantines or Christians.

'To lay down a plan of the town is impossible, the whole being concealed by trees ; but walls of the finest kind, Cyclopean blended with the Greek, as well as the beautifully squared stones of a lighter kind, are seen in every direction ; several gateways also, with their paved roads, still exist.   I observed on my first visit that the temples have been very numerous, and, from their position along the brow of the cliff, must have combined with nature to form one of the most beautiful of cities.   The extent I now find is much greater than I had imagined, and its tombs extend over miles of country I had not before seen. The beautiful gothic-formed sarcophagus-tomb, with chariots and horses upon its roof, of which I have before spoken and have given a sketch of a battle-scene upon the side, accompanied with a Lycian inscription, is again a chief object of my admiration amidst the ruins of this city. Of the ends of this monument I did not before show drawings, but gave a full description.   Beneath the rocks, at the back of the city, is a sarcophagus of the same kind, and almost as beautifully sculptured ; but this has been thrown down, and the lid now lies half-buried in the earth. Its hog's-mane is sculptured with a spirited battle-scene. Many Greek inscriptions upon pedestals are built into the walls, which may throw some light upon the history of the city ; they are mostly funereal, and belong to an age and people quite distinct from those of the many fine Lycian remains.

'Two of my days have been spent in the tedious, but, I trust, useful occupation, of copying the Lycian inscription from the obelisk I mentioned in my former volume that I had seen: this will be of service to the philologist. Having, with the assistance of a ladder, ascended to a level with the top of the monument, I discovered a curious fact: the characters cut upon the upper portion are larger and wider apart than those on the lower, thus counteracting the effect of diminution by distance, as seen from the ground. As the letters are beautifully cut, I have taken several impressions from them, to obtain fac-similes. By this inscription I hope to fix the type of an alphabet, which will be much simplified, as I find upon the various tombs about the town great varieties, though of a trifling nature, in the forms of each letter; these varieties have hitherto been considered as different characters. This long public inscription will establish the form of all the letters of an alphabet, one form only being used throughout for each letter: if this should be deciphered, it may be the means of adding information to history. The inscription exceeds two hundred and fifty lines.

'It is to be regretted that the obelisk is not perfect; time or an earthquake has split off the upper part, which lies at its foot. Two sides of this portion only remain, with inscriptions which I could copy; the upper surface being without any, and the lower facing the ground: its weight of many tons rendered it immoveable. I had the earth excavated from the obelisk itself, and came to the base, or probably the upper part of a flight of steps, as in the other obelisk-monuments of a similar construction. The characters upon the north-west side are cut in a finer and bolder style than on the others, and appear to be the most ancient.   Should any difference of date occur on this monument, I should decide that this is the commencement or original inscription upon it.

'This, which I must consider as a very important monument, appears to have on the north-east side a portion of its inscription in the early Greek language; the letters are comparatively ill cut, and extremely difficult at such an elevation to decipher; seizing favourable opportunities for the light, I have done my best to copy it faithfully, and glean from it that the subject is funereal, and that it relates to a king of Lycia; the mode of inscription makes the monument itself speak, being written in the first person. Very near to this stands the monument, similar in form, which I described in my last Journal as being near the theatre, and upon which remained the singular bas-reliefs of which I gave sketches.   On closer examination I find these to be far more interesting and ancient than I had before deemed them.   They are in very low relief, resembling in that respect the Persepolitan or Egyptian bas-reliefs.

'I have received,' continues Sir Charles FELLOWS, 'from Mr. Benjamin GIBSON of Rome a letter in reference to these bas-reliefs: his interpretation of this mysterious subject appears far the best that I have yet heard; and from finding the district to have been in all probability the burial-place of the kings, it becomes the more interesting.   Mr. GIBSON writes—"The winged figures on the corners of the tomb you have discovered in Lycia, represented flying away with children, may with every probability be well supposed to have a reference to the story of the Harpies flying away with the daughters of King PANDARUS.   This fable we find related by HOMER in the *Odyssey*, lib. xx, where they are

BOOK III,
Chap. IV.
ANOTHER
GROUP OF
ARCHÆOLO-
GISTS AND
EXPLORERS.

stated to be left orphans, and the gods as endowing them with various gifts. Juno gives them prudence, Minerva instructs them in the art of the loom, Diana confers on them tallness of person, and lastly Venus flies up to Jupiter to provide becoming husbands for them; in the mean time, the orphans being thus left unprotected, the Harpies come and 'snatch the unguarded charge away.' STRABO tells us that PANDARUS was King of Lycia, and was worshipped particularly at Pinara. This tomb becomes thus very interesting; which, if it be not the tomb of PANDARUS, shows that the story was prevalent in Lycia, and that the great author of the *Iliad* derived it from that source. With this clue, we have no difficulty in recognising Juno on the peculiar chair assigned to that goddess, and on the same side is Venus and her attendants; upon another is probably represented Diana, recognised by the hound. The seated gods are less easily distinguished. In the Harpies, at the four corners of the tomb, we have the illustration of those beings as described by the classic writers." '

*Travels and
Researches in
Asia Minor,*
pp. 336-340.

MANY SUB-
SEQUENT
DISCOVE-
RIES; (THE
DETAILS
HERE NECES-
SARILY
PASSED
OVER).

Every lateral excursion made by Sir C. FELLOWS, and by his companions in travel, added to his collection rich works of sculpture, and not a few of them added many varied and most interesting minor antiquities. But I must needs resist all temptation to enlarge on that head, though the temptation is great. The twentieth and subsequent chapters of the book itself (I refer to the *collective* but abridged '*Travels and Researches in Asia Minor*' of 1852) will abundantly repay the reader who is disposed to turn to them—whether it be for a renewed or for a new reading.

THE DIFFI-
CULTIES OF
TRANSPORT.
Jan., 1842.

When the task of removal had to be undertaken, difficulties of transport were found, under certain then existing circumstances, to be graver obstacles than had been Turkish prejudice or Turkish apathy at an earlier stage of the business. The maritime part of the duty had been entrusted to Captain GRAVES, of H.M. Ship *Beacon*. The captain left his ship at Smyrna; sailed with FELLOWS for the Xanthus, in a steam-packet; but omitted to provide himself with the needful flat-bottomed boats. When they reached the site of the marbles which were to be carried away, Captain GRAVES said he would not have any of the stores taken down the river; that stores must be obtained from Malta; and that he would take all hands away from the diggings at the beginning of March. The reader may imagine the reflections of the eager discoverer at this sudden check,—coming, as it did, at the very beginning of the burst.

He took a solitary walk of many hours, he tells us, before he could resolve upon his course of action. He saw before him, to use his own words, 'a mine of treasure.' He had willing hands to work it; ample firmans to stave off opposition; nothing deficient save boats and tackle. A year might possibly pass in awaiting them from Malta; and, meanwhile, the ignorance of the peasantry, the indiscreet curiosity of travellers, or the sudden growth of political complications, might destroy the enterprise irrecoverably.

He resolved, in his perplexity, to construct by his own exertions tackle that would suffice for the removal to the coast; got native help in addition to the willing efforts—however unscientific—of the honest sailors of the *Beacon*; succeeded in getting a portion of the precious objects of his quest to the waterside, before the arrival of the ship; and got them also strongly cased up. Then he sailed with GRAVES for Malta. The worthy captain resigned the honourable task—to him so unwelcome—into the hands of Admiral Sir Edward OWEN. A new expedition started from Malta at the end of April, and brought away seventy-eight cases of sculpture in June; leaving the splendid but too-heavy 'winged-chariot-tomb' — so called by its discoverer in one place, and elsewhere called 'horse-tomb,' but since ascertained to be the tomb of a Lycian satrap named PAIAFA; it is adorned with figures of Glaucus, or perhaps of Sarpedon, in a four-horse chariot—until next year. The seventy-eight cases were brought to England by the Queen's ship *Cambridge* in the following December.

On the fourteenth of May, 1842, the Trustees of the British Museum thus recorded their sense of Mr. FELLOWS' public services:—'The Trustees desire to express their sense of Mr. FELLOWS' public spirit, in voluntarily undertaking to lend to so distant an expedition the assistance of his local knowledge and personal co-operation. They have viewed with great satisfaction the decision and energy evinced by Mr. FELLOWS in proceeding from Smyrna to Constantinople, and obtaining the necessary authority for the removal of the marbles; as well as his judicious directions at Xanthus, by which the most desirable of the valuable monuments of antiquity formerly brought to light by him, together with several others, of scarcely less interest, now for the first time discovered and excavated, have been placed in safety, and—as the Trustees have every reason to hope — secured for the National Museum.'

This hope was more than realised. It shows the energy of FELLOWS, that the expedition to Lycia of 1841 was his *third* expedition. In 1846 he made a fourth. It was rich in discovery; but I fear somewhat exhausting to the strength of the explorer. He lived a good many years, it is true, after his return to England; but how easily he yielded when a sudden attack of illness came, I shall have the pain of showing presently.

In the interval between his third and fourth journeys to Lycia, Fellows married a fellow-townswoman, Mary, the only daughter of Francis Hart, of Nottingham, but she survived the marriage only two years. A year after her death he married the widow of William Knight, of Oatlands, in Herts. On his final return from Lycia he was knighted, as a token (and it was but a slender one) of the public gratitude for his services. At the close of October, 1860, a sudden attack of pleurisy invaded a toilworn frame. On the eighth of the following month he died, at his house in Montagu Place, London, in the sixty-first year of his age.

Book III, Chap. IV. Another Group of Archæologists and Explorers.

Taken broadly, the sculptures of Lycia may be described as works which range, in date, from the sixth century before our Lord to almost as many centuries—if we take the minor antiquities into account—after the commencement of the Christian era. Some of them rank, therefore, amongst the earliest *original* monuments of Greek art which the British Museum possesses ; and date immediately after the *casts* of the sculptures of Selinus and of Ægina.

Date and character of the monuments in the 'Lycian Gallery.'

On some of the myths and on the habits of Lycian life there has been a sharp controversy, of the merits of which I am very incompetent to speak. Narrower and narrower as my limits are becoming, I yet feel it due to a public benefactor, who can no longer speak for himself otherwise than by his works, that in these waning pages he should be permitted to supply at least a part of his own explanatory comments upon the story of his discoveries. It is one of enchaining interest to the students of classical antiquity.

The famous ' Harpy Tomb,' thinks Sir Charles Fellows, is to be enumerated as among the most ancient of the remaining works of the ' Tramilæ,' or ' Termilæ,' mentioned both by HERODOTUS and by STEPHEN of Byzantium, as well as on the Xanthian obelisk or *stelè*, now called the 'Inscribed Monument,' and numbered '141' in the Lycian Gallery of the Museum.

Sir Charles FELLOWS proceeds to say that 'the shaft, frieze, and cap of this monument, weighing more than a hundred tons, has been by an earthquake moved upon its pedestal eighteen inches towards the north-east, throwing to the ground two stones of the frieze towards the south-west: in this state I found it in 1838. In 1841 the eight stones of this frieze were placed in the Museum. The only similar art which I know in Europe is in the Albani Villa near Rome. This slab is described by WINCKELMANN as being of earlier workmanship than that of Etruria. I shall not dwell upon these works, as they were found *in situ*, and will therefore be as well understood in England as if seen at Xanthus. I may draw attention to the blue, red, and other colours still remaining upon them. The subject also being that of the family of King PANDARUS, it should ever be borne in mind that this monument stood in the metropolis of Lycia, and within twelve miles of the city of Pinara, where we are told that PANDARUS was deified. This and the neighbouring tombs stood there prior to the building of the theatre, which is probably of Greek workmanship. The usual form of this structure must have been partially sacrificed on account of these monuments, as the seats rising in the circles above the diazoma have abruptly ceased on the western side, and have not been continued towards the proscenium. Near to one of the vomitories in the south-eastern bend of the diazoma is a similar monument to the Harpy Tomb, which has had the capstone and bas-reliefs removed, and the shaft built over by the theatre. Upon one of its sides is a short Lycian inscription, and a few words referring to its repair remain upon another side in the Greek character.

'Not far from these stands the inscribed stele, which is of the highest interest; of this, which is too heavy and too much mutilated to allow, without great labour, of its removal to the Museum, I have had casts taken in plaster. From my publications you would learn that a portion of the top of this [monument], weighing several tons, had been split off by the shocks of earthquakes: of this I have also had casts taken. In excavating around the monument on the south-west, and in the opposite direction to which the top had split off, I found the capstone had been thrown which had surmounted bas-reliefs; also two fragments of a bas-relief, but I think too high to have been placed upon this stele : they are the work of the same age, and are now placed in the Museum. The most important discovery here was of the upper angles broken from the monument, and having upon them the inscription on each side, thus perfecting, as far as they extend, the beginnings and ends of the upper lines of the inscription; these original stones I have brought home, being useless and insecure, if left in fragments with the monument. The exact form of the letters of the Greek portion of this inscription, compared with many others of which I shall speak, will do much to fix a date to these works.

'Upon the point of rock on the north-west side of the Acropolis is a fine Cyclopean basement, which has probably been surmounted by a similar monument to those of which I have spoken. No trace is found of any of its fragments; and from its position, shocks in the same direction as those which have destroyed the others would have thrown this down the perpendicular cliff into the river which flows about three hundred feet beneath.

' The masses of Cyclopean foundations traced around and upon the Acropolis, have been too much worked in, and converted to the use of an after people to ascertain their original form : they certainly have not been continuous, forming a wall or defence for the Acropolis; indeed, its natural position would render this superfluous, the cliffs on the south and west are inaccessible. I observe that most of the forms are referable to vast pedestals or stoas for large monuments; and from their individual positions at various elevations, and upon angles and points, I believe that the Acropolis has been covered with the ornamented monuments of this early people. The walls and basements of these separate buildings have since been united by strong lines formed of the old materials, the most ready for the purpose, and all put together with a very excellent cement, of which I have brought away specimens. A wall of this formation, facing the south-west, attracted my attention in 1838, by displaying some sculptured animals and chariots built as material into its front. This wall we have, with great labour, owing to the hardness of the cement, entirely removed; behind a portion of it we found a fine Cyclopean wall, which had slightly inclined over from the weight of earth behind; the casing which we have re-moved strengthened it, and, connecting the old buildings with others, formed a line of fortification, probably in Roman times. From the great size of the blocks used in constructing this wall, from the similarity of the stone, as well as from the sculpture traceable upon almost the whole of them, I conclude that they must have been the ruins of monuments in the immediate neighbourhood; basements for such are on either side. The works found here are entirely those of the early people; and I may extend this remark to all found upon the Acropolis. The architectural fragments, many specimens of which I bring away, are all Lycian, and would form monuments imitative of wooden constructions—beam-ends, ties, mortices, and cornices, similar to the tombs shown in the drawings, but double the size in point of scale to any now existing; bearing this in mind, I do not think it improbable that the sculptures representing a chariot procession have filled the panels on either side; should this be the case we have nearly the whole complete. The cornice and borders of these strongly corroborate this idea. We have four somewhat triangular stones, with sitting sphinxes upon each; these would complete the two gable ends in similar form and spirit of device to the generality of the tombs of this people. There is also an angle-stone, interesting from its sculpture, and from its style and subject blending these works with the age of the "Harpy-Tomb."

'To continue with the works of the early inhabitants: We must next notice the tombs at the foot of the rocky heights at the south-eastern parts of the city : of these the most beautiful are the kind having Gothic-formed tops ; these can be seen in the various drawings. The structure generally consists of a base or pedestal which has contained bodies, the *Platas,* surmounted by a plinth or solid mass of stone, which is often sculptured; above this is a sarcophagus, generally imitative of a wood-formed cabinet, the principal receptacle for the bodies, the *Soros;* upon this is placed a Gothic lid, sometimes highly ornamented with sculpture, which also served as a place of sepulture, probably the *Isostæ.* From one of these, in which the lower parts were cut out of the solid rock, and the top had fallen and been destroyed, I have had casts taken, as the subject is intimately connected with the frieze of the wild animals on the Acropolis. On this tomb, the inscription is cut in the language of the early people. Not far distant from this is a tomb which, from the sculpture upon it, I distinguish as the " Chimæra-Tomb." The lid of this, which I found in 1840, is perfect, but had been thrown to the ground by the effect of earthquakes; the chamber from off which it had slidden was inclining towards the lid; beneath the chamber a few stones forming the foundation and step (in the same block) are alone to be found. There is here no trace of the first two stories, and from the rock approaching the surface of the ground I found no depth of earth for research. Upon the chamber of this tomb is a Lycian inscription, of which I have casts, in order that they may be used in reconstructing the monument in the Museum. The other tomb of this character, and by far the most highly ornamented, was the tomb of PAIAFA, and I call it, from its sculpture, the " Winged-Chariot-Tomb." In finding this monument, in 1838, I observed that each part had been much shaken and split by earthquake, but no portion was wanting except a fragment from the north corner. This monument combines matters of great interest, showing in itself specimens of the architecture, sculpture, and language. I have stated that this style of monument is peculiar to Lycia; and I now add, from the knowledge derived from my research in that country, that Lycia contains none but these two of this ornamental description. These differ in minor points, making the possession of each highly desirable, and I am glad that these will be placed in our National Museum. The tombs of Telmessus, Antiphellus, and Limyra, are similar in construction, but have not the sculptured tops and other ornamental finishings seen in these.

' Upon the Acropolis, and fallen into a bath, we found a pedestal having sculptured upon the side a god and goddess

within a temple, in excellent preservation. On the opposite side of the pedestal is a very singular subject, which,
had not certain points both of execution, material, and
position occurred, I should have attributed to the Byzantine age. Amongst many other animals, the object of chase
to a hunter is seen much mutilated: this may have been
the representation of a novel idea of the Chimæra: the
hind quarters of a goat remain, with a snake for its tail.
It is greatly to be regretted that the other fragments could
not be found. On observing in the ground some very
ancient forms of the Greek letters, differing from all others
found so commonly here, cut upon a slab of marble, I had
it taken up, and was delighted to find that it was a pedestal,
with a Lycian inscription upon the other side ; this will be
valuable, as showing the form of the Greek characters in
use at the age of the language of Lycia. This same type
is seen in all the bilingual inscriptions, of which we have
only casts.

‘ Of another pedestal at Tlos I have taken casts, which will
be valued from the subjects of the bas-reliefs. The pedestal
of one stone was formed of two cubes, a small one upon
a larger. The fourth side of the upper one was not sculptured. One slab of the larger cube represents in bas-
relief a view of the Acropolis of Tlos, the Troas of these
early people : probably the hero whose deeds were by this
monument commemorated, and whose name occurs twice
upon it, was engaged in the defence or capture of the
city. At Tlos I also found cut in the rock of the Acropolis a tomb with an Ionic portico. Within this are represented a panelled and ornamented door, and several
sculptured devices and animals, as shown in the drawings
and plans. On the side, and within the portico, is a very
early bas-relief of Bellerophon upon Pegasus, and probably

Book III,
Chap. IV.
Another
Group of
Archæolo-
gists and
Explorers.

Note.—The
plans refer-
red to are
appended to
the first
edition of Sir
C. Fellows'
book.

a chimæra beneath the horse; but this portion of the sculpture is unfinished, and the rock beneath is left rough; the columns of the portico are only blocked out from the rock. Of the bas-relief of Bellerophon I have casts, and the full detail of the colouring which now remains upon the figures. This is probably the earliest sculpture which we have obtained. From Cadyanda I have casts of parts of a beautiful tomb, which is so much in ruins, and shaken into fragments, that I could not even take casts of the whole of the sculptures that remain. The roof or lid is wanting. The tomb now consists of a chamber in imitation of a wooden structure, and in the panels is sculpture; surmounting this is a smaller solid block, or plinth, also sculptured, but the upper part is wanting. These bas-reliefs, of which I show many drawings in my 'Lycia,' derive great additional interest from several of the figures having near them names inscribed in two languages—the Greek and the Lycian. The casts of these, I doubt not, will be valued as important illustrations. From Myra I have casts of the whole of the figures ornamenting one of the rock-tombs. Three of these subjects from within the Portico retain so much of their original painting that I have had the casts coloured on the spot as fac-similes, and a portion of the paint is preserved for chemical examination. There are from this tomb eleven figures the size of life. Of the inscriptions of this people I have made many copies; I have had casts of one long one from the large Gothic-formed tomb at Antiphellus, also of the bilingual inscription from the same place, and of another from Levisse, near the ancient Telmessus.

' Of the age of the next works of which I must speak, and which are a large portion of the collection from Xanthus, I have great difficulty in forming an opinion. The whole were found around a basement which stands on the edge of a cliff to the south-east of the ancient Acropolis. The monument which stood upon this stoa has been thrown down by earthquake, almost the whole of its ruins falling towards the north-west. These works are of a people quite distinct from the preceding, both in their architecture, sculpture, and language: these are purely Greek. On carefully examining the whole of the architectural members of which I have specimens selected (some retaining coloured patterns upon them), as well as the position in which each of the various parts were thrown, I have, in my own mind, reconstructed the building, the whole of which was of Parian marble, and highly finished. The monument which I suppose to have crowned this basement has been either a magnificent tomb, or a monument erected as a memorial of a great victory. In re-forming this, I require the whole of the parts that we have found, and none are wanting except two stones of the larger frieze, and the fragments of the statues. The art of this sculpture is Greek, but the subjects show many peculiarities and links to the earlier works found in Lycia. The frieze, representing the taking refuge within a city, and the sally out of its walls upon the besiegers, has many points of this character. The city represented is an ancient Lycian city, and has within its walls the stelé, or monument known alone in Xanthus. The city is upon a rock ; women are seen upon the walls. The costume of the men is a longer and thinner garment than is seen in the Attic Greeks. The shields of the chiefs are curtained. The saddle-cloth of the jaded horse entering the city is precisely like the one upon the Pegasus of Bellerophon, and the conqueror and judge is an Eastern chief, with the umbrella, the emblem of Oriental royalty, held over him. The body-guard and conquering party of the chief are

Book III,
Chap. IV.
Another
Group of
Archæolo-
gists and
Explorers.

Greek soldiers. Many of these peculiarities are also seen in the larger frieze, and also in the style of the lions and statues. The form of the building, which alone I can reconcile with the remains, is a Carian monument of the Ionic order. Bearing in mind all these points, I am strongly inclined to attribute this work to the mercenaries from Æolia and Ionia, brought down by HARPAGUS to conquer the inhabitants of Xanthus, whom they are said to have utterly destroyed. This monument may have been the tomb of a chief, or erected as a memorial of the conquest of the city by HARPAGUS. No inscription has been found, or it might probably have thrown some light upon the date of this work. In the immediate neighbourhood were found the other friezes, representing hunting-scenes, a battle, offerings of various kinds and by different nations, funeral feasts, and several statues which are of the same date.' Sir Charles then concludes thus :—

'The whole of the remaining works now to be traced amidst the ruins of Xanthus are decidedly of a late date; scarcely any are to be attributed to a period preceding the Christian era, and to that age I cannot conceive the works just noticed to have belonged. A triumphal arch or gateway of the city at the foot of the cliff of which I have spoken has upon it a Greek inscription, showing it to have been erected in the reign of VESPASIAN, *A.D.* 80 : from this arch are the metopes and triglyphs now in the Museum. Through this is a pavement of flagstones leading towards the theatre. To this age I should attribute the theatre, agora, and most of the buildings which I have called Greek, and which are marked red upon the plan. To this people belong the immense quantity of mosaic pavements which have existed in all parts of the city. Almost all the small pebbles in the fields are the débris of these works. In many

*Travels and
Researches in
Asia Minor,*
pp. 429, 430
1852).

places we have found patterns remaining which are of coarse execution, but Greek in design.'

The not a whit less interesting discoveries at Halicarnassus and elsewhere, made chiefly in the years 1856, 1857, and 1858, by Mr. Charles NEWTON, now claim attention, but my present notice of them can be but very inadequate to the worth of the subject. They as richly deserve a full record as do the explorations of LAYARD or those of FELLOWS.

The earliest, in arrival, of the Halicarnassian Marbles were procured by our Ambassador at Constantinople (then Sir Stratford CANNING, now) Lord STRATFORD DE REDCLIFFE. These first-received marbles comprise twelve slabs, sculptured with the combats of Greeks and Amazons in low-relief; and were removed from the walls of the mediæval castle of Budrum, in the year 1846, with the permission, of course, of the Sublime Porte. It is a tribute all the stronger to the energy of Lord STRATFORD to find another man of energy writing, in 1841: 'I would not have been a party to the asking what—to all who have seen them' (namely, the Marbles of Halicarnassus, built into the inner walls of Budrum Castle)—'must be considered as an unreasonable request.' It took, it is true, five years for Lord STRATFORD to overcome the obstacle which to Mr. FELLOWS seemed, in 1841, quite insuperable.

In 1856, and expressly in order to a thorough exploration of the site of Halicarnassus, and of other promising parts of the Levant, Mr. Charles NEWTON, then one of the ablest of the officers of the Department of Antiquities (whose loss at the Museum, even for three or four years, was not very easily replaceable), accepted the office of British Vice-Consul at Mitylene. In 1857, he discovered

BOOK III, Chap. IV.

ANOTHER GROUP OF ARCHÆOLOGISTS AND EXPLORERS.

THE MARBLES OF HALICARNASSUS, OF CNIDUS, AND OF BRANCHIDÆ.

Travels and Researches in Asia Minor, pp. 429, 430 (1852).

THE MISSION TO THE LEVANT OF MR. CHARLES NEWTON. 1856-58.

Book III,
Chap. IV.
Another
Group of
Archæolo-
gists and
Explorers.

four additional slabs (similar to those received from the Ambassador), on the site of the world-famous mausoleum itself; several colossal statues, and portions of such; together with a multitude of architectural fragments of almost every conceivable kind; columns—mostly broken into many portions—with their bases, capitals, and entablatures, in sufficient quantity and diversity to warrant a faithful restoration of the ancient building by a competent hand.

From Didyme (near Miletus), from Cnidus, and from Branchidæ, many fine archaic figures in the round; some colossal lions; and an enormous number of fragments both of sculpture and of architecture; with many minor antiquities, various in character and in material, were successively sent to England. Mr. Charles NEWTON's narrative of his adventures at Budrum, and at several of the other places of his sojourn and excavations, is very graphic. Some portions of it are worthy to be placed side by side with the best chapters of the earlier narrative of the explorations and travelling experiences of LAYARD.

Of the most famous trophy of Mr. NEWTON's first mission to the East—the mausoleum built by Queen ARTEMISIA— the discoverer has himself more recently given this brief and striking descriptive account :—

The tomb
of Mauso-
lus at
Halicar-
nassus.

This monument, writes Mr. NEWTON, in 1869, was erected 'to contain the remains of MAUSOLUS, Prince of Caria, about *B.C.* 352. It consisted of a lofty basement, on which stood an oblong Ionic edifice, surrounded by thirty-six Ionic columns, and surmounted by a pyramid of twenty-four steps. The whole structure, a hundred and forty feet in height, was crowned by a chariot-group in white marble, in which probably stood MAUSOLUS himself, represented after his translation to the world of demigods

Guide to the
Department
of Antiqui-
ties, &c.,
pp. 74, 75.

and heroes.   The peristyle edifice which supported the
pyramids was encircled by a frieze, richly sculptured in high-
relief,' and so on.   The frieze thus mentioned is that of
which the twelve slabs were, as already mentioned, given
by Lord STRATFORD DE REDCLIFFE in 1846, four exhumed
by NEWTON himself in 1857, and one more purchased from
the Marchese SERRA, of Genoa, in 1865.   This piecemeal
acquisition of the principal frieze, by dint of researches
spread over twenty years, is not the least curious of the facts
pertaining to the story.   But the annals of the Museum
comprise ten or twelve similar instances of ultimate reunion,
after long scattering, of the parts of one whole.   They tell of
manuscripts (made perfect after the lapse of a century, it
may be) as well as of sculptures, thus toilsomely recovered.

But the Greco-Amazonian battle-frieze was not the only
frieze of the famous mausoleum.   The external walls of the
' cella' had two other friezes, of which Mr. NEWTON succeeded in recovering several fragments, some of them of
much interest.   And the mausoleum was profusely adorned
with sculptures in the round as well as with the richly
carved figures in relief, both high and low, which encircled
(in all probability) the very basement, as well as the peristyle and the cella portions of this marvellous structure.
Lions in watchful attitudes (' lions guardant,' in heraldic
phrase) stood here and there, and the fragments of these
which have been recovered testify to their variety of scale,
as well as to their number.   The names of five famous
sculptors of the later Athenian school—SCOPAS, LEOCHARES,
BRYAXIS, TIMOTHEUS, PYTHIOS—who were employed upon
the decoration of the tomb itself, or upon the chariot-group,
have been recorded, and it would seem that each of four of
these had one side of the tomb specially assigned to him.
' The material of the sculpture was Parian marble, and the

whole structure was richly ornamented with colour. The tomb of MAUSOLUS was of the class called by the Greeks *heröon*, and so greatly excelled all other sepulchral monuments in size, beauty of design, and richness of decoration, that it was reckoned one of the " Seven Wonders of the World." '

While LAYARD was unearthing Nineveh; FELLOWS bringing into the light of day the long-lost cities of Lycia; and Charles NEWTON restoring, before men's eyes, this funereal marvel of the ancient world, which had long been known (in effect) only by dim memories and traditions; Dr. Nathan DAVIS, in his turn, was exhuming Carthage and Utica. All these distinguished men were labouring, in common, for the enrichment of our National Museum, within a period of some twenty years. Three of them may be said to have been busied (in one way or other) with their self-denying tasks contemporaneously.* If we take into the account the variety, as well as the intrinsic worth, of the additions thus made to human knowledge; above all, if we duly estimate the value of those links of connection

---

* I shall not, I trust, be suspected of a want of gratitude for the eminent and most praiseworthy efforts of Mr. Davis—one of the many Americans who have returned, with liberal profuseness, the reciprocal obligations which *all* Americans owe to Britain (for their ancestry, and also for the noble interchange of benefits between parent and offspring, prior to 1776; if for nought else), if I venture to remark that the above-written passage in the text has been inserted somewhat hesitatingly, as far as it concerns the *date* of the Carthaginian explorations. No index; no summary; no marginal dates; conflicting and obscure dates, when any dates appear anywhere; no introduction, which introduces anything; scarcely any divarication of personal knowledge and experiences, from borrowed knowledge and experiences; such are some of the difficulties which await the student of *Carthage and her Remains*. Yet the book is full of deep interest; its author is, none the less, a benefactor to Britain, and to the world.

between things human and things divine, which are the most essential characteristic of some of the best of these acquisitions, it may well be said that the annals of no museum in the world can boast of such an enrichment as this, by the efforts of the travellers and the archæologists of one generation.   And all of these explorers are—in one sense or other—Britons.

On one incidental point, I have to express a hope that the reader will pardon what he may be momentarily inclined to think an over-iteration of remark.   If I have really adverted somewhat too frequently to the connection which many of these rich archæological acquisitions, of 1842-1861, present between the annals of man and the Book of God, I have this to plead, in extenuation : Certain writers pass over that connection so hurriedly as almost to lose sight of it.   And we live in an age in which some of our own countrymen—some of those among us to whom the Creator has been most bounteous in the bestowal of the glorious gifts of mind and genius—have even spoken of our best of all literary possessions as 'Jew-Records,' and 'Hebrew old-clothes.'   Those particular expressions, indeed, were employed long before the arrival of the Assyrian Marbles.   But I think I have seen them quoted since.

Among the spoils of Carthage and of Utica which we owe to Dr. Nathan Davis, are many rich mosaic pavements, of the second and third centuries of our era, and a multitude of Phœnician and Carthaginian inscriptions, extending in date over several centuries.   And it must be added that many of the antiquities, and more especially of the mosaics, excavated under Dr. Davis's instructions at Utica, were found to possess greater beauty, and a more varied interest, than most of those which were disinterred by him from amidst the ruins of Carthage. Many of these, like some of the choice treasures of Nineveh, are, in a sense, still buried—for want of room at the British Museum adequately to display them. The reader may yet, but too fitly, conceive of some of them as piteously crying out (in 1870, as in 1860)—

> ' Here have ye piled us together, and left us in cruel confusion,
> Each one pressing his fellow, and each one shading his brother ;
> None in a fitting abode, in the life-giving play of the sunshine ;
> Here in disorder we lie, like desolate bones in a charnel.'

Many other liberal benefactors to the several Archæological Departments of the Museum deserve record in this chapter. But the record must needs be a mere catalogue, not a narrative; and even the catalogue will be an abridged one.

Foremost among the discoverers of valuable remains of Greek antiquity, subsequent to most of those which have now been detailed, are to be mentioned Mr. George Dennis, who explored Sicily in 1862 and subsequent years ; and Captain T. A. B. Spratt, who travelled over Lycia and the adjacent countries, following in the footsteps of Sir Charles Fellows, and who enjoyed the advantage of the company and co-operation of two able and estimable fellow-travellers, Edward Forbes and Edward Thomas Daniell, both of whom, like their honoured precursor in Lycian exploration, have been many years lost to us.

The antiquities collected in Sicily by Dennis, at the national cost, were chiefly from the tombs. They included very many beautiful Greek vases, a collection of archaic terra-cottas, and other minor antiquities.* Some of the

---

* These were given to the Museum by Lord Russell, as Secretary of State for Foreign Affairs. Lord Russell was one of the earliest of

marbles discovered by SPRATT are of the Macedonian period, and probably productions of the school of Pergamus.

At Camerus and elsewhere, in the island of Rhodes, important excavations were carried on by Messrs. BILIOTTI and SALZMANN. These also were effected at the public charge. In the course of them nearly three hundred tombs were opened, and many choicely painted fictile vases of the best period of Greek ceramography were found. Those researches at Rhodes were the work of the years 1862, 1863, and 1864. In 1865, the excavations at Halicarnassus were resumed by order of the Trustees, and under the direction of the same explorers, and with valuable results. In 1864, an important purchase of Greek and Roman statues, and of the sculptures from the Farnese Collection at Rome, was made. In the following year came an extensive series of antiquities from the famous Collection of the late Count POURTALÉS. Of the precious objects obtained by the researches of Mr. Consul WOOD, at Ephesus, in the same and subsequent years, a brief notice will be found in Chapter VI.

the Foreign Secretaries who began a new epoch, in this department of public duty, by setting new official precedents of regard and forethought for the augmentation of the national collections.

BOOK III, CHAP. IV. ANOTHER GROUP OF ARCHÆOLOGISTS AND EXPLORERS.

Reports of British Museum; 1864, and subsequent years.

CHAPTER V.

THE FOUNDER OF THE GRENVILLE LIBRARY.

> ' He was a scholar, and a ripe and good one,
> Exceeding wise, fairspoken, and persuading;
> Crabbed, mayhap, to them that loved him not;
> But to those men that sought him, sweet as Summer.'—
> *Henry VIII.*

> 'If a man be not permitted to change his political
> opinions—when he has arrived at years of discretion—he
> must be born a SOLOMON.'—
> W. F. HOOK, *Lives of the Archbishops of Canterbury*,
> (vol. viii, p. 237).

The GRENVILLES *and their Influence on the Political Aspect of the Georgian Reigns.—The Public and Literary Life of the Right Honourable Thomas* GRENVILLE.*— History of the* GRENVILLE *Library.*

IT was the singular fortune of Thomas GRENVILLE to belong to a family which has given almost half a score of ministers to England; to possess in himself large diplomatic ability; and to have been gifted—his political opponents themselves being judges—with considerable talents for administration; and yet, in the course of a life protracted to more than ninety years, to have been an *active* diplomatist during less than one year, and to have been a Minister of State less than half a year. It is true that he was of that happy temperament which both enables and tempts a man to carve out delightful occupation for himself. He had, too, those rarely combined gifts of taste, fortune, and public spirit, which inspire their possessor with the will, and confer upon him the power, to make his personal enjoyments largely contribute (both in his own time and after it) to the enjoyments of his fellow-countrymen. It might be true, therefore, to say that Thomas GRENVILLE was the happier and the better for his exclusion, during almost forty-nine-fiftieths of his long life, from the public service. But it can hardly be rash to say that England must needs have been somewhat the worse for that exclusion.

Nor was it altogether a self-imposed exclusion. There was among its causes a curious conjunction of outward accidents and of philosophic self-resignation to their results. Untoward chances abroad twice broke off the foreign embassies of this eminent man. Unforeseen political complications amongst Whigs and semi-Whigs twice deprived him of cabinet office at home. But, no doubt, neither shipwreck at sea nor party intrigue on land would have been potent enough to keep Thomas GRENVILLE out of high State employment, but for the personal fastidiousness which withheld him from stretching out his hand, with any eagerness, to grasp it.

It would, perhaps, be hard to lay the finger on any one family recorded in the ‘ *British Peerage*’ which so long and so largely influenced our political history, in the Georgian era of it, as did that of GRENVILLE. During the century (speaking roundly) which began with the suppression of the Jacobite Rebellion of 1745, and ended with the Repeal of the Corn Laws, GRENVILLES are continually prominent in every important political struggle. The personal influence and (for lack of a plainer word) the characteristic ‘ idiosyncrasy’ of individual GRENVILLES notoriously shaped, or materially helped to shape, several measures that have had world-wide results. But perhaps the most curious feature in their political history as a family is this: At almost every great

Book III,
Chap. V.
The
Founder
of the
Grenville
Library.

crisis in affairs one GRENVILLE, of ability and prominence, is seen in tolerably active opposition to the rest of the GRENVILLES. In the political history of the man who forms the subject of this brief memoir the family peculiarity, it will be seen, came out saliently.

The political GRENVILLES were offshoots of an old stock which, in the days of eld, were richer in gallant soldiers than in peace-loving publicists. The old GRENVILLES dealt many a shrewd swordthrust for England by land and by sea, in the Tudor times, and earlier. The younger branch has been rich in statesmen and rich in scholars. Not a few of them have shone equally and at once in either path of labour.

PARENTAGE
AND EARLY
LIFE OF
THOMAS
GRENVILLE.

Thomas GRENVILLE was the second son of the Minister of GEORGE THE THIRD, George GRENVILLE,—himself the second son of Richard GRENVILLE, of Wotton, and of Hester TEMPLE (co-heiress of Richard TEMPLE, Lord Cobham, and herself created Countess TEMPLE in 1749). He was born on the thirty-first of December, 1755, and entered Parliament soon after attaining his majority. In the House of Commons he voted and acted as a follower of Lord ROCK-INGHAM and a comrade of Charles Fox, in opposition to the other GRENVILLES and the 'Grenvillite' party. Had the famous India Bill of Fox's ministry been carried into a law, Thomas GRENVILLE, it was understood, would have been the first Governor-General of India under its rule.

HIS SHORT
DIPLOMATIC
CAREER.

His first entrance into the diplomatic service was made in 1782. His mission was to Paris. Its purpose, to negotiate with Benjamin FRANKLIN a treaty of peace with America. The circumstances beneath the influence of which it was undertaken I have had occasion to advert to,

See above,
Book II,
Chap. III,
page 431.

already, in the notice of Lord SHELBURNE. It is needless to return to them now.

Thomas GRENVILLE's union in the double negotiation with Mr. OSWALD (instructed by SHELBURNE, it will be remembered, as GRENVILLE was by Fox) proved to be very distasteful to him. From the beginning it boded ill to the success of the mission. As early as the 4th of June, 1782, we find Mr. GRENVILLE writing to Fox thus :—'I entreat you earnestly to see the impossibility of my assisting you under this contrariety. . . . . . I cannot fight a daily battle with Mr. OSWALD and his Secretary.* It would be neither for the advantage of the business, for your interest, or for your credit or mine ; and, even if it was, *I* could not do it.'

The then existing arrangements of the Secretaryship of State gave the control of a negotiation with *France* to one Secretary, and of a negotiation with *America* to the other. The reader has but to call to mind the well-known political relationship between Fox and SHELBURNE in 1782, to gain a fully sufficient key to the consequent diplomatic relationship between OSWALD and Thomas GRENVILLE, when thus engaged in carrying on, abreast, a double mission at the Court of Paris. To add to the obvious embroilment, OSWALD had shortly before received from Benjamin FRANKLIN a suggestion that Britain should 'spontaneously' cede Canada, in order to enable his astute countrymen at home the better to compensate both the plundered Royalists and those among the victorious opponents of those Royalists who had, from time to time, sustained any damage at the hands of the British armies.

The most earnest entreaties, from many quarters, were used to induce GRENVILLE to remain at Paris. His political friends, and his family connections, were, on that point, alike urgent. But all entreaties were in vain. When the

* Meaning Lord Shelburne. See, heretofore, pp. 431-433.

Book III,
Chap. V.
The
Founder
of the
Grenville
Library.

news reached him of Lord Rockingham's death, and of the break-up in the Cabinet which followed, his decision was, if possible, more decided.   He still clave to Fox, while his brother, Lord Temple, accepted from Shelburne the Lieutenancy of Ireland.   A Lordship of the Treasury or the Irish Secretaryship was by turns pressed upon Mr. Grenville by Lord Temple with an earnestness which

Lord Temple to T. Grenville, 12th July.

may be called passionate.   'Let me hope,' said he, 'that you will feel that satisfaction that every [other] member of my family most earnestly feels at my acceptance of the Lieutenancy of Ireland. . . . I conjure you, by everything that you prize nearest and dearest to your heart; by the joy I have ever felt in your welfare; by the interest I have ever taken in your uneasiness; weigh well your determination; it decides the complexion of my future hours. . . . . I have staked my happiness upon this cast.'   The resolve of Thomas Grenville to adhere to the position he had taken was the cause of a family estrangement which endured for many years.   But the more a reader, familiar with the annals of the time (and especially if he be also familiar with the personal history of Lord Temple before and after), may study Lord Temple's letters of 1782, the less he is likely to wonder that the peculiar line of argument they develope failed to attain the aim they had in view.   The vein that runs through them is plainly that of personal ambition; not of an adherence—at any cost—to a sincere conviction, whether right or wrong, of public duty. Such a line of argument was, at no time, the line likely to commend itself to Thomas Grenville.   Both his virtues, and what by many politicians will be regarded as his weaknesses, alike armed him against obvious appeals to mere self-interest or self-aggrandisement.

One result—and the not unanticipated result—of the family estrangement of 1782 was that, two years later, Mr. GRENVILLE found himself to have no longer the command of a seat in Parliament. For four years to come he gave most of his leisure to a pursuit which he loved much better—as far as personal taste was concerned—namely, to the resumption of his systematic studies in classical literature. But in 1790 he was elected a burgess for the town of Aldborough. Thenceforward, and for a good many years, politics again shared his time with literature, and with those social claims and duties to which no man of his day was more keenly alive.

In 1795 a second diplomatic mission was offered to him, and it was accepted. In the interval, another and more lasting change had come across his career in Parliament. He was one of the many 'Foxites' who utterly disapproved the course which their old leader adopted in regard to the French Revolution and to the rising passion to glorify and to imitate it at home. To the 'Man of the People' (as he was very fancifully called), the English countershock to the French overturn was, in one sense, specially fatal. It ripened peculiar, though hitherto in some degree latent, weaknesses. And with these, when they became salient, Thomas GRENVILLE had really as little fellow-feeling as had Edmund BURKE. Alike both men now supported PITT, with whom, as experience increased and judgment matured, they both had always had intrinsically far more in common. And among the results of the new political relationships came a restoration of family harmony. George GRENVILLE became PITT's Foreign Secretary; Thomas GRENVILLE became PITT's Minister to the Court of Berlin. One year later, he again sat in Parliament for Buckingham.

The mission to Berlin was first impeded by a threatened shipwreck among icebergs at sea, and, when that impediment had been with difficulty overcome, the journey was again and more seriously obstructed by an actual shipwreck upon the coast of Flanders. Mr. GRENVILLE's life was exposed to imminent danger. After a desperate effort, he succeeded in saving his despatches and in scrambling to land. But he saved nothing else; and the inevitable delay enabled the French Directory to send SIÈYES to Berlin, in advance of the ambassador of Britain. The able and versatile Frenchman made the best of his priority. Mr. GRENVILLE was not found wanting in exertion, any more than in ability. But in the then posture of affairs the advantage in point of time, proved to be an advantage which no skill of fence could afterwards recover. Hence it was that the mission of 1795 became practically an abortive mission. With it ended the ambassador's diplomatic career.

Almost equally brief was his subsequent actively official career in England. On the formation of Lord GRENVILLE's Cabinet (February, 1806), no office was taken by the Premier's next brother. But on the death of Fox, six months later, he became First Lord of the Admiralty. That office he held until the formation of the Tory Government, in the month of April, 1807. It was too brief a term to give him any adequate opportunity of really evincing his administrative powers. And during almost forty remaining years of life he never took office again, contenting himself with that now nominal function (conferred on him in the year 1800), the 'Chief-Justiceship in Eyre, to the south of the river Trent,' of the profits of which, as will be seen presently, he made a noble use. That office in Eyre had once been a function of real gravity and potency. It was still a surviving link between the feudal England of the Henrys and the Edwards, on the one hand, and the industrial England of the Georges on the other. Under a king who could govern, as well as reign, the 'Chief-Justiceship in Eyre' might have shown itself, in one particular, to possess a real and precious vitality still. By possibility, the sports of twelfth-century and chase-loving monarchs might have been made to alleviate the toils, to brighten the leisure, and to lengthen the lives, of nineteenth-century and hard-toiling artisans. For in exerting the still *legal* powers (long dormant, but not abolished) of the forest justiceship, a potent check might have been provided against the profligate, although now common, abuse of the powers entrusted by Parliament to the Board of Woods and Forests. No new legislation was wanted to save many splendid tracts of forest land (over which the Crown then—and as well in 1845, as in 1800—possessed what might have been indestructible ' forestal rights'), for public enjoyment for ever. Existing laws would have sufficed. But no blame on this score lies at the charge of the then Chief Justice in Eyre. Had Mr. GRENVILLE, for example, ever conceived the idea of using the Forest Laws to preserve for the English people, we will say, Epping Forest, or any other like sylvan tract on this side of Trent, as a 'People's Park' for ever, he would have been laughed at as a Quixote. If Parliament in 1870 is fast becoming alive to the misconduct of those ' Commissioners' who have dealt with the Forestal rights of the Crown exactly in the spirit of the pettiest of village shopkeepers, rather than in the spirit of Ministers of State, there was in Mr. GRENVILLE's time scarcely the faintest whisper of any such conviction of public duty in regard to that matter. Not one Member of Parliament, I think, had ever (at that time) pointed out the gross hypocrisy, as well

BOOK III,
Chap. V.
THE
FOUNDER
OF THE
GRENVILLE
LIBRARY.

THE CHIEF
JUSTICESHIP
IN EYRE,
AND WHAT
MIGHT HAVE
COME OF ITS
PERPETUA-
TION.

as the folly, of *selling* by the hands of one public board and for a few pounds hundreds of acres of ancient and lovely woodlands, and then presently *buying*, by the hands of another public board, acres of dreary and almost unimproveable barrenness by the expenditure of several thousands of pounds, in order to provide new recreation grounds for ' public enjoyment !'

Of that forestal Chief-Justiceship Mr. GRENVILLE was the last holder. The office had been established by WILLIAM THE CONQUEROR. It was abolished by Queen VICTORIA. One of the chief pursuits of those forty years of retirement which ensued to the founder of the Grenville Library, upon the breaking up of the Grenville Administration of 1806, was book-buying and book-reading. ' A great part of my Library'—so wrote Mr. GRENVILLE, in 1845—'has been purchased by the profits of a sinecure office given me by the Public.' If that sinecure was not and, under the then circumstances, could not have been by its holder's action or foresight, made the means of preserving for public enjoyment such of the ancient forests as, early in this century, were still intact in beauty, and also lay near to crowded and more or less unhealthy towns, it was at least made the means of giving to the nation a garden for the mind. ' I feel it,' continued Mr. GRENVILLE, in his document of 1845, ' to be a debt and a duty that I should acknowledge my obligation by giving the Library so acquired to the BRITISH MUSEUM for the use of the Public.'

I have had occasion, already, to mention that many years before his death Mr. GRENVILLE formed a very high estimate of the eminent attainments and still more eminent public services of Sir A. PANIZZI. No man had a better opportunity of knowing, intimately, the merits of the then

Assistant-Keeper of the printed portion of our National Library. Mr. GRENVILLE showed his estimate in a conclusive and very characteristic way. He had earnestly supported (in the year 1835) the proposal of a Sub-committee of Trustees that Mr. PANIZZI's early services—more especially in relation to the cataloguing of what are known, at the Museum, as 'the French Tracts,' but also as to other labours—should be substantially recognised by an improvement of his salary. At a larger meeting, the recommendation of the smaller sub-committee was cordially adopted in the honorary point of view, but was set virtually aside, in respect to the 'honorarium.' That latter step Mr. GRENVILLE so resented that he rose from the table, and never sat at a Trustee meeting again. He many times afterwards visited the Museum; and I well remember the impression made upon my own mind by his noble appearance, at almost ninety years of age, on one of the latest of those visits—not very long before his death. But in the Committee Room he never once sat, during the last eleven years of his life.

The fact being so, Readers unfamiliar with the 'blue-books' will learn without surprise that a conversation between Mr. GRENVILLE and Mr. PANIZZI, in Hamilton Place, was the prelude to his noble public gift of 1846. That conversation took place in the autumn of 1845. He, in the course of it, assured Mr. PANIZZI (by that time at the head of the Printed Book Department) of his settled purpose, and evinced a desire that his Library should be preserved apart from the mass of the National Collection. He then remarked, 'You will have a great many duplicate books, and you will sell them,' speaking in a tone of inquiry. 'No,' replied PANIZZI, the 'Trustees will never sell books that are given to them.' Mr. GRENVILLE rejoined with an

BOOK III, Chap. V. THE FOUNDER OF THE GRENVILLE LIBRARY.

Minutes of Inquiry, &c., 1818, and subsequent years, pp.141, seqq.

Minutes of Evidence, as above.

CIRCUMSTANCES WHICH MARKED THE GIFT TO THE NATION OF THE GRENVILLE LIBRARY.

Ibid.; and comp. p. 780 of the *Minutes* of 1849.

BOOK III,
Chap. V.
THE
FOUNDER
OF THE
GRENVILLE
LIBRARY.

See the
Plan, here-
after.

evident relief of mind, ‘Well, so much the better.’ Long afterwards, when visiting Mr. PANIZZI in his private study, he asked the question—‘Where are you going to put my books? I see your rooms are already full.’ He was taken to the long, capacious, but certainly not very sightly, ‘slip,’ contrived by Sir R. SMIRKE on the eastern outskirt of the noble King’s Library. ‘Well,’ was the Keeper’s reply, ‘if we can’t do better, we will put them *here*; and, as you see, my room is close by. Here, for a time, they will at least be under my own eye.’ The good and generous book-lover went away with a smile on his genial face, well assured that his books would be gratefully cared for.

THE RECEP-
TION AT THE
MUSEUM
OF THE
GRENVILLE
COLLECTION.

Mr. GRENVILLE died on the 17th of December, 1846. On the day of his death it chanced that the present writer was engaged on a review-article about the history of the Museum Library. Ere many days were past it was his pleasant task to add a paragraph—the first that was written on the subject—respecting the new gift to the Public. But an accident delayed the publication of that article until the following summer.

Meanwhile, the final day of the reception of the books—a dreary, snowy day of the close of February—was, to us of the Museum Library, a sort of holiday within-doors. Very little work was done that day; but many choice rarities in literature, and some in art, were eagerly examined. All who survive will remember it as I do. To lovers of books, such a day was like a glimpse of summer sunshine interposed in the thick of winter.

To tell what little can here be told of the history and character of the Grenville Library in other words than in those well-considered and appropriate words which were employed by the man who had had so much delightful intercourse with the Collector himself, and to whom belongs a part of the merit of the gift, would be an impertinence. In his report on the accessions of the year 1847, Mr. PANIZZI wrote thus:—'It would naturally be expected that one of the editors of the "Adelphi *Homer*" would lose no opportunity of collecting the best and rarest editions of the Prince of Poets. Æsop, a favourite author of Mr. GREN-VILLE, occurs in his Library in its rarest forms; there is no doubt that the series of editions of this author in that Library is unrivalled. The great admiration which Mr. GRENVILLE felt for Cardinal XIMENES, even more on account of the splendid edition of the Polyglot *Bible* which that prelate caused to be printed at Alcala, than of his public character, made him look upon the acquisition of the *Moschus*, a book of extreme rarity, as a piece of good fortune. Among the extremely rare editions of the Latin Classics, in which the Grenville Library abounds, the unique complete copy of AZZOGUIDI's first edition of *Ovid* is a gem well deserving particular notice, and was considered on the whole, by Mr. GRENVILLE himself, the boast of his collection. The Aldine *Virgil* of 1505, the rarest of the Aldine editions of this poet, is the more welcome to the Museum as it serves to supply a lacuna; the copy mentioned in the Catalogue of the Royal Collection not having been transferred to the National Library.

'The rarest editions of English Poets claimed and obtained the special attention of Mr. GRENVILLE. Hence we find him possessing not only the first and second edition of CHAUCER's *Canterbury Tales* by CAXTON, but the only copy known of an hitherto undiscovered edition of the same work printed in 1498, by WYNKYN DE WORDE. Of SHAKESPEARE's collected Dramatic Works, the Grenville

Library contains a copy of the first edition, which, if not the finest known, is at all events surpassed by none. His strong religious feelings and his sincere attachment to the Established Church, as well as his knowledge and mastery of the English language, concurred in making him eager to possess the earliest as well as the rarest editions of the translations of the Scriptures in the vernacular tongue. He succeeded to a great extent; but what deserves particular mention is the only known fragment of the *New Testament* in English, translated by TYNDALE and ROY, which was in the press of QUENTELL, at Cologne, in 1525, when the translators were obliged to interrupt the printing, and fly to escape persecution.

'The History of the British Empire, and whatever could illustrate any of its different portions, were the subject of Mr. GRENVILLE'S unremitting research, and he allowed nothing to escape him deserving to be preserved, however rare and expensive. Hence his collection of works on the Divorce of HENRY VIII; that of Voyages and Travels, either by Englishmen, or to countries at some time more or less connected with England, or possessed by her; that of contemporary works on the gathering, advance, and defeat of the "Invincible Armada;" and that of writings on Ireland;—are more numerous, more valuable, and more interesting, than in any other collection ever made by any person on the same subjects. Among the Voyages and Travels, the collections of DE BRY and HULSIUS are the finest in the world; no other Library can boast of four such fine books as the copies of HARIOT'S *Virginia*, in Latin, German, French, and English, of the DE BRY series. And it was fitting that in Mr. GRENVILLE'S Library should be found one of the only two copies known of the first edition of this work, printed in London in 1588, wherein an account is given of a colony which had been founded by his family namesake, Sir Richard GRENVILLE.

'Conversant with the Language and Literature of Spain, as well as with that of Italy, the works of imagination by writers of those two countries are better represented in his Library than in any other out of Spain and Italy; in some branches better even than in any single Library in the countries themselves. No Italian collection can boast of such a splendid series of early editions of ARIOSTO's *Orlando*, one of Mr. GRENVILLE's favourite authors, nor, indeed, of such choice Romance Poems. The copy of the first edition of ARIOSTO is not to be matched for beauty; of that of Rome, 1533, even the existence was hitherto unknown. A perfect copy of the first complete edition of the *Morgante Maggiore*, of 1482, was also not known to exist before Mr. GRENVILLE succeeded in procuring his. Among the Spanish Romances, the copy of that of *Tirant lo Blanch*, printed at Valencia, in 1490, is as fine, as clean, and as white, as when it first issued from the press; and no second copy of this edition of a work professedly translated from English into Portuguese, and thence into Valencian, is known to exist except in the Library of the Sapienza, at Rome.

'But where there is nothing common, it is almost depreciating a collection to enumerate a few articles as rare. It is a marked feature of this Library, that Mr. GRENVILLE did not collect mere bibliographical rarities. He never aimed at having a complete set of the editions from the press of CAXTON or ALDUS; but *Chaucer* and *Gower* by CAXTON were readily purchased, as well as other works which were desirable on other accounts, besides that of having issued from the press of that printer; and, when possible, select copies were procured. Some of the rarest, and these the finest, Aldine editions were purchased by him, for the same reasons. The *Horæ* in Greek, printed by ALDUS in 16°, in 1497, is a volume which, from its language, size, and rarity, is of the greatest importance for the literary and religious history of the time when it was printed. It is therefore in Mr. GRENVILLE's Library. The *Virgil* of 1501 is not only an elegant book, but it is the first book printed with that peculiar *Italic*, known as Aldine, and the first volume which ALDUS printed, "*forma enchiridii*," as he called it, being expressly adapted to give poor scholars the means of purchasing for a small sum the works of the classical writers. This also is, therefore, among Mr. GRENVILLE's books; and of one of the two editions of *Virgil*, both dated the same year, 1514, he purchased a large paper copy, because it was the more correct of the two.

'It was the merit of the work, the elegance of the volume, the "genuine" condition of the copy, &c., which together determined Mr. GRENVILLE to purchase books printed on vellum, of which he collected nearly a hundred. He paid a very large sum for a copy of the Furioso of 1532, not because it was "on ugly vellum," as he very properly designated it, but because, knowing the importance of such an edition of such a work, and never having succeeded in procuring it on paper, he would rather have it on expensive terms and "ugly vellum," than not at all.

'By the bequest of Mr. GRENVILLE's Library, the collection of books printed on vellum now at the Museum, and comprising those formerly presented by GEORGE II, GEORGE III, and Mr. CRACHERODE, is believed to surpass that of any other National Library, except the King's Library at Paris, of which VAN PRAET justly speaks with pride, and all foreign competent and intelligent judges with envy and admiration. In justice to the Grenville Library, the list of all its vellum books ought to be here inserted.   As this cannot be done, some only of the most remarkable shall be mentioned.   These are—the Greek *Anthology* of 1494; the *Book of Hawking* of JULIANA BERNERS of 1496; the first edition of the *Bible*, known as the " Mazarine Bible," printed at Mentz about 1454; the Aldine *Dante* of 1502; the first *Rationale* of DU-RANDUS of 1459; the first edition of FISHER *On the Psalms*, of 1508; the Aldine *Horace, Juvenal, Martial*, and *Petrarca*, of 1501; the *Livy* of 1469; the *Primer of Salisbury*, printed in Paris in 1531; the *Psalter* of 1457, which supplies the place of the one now at Windsor, which belonged to the Royal Collection before it was transferred to the British Museum; the *Sforziada*, by SIMONETA, of 1490, a most splendid volume even in so splendid a Library; the *Theuerdank* of 1517; the *Aulus Gellius* and the *Vitruvius* of Giunta, printed in 1515, &c. &c.   Of this identical copy of *Vitrivius*, formerly Mr. DENT's, the author of the *Biblio-graphical Decameron* wrote, " Let the enthusiastic admirers of a genuine vellum Junta—of the amplest size and in spotless condition—resort to the choice cabinet of Mr. DENT for such a copy of this edition of Vitruvius and Frontinus." The *Aulus Gellius* is in its original state, exactly as it was when presented to LORENZO DE' MEDICI, afterwards Duke of Urbino, to whom the edition was dedicated.'

CHAPTER VI.

OTHER BENEFACTORS OF RECENT DAYS.— CREATION OF THE NEW DEPARTMENT OF BRITISH AND MEDIÆVAL ANTIQUITIES AND ETHNOGRAPHY.

> 'Amidst tablets and stones, inscribed with the straight
> and angular characters of the Runic alphabet, and similar
> articles which the vulgar might have connected with the
> exercise of the forbidden arts, ... were disposed, in
> great order, several of those curious stone axes, formed of
> green granite, which are often found in these Islands. . .
> . . . There were, moreover, to be seen amid the strange
> collection stone sacrificial knives . . . and the brazen
> implements called Celts, the purpose of which has troubled
> the repose of so many antiquaries.'—*The Pirate*, c. xxviii.

> 'A Museum of Antiquities—not of one People or period
> only, but of all races and all times—exhibits a vast com-
> parative scheme of the material productions of man. We
> are thus enabled to follow the progress of the Fine and
> Useful Arts, contemporaneously through a long period of
> time, tracing their several lines backwards till they con-
> verge at one vanishing point of the unknown Past.'—
> C. T. NEWTON (*Letter to Col. Mure*, 1853).

*Scantiness of the Notices of some Contributors to the Natural-
History Collections, and its cause.—The Duke of
BLACAS and his Museum of Greek and Roman Anti-
quities.—Hugh CUMING and his Travels and Collections
in South America.—John RUTTER CHORLEY, and his
Collection of Spanish Plays and Spanish Poetry.—
George WITT and his Collections illustrative of the
History of Obscure Superstitions.—The Ethnographical
Museum of Henry CHRISTY, and its History.—Colonial
Archæologists and British Consuls: The History of the
WOODHOUSE Collection, and of its transmittal to the*

British Museum.—Lord Napier *and the acquisition of the Abyssinian MSS. added in* 1868.—*The Travels of* Von Siebold *in Japan, and the gathering of his Japanese Library.—Felix* Slade *and his Bequests, Artistic and Archæological.*

No reader of this volume will, in the course of its perusal, have become more sensible than is its author of a want of due *proportion*, in those notices which have occasionally been given of some eminent naturalists who have conspicuously contributed to the public collections, as compared with the notices of those many archæologists and book-gatherers who, in common with the naturalists, have been fellow-workers towards the building up of our National Museum.   I feel, too, that my own ignorance of natural history is no excuse at all for so imperfect a filling-out of the plan which the title-page itself of this volume implies. I feel this all the more strongly, because I dissent entirely from those views which tend to depreciate the importance of the scientific collections, in order (very superfluously) to enhance that of the literary and artistic collections.   Far from looking at the splendid Galleries of mammals, or of birds, or of plants, as mere collections of 'book-plates,' gathered for the 'illustration' of the National Library, or from sharing the opinion that the books and the antiquities, alone, are 'what may be called the permanent departments of the British Museum' (to quote, literally, the words of a publication* issued whilst this sheet is going to press, words which seem somewhat rashly—considering whence they come—to prejudge a question of national scope, and one which it assuredly belongs alone *to Parliament* to settle),

* *A Handy-Book of the British Museum, for Every-day Readers.'* 1870 (Cassell and Co.).

I regard these scientific collections as possessing, in common with the others, the highest educational value, and as also possessing, even a little beyond some of the others, a special claim, it may be, upon the respect of Englishmen.

That speciality of claim seems to me to accrue from the fact, that two of the early FOUNDERS, and one of the most conspicuous subsequent BENEFACTORS of the Museum, were pre-eminently Naturalists. Such was COURTEN. Such was SLOANE. Such was Sir Joseph BANKS. I shall have erred greatly in my estimate of the regard habitually paid by a British Parliament to the memory of the eminent benefactors of Britain, if, in the issue, it do not become apparent that such a consideration as this will weigh heavily with those who will shortly—and after due deliberation and debate—have to decide pending questions in relation to the enlargement and to the still further improvement of the British Museum.

Be that however as it ultimately shall prove to be, if the Public should honour this volume with a favourable reception, it will be its author's endeavour (in a second edition) to supplement, by the knowledge and co-operation of others, the ignorance and the deficiencies of which he is very conscious in himself.

In resuming the notices connected with the now truly magnificent Collection of Antiquities, we have to glance at the organizing of a new 'Department' in the Museum. During at least two generations it has been, from time to time, remarked—with some surprise as well as censure—that the 'British' Museum contained no 'British' Antiquities. Sometimes this criticism has been put much too strongly, as when, for example, one of the recent biographers of WEDGWOOD thus wrote (in 1866, but referring also to a period then ninety years distant). ' At that date, *as at present*, everything native to the soil, or produced by the races who had lived and died upon it, was repudiated by those who were the rulers of the National Collection.' At that time, assuredly, there were already in the Museum a good many British beasts, British birds, and British books;—no inconsiderable part of the ' productions' of our soil and of the races born and nurtured upon it.

But, within a few months after the appearance of the criticism I have quoted, all ground for its repetition was removed by the formation of the ' Department of British and Mediæval Antiquities and Ethnography.' It is thus organized, in six separate sections :—

§ I. British Antiquities anterior to the Roman period.
II. Roman Antiquities found in Britain.
III. Anglo-Saxon Antiquities.
IV. Mediæval sculpture, carving, paintings, metal work, enamels, pottery, glass, stone ware; and implements of various kinds, and of various material.
V. Costumes, weapons, accoutrements, tools, furniture, industrial productions, &c.—both ancient and modern—of non-European races.
VI. Pre-historic Antiquities.*

To the enrichment of the fourth section of this new department of the Museum (in a small degree), as well as (much more largely) to that of the Classical Collections, the choice treasures gathered in France during two generations by successive Dukes of BLACAS largely contributed.

The first of these Dukes, Peter Lewis John Casimir de BLACAS, was born at Aulps in the year 1770. He was of a family which has been conspicuous in Provence from the beginning of the Crusades. Attaining manhood just at the eve of the Revolution, the Duke followed the French princes into

Book III,
Chap. VI.
OTHER
BENEFAC-
TORS OF
RECENT
DAYS.

Meteyard,
*Life of Josiah
Wedgwood,*
vol. ii, p. 162.

* See the notice, hereafter, of the Christy Museum.

THE BLACAS
MUSEUM
AND ITS
FOUNDERS,
1815-1860.

exile, and warmly attached himself to LEWIS THE EIGH-
TEENTH, to whom, in after years, he became the minister of
predilection, as distinguished from that monarch's many
ministers of constraint. He had, in his own day, the
reputation of being a courtier; but seems to have been, in
truth, an honest, frank, and outspeaking adviser. One
saying of his depicts quite plainly the nature of the man,
and also the nature of the work he had to do :—" If you want
to defend your Crown, you musn't run away from your
Kingdom.' Those words were spoken in 1815 ; and, as we
all know, were spoken in vain.

A statesman of that stamp—one who does *not* watch and
chronicle the shiftings of popular opinion, in order to know
with certainty what are his own opinions, or in order to
shape his own political 'principles'—rarely enjoys popularity. DE BLACAS became so little popular at home, that
the King was forced to send him, for many years, abroad.
At Rome, he negotiated the Concordat (1817-19); at
Naples, he advised an amnesty (1822), together with other
measures, some of which were too wise for the latitude. In
the interval between his two residences at the Court of
Naples, he took part in the Congress of Laybach.

The opportunities afforded by diplomacy in Italy and in
other countries were turned to intellectual and archæological, as well as to political, account. He imitated the
example of HAMILTON and of ELGIN, and that of a crowd
of his own countrymen, long anterior to either. Since his
son's death, the British Museum has, by purchase, entered
into his archæological labours almost as largely—in their
way and measure—as it has inherited the treasures of its
own enlightened ambassadors at Naples and at Constantinople.

The Duke died at Goeritz in 1839. Nine years earlier,

he had advised CHARLES X against the measures which precipitated that king into ruin; and when the obstinate monarch had to pay the sure penalty of neglecting good advice, the giver of it voluntarily took his share of the infliction. He offered to attend CHARLES into exile in 1830, as he had attended him forty years before, when in the flush of youth. He lies buried at the King's feet, in the Church of the Franciscans at Goeritz—

> ' He that can endure
> To follow, in exile, his fallen Lord,
> Doth conquer them that did his master conquer,
> And earns his place i' the story.'

The late Duke of BLACAS augmented his father's collections by many purchases of great extent and value. His special predilection was for coins and gems. In that department the combined museum of father and son soon came to rank as the finest known collection, belonging to an individual possessor. It includes seven hundred and forty-eight ancient and classical cameos and intaglios, and two hundred and three others which are either mediæval, oriental, or modern. The most precious portion of the STROZZI cabinet passed into it, as did also a choice part of the collections, respectively, of BARTH and of DE LA TURBIE. The Blacas Museum is also eminently rich in vases and paintings of various kinds; in sculptures, on every variety of material; in terracottas, and in ancient glass. Its ' silver toilet service' of a Christian Roman lady of the fifth century, named PROJECTA, has been made famous throughout Europe by the descriptive accounts which have appeared from the pen of VISCONTI and from that of LABARTE. The casket is richly chased with figure-subjects. Among them are seen figures of Venus and Cupid; of the lady herself and of her bridegroom, SECUNDUS. Roman bridesmaids, of

BOOK III,
Chap. VI.
OTHER
BENEFAC-
TORS OF
RECENT
DAYS.

HUGH
CUMING; HIS
TRAVELS
AND HIS
COLLEC-
TIONS, IN
AMERICA
AND ELSE-
WHERE.
1791.

See page 376.

indubitable flesh and blood, are mingled with the more unsubstantial forms of Nereids, riding upon Tritons.

Of the men devoted, in our own day, to the enchaining pursuits of Natural History, few better deserve a competent biographer than does Hugh CUMING, whose career, in its relation to the Museum history, has an additional interest for us from the circumstance that his course in life was partly shaped by his having attracted, in childhood, the notice of another worthy naturalist and public benefactor, Colonel George MONTAGU, of Lackham.

Young CUMING's childish fondness for picking up shells and gathering plants attracted Colonel MONTAGU's notice about the time that the boy was apprenticed to a sailmaker, living not far from the boy's native village, West Alvington, in Devon. The elder naturalist fostered the nascent passion of his young and humble imitator, and the trade of sailmaking brought CUMING, whilst still a boy, into contact with sailors. The benevolent and Nature-loving Colonel told the youngster some of the fairy tales of science; the tars spun yarns for him about the marvels of foreign parts. A few, and very few, years of work at his trade at home were followed by a voyage to South America. At Valparaiso he resumed his handicraft, but only as a step (by aid of frugality and foresight) towards saving enough of money to enable him to devote his whole being to conchology and to botany. Seven years of work under this inspiring ambition, seem to have enabled the man of five-and-thirty to retire from business, and to build himself a yacht. But his was to be no lounging yachtman's life; it was rather to resemble the life of an A.B. before the mast. The year 1827 was spent in toiling and dredging, to good purpose, amongst the islands of the South Pacific. When he returned to Valparaiso, the retired sailmaker found that he had won fame, as well as many precious rarities in conchology and botany. The Chilian Government gave him special privileges and useful credentials. He then devoted two years to the thorough exploration of the coasts extending from Chiloë to the Gulf of Conchagua. He botanized in plains, marshes and woods; he turned over shingle, and explored the crannies of the cliffs, with the patient endurance of a Californian gold-digger, and was much happier in his companions. In 1831, he returned to England, with a modest but assured livelihood, and with inexhaustible treasures in shells and plants, of which multitudes were theretofore unseen and unknown in Europe.

The year 1831 was a happy epoch for a conchologist. The Zoological Society had just gained a firm footing. BRODERIP and SOWERBY were ready to exhibit and to describe the rich shells of the Pacific. Richard OWEN was eager to anatomize the molluscs, and to write their biography. Some of the novelties brought over by CUMING in 1831 were still yielding new information thirty years afterwards; probably are yielding it still.

In 1835, Mr. CUMING returned to America. He devoted four years to an exhaustive survey of the natural history— more especially, but far from exclusively, the conchology and the botany—of the Philippine group of islands, of Malacca, Singapore, and St. Helena.

CUMING was fitted for his work not more by his scientific ardour and his patient toil-bearing, than by his amiable character. He loved children. His manner was so attractive to them that in some places to which he travelled a schoolful of children were extemporised into botanic missionaries. The joyous band would turn out for a holiday, and would spend the whole of it in searching for the plants,

Book III,
Chap. VI.
OTHER
BENEFAC-
TORS OF
RECENT
DAYS.

*Athenæum
of 1865;
Returns pre-
sented to
Parliament,
v. y.*

Book III,
Chap. VI.
Other
Benefac-
tors of
Recent
Days.

the shells, and the insects, with the general forms and appearances of which the promoter and rewarder of their voluntary labours had previously familiarised them. He returned to England with such a collection of shells as no previous investigator had brought home; and with about one hundred and thirty thousand specimens of dried plants, besides many curious specimens in other departments.

R. Owen,
*On a National
Museum of
Natural His-
tory*, pp. 53,
seqq.
Comp. *Athe-
næum* as
above, and
the Museum
returns of
1865 and
subsequent
years.

His collections had been a London marvel before he set out on his third voyage of discovery. He then possessed, I believe, almost sixteen thousand *species*, and they were regarded as a near approximation to a perfect collection, according to the knowledge of the time. If the writer of the able notice of him which the *Athenæum* published immediately after his death was rightly informed, CUMING nearly doubled that number by the results of his final voyage, and by those of subsequent purchases made in Europe.

Very naturally, strenuous efforts were made to ensure the perpetuity of this noble collection during its owner's lifetime. The history of those efforts still deserves to be told, and for more than one reason. But it cannot be told here. This inadequate notice of a most estimable man must close with the few words which, three years ago, closed Professor OWEN's annual *Report on the Progress of the Zoological Portion of the British Museum.* 'The discoveries and labours of Mr. Hugh CUMING,' he then wrote, ' do honour to his country ; the fruition of them by Naturalists of all countries now depends mainly *on the acquisition of the space required for the due arrangement, exhibition—facility of access and comparison—of the rarities which the Nation has acquired.*' And then he adds a small individual instance, as a passing illustration of the value of Mr. CUMING's lifelong pursuit—'Among the choicer rarities, ... brought from the Philippines in 1840, was a specimen of siliceous sponge (described and figured in the *Transactions of the Zoological Society*), known as *Euplectella Aspergillum*.' Up to the date of Mr. CUMING's death (tenth August, 1865), this specimen—of what, for non-zoological readers, may be likened to a sort of coral of rare beauty— brought over in 1840, was unique. In the year next after the discoverer's death, *many* fine and curious specimens were sent from the Philippines. The solitary explorer of 1839 had at length been followed by a school of explorers. Such men as CUMING live after their death, and hence the marvellous increase, within a very few years, in our knowledge of Nature, and of GOD's bounty to the world he made.

BOOK III, Chap. VI. OTHER BENEFACTORS OF RECENT DAYS.

Transactions, &c., vol. iii, p. 203.

By a man who did but little in literature, although he possessed attainments which, in some respects, seem to have surpassed those of a good many men whose lucubrations have had much publicity and vogue, a valuable addition was made a few years ago, by bequest, to the Museum Library, both in the printed and manuscript departments. Mr. John Rutter CHORLEY had collected about two hundred volumes of the Spanish poetry and drama, and had enriched them with manuscript notes, bibliographical and critical. He had also prepared chronological tables of the dramatists—writing them in Spanish, of which he was a master— together with an account of their respective works. He had, I think, contemplated, at some future time, the preparation of some such book on the Spanish theatre as that published by Mr. TICKNOR, many years ago, on Spanish literature at large. Whether the appearance of TICKNOR's valuable book deterred Mr. CHORLEY from prosecuting his purpose, I know not. Probably he was one of the many men the very extent of whose knowledge inspires a fastidiousness which prompts them to keep on increasing their

J. R. CHORLEY AND HIS COLLECTION OF THE SPANISH POETS AND DRAMATISTS.

Will of Mr. Rutter Chorley, 1866.

private store, and to defer, almost until death overtakes them, the drawing from that store for the Public. If there may really, by some dim possibility, have been here and there an inglorious HAMPDEN, or a mute SHAKESPEARE, it is very certain that there have been, in literary history and in like departments of human study, many an unknown DISRAELI, many a Tom WARTON, brimful of knowledge about poets and poetry, who never could have lived long enough to put to public use the materials he had laboriously brought together.

Of another Collector, whose pursuits lay at an opposite pole to those of Mr. CHORLEY, it would not be edifying to say very much in these pages. Some among the collections illustrative of the history of obscure superstitions (to quote the polite euphuism of one of the Museum *Returns* to Parliament) partake, in a degree, of the peculiar associations which connect themselves with the bare name of a place at which some few of them were really found—that too famous retreat of the Emperor TIBERIUS. Others of them, however, possess a real archæological value from a different point of view. All, no doubt, are characteristically illustrative, more or less, of the doings 'in the dark places of the earth,' and may point a moral, howsoever little fitted to adorn a tale.

Mr. George WITT, F.R.S., the collector of these curiosities of human error, was a surgeon who had lived much in Australia, and who, on his return from the Colonies, had retired to a provincial town in England, where, at first, he amused his leisure by gathering a small museum of natural history. Of that collection I remember to have seen a printed catalogue, but I imagine that he sold it in his lifetime, as no part of his objects of natural history came, with his other and much more eccentric museum, to the augmentation of the public stores.   Towards the close of his life he lived in London, and used to amuse himself *by* exhibiting, and by lecturing upon, what he regarded as the more racy portion of his later collections.   He chose (I am told) the hour of eleven o'clock on Sunday morning for such peculiar expositions, but I do not think that *these* 'Sunday Lectures' were regarded, either by the man who gave them or by his auditors, as especially fitted for 'the instruction of the working classes.'

Book III. Chap. VI. OTHER BENEFACTORS OF RECENT DAYS.

Of a very different calibre to Mr. George WITT was the donor of the noble Museum of Ethnography which, *for want of room at Bloomsbury*, still occupies the late donor's dwelling-house, almost two miles off.   It is not too much to say of Henry CHRISTY, that he was both an illustrious man of science and an eminent Christian.   The man whose fame as a searcher into antiquity is spread alike over Europe and America, is also remembered in many Irish cabins as one who was willing to spend, lavishly, his health and strength, as well as his money, in lifting up, from squalid beds of straw and filth, poor creatures stricken at once with famine and with fever, and so stricken as sometimes to have almost lost the semblance of humanity.   He is also remembered by Algerian peasants, by West African negroes, and by Canadian Indians for like deeds of beneficence.   When Prussian insolence and Prussian barbarity struck down Danes who were defending hearth and home, CHRISTY was again the open-handed benefactor of the oppressed.   When Turks were, in like manner, beating down by sheer brute force the Druses of Syria, Henry CHRISTY was relieving the distressed and the down-trodden in the East, with no less liberality than he had evinced a little while before in relieving them in the North of Europe.

THE CHRISTY MUSEUM AND ITS FOUNDER'S HISTORY.

Book III,
Chap. VI.
Other
Benefac-
tors of
Recent
Days.

The time which works of good-samaritanism such as these left unoccupied was given to a vast series—or rather to a succession of series—of explorations which have had already a noble result, and which will yield more and more fruit for many a year to come. The scene of them embraced Mexico, the United States, British America, Denmark, and several Departments of Southern and Western France. Their period reached from 1860—when he had just entered the fiftieth year of his age—almost to the day of his lamented and sudden death in the May of 1865. His able and beloved friend and fellow-worker LARTET was with him in the Allier, when the fatal illness struck him, at the age of fifty-four. It will be pardoned me, I trust, if in this connection I quote, once again, those thoughtful words, out of the private note-book of Lord Bacon, which I applied in a former chapter to another and more recent public loss—' Princes, ... when men deserve crowns for their performances, do not crown them below, where the deeds are performed, but call them up. So doth God, by death.'

Character
of the
Christy
Museum.

The little that need here be added as to the nature and extent of Mr. Christy's gift to the Public, will be best said in the words of the present able Curator of the Collection, Mr. A. W. Franks. But it should be first premised that the posthumous gift was only the continuation of a long series of gifts, which embraced the Museums, not of England alone, but those of Northern and of Southern Europe, and (as I think) some of those of America :—

Ancient
Europe and
part of
North
America.

Among the most important contents of the Christy Museum is a collection of stone implements from the Drift. They are the most ancient remains of human industry hitherto discovered; they include a remarkably fine series from St. Acheul, near Amiens. Antiquities found in the

Caves of Dordogne, were excavated by Mr. CHRISTY and M. LARTET, at the expense of the former. This collection is very extensive, and includes a number of drawings on reindeer bone and horn, probably some of the most ancient works of art that have been preserved. It would have been still more extensive, had it not been known that Mr. CHRISTY intended to present the unique specimens to the French Museum, an intention which the Trustees under his Will have felt bound to fulfil. The Museum includes many ancient stone implements found on the surface, in England and Ireland, France, Belgium, and Denmark. The last of these is a remarkable collection, and includes a good series from the Danish Kitchenmiddens. A few specimens from Italy are also to be found; a valuable collection from the caves at Gibraltar; and specimens from the Swiss Lakes. For convenience, a case of ancient stone implements from Asia has been placed in this room, as well as the more modern implements, dresses, and weapons of the Esquimaux of America and Asia, and of the maritime tribes of the North-West Coast of America. These furnish striking illustrations of the remains found in the Caves of Dordogne, and prove that, while the climate was similar to that of the northern countries in question, the inhabitants of that part of France must have resembled the Esquimaux in their habits and implements.

The African Collection is very extensive, and supplies a lacuna in the collections of the British Museum, where there are few objects from this continent. The same may be said of the series from the Asiatic Islands. The collection from Asia proper is not very numerous; the races now occupying that continent being generally in a more advanced state of civilization than that which especially interested Mr. CHRISTY. Attention should, however, be

Book III,
Chap. VI.
OTHER
BENEFAC-
TORS OF
RECENT
DAYS.

Franks'
Report on
Christy
Museum
(abridged).

AFRICA AND
ASIA.

called to two valuable relics from China; an Imperial State Seal carved in jade, and a set of tablets of the same material, on which has been engraved a poem by the Emperor Kien-Lung.

The Polynesian Room contains a valuable collection of weapons, ornaments, and dresses, both from the islands inhabited by the black races of the Pacific, and from those of Polynesia proper. Many of the specimens are of interest, as belonging to a state of culture which has now completely changed, and as illustrating manners and customs that have disappeared before the commerce and the teaching of Europeans.

In the ' Asian Room ' are placed the larger objects from the Pacific, such as spears, clubs, and paddles. The collection of spears is very large and interesting.

The Australian Collection is very complete, and it would not be easy to replace it, inasmuch as the native races are dwindling in most parts of that continent.

The American department in chief includes antiquities and recent implements and dresses from the North American Indians; ancient Carib implements; and recent collections from British Guiana, and other parts of South America. The most valuable part of the contents of this room is the collection of Mexican antiquities, which is not only extensive, but includes some specimens of great rarity. Among them should be especially mentioned the following:—An axe of Avanturine jade, carved into the form of a human figure; a remarkable knife of white chalcedony; a sacrificial collar formed of a hard green stone; a squatting figure, of good execution, sculptured out of a volcanic rock; and three remarkable specimens coated with polished stones. The latter consist of a wooden mask covered with a mosaic of blue stones, presumed to be turquoises, but more probably a rare form of amazon-stone; a human skull made into a mask, and coated with obsidian and the blue stone mentioned above; and a knife with a blade of flint, and with a wooden handle, sculptured to represent a Mexican divinity, and encrusted with obsidian, coral, malachite, and other precious materials. There is also a small but choice collection of Peruvian pottery.

A catalogue of the collection was privately printed by Mr. CHRISTY in 1862; but it embraces only a small part of the present collection. A more extended catalogue is in preparation.

It is due to accuracy to add that the aspect of the rooms devoted to the CHRISTY Museum in Victoria Street, and the facilities of study which they afford, are utterly unsatisfactory to real students. They are adapted only to holiday sightseers, who look and go, and but to very small groups, indeed, even of them.

Every praise is due both to the Trustees and to their officer, for having done their best, under strait and lamentable limitations, the *removal* of which is the duty of Parliament and of the Chancellor of the Exchequer, not that of the Trustees. Under the Premiership of such an eminent scholar and writer as Mr. GLADSTONE, humbler students of history and of literature would fain hope that a long-standing reproach will speedily be removed; but his ministerial surroundings are unfriendly to such anticipations. After words which we have recently heard, *from the Treasury Bench itself*, about Public Parks, there is only scanty ground for hope that much improvement can, under existing circumstances, be looked for in respect to Public Museums.

At all events, the condition, as to space, of the CHRISTY Museum in Victoria Street, no less than the condition, in that respect, of portions of the general Museum of Antiquities at Bloomsbury itself—and of nearly all our splendid national collections in Natural History—gives tenfold importance to that question of speedy enlargement or efficient reconstruction which it will be my duty rather to state, than to discuss, in the next chapter. It will be my earnest aim to state it with impartiality, and, for the most part, in better words than my own.

Next in importance—but next at a long interval—to the accessions which the Nation owes to the munificence of Henry CHRISTY, comes the bequest of Mr. James WOODHOUSE, of Corfu, the circumstances attendant upon which have much singularity.

It is only of late years (speaking comparatively) that British Consuls have become at all notable as collectors of antiquities. But when once the new fashion was set, it spread rapidly, and it may now be hoped that there will be as little lack of continuance as of speed. In Chapter V, I had to mention (though very inadequately to the worth of their labours) several Consuls in the Levant, who have eminently distinguished themselves in augmenting our National Museum. But in this chapter the reader must be introduced to a Consul who rather obstructed than promoted a worthy public object.

James WOODHOUSE was a British subject engaged in commerce, who had resided for many years at Corfu (where for a time he had filled the office of Government Secretary), and who consoled his self-imposed exile by collecting a cabinet of coins, which eventually became one of great value, and also an extensive museum of miscellaneous, but chiefly of Greek, antiquities. Repeatedly, during his lifetime, he announced his desire and purpose to perpetuate

his collection by giving it to the British Museum.   When
his health failed, he began to superintend in person the
packing up of the most valuable portions of his museum;
but illness grew upon him, and he was forced to leave off
his preparations abruptly.

A delicate circumstance connected with his family circle
seems to have combined with this regretted interruption,
by increasing illness, of his precautionary measures and
intentions (the secure fulfilling of which lay near his heart),
to make him uneasy and anxious.   He sent for a legal
friend, Dr. ZAMBELLI; told him of his plans, and also of
his fears that they might be—in the event of his sudden
death, and he felt that death was fast coming—obstructed.
ZAMBELLI told him that the person to whom his purpose
and wishes ought to be communicated, without delay, was
undoubtedly the British Consul-General, Mr. SAUNDERS.
In joint communication with both of them, a deed of gift
was prepared. 'Having been engaged,' said the donor,
'in numismatic pursuits, ... and being desirous that
the Collection of Coins *and other Antiquities* so formed by
me, should be dedicated to national purposes, I give,' and
so on.   No inventory, however, had been made when the
donor died, on the twenty-sixth of February, 1866.   Before
WOODHOUSE's death, Mr. Consul-General SAUNDERS put a
guard round the house; and, immediately after the event,
sent away all the household, taking official possession of
the whole of the effects, in the manner usual in cases of
undoubted *intestacy*.*   He then, according to his own statement, set about 'selecting such portions' of Mr. WOOD-

Book III,
Chap. VI.
OTHER
BENEFAC-
TORS OF
RECENT
DAYS.

THE CIR-
CUMSTANCES
OF THE
WOODHOUSE
BEQUEST.

---

* This, I think, has been clearly shown by the correspondence laid
before Parliament. The reader is referred to the papers of the session
of 1867, entitled *Correspondence as to the Woodhouse Collection of Antiquities*, printed by order of Lord Derby, as Foreign Secretary.

House's property as 'seemed' (to him and to a clerical friend of the collector) '*suitable* for the British Museum.'

Most naturally, when the intelligence came to the Museum, it was thought by the Trustees that Mr. Saunders had both very seriously exceeded, and very gravely fallen short of, his obvious official duty. 'Selection' was felt to have been superfluous in respect to any and every item, of every kind, belonging to the donor's museum. Just as plainly, the instant forwarding of the whole, on the other hand, was a peremptory obligation upon the British Consul.

Eventually (and by the zealous exertions of Sir A. Panizzi and of Mr. Charles Newton, respectively, on behalf of the Trustees) conclusive evidence was placed before Lord Stanley (the now Earl of Derby, and then, it will be remembered, Foreign Secretary of State) that Mr. Consul-General Saunders had divided the Woodhouse antiquities into *two* portions, and had then proceeded to allot the smaller portion to the British Museum, and the larger to the 'heirs-at-law' of the deceased. Nor is it yet quite certain that such division was *all* the division that occurred.

After long inquiries and much correspondence—as well between the Foreign Office and the Queen's Advocate, as between the Trustees and their officers on the one hand, and various persons at Corfu, including, of course, the Consul-General himself, on the other—Lord Stanley touched the point of the affair with characteristic keenness when he wrote, in his despatch to Mr. Saunders of the seventh of January, 1867 : 'Your neglect to *make an Inventory* of the effects of the deceased has been the main cause of the doubts which have been felt as to the propriety of your conduct in this matter, and of the inquiry which has been the consequence of those doubts.'

But that neglect was then incurable. And, subsequently

to the despatch thus worded, further inquiry has but made the omission more regrettable.   The making of the Inventory had been pressed on Mr. SAUNDERS' attention at the time of the Collector's death.

BOOK III,
Chap. VI.
OTHER
BENEFAC-
TORS OF
RECENT
DAYS.

That part of the WOODHOUSE Museum which came to England in 1866 included a very interesting Collection of Greek Coins, chiefly from Corcyra, Western Greece, and the Greek islands; an extensive series of rings and other personal ornaments; some ancient glass; a few medallions; a few sculptures, in marble, of doubtful antiquity; and last, but far indeed from being least acceptable, a most beautiful head of Athené in cameo, cut on a sardonyx.   It was thought by the antiquary VISCHER—who saw this fine cameo about the year 1854—that it represents the head of PHIDIAS' famous statue in gold and ivory, and therefore had a common origin with the jasper intaglio so often praised by archæologists who have seen the Imperial Cabinet at Vienna.

Newton; in
*Returns to
Parliament,*
of the year
1866.

Vischer,
*Archæologi-
sche Beiträge
aus Griechen-
land,* p. 2.

Some of my readers will remember that although war, and the calamities which commonly accompany it, have often devastated museums and libraries, it has occasionally enriched them.   Sometimes by sheer plunder, as under CATHARINE of Russia and the marshals of her predatory armies.   Sometimes by acts of genuine beneficence and public spirit, as in Ireland under BLOUNT (afterwards Earl of Devonshire); and, again, under the great Protector.   Lord NAPIER adds his honoured name to the small category of the soldiers who have justifiably turned victorious arms to the profit of learning, and the enrichment of honestly built-up national collections.   I cannot, however, but regard as utterly unworthy of the British arms and name certain

LORD
NAPIER OF
MAGDALA,
AND THE
ADDITIONS
TO THE
MUSEUM
OF THE
ANTIQUITIES
AND MSS. OF
ABYSSINIA,
1867-8.

acquisitions which were incidental to that campaign. 'Mr. HOLMES, the officer attached to the Abyssinian Expedition by the Trustees of the British Museum '—I quote exactly and literally from the ' *Accounts and Estimates* ' of last year (1869)—'collected . . . among other objects, a silver chalice and a paten bearing Æthiopic inscriptions, showing them to have been given to various churches by King THEODORE.'

I am certain to be uncontradicted when I assert, that neither the Trustees of the British Museum, nor Lord NAPIER of Magdala, instructed Mr. HOLMES to take from Christian churches in Abyssinia their sacramental plate, or their processional crosses.

It is a far pleasanter task to praise the diligence with which Mr. HOLMES executed the Commission really given him by the Trustees. He collected many specimens of Abyssinian art and industry which were fit contributions to the National Museum. In like manner, Lord NAPIER authorised the collection, partly by officers under his command, and partly by the researches of Mr. HOLMES, of a series of Abyssinian Manuscripts, extending to three hundred and thirty-nine volumes. These were given to the Museum by the then Secretary of State for India.

In the same year with the Abyssinian spoils, came a noble addition to the Art Collections of the Museum by the bequest of the late Felix SLADE, and a rich addition to the Library, by the purchase of the Japanese books collected by the late Dr. VON SIEBOLD, during the later of his two visits to Japan, a country which he so largely contributed to make well known to the rest of the world.

Felix SLADE was the younger son of Robert SLADE, in his day a well-known Proctor in Doctors' Commons. Mr. William SLADE, elder brother of Felix, had inherited the valuable estate of Halsteads in Lonsdale (Yorkshire), under the will of the last male-heir of that family, and on his early death he was succeeded by his brother, the benefactor.

Truly a 'benefactor.' To purposes of public charity he bequeathed not less than seven thousand pounds, and bequeathed that sum with wise forethought, and with Christian generality of view. He founded and munificently endowed Professorships of Art at each of the ancient Universities, and at University College in London. To the British Museum he gave the splendid bequest about to be described, which had been selected with exquisite taste, knowledge and judgment, and which, under such rare conditions of purchase, had cost him more than twenty-five thousand pounds. I describe it in the precise words—chiefly from the pen of one of his Executors—which are used in the Return to Parliament of 1869 :—' The collection of glass and other antiquities bequeathed to the Nation by the late Felix SLADE, Esq., F.S.A., includes about nine hundred and fifty specimens of ancient glass, selected with care, so as to represent most of the phases through which the art of glass-working has passed. Collected in the first instance with a view to artistic beauty alone, the series has been since gradually enriched with historical specimens, as well as with curiosities of manufacture, so as to illustrate the history of glass in all its branches.

' Of early Egyptian glass there are not many examples in the collection; one of some interest is a case for holding the *stibium*, used by the Egyptian ladies for the eye, and which is in the form of a papyrus sceptre. The later productions of Egypt are represented by some very minute specimens of mosaic glass, formed of slender filaments of various colours fused together, and cut into transverse sections.

Book III.
Chap. VI.
Other
Benefac-
tors of
Recent
Days.

'To the Phœnicians have been attributed the making of many little vases of peculiar form and ornamentation that are met with, not unfrequently, in tombs on the shores of the Mediterranean. They are of brilliant colours, with zig-zag decoration, and exhibit the same technical peculiarities, so that they must have been derived from one centre of fabrication. Of these vases there is a considerable series, showing most of the varieties of form and colour that are known.

'The collection is especially rich in vessels moulded into singular shapes, found principally in Syria and the neigh-bouring islands, and which were probably produced in the workshops of Sidon, but at a later time; possibly as late as the Roman dominion. The Museum Collections were pre-viously very ill provided with such specimens. To the same date must belong a vase handle, stamped with the name of ARTAS the Sidonian, in Greek and Latin cha-racters.

'Of Roman glass there is a great variety, as might be expected from the skill shown in glass-making during the Imperial times of Rome. Large vases were not especially sought after by Mr. SLADE, but two fine cinerary urns may be noticed, remarkable not only for their form, but for the beautiful iridescent colours with which time has clothed them. There is also a very fine amber-coloured ewer, with blue filaments round the neck, which was found in the Greek Archipelago; an elegant jug or bottle with diagonal flutings, found at Barnwell, near Cambridge, and a brown bottle, splashed with opaque white, from Germany. Of cut glass, an art which it was formerly denied that the Romans possessed, there are good examples; such, for instance, is a boat-shaped vase of deep emerald hue, and of the same make apparently as the Sacro Catino of Genoa; a

A. W. Franks,
Account of
Slade
Museum, in
the Parlia-
mentary
Returns of
1869.

bowl cut into facets, found near Merseburg, in Germany; and a cup, similarly decorated, found near Cambridge. The last two specimens are of a brilliant clear white, imitating rock crystal, a variety of glass much esteemed by the Romans. Several vessels found in Germany are remarkable for having patterns in coloured glass, trailed as it were over the surface. There are two very fine bowls of millefiori glass, one of them with patches of gold, and very numerous polished fragments illustrating the great variety and taste shown by the ancients in such vessels. Two vases exhibit designs in intaglio; one of them, a subject with figures; the other, a bowl found near Merseburg, exhibits the story of Diana and Actæon; the goddess is kneeling at a pool of water in a grotto; Actæon is looking on, and a reflection of his head with sprouting horns may be distinguished in the water at the goddess's feet; to prevent any mistake, the names of the personages, in Greek, are added. This bowl may be of a late date, probably early Byzantine. Of vases decorated in cameo, fragments alone are to be found in the collection; but as only four entire vases are known, this is not surprising. One of the fragments seems to be part of a large panel which has represented buildings, &c., and has on it remains of a Greek inscription. There are several glass cameos and intaglios, the representatives of original gems that have long since been lost; one of the cameos is a head of AUGUSTUS; another represents an Egyptian princess; whilst among the intaglios are several of great excellence; of these should particularly be noticed a blue paste representing Achilles wounded in the heel, and crouching down behind his rich shield, a gem worthy of the best period of Greek art. One of the rarest specimens in the collection is a circular medallion of glass, on which is painted a gryphon; the colours appear to be burnt in, and it is therefore a genuine specimen of ancient painting on glass, of which but three other instances are known.

'In the fourth and fifth century it was the habit to ornament the bottoms of bowls and cups with designs in gold, either fixed to the surface or enclosed between two layers of glass. These specimens have generally been found in the Catacombs of Rome; but two or three have been found at Cologne, one of which is in the collection. It is the remains of a disc of considerable size, with a central design, now destroyed; around are eight compartments, with subjects from the Old and New Testaments: Moses striking the Rock, the History of Jonah, Daniel in the Lions' Den, the Fiery Furnace, the Sacrifice of Isaac, the Nativity, and the Paralytic Man; of these, the Nativity is a very rare representation.

'Of glass of a Teutonic origin there is but one specimen in the collection, a tumbler of peculiar form, from a cemetery at Selzen, in Rhenish Hesse. Like other glasses of the time, it is so made that it cannot be put down until it has been emptied, and thus testifies to the convivial habits of the Teutons.

'Of early Byzantine glass but little is known; the bowl with Diana and Actæon, already noticed, is very probably of that period; and a Byzantine cameo with the head of CHRIST should be mentioned.

'Of glass of the middle ages, from the West of Europe, but little or nothing has been preserved save the exquisite painted glass in cathedrals and churches. Of the Eastern glass of the same period several specimens are in the collection. Among these is a very beautiful bottle, probably of the thirteenth century, decorated with a minute pattern of birds; a lamp of large size, made in Syria to hang in a mosque, bears the name of SHEIKHOO, a man of great wealth and importance in Egypt and Syria, who died in 1356, after building a mosque at Cairo.

'To a later period of the Eastern glass works may be referred an ewer of a sapphire blue, resplendent with gold arabesques, and several other richly decorated pieces, all made in Persia.

'Venice for many centuries held the foremost place among the makers of glass. Enriched, to begin with, by her very extensive trade in beads, she received gladly the Byzantine workers in glass, who had been driven out of Constantinople by the Turks. Henceforward the variety of her glass wares increased, and must have brought much profit. The earliest glass vases which can with certainty be referred to Venice are of the fifteenth century ; of these, a large covered cup with gilt ribs is remarkable for its early date and size. The two finest specimens are, however, two goblets richly ena- meled ; one of them is blue, with a triumph of Venus ; the other green, with two portraits. These were the choicest specimens in the DEBRUGE and SOLTYKOFF Collections suc- cessively, and were obtained by Mr. SLADE, for upwards of four hundred pounds, at the sale of the latter collection. Among other enameled specimens may be noticed three shallow bowls, or dishes, with heraldic devices: one has the arms of Pope LEO X, 1513-1521 ; another those of LEO- NARDO LOREDANO, Doge of Venice, 1501-1521 ; and the third the arms of FABRIZIO CARETTO, Grand Master of the Order of St. John of Jerusalem, 1513-1521.

'The blown glasses of Venice are numerous and well selected, exhibiting great beauty of outline and variety of design. Among them should be especially remarked, a very tall covered cup, surmounted with a winged serpent, from the BERNAL Collection ; and two drinking glasses, with ena- meled flowers forming the stems.

'The coloured vases display most of the hues made at Venice; ruby, purple, green, and blue, as well as an opalescent white and an opaque white, the latter often diversified with splashes of other colours. To these may be added various imitations of agate, avanturine, &c. Another peculiar fabric of Venice is well illustrated, the frosted glass belonging generally to an early period.

' In the production of millefiori glass the Venetians did not equal the ancients, either in harmony of colour or variety of design. The rosettes were formed of sections of canes, such as were employed in making beads. The specimens of this glass are rare, but there are not less than seven pieces so ornamented in the collection.

'Of lace glass, one of the most remarkable productions of Venice, and which nowhere has been carried to such perfection, there are many fine specimens, both in form and delicacy of pattern, as there are likewise of the variety called reticelle. Among the latter is a tall covered cup with snakes on the cover and in the stem; there should also be noticed a drinking glass, in the stem of which is enclosed a half sequin of the Doge Francesco Molino, 1647.

'Of unquestionably ancient French glass but few specimens are known. This adds much to the value of a goblet in the collection, with enameled portrait of Jehan Boucau and his wife Antoinette, made about 1530.

'German glass is fully represented: the earlier specimens are richly decorated with enamel, chiefly heraldic devices; they are dated 1571, 1572, &c. A few are painted like window glass, and among them is a cylindrical cup, dated 1662, on which is depicted the procession at the christening of Maximilian Emmanuel, afterwards Elector of Bavaria. The later German specimens are engraved, and some of them by artists of note. Of ruby glass, another production for which Germany was famed, there are good specimens ; one bears the cypher of JOHN GEORGE IV, Elector of Saxony, another that of FREDERICK THE FIRST. KUNCKEL, to whom these glasses are attributed, was successively in the service of both princes.

'Though glass was early made in Flanders, the most ancient specimens in the collection under this head have been regarded as Venetian glasses decorated in the Low Countries. If made at Venice, they must, from certain peculiarities of form, have been designed for the Flemish and Dutch markets. The ornaments are etched, and contain allusions to the political events of the country : for instance, the arms of the seventeen provinces chained to those of Spain, and dated 1655 ; a portrait of PHILIP IV ; WILLIAM II of Orange ; his wife, MARY OF ENGLAND ; OLDEN BARNEVELDT, &c. Some of the later specimens are engraved on the lathe in a very ornamental manner, and others delicately stippled. One of the latter bears the name of F. GREENWOOD, and others are attributed to WOLF.

' In English glass the collection is not rich, the difficulty of identifying such specimens being very great ; some of them are referred to the works at Bristol, which produced ornamental glass about a century ago.

' Some valuable additions to the collection of glass have been received from the Executors of Mr. SLADE, purchased by them out of funds set aside for the purpose. They are nineteen in number, and among them may be especially noticed a very fine Oriental bottle with elaborate patterns in gold and enamel, together with figures of huntsmen, &c. It may be referred to the fourteenth century, and was formerly in the possession of a noble family at Wurzburg. Two specimens of Chinese glass, dated in the reign of the Emperor Kien-Lung, 1736-1796; and several ancient Flemish and Dutch glasses.

'By the acquisition of the Slade Collection the series of ancient and more recent glass in the British Museum has probably become more extensive, as well as more instructive, than any other public collection of the kind, and it will afford ample materials for study both to the artist and the antiquary.

'In addition to his collection of glass, Mr. Slade has bequeathed to the Museum a small series of carvings in ivory and metal work, from Japan, which are full of the humour and quaintness which characterise the art of that country.

'He has likewise bequeathed to the Museum such of the miscellaneous works of art in his possession as should be selected by one of his Executors, Mr. Franks. The objects so selected are not numerous, but include some valuable additions to the National Collection.

'Among them may be noticed the following :—Two very beautiful Greek painted vases, œnochoæ with red figures of a fine style ; these were two of the gems of the Durand and Hope Collections successively ; also a fine tazza, with red figures very well drawn, formerly in the Rogers Collection. Two red bowls of the so-called Samian ware, with ornaments in relief; one of them was discovered near Capua, the other is believed to have been found in Germany ; an antique hand, in rock crystal, of which a drawing by Santo Bartoli is preserved in the Royal Library at Windsor, and a small Roman vase of onyx ; a panel, probably from a book cover, a fine example of German enamel of the twelfth century, from the Préaux Collection ; a very fine flask-shaped vase of Italian majolica, probably of Urbino ware, and representing battle scenes ; three elegant ewers, one of them made at Nevers, another of Avignon ware, and the third probably Venetian—all three are rare specimens; an oval plate of niello work on silver, and a silver plate engraved in the style of CRISPIN DE PASSE; three early specimens of stamped leather work, commonly termed cuirbouilli; a tile from the Alhambra, but probably belonging to the restorations made to that building in the sixteenth century.

'The value of Mr. SLADE's bequest is considerably increased by a very detailed and profusely illustrated catalogue of the Collection which, having been prepared during his lifetime, will be completed and distributed, according to his directions.

'Since the CRACHERODE bequest, which formed the nucleus of the British Museum Print Collections, no acquisition of the kind approaches the bequest of Mr. SLADE in rare and choice specimens of etchings and engravings, wherein nearly every artist of distinction is represented. The collection comprises rare specimens of impressions from Nielli and prints of the School of Baldini; fine examples of some of the best productions of Andrea Mantegna, Zoan Andrea Vavassori, Girolamo Mocetto, Giovanni Battista del Porto, Jean Duvet, Marc Antonio, with his scholars and followers, the master of the year 1466; Martin Schongauer, Israel van Meckenen, Albert Dürer, Lucas van Leyden, Hans Burgmair, Lucas Cranach, Matheus Zazinger, the Behams, Rembrandt, Vandyck, Adrian Ostade, Paul Potter, Karl du Jardin, Jan Both, N. Berghem, Agostino Caracci, Wenceslaus Hollar, Cornelius Visscher, Crispin and Simon de Passe, S. à Bolswert, Houbraken, L. Vorsterman, Jacques Callot, Claude Mellan, Nanteuil, George Wille, Faithorne, Hogarth, L. A. B. Desnoyers, F. Forster, Sir R. Strange, William Woollett, Porporati,

Book III,
Chap. VI.
OTHER
BENEFAC-
TORS OF
RECENT
DAYS.

Franks, as
above.

G. W. Reid,
in Parliamentary
Returns of
1869.

Pefetti, Pietro Anderloni, Raphael Morghen, Giuseppe Longhi, Garavaglio, and others. There are also some rare English portraits and book-illustrations.

'The specimens of binding from the Slade Collection (now placed in the Printed Book Department), continues the Report of 1869, are twenty-three in number, chiefly of foreign execution, and afford examples of the style of Padeloup, Dusseuil, Derome, and other eminent binders. One of the volumes, an edition of Paulus Æmylius, *De gestis Francorum* (Paris, 1555, 8vo), is a beautiful speci-men of the French style of the period, with the sides and back richly ornamented in the Grolier manner. An Italian translation of the works of Horace (Venice, 1581, 4to), is of French execution, richly tooled, and bears the arms of Henry III of France. A folio volume of the *Reformation der Stadt Nürnberg* (Frankfort, 1566), which is a magnifi-cent specimen of contemporary German binding, formerly belonged to the Emperor Maximilian the Second, whose arms are painted on the elegantly goffered gilt edges. An edition of Ptolemy's *Geographicæ Narrationis libri octo* (Lyons, 1541, fol.) affords a fine illustration of the Italian style of about that date. The copy of a French translation of Xenophon's *Cyropædia*, by Jacques de Vintemille (Paris, 1547, 4to), appears to have been bound for King Edward VI, of England, whose arms and cypher are on the sides, while the rose is five times worked in gold on the back. A volume of Bishop Hall's *Contemplations on the Old Testament* (London, 1626, 8vo), in olive morocco contemporary English binding, has the Royal arms in the centre of the sides, and appears to have been the dedication copy of King Charles the First.' It is proposed, con-cludes the *Report*, to exhibit some of the most beautiful specimens comprised in Mr. Slade's valuable donation, in one of the select cases in the King's Library.

Mr. SLADE also bequeathed three thousand pounds for the augmentation, by his Executors, of his Collection of Ancient Glass, and five thousand pounds to be by them expended in the restoration of the parish church of Thornton-in-Lonsdale.

Philip VON SIEBOLD was born at Wurtzburg, in February, 1796, and in the university of that town he received his education. He adopted the profession of medicine, but devoted himself largely to the study of natural history. In the joint capacity of physician and naturalist, he accompanied the Dutch Embassy to Japan in the year 1823. He was a true lover of humanity, as well as a lover of science. Many Japanese students were taught by him both the curative arts, and the passion for doing good to their fellowmen, which ought to be the condition of their exercise and practice. He won the respect of the Japanese, but his ardent pursuit of knowledge brought him into great peril.

In 1828 he was about to return to Europe, laden with scientific treasures, when he was suddenly seized and imprisoned for having procured access to an official map of the Empire, in order to improve his knowledge of its topography. His imprisonment lasted thirteen months. At last he was liberated, and ordered to do what he was just about to do when arrested. (SIEBOLD, says his biographer, *kam mit der Verbannung davon.*) But his banishment was not perpetual. In 1859, he returned. He won favour and employment from the then Tycoon. He returned to his birthplace in 1862, and died there in October, 1866.

Of his second library, Mr. WATTS wrote thus :—'The collection of Japanese books was one of two formed by Dr.

Von Siebold during his residence in, and visits to, Japan. The first of these collections, which is now at Leyden, and of which a catalogue was published in 1845, was long considered as beyond comparison the finest of its kind out of Japan and China; but the second, now in the Museum, is much superior. That at Leyden comprises five hundred and twenty-five works, that in London one thousand and eighty-eight works, in three thousand four hundred and forty-one volumes. It contains specimens of every class of literature: cyclopædias, histories, law-books, political pamphlets, novels, plays, poetry, works on science, on antiquities, on female costume, on cookery, on carpentry, and on dancing. It abounds in works illustrative of the topography of Japan, as, for instance, one, in twenty volumes, on the secular capital Yeddo, and two, in eleven volumes, on the religious capital Miaco; collections of views of Yeddo and of the volcano Fusiyama, &c. &c. There are also several dictionaries of European languages, testifying to the eagerness with which the Japanese now pursue that study. The Museum was already in possession of a second edition of an English dictionary published at Yeddo in 1866, in which the lexicographer, Hori Tatsnoskay, observes in the preface, "As the study of the English language is now becoming general in our country, we have had for some time the desire to publish a pocket dictionary of the English and Japanese languages, as an assistance to our scholars," and adds that the first edition is " entirely sold out." These dictionaries may now assist Europeans to study the language of Japan, and it is believed that the Japanese Library now in the Museum will afford unequalled opportunities for the study of its literature.'

This was the last sentence in the last official report which Mr. Watts lived to write, for the purpose of being laid before Parliament.   He died on the ninth of September, 1869, at the age of fifty-nine.   His post was not filled up until the end of December, when he was succeeded by Mr. William Brenchley RYE, who was then Senior Assistant-Keeper in the Department of Printed Books. Mr. RYE is well known in literature.   He has edited, with great ability, several works of early travel for the useful 'Hakluyt Society,'—an employment which he has often shared with his friends and Museum colleagues Messrs. Winter JONES and Richard Henry MAJOR, and with like honourable distinction in its performance.   More recently, he has increased his reputation by a book which has been largely read, and which well deserves its popularity— *England as seen by Foreigners.*   This work was published in 1865.

CHAPTER VII.

RECONSTRUCTORS AND PROJECTORS.

> 'What do we, as a nation, care about books? How much do you think we spend altogether on our Libraries, public or private, as compared with what we spend on our horses? If a man spends lavishly on his Library, you call him mad,—a Bibliomaniac. But you never call any one a Horse-maniac, though men ruin themselves every day by their losses, and you do not hear of people ruining themselves by their books. Or, to go lower still, how much do you think the contents of the bookshelves of the United Kingdom, public and private, would fetch, as compared with the contents of its wine-cellars.'—
>
> RUSKIN, *Sesame and Lilies*, pp. 75-77.

The various Projects and Plans proposed, at different times, for the Severance, the Partial Dispersion, and the Re-arrangement, of the several integral Collections which at present form 'The British Museum.'

THE first reconstructor, in imagination, of the British Museum on the plan of severing the literature from the scientific collections, was a speculative and clever Frenchman, Peter John GROSLEY, who visited it within less than six years of its being first opened to public inspection. GROSLEY expressed great admiration for much that he saw, and he also criticised some of the arrangements that seemed to him defective, with freedom but with courtesy. Some of my readers will probably think that he hit a real blot, at that time, when he said: 'The Printed Books are the weakest part of this immense collection. The building cannot contain such a Library as England can form and ought to form for the ornament of its capital. It has a building quite ready in the "Banquetting-House" [at Whitehall], and that building could be enlarged from time to time as occasion might require.'

Other writers, at various periods, have advocated the severance of collections which seemed to them too multifarious to admit of full, natural, and equable development, in common. There is perhaps no apparent reason, on the surface, why a great Nation should not be able to enlarge the most varied public collections as effectively, and as impartially, within one building, as within half a dozen buildings. Nor does there seem to be any necessary connection between the wise and liberal government of public collections, and their severance or division into many buildings, rather than their combination within a single structure. Nevertheless it is certain that many thinkers have, by some process or other, reached the conclusion that severance would favour improvement.

Seventy years after GROSLEY wrote, Thomas WATTS revived the proposition of dividing the contents of the British Museum, but he revived it in a new form. His idea was to remove the Antiquities and to retain at Montagu House both the Libraries and the Natural History Collections. 'The pictures have been removed,' wrote Mr. WATTS in 1837, 'why should not the statues follow? The collections at the Museum would then remain of an entirely homogeneous character. It would be exclusively devoted to conveying literary information; while the collection at the National Gallery would have for its object to refine and cultivate the taste.'

It was not by any oversight that Mr. WATTS spoke of the 'homogeneity' of Manuscripts, Printed Books, and Natural-History Collections. He (at the time) meant what he said. But I doubt if the naturalists would feel flattered by the reason which he gives in illustration of his opinion. 'The various curiosities accumulated at the Museum might be considered,' he continues, 'as a vast assemblage of *book-plates*, serving to illustrate and elucidate the literature of the Library.'

Be that as it may, the idea of removing either the Antiquities or the Printed Books has long ceased to be mooted.   All who now advocate severance advise, I think, that the Natural History Collections should be removed, and none other than those.   But hitherto the idea of severance, in any shape, has been uniformly repudiated both by Royal Commissions of Inquiry, and by Parliamentary Committees.   The question, however, is sure to be revived, and that speedily.   Ere long it must needs receive a final parliamentary solution—aye or no.

In this chapter I shall endeavour to state,—and as I hope with impartiality,—the main reasons which have been severally adduced, both by those who advocate a severance, and by those who recommend the continuance of the existing union of all the varied and vast Collections now at Bloomsbury.   There can be no better introduction of the subject than that which will be afforded by putting before the reader, on the one hand, a detailed and well-considered plan which contemplated the maintenance of the Museum as it is ; and, on the other, the elaborate report in favour of transferring the scientific collections to a new site,—in order to gain ample space at Bloomsbury for a great Museum of Literature and Archæology, such as should be in every point of view worthy of the British Empire,—which was approved of by a Treasury Minute more than eight years ago.

Of the several schemes and projects of extension which rest on the twofold basis of (1) the retention at Bloomsbury of nearly all the existing collections, with ample space for their prospective increase, and (2) such an effective internal rearrangement of the collections themselves as would greatly increase the public facilities of access and study, none better deserves the attention of the reader than that which was submitted in the first instance to the Trustees of the British Museum, and subsequently to Parliament (in 1860) by Mr. Edmund OLDFIELD, then a Senior Assistant in the Department of Antiquities, entrusted (in succession to Mr. C. T. NEWTON, on his proceeding to Greece) with the charge of the Greek and Roman Galleries. By this plan it is proposed to erect on the west side of the Museum a new range of Galleries for Greek and Roman Antiquities. The façade in Charlotte Street—prolonged to the house No. 4 in Bedford Square—would extend to about 440 feet in length, with an usual depth of 140, increased at the southern extremity to 190 feet. This new range would provide for the whole of the present Greek, Roman, Phœnician, and Etruscan Antiquities, and for considerable augmentations. To Assyrian Antiquities would be assigned the present Elgin Gallery, the 'Mausoleum Room,' and the 'Hellenic Room,' together with two other rooms—gained in part by new adaptations of space comprised within the existing buildings. The rooms now devoted to the Antiquities of Kouyunjik and Nimroud would then be applied to the reception of Egyptian Antiquities, together with a room to be constructed on the site of the present principal staircase. The Lycian Gallery would retain its site, with an enlargement westward. I quote Mr. OLDFIELD's own descriptive account of his project, in full, from the Appendix to the *Minutes of Evidence* of 1860.

I. *Entrance Hall.*—On the north side is a staircase, such as suggested by Mr. PANIZZI, forming the access to the galleries of Natural History.

II. Room for the first reception, unpacking, and examination of sculptures, the consideration of such as are offered for purchase, the cleaning and repairing of marbles and mosaics, and storing of pedestals, mason's apparatus, and machinery, &c.

III. *First Egyptian Room.*—The present two staircases, and the wall at the east end of the Assyrian Transept being removed, a handsome entrance would be obtained to the galleries of Antiquities. The room would be about seventy-six feet by thirty-five, and though not very well lighted, might suffice for the monuments of the first twelve dynasties of Egypt, at present in the northern vestibule and lobby, which have no very artistic character.

IV. *Second Egyptian Room.*—The monuments of the Eighteenth Dynasty would here commence. Terminating the vista from the north would be the head of Thothmes III, more advantageously seen than in its present position, where it stands in front of a doorway, and exposed to a cross light.

V. *Third Egyptian Room.*—For smaller remains of the same period. The alcoves should be removed, and a door opened on the north side.

VI. *Fourth Egyptian Room.*—To remedy the darkness of this room, an opening should be made in the ceiling, inclosed by a balustrade in the room above (*v.* Plan of Upper Floor), and covered with glass; whilst the roof of this upper room should be lightened, at least in the central compartment, by substituting glass for its present heavy ceiling. The small space thus sacrificed in the floor of the upper room would be a less serious loss than the virtual uselessness of so large an apartment below. With the proposed improvement in the lighting, the Fourth Egyptian Room would be well adapted for the colossal monuments of Amenophis III; without it, the room could hardly serve for any purpose but a passage.

VII. *Fifth Egyptian Room.*—In the middle would be arranged, in two rows, the remaining sculptures of the Eighteenth and part of those of the Nineteenth Dynasty. In the recesses between the pilasters might be fixed wall cases, which would rather improve than impair the architectural effect of the room, and for which the light is well adapted, the rays from the opposite windows striking sufficiently low to obviate the shadow occasioned by shelves in rooms lighted from above. Such cases would contain small objects from the Egyptian collection now on the Upper Floor.

VIII. *Sixth Egyptian Room.*—This room, originally ill lighted, has been further darkened by the new Reading Room. erected within a few yards of its windows. If, however, an opening were made in the ceiling (as proposed for Room VI, and if the roof of the room above were somewhat modified, light might be thrown both on the magnificent bust of Rameses II and on the east wall of the room. The middle window in that wall, which furnishes no available light, might then be blocked up; and before it might stand the cast from the head of the colossus at Abousimbul, now placed over a door in the northern vestibule, but which ought, in any re-arrangement, to be united with the other monuments of Rameses II, and which would finely terminate the vista, looking from the west.

IX. *Seventh Egyptian Room.*—Here would be the sculptures, both of the native dynasties posterior to the Nineteenth, and of the Ptolemaic and Roman periods, which at present occupy the southern Egyptian Gallery. In the recesses between the pilasters might be wall cases.

X. *Eighth Egyptian Room.*—This, and the two succeeding rooms, would be appropriated to smaller Egyptian remains. The light on the western side of these rooms falls so nearly vertically, from the overshadowing mass of building adjoining, that wall cases would have their contents completely thrown into shade by the shelves, or by the tops of the cases. Objects in the middle of the room, on the other hand, would be in uninterrupted light. It is, therefore, proposed to place against the walls inscribed tablets, which are best seen under an acutely striking light; painted plaster friezes, which, from their strong colours and coarse execution, do not require much light; and framed papyri, which are liable to injury from exposure to powerful light. Along the centre of the room would be arranged mummies, and mummy cases, in glass frames, with table cases for scarabæi, and other small objects, which are most conveniently exhibited on flat or sloping surfaces.

XI. *Ninth Egyptian Room.*—The thoroughfare is here too great for objects to be conveniently arranged in the centre; but the walls might be occupied as in the preceding room.

XII. *Tenth Egyptian Room.*—To be arranged similarly to the Eighth.

Summary of the Accommodation provided in the plan for Egyptian Antiquities :—

1. The large sculptures would gain Rooms III, IV, and VI, in lieu of the northern vestibule.

2. The inscribed tablets, which at present occupy the recesses of Rooms VII, VIII, IX, containing four hundred and twenty-two linear feet of wall space, and the walls of the northern vestibule, containing about eighty feet, or altogether about five hundred and two feet, would share with the framed papyri and painted plaster friezes the walls of Rooms III, IV, V, VI, VIII, X, XI, XII, containing altogether about nine hundred and sixty feet.

3. The mummies, overcrowded in a room containing two thousand and fourteen square feet of available open space, and the coffins in the present 'Egyptian Ante-room,' would be arranged, with several table cases, in Rooms X and XII, containing altogether about four thousand and eighty square feet.

4. The small objects, now in wall cases extending to two hundred and

thirty-seven feet of linear measurement, and in three table cases, would be arranged in wall cases, extending to three hundred and eighty-three feet, and in several table cases, of which the exact extent cannot be fixed.

The additional space here provided for large Egyptian sculptures is not so much needed for the present as is the case in some other series; but the greater comparative difficulty of moving objects so bulky makes it advisable to secure, as far as possible, the permanence of any re-arrangement, by leaving room for the probable incorporations of future years. The accommodation provided for smaller objects is little more than they already require for advantageous display.

XIII. *First Assyrian or Nimroud Room.*—This room, on the site of the basement-room, would be formed by demolishing the small room, with the adjoining students' room and staircase; by extending over their site the glass roof of room; by throwing a floor, on a continuous level with those of the adjoining galleries, and supported upon iron pillars, over so much of room as is coloured brown in the plan; and by carrying up thin partitions from this floor to the glass roof, so as to inclose a new apartment. This apartment would, at the south end, extend across the whole breadth of room, but elsewhere it would be limited to a central space, nineteen feet wide, corresponding to the present central compartment of room, so as to leave open an area of ten feet wide on each side. The open areas would serve to light both the whole room below, of which the central portion would be partially obscured by the new structure, and also the rooms in the adjoining base-ments, which, though no longer used for exhibition, might be serviceable for other subordinate purposes. In one of the open areas might be a private staircase to the basement. Room XIII would be considerably loftier than the present 'Nimroud Side Gallery,' and it would contain two thousand nine hundred and seventy superficial feet, and three hun-dred and fourteen linear feet of wall-space, instead of two thousand one hundred and seventy-six superficial feet, and two hundred and seventy-eight feet of wall-space. In this new room would be placed the earliest of the Assyrian monuments, those of Sardanapalus I; at the south end those found in the two small temples at Nimroud, including the colossal lion, the arched monolith and altar, and the mythological figures from a doorway; in the northern portion, the sculptures from the North-west Palace at Nimroud, including the small winged lion and bull, now in room.

XIV. *Second Assyrian Room.*—This would contain a continuation of the series from Nimroud. On the west side the colossal winged lions now in the western compartment of the Assyrian Transept, which would complete the monuments of Sardanapalus I; in other parts of the room, the few but important sculptures of Divanubara, Shammaz-Phal, and Pul, now somewhat scattered for want of the requisite accommodation in room, but for which there would here be ample space, and an advantageous light.

XV. A proposed new room, to be entitled the *Third Assyrian or Khorsabad Room*, the Assistant-Keeper's study being removed, and accommodation being provided for him elsewhere. The room might be forty-seven feet by forty, about the same height as XIV, and similarly lighted by a central skylight; beneath it would be a basement room for the uses of the establishment. Room XV would contain, first, the bas-reliefs of Tiglathpileser II from the South-west edifice of Nimroud; and secondly, the Khorsabad collection, or monuments of Sargina, which is next in chronological order to the Nimroud collection. The two colossal bulls of Sargina are marked in the plan as facing each other, an arrangement common at Khorsabad. Deducting space for the bulls, upwards of eighty linear feet of wall-surface would remain in the room, which is considerably more than the bas-reliefs of Tiglathpileser and Sargina require. The new building would necessarily obscure some of the windows of the adjoining basement, but this is of minor importance; and the evil might be diminished on the western and southern side, by leaving open spaces in the floor behind each of the colossal bulls. Between the bulls would be a passage to

XVI. *Fourth Assyrian or Sennacherib Room.*—Here would be the first part of the collection discovered at Koyunjik, the monuments of Sennacherib, now inconveniently divided, and arranged partly in the 'Koyunjik Gallery,' and partly in the 'Assyrian Basement Room.' These monuments consist, almost entirely, of bas-reliefs, extending as at present arranged, to about three hundred and fifty-one feet (two hundred and eight on the ground floor, and one hundred and forty-three in the basement). In a lofty and wide room, however, such as XVI, an upper row of bas-reliefs might be introduced over many of the smaller slabs, now arranged in a single row only; by this means the sculptures of Sennacherib might all be included on the east, west, and north sides of the room, containing three hundred and seventeen linear feet of wall-space, leaving the south side, or twenty-seven feet, for sculptures of Sardanapalus III, the last monarch of the Assyrian series. In the centre of the room would be glass cases for the numerous tablets, cylinders, and other small objects of this collection, which it is most instructive to exhibit in connection with the sculptures. The only architectural alteration desirable in the room would be to open skylights in the lateral portion of the roof, and to close those in the central, in order to obtain a sharper light, upon the principle so successfully adopted in the present 'Nimroud Side Gallery.'

XVII. *Fifth Assyrian Room.*—Here would be the continuation of the monuments of Sardanapalus III, which conclude the Assyrian department; they are at present divided like those of Sennacherib, and part exhibited in the 'Koyunjik Gallery,' part in the basement room; altogether they now extend to three hundred and seventy-three feet; but as the greater part might, in Room XVII, be very well arranged in double rows, and some of those in single rows might, without injury, be less widely spread, two hundred and twenty-five feet would suffice for their exhibition; of this space twenty-seven feet would be supplied by Room XVI, and the remainder by XVII. The centre of the room should be appropriated as the preceding, and the lighting similarly modified.

SUMMARY OF THE ACCOMMODATION PROVIDED IN THE PLAN FOR ASSYRIAN ANTIQUITIES.

Amount of Wall-space now in use for Assyrian Bas-reliefs.		*Amount of Wall-space in the Plan for Assyrian Bas-reliefs.*	
	Linear feet.		Linear feet.
Nimroud Side Gallery	. 278	Room XIII . .	. 314
Nimroud Central Saloon	. 82	„ XIV . .	. 95
Assyrian Transept .	. 125	„ XV . . .	. 145
Koyunjik Gallery .	. 242	„ XVI . . .	. 344
Assyrian Basement Room	. 243	„ XVII . . .	. 199
	970		1,097
Bas-reliefs in the middle of			
Basement Room .	. 254		
	1,224		

It thus appears that the wall-space provided in the plan, though one hundred and twenty-seven feet more than the wall-space in the existing rooms, falls short by one hundred and twenty-seven feet of the total linear extent of the bas-reliefs, as now arranged. In lieu, however, of placing slabs in the middle of a gallery, as is done in the basement room, and as it would likewise be possible to do in XVI or XVII, it is thought better, in these last rooms, to provide the additional space by simply carrying up the slabs to a greater height.

The space for central cases for small objects, which is at present four thousand and eighty square feet in rooms would be eight thousand one hundred and seventy square feet in Rooms XVI and XVII, an amount so abundant as to supersede the necessity for any wall-cases.

The accommodation here provided for Assyrian antiquities is little more in quantity, though much better in quality, than the present.

But this is nearly the only branch of the archæological collections to which there seems little probability of future additions. If, contrary to expectation, any such should be made, a supplemental room might be built on the vacant space to the north of the Assyrian galleries.

XVIII. *Persian Room.*—The sculptures to be here exhibited, which are all bas-reliefs, would probably not occupy more than half the wall-space, which is forty-seven linear feet. They belong chiefly to the sixth century, B.C., and properly therefore succeed the Assyrian, which range from the tenth to the seventh century, B.C.

XIX. *Lycian Gallery.*—It is intended to reserve this room for the monuments peculiarly characteristic of Lycia, and to transfer to the Greek galleries those in which the Greek element is predominant; such as, particularly, the sculptures of the Ionic trophy monument or *heroum* from Xanthus, now scattered over the room, and, if necessary, the casts from the rock tomb at Myra. This would leave abundant space for the purely Lycian remains. The harpy tomb, of which the bas-reliefs furnish a very important illustration of archaic Greek art, might best be placed in an isolated position near the entrance to the Greek galleries, where it would be favourably lighted and conspicuously seen. Its present place might be filled by the rude sarcophagus with sculptures of lions. The lighting of the Lycian room, which is very defective, should be improved by an alteration in the roof; but it is thought better not to enter into the details of such alteration in the present paper.

XX. *First Greek or Inscription Room.*—The room beneath this being supposed to be withdrawn from exhibition, the staircase at the west end should be separated by a partition, and entered through a private door. All Greek inscriptions, except the sepulchral, and such as are engraved on architectural or sculptural monuments, would be here collected.

At this point the new buildings commence with—

XXI. *Second Greek or Branchidæ Room*, thirty feet by twenty-four.—The height both of this and the four succeeding rooms should be about twenty feet. This would contain the earliest Greek sculptures, of which the principal are those procured by Mr. NEWTON from Branchidæ. The ten seated statues would be arranged on each side, as in the 'Sacred Way' at that place, and the recumbent inscribed lion and the sphinx placed at the end of the room.

XXII. *Third Greek Room*, twenty-four feet by seventeen.—This would contain other archaic works, including the casts from Selinus.

XXIII. *Fourth Greek or Æginetan Room*, thirty-eight feet by twenty-four.—Here would be fixed, in two recesses, the restorations of the two pedimental groups from Ægina, which are exactly of the length of this room, and which might be placed at a more convenient level for examination than their present elevated position in room.

XXIV. *Fifth Greek Room*, seventeen feet by twenty-four.—On a pedestal, facing the great Greek gallery, might stand the semi-archaic Apollo, from Byzantium.

XXV. *Sixth Greek or Phigaleian Room*, thirty-eight feet by twenty-four.—Here would be the casts from the Temple of Theseus, and the sculptures and casts from the Temple of Wingless Victory, both of the middle of the fifth century, B.C.; also the Phigaleian collection, which is a somewhat later production of the same school. The friezes, arranged in two rows, would just fill the room.

XXVI. *Seventh Greek or Parthenon Room.*—Here would commence the grand suite of galleries for large sculptures, of which the general breadth would be forty-two feet, and the height from thirty to thirty-five feet. By its side would run a secondary suite, twenty feet wide, and from fifteen to twenty feet high, for minor specimens, of which the interest generally is rather archæological than artistic. These latter objects are both more conveniently classified, and more favourably seen, in small rooms; if placed in large galleries, beside grand monumental works, they lose importance themselves, whilst they fritter away the effect of what is really more valuable. The Seventh Greek Room, which is two hundred and forty-one feet long, would contain only the remains of the Parthenon; which might be arranged as indicated in the Plan, so as at once to keep the pedimental groups and the frieze from interfering with each other, and to distinguish, more accurately than is now done, the original connection or disconnection of the several slabs of the frieze. As we possess the entire frieze from the east end of the temple, and casts of the entire frieze from the west, these two are here arranged opposite each other, towards the middle of the two side walls of the room. On either side are the slabs from the north and south flanks of the temple, which are mostly disconnected. In front of the casts from the west is a proposed full-sized model of part of the entablature, supported by one original and five restored capitals, with the upper parts of their shafts, and incorporating ten of the metopes, so as to explain their original combination with the architecture. The total height of this model might be about eighteen feet. The metopes not included in it should be attached to the wall opposite, over the frieze. The finest of the pedimental groups would face the grand entrance from the Lycian Gallery, through which the whole might be seen in one view, from any distance less than forty-eight feet. If it were desired to retain the two small models of the Parthenon in the room, they might stand near the south end.

XXVII. *Eighth Greek or Erechtheum Room*, sixty-five feet by twenty-six, for monuments of the era between Phidias and Scopas, of which the principal are the remains of the Erechtheum.

XXVIII. *Ninth Greek, or Mausoleum Room*, one hundred and twenty feet in length, forty-two in breadth, and eighty across the transept.—

Here would be, 1. The marbles procured by Lord STRATFORD and Mr. NEWTON, from the Mausoleum of Halicarnassus; in the west transept, the group from the *quadriga*, and in the southern part of the room the other important sculptural and architectural remains of the building, including the frieze. 2. In the east transept, the colossal lion from Cnidus, with a few other sculptures of the same school. 3. In the northern part of the room, the Xanthian Ionic monument, here placed for comparison with the remains of the Mausoleum. The whole upper portion of this monument, commencing with the higher of the two friezes which surrounded the original base, might be reconstructed, though not restored, and would form a striking termination to the vista through the galleries. The lower frieze might be arranged against the adjoining walls of the room.

XXIX. *Tenth Greek Room.*—Having thus passed through the great monumental series of Greek sculptures in chronological order, the visitor would return south by the side rooms, containing minor remains of the same school. The Tenth Greek Room would be forty-two feet by twenty, and would contain the latest of the smaller sculptures.

XXX. *Eleventh Greek Room*, thirty-three feet by twenty.—This should be appropriated to the small fragments from the Mausoleum, which would thus be in immediate connection with its larger sculptures, without impairing their grandeur of effect.

XXXI, XXXII. *Twelfth and Thirteenth Greek Rooms*, together one hundred and thirty-five feet in length and twenty in breadth.—The exact position of the wall separating these rooms might be reserved till the arrangement of their contents was settled. In one might be architectural fragments, from buildings not represented in the large galleries; in the other, small tablets, votive offerings, altars, and other minor sculptures.

XXXIII. *Fourteenth Greek or Sepulchral Room*, ninety-three feet by eighteen.—Here would be all the Greek sepulchral monuments now in the basement. The casts from the sculptured tomb at Myra, of which the style is more Greek than Lycian, might also be here placed, as indicated in the plan, in case it should be thought desirable to remove them from the Lycian Room, though the expediency of this transfer may perhaps be doubted. Wherever placed, these casts ought to be so put together as to explain the true arrangement of the originals.

[Then follows a Summary of the Accommodation provided in the Plan for Greek Sculptures, amounting to a superficial area of twenty-seven thousand four hundred and ten square feet, and to two thousand one hundred and ninety-one lineal feet of wall-space.]

XXXIV. *Etruscan Room.*—The next parallel on the ground floor would be devoted to the monuments of ancient Italy. The earliest are the Etruscan, which, being altogether taken from tombs, would properly

BOOK III, Chap. VII. RECONSTRUCTORS AND PROJECTORS.

MR. OLDFIELD'S PROJECT OF RECONSTRUCTION (1854-1860)—*continued.*

TENTH GREEK ROOM.

ELEVENTH GREEK ROOM.

TWELFTH AND THIRTEENTH GREEK ROOMS.

FOURTEENTH GREEK ROOM.

ETRUSCAN ROOM.

be placed adjacent, on the one side to the Greek, on the other to the Roman, sepulchral collections. The principal portion of the Etruscan Room would be fifty-five feet by forty, with additional recesses at the south end, the whole about twenty feet high. Two rows of pilasters would divide the room into three compartments, the central for the gangway, the other two to be fitted up as a series of tombs, of which the sides would be formed of the mural restorations, with fac-similes of paintings from Corneto and Vulci. Within these restored tombs would be such sarcophagi as we possess, found in the tombs themselves. The fac-similes of the painted roofs of two of the tombs might be fixed above them, at such a height as not to obstruct the light. In the central compartment, which contains six shallow recesses between the pilasters, might be monuments from various tombs other than those here restored.

XXXV. *Staircase Room*, forty feet by thirty, and of the same height as the three united stories of the western galleries.—Four successive flights of steps would be required to reach each floor. The landings between the first and second, and between the third and fourth flights, might each be supported by Caryatid or Atlantic figures, which would give the whole composition an ornamental effect, as seen from the east side. Beneath one side of this staircase might be a private one leading to the western basement.

To the north is another private staircase, conducting to the basement under the Greek galleries. The adjoining passage leads to—

XXXVI. *First Græco-Roman Room.*—The Etruscan monuments are succeeded chronologically by the Græco-Roman, here placed so as to adjoin the galleries both of Greek and of Roman art. In accordance with the character of Græco-Roman sculpture, the apartments containing it should be somewhat ornamentally constructed and arranged, as in the great continental museums, where works of this class form the staple of the collections. The position of the principal objects in all this series of rooms is marked in the plan, without distinguishing them individually, as none are of such a character as to require any special architectural provision. The first room is one hundred and six feet by twenty-six, exclusive of the alcoves. Its height need not, for the display of statuary, exceed twenty feet; but if, for architectural effect, a vaulted ceiling is preferred, the height must be increased. In the Braccio Nuovo, in the Vatican Museum, which is probably the finest gallery of this kind in Europe, and has a cylindrical vault, with a central skylight, the proportion of height to breadth is about thirty-seven feet to twenty-seven; but in the darker climate of London the height should not, if possible, exceed the breadth.

XXXVII. *Second Græco-Roman Room, or Rotunda*, sixty feet in diameter, and about sixty feet high in the centre, being surmounted by a hemispherical dome.—This room is, with slight variations, and on a somewhat smaller scale, a copy of the Rotunda in the Museum of Berlin, an apartment universally admired for its architectural beauty, and only defective as a hall for sculpture from the unnecessary smallness of the central skylight. The entablature over the columns would support a gallery, opening into the first floor of the western buildings.

XXXVIII. *Third Græco-Roman Room*, similar to the first, but only one hundred and one feet long, exclusive of the northern alcove.

The spaces between the lateral alcoves on the east side of the First and Third Græco-Roman Rooms might either be covered with glass, or left open for ventilation, though the second arrangement would involve a provision for the drainage below.

The amount of accommodation for Græco-Roman sculptures cannot, from the form of the rooms, be stated with the same exactness as that for the Greek. Exclusive of the alcoves, there would be in the—

	Superficial Area.	Length of Wall-space.
First Gallery . .	2,756 square feet.	180 linear feet.
Third Gallery . .	2,626 ,,	152 ,,
	5,382 ,,	332 ,,

The Rotunda would not have available space in proportion to its size. Twelve statues or busts between the columns, and perhaps a large sculpture in the centre, would be the natural complement of the room. The wall-space behind the columns would not be available for sculpture. The total accommodation in the three rooms would amply suffice for our present collection, even somewhat enlarged. As it increased, however, further space might be obtained by erecting in the first and third rooms transverse walls, opposite the alcoves in the Roman galleries, thus subdividing the first room into three principal compartments, with a small lobby at each end, and the third into three compartments (of which the most northern would need some modification), with a lobby at the south end. The doorways through these walls might be twelve feet wide, so as to preserve the continuous appearance of the suite; and they would still leave one hundred and twelve feet of additional wall-space in the first room, and eighty-four in the third. The lighting would be somewhat improved by such an alteration.

The last suite of galleries on the ground floor would contain the Roman and Phœnician remains. To avoid any obscuration from the houses on the west side of Charlotte Street, the windows should be as high in the wall as possible, and as broad as architectural propriety

Book III,
Chap. VII.
Recon-
structors
and Pro-
jectors.

Mr.
Oldfield's
Project of
Recon-
struction
(1858-1860)—
continued.

Third
Græco-
Roman
Room.

Summary of
accommoda-
tion for
Græco-
Roman
Sculp-
tures.

Means of
future en-
largement.

Western
Galleries.

would admit, whilst the rooms should be not less than twenty-five feet high.

XXXIX. *First Roman Room*, one hundred and ten feet by twenty-eight, exclusive of the alcoves.—It would contain mosaics, including those from Carthage, and miscellaneous sculptures, altars, architectural fragments, &c.; the mosaics indifferently placed on all sides of the room, the sculptures on the east side and against the two end walls.

XL. *Hall*, fifty-six feet by seventeen.—Here might be an entrance from Charlotte Street, which on many occasions would furnish a convenient relief to the principal entrance to the Museum. It would open immediately into the Rotunda, and through the vista beyond would be seen, in the distance, the cast of the colossal head from Abousimbul. Within the two abutments of the Rotunda would be recesses for the attendants to sell catalogues, receive umbrellas, &c.

XLI. *Second Roman or Iconographical Room*, fifty-four feet by twenty-eight, without the alcoves.—This would contain the series of portrait statues and busts, in chronological order. The west, or dark side of the room, could only be used for very inferior sculptures.

XLII. *Third (or Anglo-) Roman Room*, the same size as the preceding, for Roman monuments found in this country. The rude character of many would admit of placing them on the west side.

XLIII. *Fourth Roman or Sepulchral Room*, eighty-two feet by twenty-six, containing Roman sarcophagi for which the west side might be partially available, and sepulchral cippi, and inscriptions. At the north-east angle would be a Columbarium, twenty-three feet by fourteen, fitted up like that in the present Sepulchral Basement Room, but with the advantage of a skylight.

[Then follows a Summary of Accommodation provided in the plan for Roman Sculptures, amounting to a superficial area (without alcoves) of eight thousand five hundred and fifty-eight square feet, and seven hundred and seventeen linear feet of wall-space.]

The first three rooms, when their contents sufficiently increased, would admit of an easy alteration, which would not merely increase the wall-space, but much improve the lighting, by simply inserting transverse walls between each window. Against these walls the sculptures would have a true side light, whilst those against the east wall would be protected from double lights. It may even be doubted whether such an arrangement should not be adopted in the first instance, without waiting till the additional accommodation is actually required.

XLIV. *Phœnician Room*, twenty-six feet square.—Here would be the *stelæ* and bas reliefs from Carthage and its vicinity, with the few Punic inscriptions which we possess. The room contains six hundred and seventy-six superficial feet, and eighty-eight of wall-space.

XLV. A similar room to the preceding, which, in case of necessity, might serve for extending the Phœnician collection. In the mean time it might perhaps be used for exhibiting such miscellaneous inferior sculptures as could be advantageously weeded from the regular series, though circumstances might temporarily prevent their removal from the Museum. In such case it might be entitled 'Supplemental Room.'

In accordance with a suggestion made in the Committee now sitting, the writer has added to the new buildings proposed in his plan another story, or second floor, over the first. The advantage of this is, that it would provide for objects which it might be more costly or inconvenient to accommodate elsewhere. But it involves necessarily two evils: 1. That the height of the second floor, involving an ascent of perhaps nearly one hundred steps (though this is not more than is common in continental museums), might excite complaint in English visitors. 2. That so lofty a building, by excluding all oblique rays from the east side of the Græco-Roman galleries, would make the light on the statues and busts there placed somewhat too vertical.

With regard to the collections to be provided for on the upper floors, it is here assumed, though of course without any express authority, that Ethnography and Oriental Antiquities would be removed from the Museum, and better accommodated elsewhere. The British and Mediæval Collections, however, are supposed to be retained; if they are removed, a modification of this plan must in consequence be made.

The apartments should all be about eighteen feet high, the windows of the same breadth as those below, but, except in the Terracotta Room, only about eight feet high, and as near the ceiling as possible. On the east side should be corresponding windows, so that each wall would be illuminated; for cross lights, though so injurious to sculptures, are generally desirable for galleries filled with wall-cases. All the windows should have ground glass, to prevent injury to the collections from the sun.

1. *Vase Gallery.*—Two hundred and twenty-two feet long, the southern half twenty-six feet wide, and the northern twenty-eight feet. The wall-cases should be about eight feet high, like those in our First Vase Room; and the transverse projections, flanked by pilasters, would be only of the same height, so as not to shut out the view of the upper part of the gallery; having glass on each side, they would serve for vases with double paintings, such as we now exhibit only in dwarf central cases. The most important vases should stand isolated on tables, or pedestals, on each side the gangway; as in the present arrangement of the Temple Collection. Although the superficial area of this gallery (five thousand nine hundred and ninety-two feet) is little more than a third greater than that occupied by vases in the present buildings (four thousand three hundred and twenty-one feet), the amount of accommodation it would afford is nearly double. For the present wall-

cases, eight feet high, extend to one hundred and forty-six feet of linear measurement; those ten feet high will, when the collection is fully arranged, extend to eighty-four feet; the whole therefore may be reckoned as equivalent to two hundred and fifty-one feet of cases, eight feet high. The total extent, however, of such wall-cases in the proposed gallery is four hundred and fifty-five feet. The projections also, with the tables and pedestals, may safely be estimated as providing twice the accommodation for vases painted on both sides which is now furnished by the dwarf central cases, besides exhibiting them much more conveniently. It should be added that the vases would be better lighted than at present; whilst the length and comparative openness of the gallery would produce a more striking impression on the passing visitor.

The accommodation here provided being so ample, it might be desirable to appropriate one compartment of the gallery to an exclusively Etruscan Collection, comprising not merely the pottery of the Etruscans, properly so called, but that for which they were really more distinguished in ancient times, their bronze and other metal work.

2. *Terracotta Room.*—Fifty-six feet by seventeen. As no windows could be made on the east side, there should be no cases on the west; but the western windows, which do not correspond with the others of this story, should extend from near the ceiling to four or five feet from the floor. A sloping case might then be placed in each window, for lamps and other small objects, requiring a strong light. Against the east wall should be cases for vases, and other large objects.

3. *Gallery of the Rotunda.*—From one hundred and eighty to one hundred and ninety feet in circumference, and about nine feet wide. The powerful light from the centre of the dome would be favourable to terracotta statuettes and bas-reliefs, which could all be contained in shallow wall-cases, that would not materially narrow the gangway.* The Townley Collection of bas-reliefs, now in the Second Vase Room, might be arranged in panels all round, so as to produce a decorative effect, agreeable to their original destination.

The entire space provided in these two rooms is much more than our terracottas can absolutely require; but this will facilitate an ornamental arrangement of the collection, appropriate to the character of the larger room. The small spaces between the Rotunda and the main building would serve for closets.

4. *Glass Room,* twenty-eight feet by twenty-six.—The fittings proper for glass being different from those of terracottas, it is desirable to give

---

* In the accompanying Plan (of the Parliamentary Report, 1860), pilasters of unnecessary size have been inadvertently introduced into this gallery, reducing both the extent of the wall-cases, and the breadth of the gangway, in a manner never intended.

it a separate room. This should be similarly arranged to the Vase Gallery, with wall-cases eight feet high, and table-cases in the centre.

5. *Bronze Gallery*, three apartments united; together eighty-two feet by twenty-eight.—As the advantage of a skylight for the bronze statuettes is necessarily sacrificed by the adoption of an upper floor, it would be best to place them, as far as possible, against each side of the transverse projections, separating those sides by internal partitions, and employing some contrivance to protect the bronzes from the cross light of the further windows, an arrangement possible with small objects in glass cases, though not with large statuary. In the middle of the gallery might be table-cases, placed longitudinally, or important objects on pedestals. The increase of accommodation in the Bronze Gallery, as in the Vase Gallery, is more than proportionate to the increase of space. Though the superficial area is only two thousand two hundred and ninety-six feet, in lieu of our present quantity, two thousand and twenty-one, the extent of wall-cases, which now is only one hundred and thirty-eight feet, would, even allowing doorways of twelve feet wide between each of these compartments, be increased to two hundred and fifty feet, equivalent, after allowing for the difference in height of the cases, to two hundred feet. This, if the Etruscan bronzes were transferred as already suggested, would liberally provide for the Greek and Roman Collection.

Each room should be fifteen to eighteen feet high; the windows exclusively on the east side, and extending from the ceiling to four or five feet from the floor. As the aspect is nearly N.E., the sun could not be injurious, and the glass of the windows, therefore, had better be unground.

1. *British Rooms*, each twenty-seven feet by twenty-six.—That which adjoins the staircase (and, if necessary, those on each side), should be lighted from the roof, and have wall-cases all round, with a separate case in the centre. The other rooms should have wall-cases on the west side, and shallower cases against the transverse walls. Two long table-cases in each room might extend from the windows to a line with the doorway.

2. *Mediæval Rooms*, each twenty-eight feet by twenty-seven, and similarly arranged to the British.—Though the entire superficial area in the British and Mediæval Rooms is only five thousand and seventy-two feet, in lieu of four thousand and forty-six, the amount in the present building, yet the wall-space is four hundred and sixty-six feet, instead of only two hundred and ninety-seven, and the cases, having no windows above, might, if necessary, be made ten feet high, like the present. The gain in table-cases would be much greater. In lieu of six, there would be twelve, each sixteen or eighteen feet long, instead of ten; whilst the central case in the room adjoining the staircase might be at least as

capacious as the large separate case in the present British and Mediæval Room. The lighting would throughout be more advantageous for these collections than at present; and the rooms, from the character of the windows, might be bright instead of gloomy.

3. *Gem Room.*—As the contents of this and the succeeding room have more or less intrinsic value, an iron door might be placed at the end of the Mediæval Gallery, to be open only when the public are admitted to the Museum. The Gem Room, twenty-eight feet by twenty-seven, would be fitted like the preceding. The gems would occupy the table-cases, which would accommodate a far larger collection than ours, and would exhibit them in the best possible light for such objects. In the wall-cases might be displayed the gold and silver ornaments, which would have much more space than as now arranged, though in a room only of the same size.

4. *Coin and Medal Gallery*, fifty-six feet by seventeen.—As the dome of the Rotunda would only rise a few feet above the floor of this gallery, and would, from its curvature, recede to a distance of several feet, windows on the east side would be quite unobstructed. In each might stand a table-case, six or seven feet long, on which would be exhibited, under glass, a series of coins and medals which, though not the most valuable of our collection in the eyes of a numismatist, would suffice to give the public an interesting and instructive view of the monetary art. In the drawers of these cases might be kept the moulds and casts of the Coin Collection. Against the side walls might be upright cases, or frames, for extending the exhibition; but the walls facing the windows, having a front light, would be unsuitable for coins or medals, and must be employed for some other purpose.

5. The rooms which remain would be a private suite for the Coin Department. The present rooms of that department are arranged in an order the reverse of what is best for security and convenience, the coins being kept in an outer room, which must be passed in going either to the Keeper's study, or to the Ornament Room, a room open to all persons merely on application. In the accompanying plan the contents of the Ornament Room have been transferred to the Gem Room; and the Keeper's study is placed near the beginning of the private suite.

Outer Coin Room, twenty-eight feet by twenty-seven, for the freer exhibition of coins to properly introduced persons, for the use of artists copying coins or other minute objects, and all other purposes now served by the Medal Room, except the custody of the collection, and work of the department.

Inner Coin Room, fifty-five feet by twenty-eight, secured by a strong iron door, of which the Keeper, Assistant-Keeper, and Principal-Librarian, would alone have keys.—In this room, to which none but the departmental staff would be admitted, the coins and medals would be preserved, arranged, and catalogued; they would be carried hence by the officers into the Outer Room when required for inspection. The room is somewhat more than half as large again as the present Medal Room; and as the absence of visitors, and of the barriers their presence now requires, would leave the whole space free, there would be ample accommodation for any probable enlargement of the collection. The library of the department might be arranged partly in this, partly in the Outer Room.

Of the apartments reserved as private, two are placed at the south end of the first and second floors, and each of these might, if necessary, be subdivided into two small studies, each twenty-six feet by thirteen, for the use either of officers or students. Private rooms are, however, required on the ground floor, to replace the female students' room, and the Assistant-Keeper's study, proposed to be removed for the new Nimroud and Khorsabad Galleries. The most effectual provision for these and other wants would be one which has been suggested during the present inquiry, namely, to transfer to the Department of Antiquities the several rooms now occupied as the Trustees' Room and adjoining offices, and to remove the official establishment to new rooms to be erected on the east side of the Museum. Should this be found impracticable, the present Insect Room, and adjoining studies, might, in the event of the transfer of this part of the Zoological Department to the upper floor, furnish the required accommodation. In default of both these alternatives, rooms might be constructed north of the new Assyrian Galleries, though, in the opinion of the writer, this ground should only be built over as a last resort.

The basement, both of the old and new buildings, would, though unfitted for exhibition, and shut up from the public, be more or less available for workshops, storing-places, retiring-rooms, &c. No part of the existing basement would be made altogether useless, though the rooms under the present Greek Galleries would all be somewhat darkened. The basement under the new buildings may, with reference to lighting, be divided into three classes:—1. The rooms under the first six or small Greek Rooms, the south end of the Etruscan Room, and the north end of the Greek Galleries, would all have ordinary windows, and be better lighted than any part of the basement now used for the purposes mentioned. 2. The rooms under the Roman Galleries, which would also have windows, would be less well lighted than the preceding, being some feet below the level of Charlotte Street, and being further somewhat obscured by the grating over the area, and the parapet to screen it from passengers in the street, which would both probably be thought necessary. 3. The basement under the Græco-Roman, and greater part of the small Greek Galleries, would receive

Book III,
Chap. VII.
Recon-
structors
and Pro-
jectors.

Mr.
Oldfield's
Project of
Recon-
struction
(1858-1860)—
continued.

Private
Rooms in
Plan.
Others
suggested.

Use of
basement.

Lighting of
basement.

BOOK III,
CHAP. VII.
RECON-
STRUCTORS
AND PRO-
JECTORS.

MR.
OLDFIELD'S
PROJECT OF
RECON-
STRUCTION
(1858-1860)—
continued.

SUMMARY OF
SPACE FOR
ANTIQUI-
TIES.

EXTRA
SPACE.

SPACE IN
BASEMENT.

SPACE
TRANS-
FERRED TO
NATURAL
HISTORY.

PUBLIC
GALLERIES.

STUDIES FOR
OFFICERS
AND STU-
DENTS.

SUGGESTION
FOR IN-
CREASING
THOSE FOR
STUDENTS.

a partial light from the openings between them. To increase this, however, and to furnish the only light to the basement under the Fourteenth Greek Room, and the apartments adjoining its west side, panels of strong glass or open metal work might be inserted at convenient places in the various floors, and serve rather as an ornament to them. With the aid of some such arrangement, the last-mentioned portions of the basement would serve as storing-rooms; in default of it, they could merely be available for any apparatus used in heating or ventilation.

[Then follows a General Summary of Additional Space provided for the Collections of Antiquities, amounting to a net addition of forty-one thousand nine hundred and fifty-six square feet of superficial area.]

This is somewhat less than the additional space demanded in the estimate supplied to the Committee by Mr. HAWKINS; but it supposes the removal of the Oriental and Ethnographical Collections, which Mr. HAWKINS, when considering only the existing department, and not the question of its modification, included in its contents.

In addition, however, to the space provided for the collections, the new buildings would comprise about eight thousand six hundred feet on the three principal floors, for studies, closets, staircases, &c.

The space in the basement it is unnecessary to estimate in detail, being manifestly superabundant for its purpose.

The Plan of the Upper Floors shows the accommodation which might be provided, upon the present scheme, for the Departments of Natural History, by transferring to them the galleries and studies on that floor now occupied by Antiquities, and constructing an upper room on the site of the staircase, to unite the Central Saloon (Return 379, Plan 18, No. 1), into which the new principal staircase would conduct, with the galleries so transferred. The apportionment of the space amongst the different collections of Natural History must be left to more competent authorities than the present writer. He may, however, add a few words on the general character of the apartments comprehended in the transfer. The public galleries are similar to the present Zoological Galleries, not merely in their structure, but in their fittings. The wall-cases, therefore, might be available, without alteration, for the new collections; and the central cases might either be retained for Natural History, or removed to the new upper floors for Antiquities, as was found more convenient. The present Medal and Ornament Rooms might serve for the use of students, whilst the four private studies numbered 6, 7, 10, and 10 in Plan 18, would be used by the officers. The rooms for students might, if necessary, be further increased by a trifling alteration, in the event of the official establishment being transferred to the east of the Museum. In place of the closet adjoining the Medal Room, a private staircase might descend by a few steps to the entresol below, the whole of which might then be made an appendage to the upper, instead of the lower floor, and would furnish two convenient rooms for students, over those numbered 4 and 6 in Plan 17. The same staircase, falling in with one already existing between the entresol and Secretary's Office, would supply a private communication between the upper and lower floors, in lieu of that abolished for the construction of the First Egyptian Room (III, 69).

The total area of the apartments transferred to Natural History may be summarily stated thus:—

		Without Entresol.	With Entresol.
Public Galleries :			
Present Galleries of Antiquities	.	19,185	
Proposed room over III (69)	.	2,660	
		21,845	21,845
Students' Working Rooms	. . . .	1,749	3,168
Officers' Studies	. . . . .	868	868
Closets, Passages, and Staircase	. . .	936	1,557
Total addition	. . . . .	25,398	27,438

Independently of the increased accommodation, the advantage of acquiring for Natural History the exclusive possession of the upper floor is obvious and unquestionable, though the gain is not limited to that department. By separating its galleries entirely from those of Antiquities, the practical superintendence of each would be simplified; one department would no longer be a necessary thoroughfare to another; the confusion of ideas experienced by ordinary visitors from the juxtaposition of collections so incongruous would be avoided; and as each department would have a separate entrance, a facility would be given for varying their periods or regulations of admission, as the circumstances of each might at any time require; considerations which must hereafter acquire increasing weight in proportion to the increasing magnitude of the Museum.

The ground immediately round the Museum, on the average of its three sides, is valued in the Report of the Special Committee of Trustees (twenty-sixth November, 1859), at about forty-three thousand five hundred pounds per acre. The houses in Charlotte Street are inferior in character to those on the other two sides, and might doubtless be purchased at a proportionately less price; but the writer, being anxious to err only on the safe side, assumes the average price as necessary. The ground proposed to be taken is about four hundred and fifty feet long, by a breadth generally of one hundred and fifty feet, but at the south end not exceeding one hundred and ten feet; so that the total area is about sixty-four thousand seven hundred square feet, or somewhat less than an acre and a half. The price, therefore, may be set down at sixty-five thousand pounds.

Buildings are estimated in the same report to cost about two pounds per square foot, reckoned upon the total internal area of the principal floors, without the basement. This calculation is founded on buildings consisting of a basement, a ground floor, and one upper floor. The buildings proposed by the writer are in one respect more costly than these, as their basements bear a larger proportion to those floors on which the cost is calculated. But in two other respects they are more economical:—1. Because they include, in one part, a second floor, which swells the space from which the expense is calculated, without involving any addition to the basement. 2. Because some of the galleries on the ground floor are not really separate buildings, but parts of a single block of buildings, subdivided merely by partition walls. On the whole, therefore, the estimate of two pounds per foot seems the safest basis of calculation.

Now the quantity of internal area or floor space in the proposed new buildings is—

For the collections . . .	71,760	square feet.
For studies, staircases, &c. . .	8,600	,,
Total . .	80,360	,,

This gives, therefore, one hundred and sixty thousand seven hundred and twenty pounds for buildings, which, added to sixty-five thousand pounds for ground, would amount to two hundred and twenty-five thousand seven hundred and twenty pounds. A further sum must be added for alterations of the existing building, particularly for the removal and reconstruction of the staircase, and the formation of the two rooms described as III (69) and XIII (15). Assuming the expense of these alterations, quite conjecturally, at ten thousand pounds, the total cost would be two hundred and thirty-five thousand seven hundred and twenty pounds. The largeness of the valuation allowed for the ground gives reason to believe that the actual expense of ground and buildings would not exceed, and might probably fall short of, this estimate.

[In concluding his remarks on this plan of reconstruction, Mr. Oldfield points out that if ever hereafter further extensions should be required, they might be obtained without material disturbance of the proposed galleries. For Antiquities, one or more additional houses might be purchased either in Bedford Square, commencing with No. 4, or in Charlotte Street, commencing with No. 3. The former would be required for the prolongation of the Greek, Græco-Roman, or Roman Galleries; the latter for the Etruscan or Phœnician.   For the minor collections on the upper floors either side would be equally appropriate.   If further space were needed for Natural History, galleries might be built as suggested by Professor MASKELYNE, extending either northwards to Montague Place, or eastwards to Montague Street, as found convenient.]

To the clear and forcible exposition of his plan, thus given by its framer in the paper submitted to the Committee of 1860, many further elucidations were added in evidence. But enough has already been quoted for the perfect intelligibility of the plans so proposed for the sanction of the Trustees and of Parliament. 'I think,' said Mr. OLDFIELD, when questioned, in the Committee, as to the extent of provision *for the probable future* requirements of the Museum, 'the proper mode is to secure so much space as will at least meet those demands which are likely to occur during the construction of the building; and then, above all, to adopt a system of construction which would at any future time admit of an extension, without derangement of that which now exists, and so would obviate the very great expense and inconvenience which has hitherto occurred from alterations and reconstructions.'

In reporting upon this plan, originally framed in 1858, the Committee of 1860, after comparing with it two other but only partial plans of extension and rearrangement, prepared respectively by Mr. Sydney SMIRKE and by Mr. Nevil STORY-MASKELYNE, observe: 'Your Committee have reason to think that if any of these plans were adopted— involving the [immediate] purchase of not more than two acres of land, with the [immediately] requisite buildings and alterations—the cost would not exceed three hundred thousand pounds.   If, however, only this limited portion of land should be at once acquired, it is probable that the price of what remains would be enhanced.   If the whole were to be purchased, as your Committee have already recommended, the cost above stated would be, of course, increased.'

The recommendation here referred to has been already quoted in a preceding chapter, together with a statement of the grounds on which it was based.

The only additional elucidation, on this head, which it seems necessary to give may be found in a passage of the evidence of one of the Trustees, Sir Roderick MURCHISON, who, in 1858, with other eminent men of science, presented a Memorial to the then Chancellor of the Exchequer, praying that the British Museum might *not* be dismembered by any transference of the Natural History Collections to another locality.   After saying : ' I entirely coincide still in every opinion that was expressed in that Memorial, and I have since seen additional and stronger reasons for wishing that [its prayer] should be supported,' Sir Roderick added : ' When it was brought before us [that is, before a Sub-Committee of Trustees] in evidence, that if we were largely to extend the British Museum at once *in situ*, and that as large a building were to be made *in situ* as might be made at Kensington, we then learned that the expense would be greater.   But I have since seen good grounds to believe that by purchasing the ground rents or the land, to north, east, or west, of the Museum, according to a plan which I believe has now been prepared and laid before the members of the Committee [referring to that of Mr. OLDFIELD, just described], and availing ourselves of the gradual * power of enlargement . . . . . the Nation would be put to a much less expense for several years to come, and would in the end realise all those objects which it is the aim † of men of science to obtain.'

---

* Printed by oversight ' general ' in the *Minutes of Evidence*.
† Printed ' object ' in *Minutes of Evidence*, as above.

The chief alternative plan is based on the transference of the Natural History Collections to an entirely new site, and on the devotion to the uses of the Literary and Archæological Departments of the Museum of the whole of the space so freed from the scientific departments.

The Committee of 1860 condemned this plan in the main (but only, as it seems, by a single voice upon a division), but what that Committee had under consideration was only the first form into which the plan of separation had been shaped. At the end of the year 1861 and beginning of 1862, that plan was again brought before a Sub-Committee of the Trustees, at the express instance of the Lords of Her Majesty's Treasury, and it was thus reported upon:—

Your Committee, to whom it has been referred to consider the best manner of carrying into effect the Treasury Minute of the thirteenth of November, 1861, and the Resolution passed at the special general meeting of the third of December of the same year, have unanimously agreed to the following report:*—

The Lords Commissioners of Her Majesty's Treasury state in that Minute, 'That, in their judgment, some of the collections ought to be removed from the present buildings, and that they will be prepared to make proposals at the proper time to the Royal Commissioners of the Exhibition of 1851, with a view to the provision, on the estate of the Commissioners, of space and buildings, which shall be adequate to receive in particular, at first the Mineralogical, Geological, and Palæontological Collections, and ultimately, in case it shall be thought desirable, all those of the Natural History Departments.' Their Lordships, after having invited the Trustees to prosecute the further examination of the question, continue as follows:—'It will have to be considered what other or minor branches of the collections may, with propriety or advantage, be removed to other sites, or even made over, if in any case it might seem proper, to other establishments.'

---

* It is to this Report of 1862 that the accompanying lithographic fac-similes of the original illustrative plans belong. Two of them show the then existing arrangements of the principal floors; the other two show the then proposed alterations and re-arrangements.

Your Committee have, therefore, thought it their duty at the outset to examine whether all the Natural History Collections, viz. the Zoological and Botanical, in addition to the Geological, Palæontological, and Mineralogical, specified in the Treasury Minute, might with propriety and advantage be removed from the present British Museum buildings. The importance, as regards science, of preserving together all objects of Natural History, was forcibly urged by Sir R. Murchison, at the special general meeting of the third of December. In a Memorial laid before the Chancellor of the Exchequer in 1858, and signed by more than one hundred and twenty eminent promoters and cultivators of science,* it was represented 'that as the chief end and aim of natural history is to demonstrate the harmony which pervades the whole, and the unity of principle, which bespeaks the unity of the Creative Cause, it is essential that the different classes of natural objects should be preserved in juxtaposition under the roof of one great building.' Your Committee concur in this opinion, and they have come to the conclusion that it is essential to the advantage of science and of the collections which are to remain in Bloomsbury, that the removal of all the objects of Natural History should take place, and, as far as practicable, should be simultaneously effected.

With regard to Botany, it is a question whether the existence of the Royal Botanical Gardens at Kew does not suggest an exception as to the place to which the British Museum Botanical Collection should be removed, reserving a small series for the illustration of fossil Botany, in connexion with Palæontology.

It is to be kept in view that the removal of the Palæontology, Geology, and Mineralogy, would leave unoccupied only two very inconveniently placed rooms in the basement, besides the north half of the north gallery on the upper floor (about four hundred feet in length, by thirty-six in width); whereas the recently imported marbles from Halicarnassus, Cnidus, Geronta, and Cyrene, fill completely the space under the colonnade, extending to about five hundred and forty feet in length. Nor can your Committee omit to add, that should the removal of the Botany and Zoology be delayed, the final and systematic arrangement of the collections which are to remain must be equally delayed; while, if any portions of these were removed to other situations in the Museum, or their final transfer postponed, many of the objects retained would have again to be shifted for the sake of congruity and economy of space.

It is, therefore, recommended by your Committee, that all the Natural History Collections be speedily and simultaneously removed.

Together with these the Ethnological Collection ought to be provided

---

* Parliamentary Return, No. 456, of the Session 1858.

for elsewhere. Most of the objects which it contains have no affinity with those which are contained in the other parts of the Museum, nor is the collection worthy of this country for its extent, nor yet, owing to its exceptional character, is it brought together in a methodical and instructive manner. Occupying but a secondary place in the British Museum, it cannot obtain either the space or the attention which it might obtain, were it not surrounded and cast into the shade by a vast number of splendid and interesting objects which have irresistible claims to preference. Mr. HAWKINS was of opinion, ' that if Ethnography be retained,' it would be necessary to quadruple the space for its exhibition. The Select Committee in their report (p. vii), state that ' they have received evidence from every witness examined on this subject in favour of the removal of the Ethnographical Collection.' If it were to be retained, an area of ten thousand feet (same report, p. xi) would be required. Your Committee cannot, therefore, hesitate to recommend the removal of the Ethnographical Collection to a fitter place. Nor can they hesitate in proposing the removal, from the present Ornithological Gallery, of the Collection of Portraits hanging on the walls above the presses containing the stuffed birds. Those paintings having no connexion with the objects for the preservation of which the Museum was founded, would never have been placed there had there been a National Portrait Gallery in existence for their reception.

The following is a detailed statement of the space which would be left vacant in various parts of the Museum by the removal of the above collections. . . . .

Then follows an enumeration, first, of the space left vacant by the removal of the Geological, Palæontological, and Mineralogical Collections, amounting in the whole to an area of twenty thousand one hundred and thirty-five feet; secondly, of the space left vacant by the removal of the Zoological Collection, amounting to an area of thirty-five thousand four hundred and twenty-eight feet; thirdly, of the space left vacant by the removal of the Botanical Collection, amounting to five thousand nine hundred feet; and, finally, of the space left vacant by the removal of the Ethnological Collection, namely, a room on the south side of the upper floor, marked ' 3 ' on the plan, ninety-four feet by twenty-four, giving an area of two thousand two hundred and fifty-six feet; and giving, in the whole, an aggregate area of sixty-five thousand and seventy-nine feet.

Having enumerated the collections which might, with propriety and advantage, be removed from the British Museum, and stated the extent of new accommodation which would consequently be gained for other collections, the Committee proceeded to consider, in the words of the Treasury Minute, 'the two important questions—first, of such final enlargement and alterations of the present buildings as the site may still admit, and as may be conducive to the best arrangement of the interior; secondly, of the redistribution of the augmented space among the several collections that are to remain permanently at the Museum, among which, of course, my Lords give the chief place to the Library Departments and the Antiquities.'

The Committee, agreeing with their Lordships that the chief claims in the redistribution of the augmented space are those of the Antiquities and of the Library Departments, then proceed to say that—

They have thought themselves bound also to pay attention to certain other important purposes, to which a portion of the space to be obtained by alterations within and by building on some remaining spots of un-occupied ground, might be beneficially applied.

Your Committee have, in the first place, had their attention drawn to that part of the existing buildings appropriated to the administrative department of the Museum. The want of space for clerks, for Museum publications, for stationery, for the archives of the Trust, for papers of all descriptions, for the transaction of business with officers and servants of the Trustees, and with tradesmen, as well as the want of a waiting-room for strangers of all ranks who have to attend on the Trustees, or wish to have interviews with their chief officer or any of the persons attached to his office, is the cause of great embarrassment and discomfort. To which is to be added the inconvenience caused by the unsuitable arrangement of the rooms, which renders those who occupy them liable to perpetual interruptions. Moreover, by the strict rule forbidding the admission of artificial light into the Museum, the period of available working time is occasionally much abridged. Another site must be found for this department; there are no means of providing on its present site against the evils above mentioned.

In the next place, your Committee have taken into consideration the absolute necessity of providing for the exhibition of specimens of coins and medals, always intended by the Trustees, but never carried into effect for want of space. And not only a selection of coins and medals, but also one of gems, cameos, and valuable ornaments, should be exhibited to Museum visitors. The want of room for such a purpose is the source of great trouble and inconvenience. The present Medal Room is much too confined even for the arrangement and preservation of its contents, and for such accommodation of its officers as is necessary to enable them to perform properly their duties. Moreover, as visitors cannot be indiscriminately admitted to the Ornament Room, still less to the Medal Room, such of them as do not take the proper steps for gaining access to those rooms are debarred from seeing even specimens of objects which acquire a peculiar interest in proportion to the strictness with which they are guarded. The general visitors should have an opportunity of satisfying their laudable curiosity by seeing a good selection of coins, just as they can at the present time see interesting specimens of manuscripts and printed books; scholars and persons who have special reasons for examining coins leisurely and minutely, ought to have the means of doing so comfortably under proper regulations, and in a separate room, in the same manner as readers are allowed to use books; but no stranger should be admitted into the room where the Collection of Coins and Medals is preserved unless in rare and exceptional cases, and always in the presence of the Principal Librarian, or the keeper of the department.

In the third place, your Committee, being aware of the importance of space for the due exhibition of prints and drawings, and of the repeated complaints of the keeper of that department, who cannot find room wherein to arrange the collection so as to have it safely preserved as well as readily accessible, have given their best attention to those complaints. Most of the inconveniences which are felt by visitors, as well as by Museum officers, in the existing Medal Room, are equally felt in the existing Print Room; and many of the wants which it is suggested should be provided for to make the Collection of Coins and Medals as useful and instructive as it ought to be in a great national institution, are wants against which provision must be made in order to render equally useful and instructive the Collection of Prints and Drawings. These wants are ample space for classing, arranging, and preserving the bulk of the collection, as well as ample space wherein to exhibit, for the amusement and instruction of the public generally, such a selection of prints and drawings as may be calculated to give a general notion of both arts from their infancy to comparatively modern times, in various countries, and according to the style of the most celebrated masters. Studies should likewise be provided for the keeper, and also for an assistant-keeper, in this department, as well as accommodation for artists who come to copy or study critically any of the objects, or classes of objects, forming part of this collection, and for those who come for the purpose of researches requiring less minute attention, and who desire to see a variety of prints and drawings in succession.

In the fourth place, your Committee have taken into consideration the want of space for carrying on the binding of the Museum books. The Collection of Manuscripts, and, much more, that of Printed Books, have of late years been increasing with unexampled rapidity; but the bookbinders' accommodation has not been increased in a corresponding ratio. The damage caused, particularly to new books, placed unbound in the readers' hands, may well be conceived; and the Trustees were compelled, by the necessity of the case, to sanction an expedient of doubtful legality, by allowing a large number of books, which in case of misfortune might be easily replaced at a comparatively small outlay, to be taken out of the Museum to be bound in a house immediately opposite to it, hired by the bookbinder. Your Committee think that such an arrangement, avowedly a temporary one, ought not to continue a moment longer than is unavoidable; and that adequate provision should be made as speedily as possible within the Museum premises for binding all books belonging to the Trust.

Your Committee will now proceed to consider the questions of the final enlargement and alterations of the present buildings, and of the redistribution of the augmented space for the several purposes above mentioned. In making the following proposals, your Committee have kept in view the principle that it would not be advisable for the Trustees to appropriate specifically to particular objects any particular space. They will, therefore, as much as possible, confine themselves to stating how the augmented space should be generally redistributed among the remaining collections, giving the chief place to the Antiquities and Library; the arrangement of the particular objects or classes of objects should rest on the responsibility of the head of each department, who would in due time submit his views to the Trustees. Your Committee also wish it to be clearly understood that the structural details herein suggested or implied, must be considered liable to such modifications as the farther development of the scheme may require.

In the building as now arranged, the principal staircase (No. 69 on the plan of the ground floor) is situated on the left in the Entrance Hall (No. 2); opposite to the entrance is the corridor (No. 80) leading to the Reading-Room; east and west of that corridor, between the main building and the new Library, there is an area (No. 70 and 79) about thirty feet wide unoccupied. It has long been suggested that the prin-

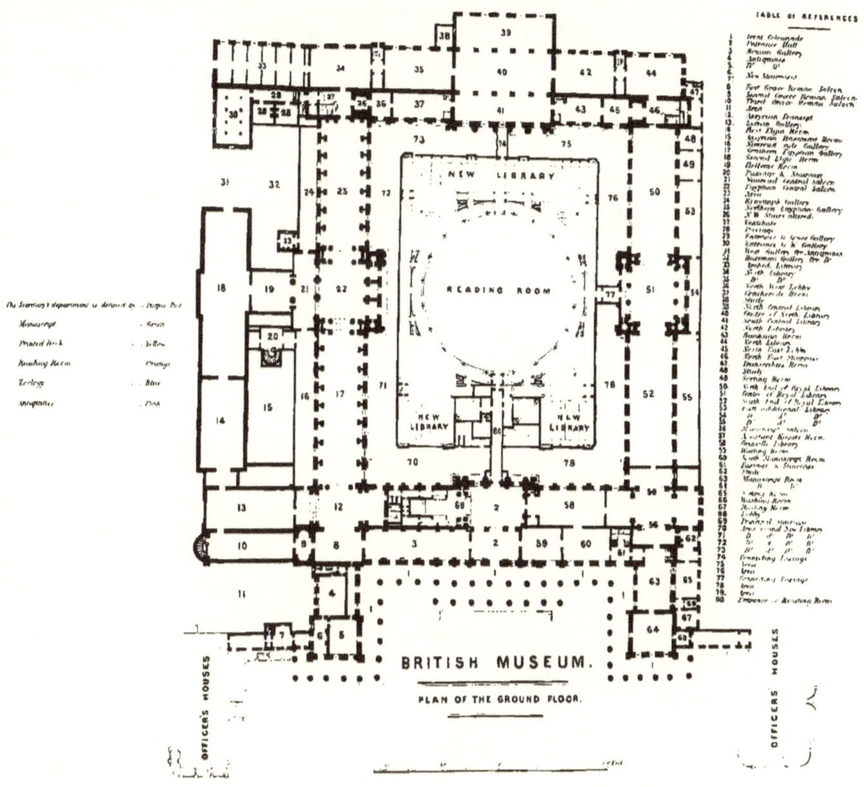

NEW LIBRARY
READING ROOM
NEW LIBRARY
NEW LIBRARY
BRITISH MUSEUM.
PLAN OF THE GROUND FLOOR.
OFFICER'S HOUSES
OFFICERS HOUSES
TABLE OF REFERENCES

cipal staircase should be removed from No. 69, and that two staircases *Book III,*
be erected on the area 70 and 79, one on each side of No. 80.   The hall *Chap. VII.*
entrance (No. 2) would be lighted by the skylight already existing in *Recon-*
the roof, and by a corresponding opening to be made in the upper floor. *structors and Pro-*
The site of the principal staircase, No. 69, would be occupied by a large *jectors.*
room, seventy-five feet by thirty-five, giving an area of two thousand
six hundred and twenty-five feet, exactly like the one opposite to it (No.
58) in height as in every other respect, with a floor on a level with the
rest of the building.

There are blank windows on the north side of the principal staircase *Present*
that would have to be cut through to light the new room, and additional *Roman*
light could be admitted if necessary.   On the south of the projected *Gallery.*
new room is a narrow room, ninety-four feet by twenty-four (No. 3),
designated as the Roman Gallery, the light of which is very defective,
especially on the side of the windows opening under the front colonnade.   The Collections of Antiquities contain some large objects, more
interesting archæologically than artistically, for which light on each
side of them is very desirable.   If the wall now separating the staircase
from No. 3 were removed, and pilasters or columns substituted (the
upper part of that wall in the floor above might likewise be removed if
desirable), a room ninety-four feet by sixty, giving an area of five thousand six hundred and forty feet, admirably adapted for antiquities of
this kind, would be obtained.

At the western extremity of the Roman Gallery (No. 3), and turning *Trustees'*
southward, are the Trustees' room (No. 4), two rooms for clerks (No. 5 *present*
and 6), and the study of the Principal-Librarian (No. 7).   It is proposed *Offices.*
to remove all the partition walls inside the space occupied by No. 4, 6,
and 5, and by the corridor on the east of No. 4, and to open windows on
the west side at the same height, and uniform with those in the gallery
No. 17, of which this part of the building would then be a continuation,
opening a communication like that on the corresponding side on the
east (between No. 56 and 63).   The Egyptian Gallery might thus be
extended to the total length of four hundred and sixty-five feet.

By removing the corridor and study No. 7, as well as the projection *New build-*
on the north side of the house now occupied by Mr. CARPENTER, so far *ings on*
west as the point at which it would intersect a prolongation to the south *No. 11.*
of the west wall of the first Elgin Room, a plot of unoccupied ground,
one hundred feet by seventy-five, might be turned to great advantage.
The interior arrangement of this newly acquired space would depend on
the purposes to which the Trustees should think fit to apply it; whether,
for instance, it might be advisable to throw into it the third Græco-
Roman Saloon (No. 10), which is now by common consent too narrow,
or whether the western part of that plot of ground had not better be
set out as a continuation of the Elgin Room, which should be carried

through the end of the above room (No. 10) and of the Lycian Room (No. 13). Before finally deciding this point it would be imperative to determine what is to be done with the Lycian Room, which is in an unfinished state, because it neither is nor ever was large enough for the collection for which it was intended; whilst, on the other hand, it contains objects which ought never to have been placed there, and which ought to be removed. Until the keeper of the department has before him a correct plan of all the space which he may eventually have at his disposal, and until he has well considered how the objects to be placed ought to be arranged, he cannot give a decided opinion upon any scheme for building on the plot now under consideration. For the present purpose it is enough to say that the Trustees' room and those annexed (No. 4, 5, and 6), giving an area of about two thousand nine hundred and fifty feet on the ground floor, and a large piece of ground, one hundred feet by seventy-five, may be beneficially applied to the Department of Antiquities.

No. 14 and 18 are the two Elgin Rooms, containing the finest reliques of Greek art in existence, which have remained unarranged for years, owing to the difficulties which the space hitherto available presented for their definitive arrangement, and to the uncertainty of the final appropriation of the space No. 31. It seems, however, to be generally admitted that on the unoccupied plot of ground, No. 31, a continuation of the second Elgin Room should be erected of the same width, to include the Print Room, the floor of which should be lowered to the general level of the Museum ground floor, and its width extended westward about seven feet. Another gallery might thus be formed altogether four hundred and seventy-five feet long and thirty-seven wide. Should it not extend farther than the southern extremity of the first Elgin Room (No. 14), its length would be three hundred and thirty feet. The plot of ground, No. 32, ought also to be applied to the accommodation of Antiquities. The study No. 23 should be done away with. The two lower flights of the N.W. staircase, No. 27, should be taken down and reconstructed in No. 26 and 36, with the necessary alterations to reconnect them with the two upper flights, which would remain as they are now. The studies No. 28, and passage No. 29, should be cleared away, as well as those above them, together with the lower part of the western wall of No. 27, the southern wall of that space being continued to No. 30, thus forming a passage or gallery, about twenty-two feet wide, for communication between the Northern Egyptian Gallery and the new gallery to be erected at the north of the Elgin Rooms. From the new passage thus formed there should be an opening on the south side, and a flight of steps to descend to the gallery which is to be built on No. 32. There would be room under the new staircase, in the space No. 36, to form an additional study for the Printed Book

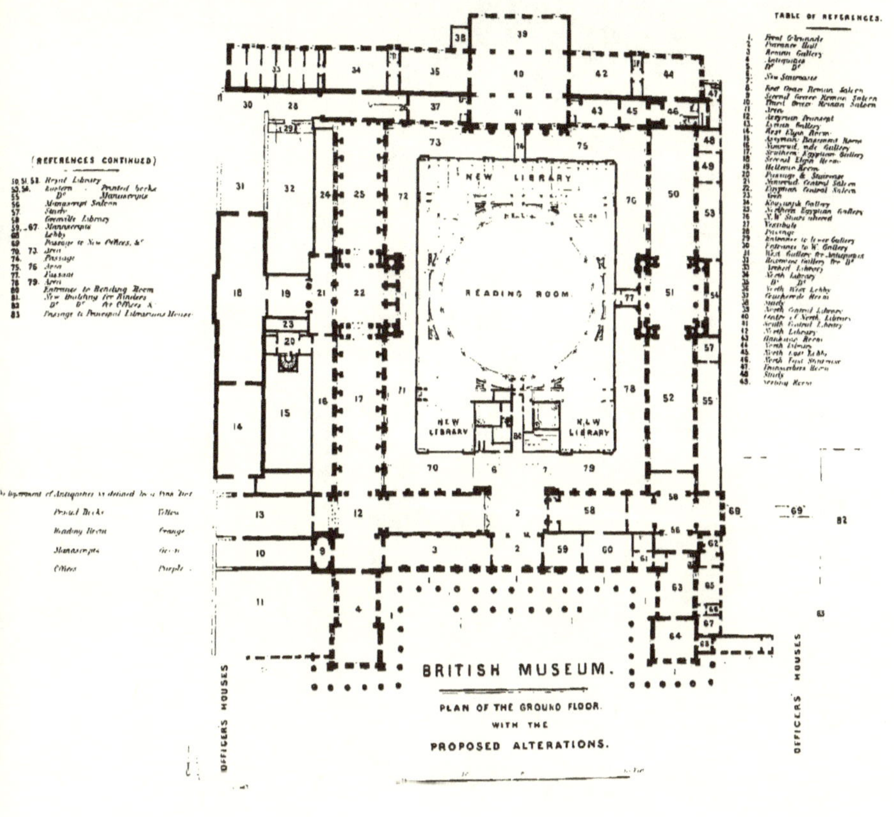

BRITISH MUSEUM.
PLAN OF THE GROUND FLOOR.
WITH THE
PROPOSED ALTERATIONS.
NEW LIBRARY
READING ROOM
NEW LIBRARY
N. W. LIBRARY
OFFICERS HOUSES
OFFICERS HOUSES
TABLE OF REFERENCES.
1. Front Colonnade
2. Entrance Hall
3. Roman Gallery
4. Antiquities
5. Do. Do.
7. New Staircases
8. First Graeco Roman Saloon
9. Second Graeco Roman Saloon
10. Third Graeco Roman Saloon
11. Area
12. Assyrian Transept
13. Lycian Gallery
14. First Elgin Room
15. Assyrian Basement Room
16. Nimroud side Gallery
17. Southern Egyptian Gallery
18. Second Elgin Room
19. Hellenic Room
20. Passage & Staircase
21. Nimroud Central Saloon
22. Egyptian Central Saloon
23. Area
24. Kouyunjik Gallery
25. Northern Egyptian Gallery
26. N. W. Stairs altered
27. Vestibule
28. Passage
29. Entrance to lower Gallery
30. Entrance to W. Gallery
31. West Gallery for Antiquities
32. Basement Gallery for Do.
33. Arched Library
34. North Library
35. Do. Do.
36. North West Lobby
37. Grenville Room
38. Study
39. North Central Library
40. Centre of North Library
41. South Central Library
42. North Library
43. Banksian Room
44. South Library
45. North East Lobby
46. North East Staircase
47. Transcribers Room
48. Study
49. Writing Room

(REFERENCES CONTINUED)
50. 51. 52. Royal Library
53. 54. Eastern   Printed books
55. Do.   Manuscripts
56. Manuscript Saloon
57. Study
58. Grenville Library
59. — 67. Manuscripts
68. Lobby
69. Passage to New Offices, &c.
70. 73. Area
74. Passage
75. 76. Area
77. Passage
78. 79. Area
80. Entrance to Reading Room
81. New Building for Binders
82. Do. Do. for Offices &c.
83. Passage to Principal Librarian's House

Department of Antiquities is denoted by a fine Tint
Printed Books   Yellow
Reading Room   Orange
Manuscripts   Green
Offices   Purple

Department, where it is much wanted. Upon No. 32, a gallery should be erected from the basement, like the Assyrian Gallery, No. 15, to both of which access might be had by two handsome staircases, descending north and south of No. 19, from which it is taken for granted the Phigaleian Marbles and other objects, now there, would be removed, the central space being applied to better purposes.

It does not appear to your Committee that any farther accommodation for Antiquities can be procured on the ground-floor, without interfering with rooms now appropriated to the Library.

On the north side of the upper floor, all that portion marked 21, 32, 31, 30, 29, 33, 28, and 27, on the plan of that floor, now occupied by Geology, Palæontology, and Mineralogy, should be transferred to the Antiquities. It would be desirable to remove the two studies, marked 21, at the western extremity of that floor, and to add so much more space to the gallery for exhibition.

But before proceeding farther, your Committee wish to make one or two remarks on the advantages which all the galleries on the upper floor offer for the exhibition of Antiquities, even of considerable size and weight, were any of the space on this floor wanted for such objects. With respect to light, as all these galleries may, if requisite, be lighted by skylights (those on the east and west being so already), they will so far meet with the approbation of those who are considered judges of the kind of light peculiarly required for the exhibition of sculptures. The size of the rooms gives ample space for the public exhibition of Antiquities, including statues, not much less than life-size, if necessary; whilst the galleries, though lofty, will not dwarf them. Competent critics have pronounced that it is a mistake to suppose that all sculptures look better in magnificent rooms. The solidity of the Museum building, throughout, leaves no doubt of its upper floor being strong enough to receive ordinary marble statues, not to speak of busts and smaller objects. The floor of the western end of the northern gallery, marked No. 21 and 32 on the plan, offers extra solidity, as it rests on substantial walls at intervals of twelve feet from each other. Your Committee have been assured by their architect that a mass of marble, weighing several tons, might be safely deposited on any part of that floor.

With respect to the northernmost central portion (No. 33) of the gallery now under consideration, it could not be better applied than to studies for the officers of the Department of Antiquities. Five such studies might be formed therein, each eighteen feet by sixteen, opening on a corridor six feet wide and eighty-four long, in which might be kept the Departmental Collection of Books for the common daily use of the occupiers of those studies.

The whole of the eastern side of the upper floor, including rooms 35 to

40 (all Zoology), together with the rooms marked 41 (Zoology), 42, 43 (Botany), 1 (Zoology), 2 (the site of the principal staircase, as well as the smaller staircase on the west of it), and finally No. 3 (Ethnography), should be transferred to the Departments of Antiquities; subject to the consideration whether the rooms No. 42 and 43 might not be reserved for the Department of Manuscripts, if at any time required. Space is wanted, not only for Antiquities now unprovided with any accommodation, but also for the display of future additions, and for the better arrangement of what is now unsatisfactorily exhibited, either too far from the eye or in dark corners. A large number of objects, to be seen as they ought to be, must be spread over twice the space which they fill at present; a great many more, now placed where they cannot be seen at all, ought to be removed to more suitable situations. The whole of the

west side—that is, rooms 9 to 15—would continue to be applied to the exhibition of Antiquities; it is not, however, to be assumed that the objects now there would necessarily be left where they are, nor yet that, for instance, Egyptian Antiquities should necessarily occupy the same galleries which they occupy at present. From room No. 14 must be removed either the Egyptian Antiquities now in it, or the Temple Collection, which was placed there from absolute necessity, there being no other space whatever where it could be exhibited. The British and Mediæval Collections would probably have to be removed to some other part of the upper floor, now occupied, or which it is now proposed should be occupied, by Antiquities, where the transition would be less abrupt than from Egyptian to Mediæval.

As before suggested, space should be set apart for the exhibition of Coins and Medals, besides that which is required for their safe custody, arrangement, and study. Your Committee will presently state how the latter ought to be provided for. As to the public exhibition of coins, the three rooms, 8, 5, and 4, in which the coins, medals, gems, &c., are now kept, would be admirably adapted for the purpose, after the internal partition walls are removed. It would be desirable to preserve the two rooms, 6 and 7, the one as a study for an assistant, who should be always at hand to give information connected with the coins exhibited close by, and to answer such questions as would not require reference to the general collection; the other as a waiting-room, to which a stranger might be more safely and freely admitted, on the understanding that nothing valuable be kept in it, whilst admission to the assistant's room should be much more sparingly granted. An obvious reason for applying this part of the premises to the above purpose is, that it is provided with special doors, windows, and locks, for the safety of the present contents. And as the objects which it is proposed should be therein exhibited would be of some considerable value, advantage should be taken of the existing arrangements for their security. It is to be noted

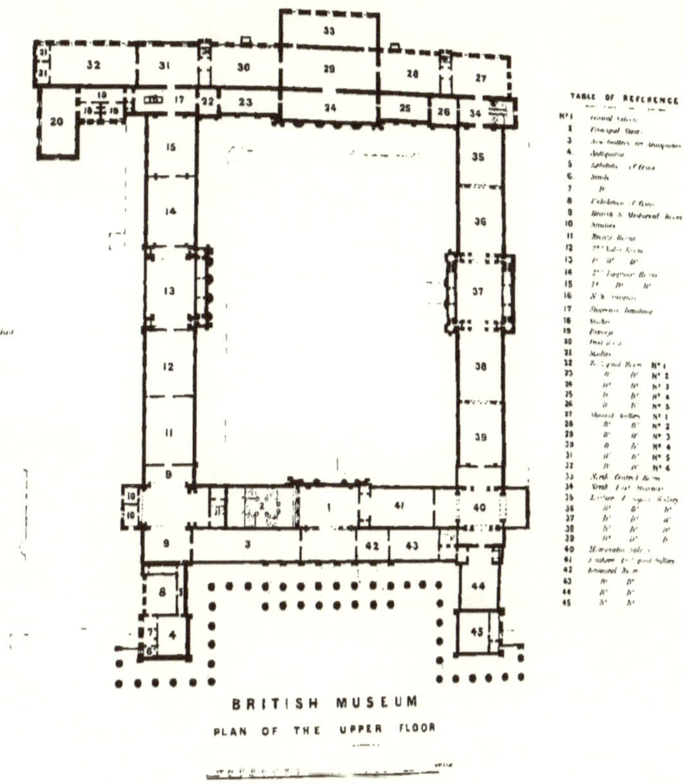

Nº III
TABLE OF REFERENCE
Nº 1 General Salon
2 Principal Stair
3 New Gallery for Antiquities
4 Antiquities
5 Antiquities of Greece
6 Scrolls
7 Dº
8 Exhibition of Greece
9 British & Medieval Room
10 Antiquities
11 Mineral Room
12 2d Salon Room
13 Dº Dº Dº
14 2d Zoological Room
15 Dº Dº Dº
16 Nº 14 entrance
17 Staircase landing
18 Studies
19 Passage
20 Reading
21 Studies
22 Zoological Room Nº 1
23 Dº Dº Nº 2
24 Dº Dº Nº 3
25 Dº Dº Nº 4
26 Dº Dº Nº 5
27 Mineral Gallery Nº 1
28 Dº Dº Nº 2
29 Dº Dº Nº 3
30 Dº Dº Nº 4
31 Dº Dº Nº 5
32 Dº Dº Nº 6
33 North Central Room
34 North East Staircase
35 Lecture of Natural History
36 Dº Dº Dº
37 Dº Dº Dº
38 Dº Dº Dº
39 Dº Dº Dº
40 Horizontal Salon
41 Southern Zoological Gallery
42 Botanical Room
43 Dº Dº
44 Dº Dº
45 Dº Dº

Antiquities & delivered by the Posch head
Egyptian   Blue
Mineralogy   Brown
Antiques   Bay Head
Fossil   Grey

32 31 30 29 28 27
20 19 18 17 22 23 24 25 26 34
15
14
13
12
11
9
10
9
8
7 4
6
35
36
37
38
39
40
44
45
41 42 43 1 2 3

BRITISH MUSEUM
PLAN OF THE UPPER FLOOR

that this exhibition would not interfere with the arrangement of any Collection of Antiquities, with none of which could the coins and medals properly mix, although so nearly allied to them.

The corresponding part of the upper floor on the south-east corner, No. 44 and 45, is perfectly well adapted for the exhibition of prints and drawings. As to space for the arrangement and preservation of the prints and drawings, for the tranquil examination and study of them, for the studies of the officers, &c., your Committee will presently lay before you their views.

Your Committee have endeavoured to show how far a portion of the new accommodation to be gained by removing the Natural History and Ethnographical Collections, by alterations within the now existing buildings, and by building on some remaining spots of unoccupied ground, may with propriety and advantage be applied to the Departments of Oriental, Mediæval, and Classical Antiquities, of the Coins and Medals, and of the Prints and Drawings; your Committee will now show what part of that accommodation might be made available for Printed Books and Manuscripts.

When the erection of the new Library and Reading-Room was suggested, it was stated that that Library would hold eight hundred thousand volumes; that is, the annual increase for forty years, calculating that increase at twenty thousand volumes. But the annual increase has been, during the last five years, at the rate of upwards of thirty thousand volumes, and during the last four years at the rate of about thirty-five thousand, which number, however, is ultimately reduced by the practice of binding two or more volumes of the same work in one; while, on the other hand, the new building will certainly contain two hundred thousand volumes more than it was originally estimated to hold; so that if the present rate of increase continues, as it ought, the new Library will be full in about twenty-five years from this date. It was necessary to say thus much, as a notion seems prevalent that a great deal more was promised when that building was suggested, and that the number of books, which that new Library can hold, may reach an almost fabulous quantity, and the space be sufficient for an extravagant number of years.

The rooms on the basement floor of the north side, both marked 15 on the plan of that floor, and now occupied by Geology, cannot be otherwise appropriated than to the Department of Printed Books; the same is to be said of the seven small rooms, marked 17, now used for Geology, as well as of rooms 18 and 19 on the east side, now used for Zoology; all these rooms are immediately under the Department of Printed Books, and naturally belong to it. The rooms marked 13, 14, and 16, from west to east, were formerly appropriated to the Department of Printed Books, to which they should now be restored. When the first importation of Halicarnassian Antiquities took place, they were deposited temporarily in these rooms, as no other space whatever could be found in which to shelter and unpack them. In this space are now arranged the Inscriptions, which have had to be removed from under the colonnade to make room for the Marbles recently arrived from Cyrene. Appropriate space for the Inscriptions will be found without difficulty in the Department of Antiquities, enlarged according to the foregoing suggestions, or, at all events, in the basement, either now existing or to be built under the galleries for Antiquities on the west side of the Museum, where sufficient light may be procured for objects like these, which are of no great interest to sight-seers, and therefore need not be publicly exhibited; enough that they be easily accessible to the small number of antiquarians and scholars who may wish to examine them.

The north galleries on the upper floor are divided lengthways, from east to west, into two portions; that now containing Zoological Collections (No. 22 to 26) can be advantageously appropriated to the Department of Printed Books when required. The volumes placed there can be easily lowered down and returned through a hoisting apparatus to be placed at either the south-east or south-west corner of No. 24, immediately above No. 41 on the ground floor—the nearest point of any in the main Library to the Reading-Room. By these various alterations space would be provided for about two hundred and fifty thousand printed volumes, in addition to that which still remains available in that department, from which, however, space for about fifty thousand volumes would have to be deducted, as will be presently shown.

Although there is now space remaining in the Department of Manuscripts for the accommodation of twelve thousand volumes, and although the annual average increase of manuscript volumes may be safely reckoned at less than six hundred and fifty, your Committee have, nevertheless, felt that prospective increased accommodation should now be provided, not only for the Collection of Manuscripts, but still more for artists and readers who have occasion to refer to select manuscripts, as well as for assistants, of whom two, together with one attendant and eight readers, are pent up in a space of thirty feet by twenty-three, crowded with tables, chairs, &c., which scarcely allow room for moving from one place to another or for access to the officers' study on each side. The Head of the Department of Manuscripts has recently represented to the Trustees his want of six assistants; but he has, at the same time, been obliged to state that, if appointed, he should not know where to place them. The Trustees have complied with his request, to the extent of granting two new assistants; and he will experience great difficulty in placing the two who are to be appointed. Add to this, the interruption to which each of these persons is unavoidably liable from

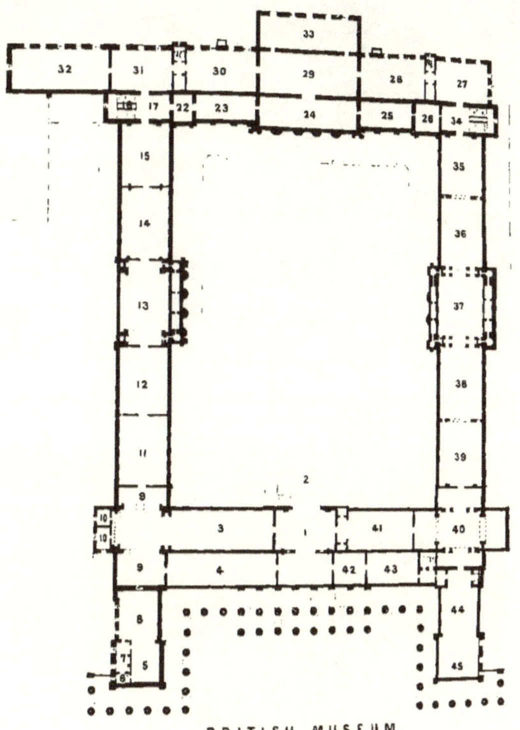

BRITISH MUSEUM.
PLAN OF THE UPPER FLOOR WITH THE PROPOSED ALTERATIONS.

each of the others in the performance of his duties and occupations, owing chiefly to the narrow space in which they are confined.

On account of its locality, the Department of Manuscripts cannot derive any direct advantage from the removal of the Natural History Collections; no space which will thus become vacant can be rendered available for the purpose of remedying the inconveniences here stated. As, however, the Department of Printed Books obtains the additional accommodation before mentioned, a portion of the space now occupied by Printed Books, very conveniently situated to supply the wants of the Department of Manuscripts, ought to be transferred to this department.

It is, therefore, proposed that the study, marked No. 57 on the ground-floor plan, be removed to the north end of No. 55, now occupied by Printed Books, and that the site of No. 55 be attached to the Department of Manuscripts. In that gallery, one hundred and fifteen by eighteen, excellent accommodation, with abundance of light, would be found for twenty thousand manuscript volumes—for fifteen students at least (this number is ample if admission be strictly and *bonâ fide* limited to the class of persons for whom it is intended) at separate seats, each having a table space of two feet and a half in depth and four in length,—and for ten assistants or more, admirably placed for superintendence. The area of the eastern recess of No. 56 would then be quite clear, and available for the exhibition of manuscripts, like the western recess in the same room. And when as large an exhibition of manuscripts as the space permits is accessible to the public (and still more accommodation for this exhibition might be found in the present Department of Manuscripts), the same restrictions as have been suggested with respect to coins and to prints ought to be imposed on the handling of select manuscripts.

It now remains to find space wherein to provide proper accommodation for the binder, as well as for the Trustees' offices, for the Collection of Prints and for the Collection of Coins.

On the east side of the roadway parallel to the Department of Manuscripts, there is a piece of ground extending to Montague Street on the east, to the house No. 30, in that same street towards the north, and to the Principal-Librarian's house on the south. On a portion of this ground stands an old building, now partly appropriated to the binder and partly used as a guard-house; the remainder forms the garden attached to the residence of the Principal-Librarian. It appears to your Committee that by substituting a new building for the one existing, and by building on the greater part of the garden, ample accommodation will be found for what is wanted. Your Committee cannot abstain from mentioning that this great sacrifice of personal convenience on the part of the Principal-Librarian was suggested and brought under their notice by that officer himself.

It was some years ago suggested by the Government that the military guard might be dispensed with at the Museum; at times when the services of the army were pressingly required, it was felt that soldiers might be more usefully employed than in being kept for mere show at the Museum. It was, however, thought that on removing the military guard, better provision should be made for the safety of the Museum.

Then follow various details of minor consequence; to which succeed an enumeration of the additional space gained for the Collections of Printed Books, Manuscripts, Prints and Drawings, Antiquities, Coins and Medals, as well as for offices, store-rooms, bookbinders' shops, &c., by the proposed alterations, as respects each of the several Departments of Printed Books, Manuscripts, and Antiquities; and a summary of the whole, from which it appears that the additional space gained by the Department of Printed Books amounts to an area of seventeen thousand eight hundred and three square feet; that the additional space gained by the Department of Antiquities amounts to sixty-seven thousand six hundred and ninety-two square feet; and, finally, that the additional space gained by the Department of Manuscripts amounts to three thousand four hundred and thirty square feet.

RECAPITULATION.

	Present Space.	Proposed Addition.	Proposed Deduction.	Proposed Total.
PRINTED BOOKS.				
Basement	33,998	14,667	. .	48,665
Ground floor	83,748	. .	2,070	81,678
Upper floor	. .	5,206	. .	5,206
	117,746	19,873	2,070	135,549
MANUSCRIPTS.				
Basement	210	1,360	. .	1,570
Ground floor	12,968	2,070	. .	15,038
	13,178	3,430	. .	16,608
ANTIQUITIES.				
Basement	33,868	16,036	6,767	43,137
Ground floor	39,334	13,775	. .	53,109
Upper floor . . 21,532				
Less Coins and Medals 2,950				
	18,582	44,648	. .	63,230
	91,784	74,459	6,767	159,476
COINS AND MEDALS.				
Upper floor	2,950	—	—	—
New building	. .	4,950	—	—
	2,950	4,950	. .	7,900
PRINTS AND DRAWINGS.				
Upper floor	2,600	3,204	2,600	—
New building	. .	4,950	—	—
	2,600	8,154	2,600	8,154
COMMITTEE ROOM, OFFICES, STORES, &c.				
Basement	1,290	. .	1,290	—
Ground floor	3,565	. .	3,565	—
Upper floor	1,869	. .	1,869	—
New Building (Basement)	. .	5,400	—	—
„ (Ground)	. .	4,950	—	—
	6,724	10,350	6,724	10,350
BINDERS.				
Basement	1,360	. .	1,360	—
Detached building	3,179	. .	3,179	—
New building	. .	7,760	—	—
	4,539	7,760	4,539	7,760

Your Committee, proceeds the Report, do not think it necessary to give the particulars of the accommodation which the unappropriated portions of the basement floor would afford for the preservation of moulds, as well as for the formatore, for making and preserving casts of statues and other large objects, as well as of gems and seals, and also for providing such decent and suitable conveniences as the health and comfort of the thousands who visit the Museum absolutely require.

It is, perhaps, unnecessary to do more than simply to remind the Trustees that the want of space at the Museum has been felt and has been urged on the Government for several years past, and that during the last four or five years the additions to the Collections of Antiquities have been so rapid and so numerous, as to render it impossible to do more than provide for them temporary shelter at a considerable expense, and to the great disfigurement of the noble façade which entitles the

Museum to claim rank among the most classical buildings of modern times. Should the above proposals of your Committee meet with the approbation of the Trustees and the sanction of the Government, they ought to be carried into effect without delay. The Government would, doubtless, lose no time in providing a proper building for the reception of such collections as are to be removed from the Museum; until this removal has taken place, no re-distribution of the vacated space can be undertaken; but the new structures proposed to be erected on ground now unoccupied ought to be proceeded with at once, that they might be rendered available as speedily as possible.

Your Committee are of opinion that the new building facing Montague Street, the building for the bookbinder, the building intended to be erected on the ground now vacant between the Elgin Room and the Print Room, and the construction of the new principal staircases, should be commenced immediately. The building intended to be erected on the vacant ground on the west of the Trustees' Room (No. 11 on the plan), must, necessarily, be postponed for awhile. The alterations which might and ought to be rapidly completed, are those which will be required on the east side of the King's Library (No. 55 and 57), to transfer the gallery to the Department of MSS. from that of Printed Books.

The Lords Commissioners of Her Majesty's Treasury state that 'they will be prepared to enter upon the details of these questions in communication with the Trustees, and even, if it should be desired, to offer suggestions upon them.' Your Committee are of opinion that the proffered assistance should be at once accepted; and that in order to derive all possible advantage from that assistance a small Committee of Trustees should be appointed to carry on the necessary communications with the Treasury, either verbally or otherwise, and to consider with their Lordships all suggestions that might be offered respecting the points touched upon in this Report, and their details. This Committee would be similar to that which the Trustees requested the Treasury to appoint, by letter of the twentieth of June, 1829, and which was afterwards appointed by the Trustees themselves, with the approbation of their Lordships, to direct and superintend, not only the works then in progress, but those to be afterwards undertaken.

On the tenth of February, 1862—after the communication of this Report to each of the Trustees individually—the recommendations of the Sub-Committee were unanimously approved, at a Special General Meeting of the Trustees, at which twenty-four members of the Board were present. After the adoption of the plans thus accepted, another Sub-Committee of Trustees was appointed to confer with the Treasury in order to their realisation.

Before Parliament, this plan of severance and of re-arrangement—after some modifications of detail which are too unimportant for remark—was supported, in 1862, with the whole influence of the Government. But it failed to win any adequate amount either of parliamentary or of public favour. Some men doubted if the estimated saving, as between building at Bloomsbury and building at Kensington, would or could be realized. Others denied that the evils or inconveniences attendant upon severance would be compensated by any adequate gain on other points. The popularity of the Natural History Collections; the facilities of access to Great Russell Street; the weighty—though far from unanimous—expressions of opinion from eminent men of science in favour of continuance and enlargement, rather than of severance and removal; all these and other objections were raised, and were more or less dwelt upon, both in the House of Commons and in scientific circles out of doors, scarcely less entitled to discuss a national question of this kind. The Commons eventually decided against the project by their vote of the 19th May, 1862.

Substantially,—and in spite of small subsequent additions from time to time to the buildings at Bloomsbury— the question of 1862 is still the question of 1870. As I have said, it has been my object to state that question rather than to discuss it.

Should it seem, after full examination, that good government may be better maintained, and adequate space for growth be efficiently provided, by enlarging the existing Museum, would it be worthy of Britain to allow the additional expenditure of a few scores of thousands of pounds—an expenditure which would be spread over the taxation of many years—to preponderate in the final vote of Parliament over larger and more enduring considerations?

In the session of 1866 Mr. Spencer WALPOLE spoke thus: ' You must either determine to separate the Collections now in the Museum, or buy more land in Bloomsbury. . . . . . . I have always been for keeping them together. I am, however, perfectly willing to take either course, provided you do not heap those stores one on another—as at present,' (July, 1866)—' in such a manner as to render them really not so available as they ought to be to those who wish to make them objects of study.' Few men are so well entitled to speak, authoritatively, on the question— because few have given such an amount of time and labour to its consideration.

By every available and legitimate expression of opinion the Trustees have acted in the spirit of this remark, made almost four years since, by one of the most eminent of their number. The words are, unfortunately, as apposite in March, 1870, as they were in July, 1866.

THE END.

GENERAL INDEX.

X.

Xanthus and its sculptured monuments, Discovery by Sir C. Fellows of, 645 *seqq.*

Y.

PRINTED BY J. E. ADLARD, BARTHOLOMEW CLOSE.

www.ingramcontent.com/pod-product-compliance
Lightning Source LLC
Chambersburg PA
CBHW021548110726
47902CB00004B/1074